Praise for Candace Calvert

"Only a master storyteller can transform a villain into a complex and interesting woman. Don't miss out on Sloane's story in *Maybe It's You* and the wonderful conclusion to the Crisis Team trilogy. I loved these books!"

—JORDYN REDWOOD, author of the Bloodline trilogy and *Fractured Memory*

"With her latest novel, Candace Calvert easily defends her title as Queen of Medical Hope Opera. *Maybe It's You* combines authentic medical scenarios, ongoing and believable romance, and suspense enough to keep you turning pages long into the night. Well done."

—RICHARD L. MABRY, MD, bestselling author of medical suspense with heart

"Sincere in matters of love and faith, *Step by Step* weaves a realistically wholesome tale."

—*FOREWORD* magazine

"Fans of Dee Henderson and *Grey's Anatomy* will love this wonderfully sweet, healing story about finding one's way back to love after losing everything. Candace knows how to minister to her readers while keeping them on the edge of their seats—I'm adding this winner to my library of Candace Calvert bestsellers!"

—SUSAN MAY WARREN, RITA and Christy Award–winning author of the Christiansen Family series

"Candace C   es, as she continues t   mance writer."

—*BOOKI*

"Wow. Calvert really captures the intensity of the drama that our crisis volunteers face out on the streets with cops and firefighters every day. *By Your Side* will be my standard gift this year for every occasion, and even for no occasion."

—DAVID VINCENT, director of US Crisis Care, on *By Your Side*

"[*By Your Side*] is a wonderful love story, a super tribute to emergency workers in general, to chaplains specifically, and an honest portrayal of faith in the lives of hurting people."

—JANICE CANTORE, author of *Drawing Fire*, *Critical Pursuit*, and *Accused*

"Believable and endearing characters alongside family disputes and critical medical crises make [*Life Support*] hard to put down."

—*ROMANTIC TIMES*

"Just like an outstanding episode of *Grey's Anatomy*, *Trauma Plan* weaves medical, community, and personal issues with blossoming romance and strands of mystery."

—*BOOKLIST*

"Calvert . . . infuses her story with detailed medical procedures and terminology along with honest questions about faith that anyone might ask in the face of difficulties. The characters are likable and receive rich and thorough development in this enjoyable 'hope opera' page-turner."

—*PUBLISHERS WEEKLY* ON *TRAUMA PLAN*

"If you need an infusion of hospital drama, *Code Triage* is just the prescription."

—IRENE HANNON, bestselling author of the Heroes of Quantico series

MAYBE IT'S YOU

maybe
it's you

CRISIS TEAM

CANDACE CALVERT

TYNDALE HOUSE PUBLISHERS, INC., CAROL STREAM, ILLINOIS

Visit Tyndale online at www.tyndale.com.

Visit Candace Calvert's website at www.candacecalvert.com.

TYNDALE and Tyndale's quill logo are registered trademarks of Tyndale House Publishers, Inc.

Maybe It's You

Cover designed by Tobias' Outerwear for Books

Edited by Sarah Mason Rische

Published in association with the literary agency of Natasha Kern Literary Agency, Inc., P.O. Box 1069, White Salmon, WA 98672.

Maybe It's You is a work of fiction. Where real people, events, establishments, organizations, or locales appear, they are used fictitiously. All other elements of the novel are drawn from the author's imagination.

For information about special discounts for bulk purchases, please contact Tyndale House Publishers at csresponse@tyndale.com or call 800-323-9400.

Library of Congress Cataloging-in-Publication Data
Names: Calvert, Candace, date, author.
Title: Maybe it's you / Candace Calvert.
Description: Carol Stream, Illinois : Tyndale House Publishers, Inc., [2017] | Series: Crisis team
Identifiers: LCCN 2016028469 | ISBN 9781414390369 (softcover)
Subjects: LCSH: Man-woman relationships—Fiction. | GSAFD: Christian fiction. | Love stories.
Classification: LCC PS3603.A4463 M39 2017 | DDC 813/.6—dc23 LC record available at https://lccn.loc.gov/2016028469

Printed in the United States of America

23 22 21 20 19 18 17
7   6   5   4   3   2   1

For our grandchildren:
true treasure . . . and fondest hope.

I praise you because I am fearfully and wonderfully made;

your works are wonderful, I know that full well.

PSALM 139:14

1

"YOUR RELATION TO THE INMATE?"

Sloane Ferrell's stomach tensed. "He's my stepfather," she confirmed, lips brushing her cell phone in a whisper. "It was . . . manslaughter."

She glanced past a grouping of palm trees toward the peach stucco entrance to Los Angeles Hope hospital's emergency department. Would she ever stop peering over her shoulder—watching her back? This past year it had felt as necessary as breathing and was the biggest part of why she'd left San Diego. New zip code, new living space, new job . . . a paper trail painstakingly shredded. She'd done all that, and thankfully, the last few months had been uneventful. Right now Sloane was simply concerned that a fellow ER nurse would join her at any moment. She'd said something about

1

taking their break together. This return call from California State Prison couldn't have come at a more awkward—

"We don't have you listed," the office assistant announced. Her tone was as friendly as the slam of a cell door. "It had to be arranged in advance and approved."

"I did that—and I was," Sloane insisted over the distant whine-hum of saws; preliminary work had begun on the new hospital wing. "I was promised a chance to speak at the parole hearing. My name *has* to be on the list. Could you check again?"

"Hang on."

Sloane closed her eyes and let the late September sun warm her face, a light breeze sifting strands of her dark hair. She pretended the construction sounds were ocean waves, imagining salt-laden moisture on her skin and the keening calls of gulls. She missed San Diego, even if it had started out as a place to escape to—and ended up as one more place to run from. Her fingertips found the still-pink scar around her left eye, from the accident that could have killed her. The short time in San Diego had changed her life, but how that would play out remained to be seen. Nothing was guaranteed. Especially not for someone like Sloane. Life had taught her that in strokes as bold as freeway graffiti. But right now all that mattered was—

"Nope," the woman reported. "I've checked twice. Nobody by the name of Ferrell on the list."

Sloane blinked. "It's . . . Wilder."

"You said Ferrell."

I did? Sloane bit back a groan. "It's Ferrell now. When I filled out the paperwork, it was Wilder." New zip code, new name. "I'm sorry; I forgot. But I'm sure you'll find me under that name. Wilder. *W-i-l-d*—"

"Sloane!"

She turned, saw her friend waving.

Harper Tatum strode forward, long hair tossed by the breeze and stethoscope swinging against her watermelon-red scrub top. A Los Angeles native—an "Angeleno"—she was honey blonde, long limbed, and as effervescent as a shaken can of soda. Nothing at all like Sloane. This nurse's smile appeared in a TV commercial for whitening toothpaste, and she'd recently been signed as a foot model for a local day spa's magazine ad. *"Grasping fame, tooth and nail,"* Harper liked to joke. She was a sharp, skilled nurse every hour of every shift, and a model and aspiring actress every off-duty moment—until her student loans were paid in full.

Sloane returned Harper's wave and then hurried to wrap things up with the woman on the phone. "Got to go. It's Wilder, Sloane Wilder. Find me."

Find me? She almost choked on the irony.

"Hey," she said as Harper took a seat across from her at the visitors' table.

"Hey yourself, pal."

Sloane smiled. It was hard not to like this nurse—one of the few things she didn't have to overthink or completely fabricate. Not even six months ago, she'd have shot the gregarious coworker a back-off look. "They let you out."

"Finally." Harper pointed at Sloane's phone on the red-tile table. "I interrupted you. Anybody date-worthy?"

"No such luck." Sloane feigned a casual shrug, reminding herself that real friends were too much of a risk. She couldn't imagine telling Harper she'd changed her name to avoid the dangerous consequences of her last serious relationship. Or that the only "date" she cared about was a parole board hearing at the state prison.

"Nothing like the soul-soothing ambience of power tools," Harper pronounced over the staccato whap-thwack of a pneumatic nail gun. "Though I do like the contrast: men in hard hats, steel-toed boots, and layers of sawdust making it happen, while—" she nodded toward the ER doors behind them—"our man in a sports jacket and khakis hustles to get it all funded."

Sloane saw what Harper did: Micah Prescott, the assistant director of the hospital's marketing and public relations department. He was early thirties, probably, with a lean build, sandy hair, sunglasses, and an undoubtedly practiced smile. An ad man with a well-appointed office a safe distance from stat pages and messy trauma, who preferred cash procurement over lifesaving. It was the kind of career that required finesse, charm, and an aptitude for creative spin. Unfortunately, Sloane knew the type far too well. Micah Prescott was the kind of person she tried to avoid at all costs.

Harper watched as the marketing man was joined by two young men with cameras slung over their shoulders. "It's still five months until the official launch of the Face of Hope campaign, but Micah's already stirring things up and getting interest from the media. Of course, he's no rookie when it comes to publicity. With his connections and all."

Apparently the extended Prescott family was involved in the music industry—Christian recording artists and performers. Enormously popular, Harper had said more than once. Not surprisingly, Sloane had never heard of them. She only knew that she didn't like the intrusive scrutiny this marketing campaign brought with it—a "star search" for an employee who best personified the spirit of the hospital's mission. The campaign kickoff had coincided with the groundbreaking for the new wing, an event headlined by a megastar film couple, an impressive sampling from the roster of the Los Angeles Lakers, and a former First Lady of California. The event immediately spawned rallies with staff, endless surveys, and photo shoots. There were days it felt more like a casting call than a workplace. Sloane avoided all of it as best she could. This past year had taught her that a low profile meant safety.

"Imagine it: your face on a billboard," Harper said, sweeping her hand in an arc as if the palm trees had been magically replaced by those old spotlights at movie premieres. "The Face of Hope. Looking down on the freeway. The 405 or the 101—both maybe. Thousands and thousands of people seeing it every day, for hours at a time, LA traffic being what it is. And smog willing." Her brow puckered. "You don't look too thrilled by the idea."

"I'll pass," Sloane told her, feeling a prickle of panic. Ridiculous—it would never happen. Besides, she'd changed her name, and there had been no threatening calls in months. If she got caught in the background of some publicity photo, no one would notice. "Anyway, I'm still on probation as a new hire. You're a far more likely candidate. You're comfortable in front of a camera and—"

"And you are drop-dead gorgeous, my friend." Harper wrinkled her nose. "I probably shouldn't say 'drop dead,' considering our line of work. But I'm not kidding. The last woman to claim eyes like that was Liz Taylor. And even if you do your best to hide your light under a bushel, it's there. Not just looks. The real deal." Harper's expression turned best-friend kind. "I see how you are with the patients. Especially our lost souls, people with nobody and nothing—and bad choices up to their eyeballs. Most of us draw straws to avoid dealing with them. But it's like you champion those people, Sloane. And you're not afraid to butt heads with management or stretch some policies to do that."

"Butt heads?" Sloane grimaced. "Did I mention probation?"

Harper laughed. "I don't think there's going to be a problem. I'm on the performance review committee."

Sloane hoped her smile wasn't as weak as it felt. This nurse was intent on making her into a Mother Teresa, when nothing could be further from the truth. What was altruistic about simply recognizing her own kind? Poor choices? How many had she made in her thirty-two years—how many more would tempt her? Someone like Harper would never understand. And right now Sloane's priority was simple: be there, Wilder or Ferrell, to make herself heard at Bob Bullard's parole hearing. Nothing felt more important. That and the very real need to travel under the radar. Close relationships, friendships or otherwise, fit nowhere in that plan.

"We should get together away from the hospital sometime," Harper suggested, glancing toward the parking lot as a car with a noisy muffler screeched to the curb. "A movie, maybe. Or out to eat. I've heard good things about The Misfit in Santa Monica. They start happy hour at like noon. Five-dollar lunch specials, and it's all done sort of vintage French literary decor, with card catalogs, shelves of old books, and those tall tin ceilings." Her toothpaste smile gleamed. "You even get a free chocolate chip–sea salt cookie along with the bill for your cocktails and—"

"I don't drink," Sloane said in a rush, hating that it sounded rude.

"I don't either, really. I just thought . . ."

"My evenings are pretty booked. Because . . ." Sloane hesitated. Lying used to be much easier. "I'm taking some classes."

"No problem—good for you." Harper looked toward what sounded like a disturbance at the curb. That same car. "What's going on over there?"

"I can't tell for sure." Sloane stared, thinking it must be an argument—a man's voice rose above the background construction noises. A young woman wearing a black cap over pink hair opened the car's passenger door and attempted to slide out. Sloane stood, getting a bad feeling about the situation.

"Do they need help?" Harper asked, craning her neck to see. "It looks like that man is—"

"No!" the young woman shrieked, struggling to stand as the driver leaned across the passenger seat and gave her arm a savage yank. She dropped to one knee on the cement curb and pulled back, beginning to sob. The man grabbed a handful of her T-shirt, jerking her backward. She screamed again. "Stop! Let me go!"

Harper gasped, rising to her feet.

The car rolled forward, half-dragging the girl. "Help!"

"Call 911!" Sloane ordered, then bolted for the parking lot.

2

"I'VE GOT YOU—EASY; don't move yet." Sloane's rushed attempt to reassure the sprawled victim was obliterated by engine roar as the assailant's car peeled away. She blinked against exhaust and fine debris flung by the squealing tires.

"Get the license plate!" someone shouted, thudding footfalls adding to the chaos of the scene as witnesses seemed to arrive from everywhere.

"What happened?" A woman's voice in the clutch of gawkers. "Was that guy snatching her? A kidnapping? He nearly ran her down!"

"I think it was an older Honda Civic."

"No," another person challenged. "A Toyota."

"How's the girl? Is she okay?"

Sloane shifted her kneeling position on the curb, frowning

at the onlookers. Where was hospital security? And was that Prescott with those reporters—*taking photos?* Really?

Sirens wailed somewhere in the distance.

"You're safe now," Sloane assured the girl. She was dazed, pale, and seemed much younger up close. A teenager, probably. "I'm a nurse. Does your neck hurt?"

"No."

Blue eyes met Sloane's, their heavy liner and mascara smeared by tears. Raw, bleeding abrasions marked the girl's forehead and cheek. She was thin and, with that disheveled pink hair and a pierced eyebrow, looked like a doll tossed in a Goodwill bin. The girl dragged her fingers over her hair. "Where's my hat?"

"We'll find it," Sloane promised, slipping an arm around her shoulders as she attempted to sit up. "Easy now. Let me do most of it."

"We've got a wheelchair here," Harper offered. "Thanks, Jerry," she added, acknowledging the maintenance man who'd run to grab it. She pushed the chair closer. "Let me get these brakes locked."

"No wheelchair," the girl said, standing now. She stared, eyes wide, at the gathering of curious onlookers. "I'm fine. No problem."

"Here's her hat." Micah Prescott held out the dusty newsboy cap to Sloane. The man's usual smooth smile had been replaced by an expression of concern. Sloane wouldn't bet money, but it almost looked genuine. His voice was deep, calm. "You're taking her to the ER?"

"Yes."

"No," the girl insisted, claiming the cap from Sloane. "I'm fine. I'll go now."

"Hey! Hold on a minute." One of the reporters, a sun-tanned blond with curly hair and a long-lens camera in his hands, pushed forward like he intended to become the second man in ten minutes to accost this kid. "You knew that guy?"

"No." The girl's brows pinched. "He just offered me a ride and . . . um . . ."

"What exactly happened?" the reporter pressed. "And what's your name? Why did he bring you—?"

"Back off!" Sloane glared at the man, then turned to Micah to include him in the warning. "Tell them to go away. All of them. No cameras, no questions."

The girl took a step, grimaced with observable pain. *"Aagh."*

Sloane steadied her. "Your knee?"

"Hip, I think. Scraped maybe. No big deal." The girl lifted her chin. "I'm good."

Tough girl. Sloane knew that defense.

"I'm Sloane," she said, offering a small smile. "And you're . . . ?"

"I'm . . ." The girl looked around. The onlookers were leaving. Harper hung back a discreet distance. The girl's gaze dropped to Sloane's hospital ID badge. It was turned backward, something Sloane always did if she went outside the hospital. One more small stab at safety.

"I'm a nurse," Sloane assured, seeing the girl's wariness. She turned her ID badge around and tapped it. "Sloane from the ER."

"I'm Zoey," the girl said finally. "Zoey . . . Jones."

Jones. Right. And I'm a Ferrell.

"All right then, Zoey," Sloane told her. "How about if we go inside, make sure you're not hurt. Maybe find you some food?"

Zoey's pierced brow rose a fraction. "I could eat something, I guess."

"Good."

"No wheelchair."

"Got it." Sloane waved Harper on, then turned back to her unexpected patient. "It's not far to the ER. Lean on me if you need to."

"You'll never learn, Coop." Micah shook his head at the reporter's smirk. And his pitiful beard. Cooper Vance's effort to grow one wasn't going well; it looked like a patchy lawn subjected to years of California drought. Micah had seen the guy through more than a few attempts to make himself appear older, professionally seasoned. None more successful than this. He still looked like the weekend surf bum he was. They were both thirty-two and had met at UCLA, back when they had matching fires in their bellies for journalism. Coop was still chasing the dream—and still letting Micah spring for meal tabs. "You'll never get the story by getting in someone's face. One of these days I'll read you've been knocked flat by Justin Bieber . . . or a royal nanny."

"Nanny?" Cooper laughed against the lid of his Starbucks cup. "First, I'm no paparazzo—too much competition, no glory. I'm a serious journalist. Keeping our community informed about treadmill safety, low-water landscaping . . ."

Coop had finally landed a much-anticipated position at the *Times*, but it was somewhere down the staff list. And in the Lifestyle section. So far down the list, Coop liked to complain, that if he actually had an office, it would echo like the bottom of a well. Bylines were scarce. None of it fit with his plan to climb the ranks toward becoming a renowned journalist. He envisioned himself reporting via Skype on prime-time TV from hot spots around the globe. And had been jealous to the core when, several years back, Micah was given the opportunity to work with an embedded news team in Afghanistan. Coop had finally stopped asking why he wouldn't talk about it. Their friendship wasn't close enough for real confidences, but then again, Micah didn't talk to *anyone* about that time.

"Nope, probably don't need to worry I'm going to get myself into a brawl chasing a hot story. Although . . ." Coop peered down the hospital walkway toward the parking lot curb. "That was a close call out there. With your nurse."

My nurse?

The fact was, Micah had never had a conversation with Sloane Ferrell until today. If *"Here's her hat"* qualified as conversation. He'd spent a fair amount of time in and around the emergency department since the Face of Hope campaign started—had been pretty much forced to—but this nurse always managed to avoid him. It didn't seem accidental. She was like an apparition, hustling, efficient . . . an ever-dynamic gyroscope in scrubs. She disappeared whenever he came near. Out there in the parking lot was the nearest Micah had ever been to Sloane. Up close, within arm's reach. He'd have to admit it was worth the wait.

"Hard to imagine," Coop added, with a spreading smile, "that frosty-blue eyes can shoot fire. I think I got scorched."

Micah shook his head, pretending he hadn't been remembering those eyes himself. "You were interfering with patient care. No good nurse is going to let that happen."

"That kid wasn't a patient. Not yet. She was a victim. Maybe even an attempted kidnap victim. That's legitimate news."

13

Coop lifted his phone from his pocket, checked the screen. "No news yet on a BOLO for the perp's car. PD will probably want to review hospital security footage." He tossed his coffee cup in the trash and looked at the ER doors. "They should be here anytime to interview that girl. And the witnesses. I'll wait. There's a story here somewhere. I smell it."

Micah was thinking of a story too. But more along the lines of "LA Hope Nurse Saves Kidnap Victim." Sloane Ferrell couldn't be more than a few inches over five feet tall, maybe 110 pounds, but she'd launched herself like a drone missile into that hostile situation. She hadn't hesitated to put herself in harm's way to protect a stranger. Very few people did that, ran toward danger instead of away. It was heroic. And it should be recognized. That it could boost—help repair—the public image of Los Angeles Hope hospital during a major fund-raising campaign would be a bonus. And might even score Micah some points. The director of PR and marketing, his boss, was on a few weeks' leave after the birth of his first child. It was effectively Micah's chance to shine or flame out. That he was still ambivalent about this job didn't matter; he needed it.

"Your PIO will give a statement?" Cooper asked, glancing at his phone once more. "After the girl is examined and questioned by law enforcement?"

"It could happen." Micah had already sent her a message. "May take a while though."

"No problem. I could run over to North Alvarado and catch the Taco Zone truck," the reporter said, referencing a hipster-choice mobile eatery. "Grab some of that suadero and salsa verde you like."

That I *like?*

Micah recognized the gambit and tried to shake off a prickle of irritation he felt more and more these days. Cooper Vance helped pay for his grandmother's costly assisted-living apartment. And stopped by faithfully to clean up after her three cats, one of which consistently chose fake potted plants over the litter box. Micah could spring for Mexican.

"Don't forget our chips," he said as he reached for his wallet. "Wait for a fresh batch—it's worth it."

"For sure."

He watched Cooper head back across the parking lot, then checked his own phone. No update from Fiona, the hospital's public information officer. She was good about keeping him in the loop. The uniformed officers were likely still looking for the assailant's car. Coop was undoubtedly right: because it had seemed like an attempted abduction, detectives would be here to do interviews. If Micah was going to speak with Sloane Ferrell, it would have to be soon. He recalled what his friend said about eyes that could shoot fire. Probably true. But this was about the hospital's image. And his own career. He'd have to risk it.

"Sorry. Almost finished." Sloane lifted the stainless-steel forceps away from Zoey's cheek. The girl lay on the exam table, still wearing her baggy jeans and scuffed ankle boots; she'd agreed to a patient gown but refused an examination of her hip, saying it was fine now. She wouldn't let the doctor inject Xylocaine around the abrasions on her face, either—didn't like needles. Unfortunately, the alternative numbing gel proved to be less effective than Sloane had hoped. But Zoey had been stoic, barely a wince.

"I know it stings, but there's less chance of scarring if we get these clean," Sloane explained. "The scrape at your hairline is superficial, but this spot over your cheekbone is deeper than it looked and had some specks from the asphalt."

"It's fine—no big deal."

Not fooling me, kiddo.

It was anything but fine. Not the abrasions; those would heal. But everything about this child—she couldn't possibly be the nineteen years she'd claimed—whispered today's scary incident was simply one more in a long line of troubles. Sloane wasn't going to flatter herself that Zoey's lying on this gurney was a credit to her own bedside manner. It had everything to do with a bag of barbecue chips and a turkey sandwich—two turkey sandwiches. If the girl hadn't been so hungry, she'd be on the interstate thumbing another ride.

"Thank you." Zoey's whisper was barely audible over the noise outside the exam room door. The usual emergency department racket and a new series of overhead pages for respiratory therapy. She blinked up at Sloane as a trickle of numbing gel slid like a snail trail into her dyed-pink hairline. "You didn't have to come out there and help me. It wasn't like it's part of your job."

"No . . . not really." Sloane dropped the forceps onto a small tray of surgical instruments and stripped off her sterile gloves. "Let's just say I've been in a few tight spots myself. If I can help somebody out, I'm gonna do that."

"Yeah . . ." Zoey's lips tugged toward a smile for the first time. "Then you took on that dude with the camera. Seems like you've done that before too."

Sloane shrugged. "Not a fan of folks who invade people's privacy."

"For sure. But that taller guy with the sunglasses, the one who found my hat—he wasn't half-bad to look at. For a reporter."

Sloane shook her head. "Not a reporter. He's the hospital's marketing guy."

"Same difference. Snoopy and pushy."

"Yep," Sloane agreed.

Zoey's gaze lingered on Sloane's ID badge. "Ferrell . . . Irish, right?"

"Uh . . . somewhere back there, I guess." Did anyone ever consider the heritage aspect of a fake name? "Okay then," Sloane said, changing the subject. "We're pretty much finished here."

Zoey let Sloane help her to a sitting position, then glanced toward the exam room door as if to assess their privacy. "There isn't any more to say about what happened," she said, lowering her voice some. "I was on my way to Bakersfield to stay with a friend for a while. My ride backed out at the last minute and I don't have a car."

"You hitched a ride."

"Yeah, so?" She crossed her arms. "I'm not stupid. I know girls end up in Dumpsters. I'm careful, okay?" Zoey hesitated, then continued. "That guy seemed all right. For maybe fifty miles. And then his grubby hand was crawling up my leg."

Sloane's stomach twisted.

"I saw the hospital sign. So I faked belly pains. I told him I had a serious 'female problem' and I needed to get to an ER. I figured he'd drop me off and I'd go in one door and out the other." Zoey shook her head. "I had to go and mouth off at the last minute. Tell him what I thought of creeps like him."

"And he tried to pull you back into the car."

"Could have, maybe. If you hadn't come running like a bat out of—"

"Sloane!" Harper's face appeared at the door. "Code 3 trauma pulling up. Two stabbing victims. One under CPR."

"On my way." Sloane turned to Zoey. "Hang out for a few. We still need to dress those wounds."

"Save the world. I'm good here."

3

"NOTHING. NO PALPABLE PULSES, carotid or femoral," Sloane reported as the physician studied the deceiving display on the trauma room cardiac monitor: marching electric complexes that looked like viable heart activity. And should have been, if most of this young man's blood weren't congealing in a garbage-strewn alley somewhere. His face was the same shade of gray as his hooded sweatshirt, shredded by a paramedic's trauma scissors. Only a trickle of blood oozed from the deep wound beneath his left nipple. A scant trickle but still red in color since aggressive fluid resuscitation was contraindicated in a penetrating wound of the heart. As was flogging the organ with repeated doses of adrenaline. Even cardiac compressions could be viewed as controversial. . . .

A penetrating wound to the heart. It had to have been a horrible scene.

Sloane could imagine the frustration of the medics. Their patient dying before their eyes and so many of their lifesaving protocols ineffective. A trauma like this was load and go, lights and sirens, praying all the way—for people who did that sort of thing. She glanced at the gold chain around the young man's neck. A crucifix lay against his pale shoulder, glued to a skull tattoo by dried blood.

"Start compressions?" the tech asked.

"Hang on." The physician's gaze moved past the ultrasound equipment to an open and ready emergency thoracotomy tray. He turned to the paramedic who'd attended the patient on scene. "No signs of life in the field? During transport? Give me a reason to crack this kid's chest."

"No pulse," the medic confirmed, repeating his initial report, "no respiratory effort. Unknown down time. Pale, warm. No response to compressions and respiratory support. Monitor showed PEA throughout. Pupils like they are now. There were no eyewitnesses except for the other victim." The assailant, reportedly a rival gang member, was the ER's other patient—less seriously injured and unwilling to give any details.

"Seventeen minutes," the paramedic added, checking the trauma room clock, "since we arrived on scene. Maybe fourteen since we tubed him."

An endotracheal tube down the young man's throat and past his vocal cords. At least they'd been able to secure an airway.

"Seventeen minutes . . . ," the physician muttered, checking the monitor again.

A few seconds of silence accentuated the whoosh of oxygen

as a respiratory therapist squeezed the football-shaped Ambu bag delivering oxygen to the victim's lungs.

"Okay then." The physician pressed his fingers deep against his patient's femoral artery as he watched the monitor complexes one more time. A wide, utterly useless and slowing pattern on a field of black, too much like a fading comet in the night sky. "Any family?"

"None yet," Harper answered, sadness in her expression. "The crisis responders were called. They'll be involved with notifications."

"Stop bagging," the physician ordered, nodding to the respiratory therapist. "We're done here." He shook his head, mumbled something about useless pride, waste . . . and no respect for the value of life. "Time of death: 14:47."

Micah scrolled down the text one more time: a request from LAPD for community crisis responders to assist after a violent crime. They would provide support to any family of victims after this gang-related stabbing incident. Maybe they'd be doing a death notification; he'd just seen one of the victims rushed to the ER under CPR. From what he'd already heard, it didn't sound good. He felt for the families—and for the crisis team, trained volunteers who put themselves out there to offer help in the aftermath of life-altering tragedy. He'd heard the term *"emotional paramedics"* used more than once. Micah had to agree with that.

He knew how tough it was and how valuable a service the crisis volunteers provided, because for a minimum of twenty hours a month, it was exactly what he did. After his regular work hours at the hospital and on his days off. Lately, any opportunity he got. Unsure as he was about the marketing job, Micah was as certain crisis work was where he belonged. He'd gone through the training with California Crisis Care several years back. After Afghanistan. It had come at a time when finding something that satisfied his soul became all-important, maybe even his own lifeline of hope. He'd made the decision and then wasn't certain he'd survive the training; it picked at every scab he thought he'd healed. But it had been worth it. And now he was extending a lifeline to others every time he pulled on that crisis volunteer jacket and showed up to support a grieving elderly spouse, a mother who lost her baby to SIDS, the family of a suicide victim or homicide victim . . . It was the most important work he'd ever done. But it was his day job that paid the bills; it was high time he proved himself there, too.

Right now that meant checking in with that frosty-fiery nurse, Sloane Ferrell. There were a few things he needed to talk over with her.

"I'm glad it's you, not me, dealing with that other gangster," Sloane told Harper. "I'm not sure I could act all 'poor baby' over a minor flesh wound after pulling the ET tube and zipping his victim into a body bag."

Harper connected with Sloane's gaze. "If anyone could do it, you could—angel of the misunderstood and downtrodden."

Angel?

"Not when we're talking assault and murder," Sloane said. "Maybe I haven't always drawn enough lines in my life, but that one is huge and in permanent marker. Underlined." She thought of her whispered conversation with the office assistant at the state prison. "I'll leave the 'angelic' TLC to you."

"You're making that Misfit bar sound better and better. Happy hour munchies, ocean breeze . . . free cookies?"

"Your misfit is waiting in trauma room 9. And I still have my would-be kidnap victim. She needs a champion. That's where I'll be."

"Right." Harper lifted a brow. "After your chat with marketing."

"Huh?"

"Over there, signaling to you. Maybe we'll be seeing you on a billboard?"

Sloane turned.

Micah Prescott.

Great.

She had no illusions that the man wanted her image on a freeway sign. This had to be about their exchange at the parking lot curb when she'd basically told him to butt out. That's why he was standing in the corridor, ridiculously good-looking and foolishly well-dressed for a department that prided itself on blood spatter and worse. No sunglasses, no easy smile, but definitely an expression of cool control. As if Micah Prescott, assistant director of marketing and public relations, had just taped a sign to the ER wall that read, *Keep Calm and Play the Game.*

Fat chance.

"I'm too busy," Sloane told him, her dismissal saying it didn't matter what Micah wanted; she wasn't going to be part of it. "No time to talk," she added, glancing past him toward a patient room. "I need to finish up with a patient."

"Zoey Jones?"

Sloane's small frown confirmed it.

"She's exactly why I wanted to speak with you," Micah explained, struck again by the nurse's physical presence. Attractive, but more than that—a powerhouse in a small package, with those compelling eyes . . . "Zoey Jones," he explained. "And what happened in the parking lot."

"If you're expecting an apology, you're wasting your time. And mine." A small pinch of Sloane's dark brows hinted she regretted the words. Maybe. "Look. The last thing that kid needed was a crowd of gawkers. Or worse, being manhandled by media. Just because she needed help doesn't mean she's fair game. A person's private life isn't up for grabs as some kind of spectator sport. And if you're going to argue that HIPAA rights don't apply until—"

"I'm not."

Her lashes, black as newspaper ink, flicked, but she held his gaze.

"I'm not here for an apology. Or to argue," Micah insisted, caught off guard by her preemptive hostility. Best to temper that with some praise—easy enough since she more than deserved it. "I only wanted to say what you did out there was impressive. Not many people would." She swallowed, but the blue eyes didn't blink. "People pull out their phones and snap pictures first, think of calling 911 second. Or third, after posting to social media. They're not willing to wade into the mess of someone else's life. They watch."

"Why are you telling me this?"

"I noticed, that's all. I respect what you did. Admire it." Micah was sure he saw wariness in her eyes. He was probably laying it on too thick. And she was smart, maybe even street-smart. There was something beneath the beauty that hinted at it. "Who knows what might have happened if you hadn't stepped up. It took courage. I think everyone out there would say that. It's the reason the reporters—"

"Stop. I don't want to talk about reporters or rehash any of this. It's over and I have work to do."

"So do I," Micah countered, his patience wearing thin. "And right now you're making it a lot harder. Maybe you're not ready to give a statement, but just so you know, it might not be over. People will talk. Someone will ask for the name of the nurse who—"

"No." The frosty eyes held his, fully armed. "That's not okay. Not happening."

"It hasn't happened," Micah told her, trying to keep the irritation out of his voice. He was getting nowhere and had a hunch she was a split second from sprinting away—or lashing out. Her expression made him think of warnings about cornered animals. "No one's been given your name." He looked down the hall toward the trauma rooms. "It's possible media inquiries will be focused on the gang incident now."

"Yes." There was more than a hint of relief in Sloane's expression. "Murder always gets top billing."

Micah knew better than to ask, but this meant at least one of the gangsters was dead. His crisis team would be handling a death notification.

"I need to get back to Zoey," she announced as a trio of police officers strode by. They were accompanied by a man in a suit, most likely a detective. "If she wants someone with her when they take the police report, I'll do that."

Once again, Micah had the sense this woman's compassion sprang from more than her training. Not that she'd ever reveal it, and getting to know her wasn't part of his plan. Good thing to remember.

"So . . . we're done here," Sloane added, taking a step away.

"Right," Micah said finally. "I'll see you around."

Sloane's expression said she couldn't imagine why. And wouldn't want to. "Probably," she conceded. "Small medical world."

As she walked away, it occurred to Micah that maybe he'd lied about no one asking her identity or having it. Coop had asked and Micah had readily supplied Sloane's full name. Friend to friend, not official. But he'd done it. And the eager reporter would be back any minute with a sack of Taco Zone specialties. Unless he'd been sidetracked by a phone alert regarding the gang incident. In which case Coop would already be outside the ER, vying with other reporters for details on the story. Sloane was right: murder trumped attempted abduction. And heroism.

Still, there had to be a way to spin Sloane Ferrell's selfless good deed into a hefty plug for the hospital. Like it or not, it was his job.

―――――――

Sloane covered the short distance to Zoey's exam room, trying to convince herself she'd kept her cool with the marketing man. Too many times in the past she'd gone all bristly-ballistic and struck out, losing her credibility and once, in San Diego, very nearly losing her job. It had been ugly and the lead-in to things she'd rather forget. The fact was, no one would ever understand her need to protect and defend people who'd been kicked around and victimized. But she had to. Anything else would be a denial of where she'd been and who she was. She was tap-dancing as fast as she could to present herself as someone else in this confusing new life, but though her name tag said otherwise, not so deep down she was still Ronda Sloane Wilder—and everything that came with that.

She pasted on a smile for a police officer passing by, at the least the fourth she'd seen. Here to interview the other gang member probably. Or . . .

She hoped he hadn't already been in to talk with Zoey. Pink hair and tough attitude aside, the girl was dealing with a world of hurt. So young to have to accept those kinds of realities, but Sloane understood and then some.

Happiness was a fairy tale. She couldn't afford to waste time mooning over it. Or believing men like Micah Prescott. His words about courage, that fleeting sincerity in his warm brown eyes . . . For a short moment it had almost felt good. But it was a lie, not that different from the kindness of the man who'd given Zoey Jones a ride. Then pegged her as suitable prey.

"Zoey?" Sloane knocked on the door, knocked again, and then opened it. "I'm back and—" The exam table was empty except for the discarded patient gown. "Zoey?"

Sloane whipped around and peered down the hall toward the bathroom.

"Looking for that young lady from the parking lot?"

"Yes, I . . ." Sloane recognized the fiftysomething maintenance worker who'd helped Harper with the wheelchair. Jerry. Round face, graying temples, earnest eyes, always a pencil wedged over one ear and always smiling—except right now. "Have you seen her?"

"Maybe a couple of minutes ago. She came out of her room, looking sort of nervous. I asked if she needed a nurse. She said no, she was all finished here."

"Which way did she go?"

Jerry pointed.

"Thanks," Sloane told him, beginning to jog down the corridor toward the exit. *Nervous.* Sure she was. Sirens, the whole department swarming with cops—Zoey would absolutely be finished with that. Sloane couldn't blame her a bit. But the girl still needed those bandages and instructions.

She pushed through the double doors, strode past the visitors' tables, scanned the parking lot and the busy, palm-lined street beyond. No sign of—

"Ma'am?"

Sloane turned, startled for a moment. A man in a suit. Badge on his belt.

"Detective Mendoza, LAPD," he said, his gaze flicking to her name tag. "You're Sloane Ferrell?"

Her pulse hiked. "Uh . . . yes."

"Good." The detective offered a reflexive smile. "I'll need you to answer some questions."

4

SAFE.

Sloane slid the chain into place, its brass still shiny against the oily-dark surface of the front door. It was an arched wooden door, stained walnut with black iron fittings, forged nail heads, and a small, square window protected by a matching iron grille. The kind of door that belonged in a castle, not a tiny rental cottage tucked beside a retiree's Los Angeles garage. Sloane had never cared about doors, never given them much thought beyond what they locked out, but this one had enchanted her the moment she'd seen it. Sort of an Old World welcome to a new life. That her landlady, the owner and occupant of the main house, had been okay with Sloane's Home Depot security chain—even loaned her a flower-embellished hammer to install it—made this dwelling choice seem fated somehow. Three locks, a landlady who respected privacy, a short drive to the hospital, and . . .

"Hey, you," Sloane said, smiling as the black cat—still a kitten, really—trotted toward her, springy, ballet-light, and uttering a raspy meow with each footfall. She laughed as Marty's yellow eyes blinked up at her, then bent down and scooped him up. He butted his velvety head beneath her jaw and nipped playfully at Sloane's chin before settling against her scrub top with a rumbling purr. "You don't fool me, mister," she told him, walking toward the kitchen. "All I'm worth to you is a three-ounce can of Grilled Chicken Feast."

An image came to mind: Zoey wolfing down those turkey sandwiches. At least the girl had gone AWOL with a full stomach. Her tetanus shots were up-to-date—if she'd told the truth. Sloane felt certain the few bits of information she'd shared about herself were mostly fictional. *Because it takes one to know one?* Probably. She shouldn't have been surprised Zoey took off; when the clerk said something about a police detective wanting to interview witnesses, the girl's eyes had gone wide. California had laws against hitchhiking, but Sloane would bet it was more than that.

"Fine. Be that way," she chided as Marty sprang from her arms to the dark hardwood floor, collar tags jingling. "But see if you can be patient while I get your food into the dish."

The detective had been patient interviewing Sloane, though her answers were far less helpful than he'd hoped. Yes, she'd seen the incident in the parking lot—some of it, not all. She didn't know cars well enough to ID the make or model. She'd been looking at the girl. The driver, the man, had been in shadow for the most part. Late thirties, maybe; white probably. Sunglasses, knit hat pulled down over . . . blond hair?

She'd danced around the questions as best she could.

"*Yes, Ferrell.* F-e-r-r-e-l-l." She didn't tell the detective it was newly changed. Or that she'd chosen it because of its similarity to *feral*, another word for *wild*. It had seemed clever at the time. Now it was just one more sandbag in a bunker of lies.

Sloane didn't tell him, either, that she'd changed her name because she didn't want her ex-fiancé, Paul Stryker, to track her down. Or, worse by far, for his former associates—mobsters, she'd been horrified to discover—to find her. And use her, Paul had warned a dozen times, to exact revenge for his unpaid gambling debts. It had seemed surreal initially, darkly laughable and so much like any number of Paul's whopper tales. Then the threatening phone calls started and Sloane's car was forced off the road—and over a cliff. Though her vehicle seemed the primary target, the incident had occurred in rush hour traffic and involved other cars. Two people were killed. They'd never identified the driver of the at-fault vehicle, a stolen car. It had been found abandoned. And set on fire.

"*Arson . . . it's their trademark,*" Paul's last phone message had warned. Sloane knew him well enough to recognize the fear choking his usual cocky bravado.

She'd never admitted her unwelcome connection to organized crime to the accident investigators, still hoping against reason that it had been coincidental. But when the calls started again—and she'd recovered enough from extensive injuries—Sloane packed up her cat and fled San Diego. The last she heard, the incident was still being investigated as a joyride gone bad. She wanted it to stay that way, unsolved and unconnected to her. It gave her at least a small sense of peace. These last months, Sloane was sleeping better. Going about her life with less fear that someone would show up on the porch and—

A rap at the door made her drop the cat food can.

"Sloane? It's Celeste. You've got mail."

"Coming!" Sloane peeled off the can lid, filled Marty's dish, and set it on the floor. "Be right there."

Door lock, dead bolt, brass chain. Slow breath. Better.

"Hey, Celeste." Sloane found a smile, easier because her landlady's six-year-old granddaughter was also there. Big eyes, bigger grin, and masses of taffy-colored curls. "And *heeey*, Piper."

"We brought your boxth," the child announced, lisping a little after her double donation to the tooth fairy. She pointed to the cardboard carton lying on the steps and her big eyes got bigger. "The one with the Lucky Charms lepper-kon on it."

"Not quite the first of the month," Celeste confirmed, swiping at her unruly hair—a gray edition of the family curls. Her plump face lit with a teasing smile. "General Mills is more punctual than Social Security."

"Never miss a month."

It wasn't true; they still owed Sloane a shipment—there had been some initial confusion when she changed her name. The company would eventually make it right, and Celeste would dutifully walk the rainbow-colored box back to Sloane's porch. A necessary arrangement, Celeste had explained at their first meeting, since the cottage didn't have its own address. Mail was delivered to the main house. In truth, Sloane had been relieved at this added privacy. And that Celeste had said, "No problem" when she explained there would also be a monthly delivery of a box filled with assorted cereals, toaster pastries, and lately, some new "natural" and gluten-free products.

The landlady listened to Sloane's offhand explanation of having won a lifetime supply of Lucky Charms as a child and never questioned it. The same way she hadn't questioned Sloane's name change since the initial lease application, or why she preferred to pay rent in cash, or why, in nearly five months of living here, her tenant never had a visitor. Celeste didn't pry, snoop, or hover. The fact that she was an LA Hope retiree, after forty years as a PBX operator, even gave them something in common. And made it unnecessary for Sloane to explain her odd hours, overtime shifts, or emergency calls.

"Which one is your favorite?" Piper asked, squatting down to tap her finger over a neon-bright image of the leprechaun's cereal bowl. "Of all of them."

"I don't know," Sloane told her, suddenly uncomfortable. Why on earth did she still have these delivered? Twenty-six years . . . "Maybe the breakfast bars."

"Not that." Piper's doe eyes peered up at Sloane. "I meant your favorite Lucky Charm. The hearts, shamrocks, moons, or—"

"I hate marshmallows," Sloane interrupted, instantly ashamed when the child's brow puckered. "I mean . . . I try to be careful about sugar."

"And so do we," Celeste said gently, taking her granddaughter by the hand. "Which reminds me, I promised your mother I'd feed you dinner, sweetie. Mommy has her new class after work tonight." Celeste handed Sloane the small stack of envelopes. "You, too?"

"Me?"

"Class." Celeste smiled. "Is this a class night?"

"My evenings are pretty booked. . . . I'm taking some classes."

"No," Sloane said, shame taking a second swipe. "Tomorrow night."

"Good. Maybe you can put your feet up and relax a little. I know how hard that hospital can work a person."

"Yes." Sloane sighed. "It's been a long day."

She thanked Piper for her offer to carry the General Mills box inside but said she could manage it herself. She watched the two walk back toward the main house, stopping briefly beside a small, raised garden bed so the little girl could perform what appeared to be some of her Kids' Karate moves— with an added double pirouette. Her innocent, happy giggles floated back on the breeze. A child free to be a child. An ache crowded Sloane's throat.

She carried the cereal carton into the house, closed the door, and locked it.

———

"But it's not quite Lifestyle copy," Micah said, watching as Coop munched through the last of an enormous stack of fried onion rings. He'd actually made good on a rare offer to buy Micah a burger. Something about gas prices being down and an incredible deal on clumping kitty litter having put extra cash in his pocket. Micah wasn't going to question it, but sharing two meals with Cooper Vance in the same day said too much about his meager social life. "You're working up a feature on prisons?"

"Yep." Coop's shredded-wheat beard was littered with crumbs. "Very popular."

Micah stared at him.

"I'm serious. Reality TV, movies. Anything 'prison' is an instant hit." Coop grinned. "Add a mob element, pure gold."

"You're losing me. And you're a long way from treadmills and xeriscape, which, by the way, buy your gasoline and cat litter."

Coop frowned. "I'm not forgetting that, but you know me. Always scratching for the next big thing. The story behind the story, something to get excited about. You don't make it in this business if you don't go that extra million miles."

"And some of those miles are taking you to State Prison?"

"A lot lately. I know someone there." He laughed at Micah's expression and picked up his glass of microbrew beer. "Not an inmate. Someone in the parole office. She lets me know if anything interesting is coming up. I don't care about usual stuff like burglary or drugs—dime a dozen. But they have this dude who's in for criminal fraud only because they couldn't get him for meatier crimes up and down the state. Human trafficking, illegal gambling, arson . . . I've been working on this for a while. I don't mind doing research, putting two and two together."

"If it adds up to a *Times* byline."

"Sure." Coop shrugged. "I'll start with that."

Micah shook his head. Coop wasn't wasting a minute moping over the fact that nothing had panned out for him with the gang stabbing incident. TV news had been all over that one. And with the disappearance of Zoey Jones, the abduction story was put on hold as well. As far as Coop was concerned, that was. "We really are in different camps now," Micah mused.

"What do you mean?" Coop filched one of Micah's fries.

"You're out there looking for trouble, hoping you find it so you can blow things wide-open. Get the scoop, boost your career. And I'm . . ." Micah's laugh was halfhearted. "I'm doing everything I can to put a happy face on LA Hope. Showcase our dedicated staff, prove once and for all that we're the hospital with real heart. Or at least put to rest all that bad press from a couple of years back."

"Don't blame the press. It was your chief of staff who got falling-down drunk, climbed into his Lexus, and mowed people down like bowling pins." Coop grimaced. "Sorry, buddy—too close to home."

It was. Micah's younger cousin Stephen, in every way a brother, had died in a car driven by an intoxicated college classmate—two twenty-year-olds in a twisted mass of metal. The driver survived, but Stephen's lifeless body was almost too damaged to identify. To say it had changed the Prescott family's lives was a gross understatement. It affected Micah's own like a near-fatal bloodletting. He hated drunks.

"No problem. I know what you meant," Micah told his friend. "It didn't help the hospital's image that the ER staff did everything they could to interfere with the initial investigation. There were a lot of bad actors in that incident."

"And heads rolled."

"Fourteen people fired." Micah reached for his Coke. "Now if I want to keep my job, I need to run a campaign that gets the Excellence in Aging wing funded and has everybody applauding the new Face of Hope."

"Prison sounds easier."

Micah shrugged. "I'm working on a few things."

Like a heroic nurse?

He thought of Sloane Ferrell running toward the parking lot to save that girl from a would-be abductor. Then remembered her reaction to the reporters and their conversation later in the ER corridor. She was obviously a private person, but he'd find a way to make this work to the hospital's advantage. He'd talk with the PIO, get her take on it. After all, Sloane was a new employee, still on probation; having some positive attention would be a benefit. He'd manage to convince her of that.

"It's okay. We're good," Sloane told her cat. He'd just completed his dinnertime obstacle course: kitchen floor to kitchen counter, tags jingling as he vaulted onward to kitchen table. Then to his perch, a discreet but still advantageous distance from Sloane's plate. His eyes moved like a tennis spectator's each time she lifted her fork. She glanced at her laptop again. "No e-mails, no texts or phone messages. That makes . . ." Sloane did the mental calculation. "More than four months we've been in the clear."

In hiding.

She shoved the thought aside, telling herself this was what it felt like to be free. The price was more than worth it. Last she'd heard, Paul was in Mexico. He'd had to go farther than she did to stay ahead of the men intent on "persuading" him to make good on loans from that illegal enterprise in Sacramento. Paul had managed to entice several city firefighters into what he'd described to Sloane as a friendly game of poker. It became a nightmare that ultimately threatened careers, relationships . . . and lives.

She reached for her lemon water in its plastic tumbler, one of a set in rainbow colors. She didn't like drinking from plastic, not from fear of toxic chemicals but because of the way it made things taste, feel. Celeste had provided a small collection of kitchen things, including a set of vintage rooster canisters and a matching apron. But the only alternatives to the plastic tumblers, besides some smallish coffee mugs, were wineglasses. Up on the top shelf—three. Not fine crystal, not even close. But sparkling, translucent, alluring, and too much like a glass door to a familiar escape. They needed to stay high on that shelf; Sloane was as wary of having a wineglass in her hand as she was about giving out her address. Plastic was ugly but safe.

"When it's been a year," she told Marty, "I'll spring for a set of water goblets like the ones I saw in that World Market ad. Heavy sea glass with all the little bubbles."

Sloane's phone buzzed against the tabletop. She lifted it, saw the number, and her breath released, a frisson of lingering anxiety replaced by relief. It was a response to her earlier call to the prison.

"Yes, hello," she said, not caring that Marty's paw had swiped the last few bits of her baked chicken. The spoiled rescue kitten still boasted survival skills. "This is Sloane Ferrell."

"Miss Ferrell, Marcie Dumler at State Prison. We spoke earlier."

"Right." Sloane's heart rate ticked upward. *Please . . .*

"Your name change caused some initial confusion," the woman began, an obvious rebuke. "But we have confirmed you are on the approved list to be present at the hearing for Robert Bullard on October 17 at 0900—that's 9 a.m."

"Yes." Sloane listened as the woman recited the address, policy, and basic visitation procedure. The complete instructions could be found online. "I understand," she said, a fuzzy image of her stepfather's face coming to mind. It had been so many years. Would she even recognize him? "And I'll be allowed to speak? I was told I could."

"I have a notation of that, yes. But you must understand—" her tone took on the effect of a police pat down—"that the board may make changes to the agenda. Because of time or unforeseen situations."

"But most likely I'll get to?" She hated that her voice sounded like a pleading child's. "I really need this chance."

"Of course." Marcie's voice softened as if there were actual pumping ventricles beneath the penitentiary crust. "I understand you want to show your support. Fathers and daughters have such a strong bond."

What? "But he isn't—"

"I'm not privy to decisions made here," the woman continued, oblivious. "Nor would I make any predictions. But I've been at this prison for nineteen years and I hear things. Let's just say Mr. Bullard's early release would come as no surprise. That's not in any way official, but I hope it helps you."

"Um, yes . . . thank you," Sloane said, ending the call.

She took a sip of her water, tasted the acrid plastic. Then closed her eyes for a moment and wondered if there would ever be sea glass days. If she'd ever know any real peace.

"I hope it helps you."

It did help, but not in the way Marcie Dumler assumed. The possibility that Bob Bullard's sentence could be cut short by two full years made Sloane sick. And more determined than ever to stop it. Ten years ago her testimony had helped convince a jury to put her stepfather behind bars. Even then, the sentence wasn't nearly harsh enough. For this man to skip out on it now would be the worst kind of injustice. He didn't deserve to walk free. Not after . . .

You killed my mother.

5

"I'M GOING TO GIVE YOU more happy juice," Sloane told her patient as she reached for the syringe of analgesic. "Don't move. We need you just like that: facedown, sandbag under your collarbone." She shook her head, knowing a layperson would think this was some nasty form of torture. "Juice" or not, there was no happy going on here.

The young man lay stripped to the waist on the exam table, sweat beading on his sun-browned skin and muscles quivering with pain. The right shoulder looked different from the left, its angles flattened and the substantial deltoid muscle not quite normal. According to the history, the injury happened by way of an impressive beach volleyball spike followed by a headlong crash into another player. It resulted in anterior

displacement of the head of the humerus—a shoulder dislocation. Not this patient's first.

"That's good, Mark. I know it's hard, but just let your arm
dangle."

"I'm . . . trying. This is like torture."

You said it, buddy.

Today's ER doc preferred Stimson's method for reducing
the dislocation: patient prone on a table, affected arm hanging off the edge with a ten-pound weight attached to the
wrist. Stretch, groan, pull. Something akin to the old medie-
val rack in piecemeal fashion. The theory was that once the
limb ceased its painful spasms, the joint would spontaneously
move into normal alignment. Stretch, groan, stretch . . . pop.
All better. Special sling, out the door. But it had been more
than fifteen minutes and—

"It's . . . not . . . working," the man groaned again, a rivulet
of sweat trickling down his pale face. "I'm afraid I'm going to
puke. I'm sorry, but it's never been this bad before. I usually
pop it right back in myself."

"Slow, deep breath," Sloane advised. "Hang in there. I'm
injecting the medication now."

"I don't feel it. I can't do this. I need . . . *mmmph.*" The
young man's moan morphed into a half snore and his body
relaxed, the weights lugging toward the floor. Sloane cycled
the blood pressure cuff, made note of the heart rate and
steadily beeping oxygen monitor. It was taking a lot of meds
to get this man's muscles relaxed. He was a big guy, a firefighter. When the ER doctor mentioned the possibility of
future shoulder surgery, he'd insisted it wouldn't be possible.
He was on track to take the captain's exam; nothing was more
important than that.

Sloane closed her eyes against an intruding memory and the sadness and shame that always came with it. Sacramento and another man with ambitions. Another of her monumental mistakes. Some things could never be left behind. There was no way to get life into "normal alignment" by slowly stretching it out with weights. Or burdens.

"Hey . . . wow." Mark's heavy-lidded eyes met Sloane's. "Something popped."

"Great," she said, agreeing the shoulder looked much improved. She gave his arm a pat. "Hang tight and don't move yet. I'll get the doctor to come have a look. And then we can—"

"Sloane?" Harper peeked into the room. "Should I take over here so you can get to that meeting? It's close to 2:15."

"Right. Thanks. I almost forgot."

She'd definitely tried to. Everything hinged on keeping her life private; an unexplained summons by the hospital's public information officer couldn't be more at odds with that goal. Unfortunately, Sloane had a hunch where this was headed. She didn't like it one bit.

———

Beautiful and immediately hostile. One glimpse told Micah he'd underestimated this challenge.

"I should have known you were behind it," Sloane said, finding him sitting alone in Fiona's office. "Is our PIO even coming? Or was this a diversion tactic?"

"Diversion?"

Sloane crossed her arms. "Because you figured I wouldn't come if I knew it was you."

"No . . ." She was right; the meeting was Micah's idea. But right now he was more concerned that this hostility was . . .

personal? It sure felt like it. He pulled out an adjacent chair, expecting her to refuse it. She didn't disappoint. Color infused her cheeks. Attractive if she wasn't assuming a battle stance. "There's no 'tactic.' Fiona called us both here."

"And . . . ?" She glanced around.

"She just texted me. She'll be late. She said to make ourselves at home. There's coffee. And that tray of muffins."

Sloane's dark brows pinched. "Seriously? Muffins?"

Micah cleared his throat, more surprised by her disrespect for baked goods than for his offer of seating. Hospital staff were notorious snackers; ask any sharp sales rep. It wasn't as if he'd asked her to nibble crumbs from his palm, for crying out loud. "Look, I didn't call the meeting, but I'm sure you've guessed it's about the incident with that girl."

"I gave a full report to the police."

That was a stretch. Micah overheard the detective complain he'd once prodded more information from a troupe of mimes.

"Fiona's responsibility is to the hospital," he explained, rising from his chair. He realized immediately that it was a mistake; she probably viewed it as an intimidation tactic. He was taller by a head—and she'd just squared her shoulders. "A PIO needs to be able to relay information to the media, answer queries."

"Have there been?" There was the faintest suggestion of nervousness in Sloane's expression. "Queries?"

"I think so—I know so," Micah told her honestly. "I had a call from the *Times* and referred it to Fiona. I believe she received a couple of calls directly. My best guess is that at least a dozen witnesses called 911 from our parking lot. It stirs things up. And requires Fiona to make a statement that both speaks the truth and presents the hospital in the most positive light. A big part of a PIO's job is to put a face on the organization."

Sloane frowned. "You seem to be obsessed with faces."

And you want to fight. Not going to oblige. Micah made himself take a slow breath, a crisis team method borrowed from combat training. Who knew he'd need it to deal with a nurse?

"I think," he said finally, "what Fiona will want is a simple statement. But moreover, she'd like to be able to personalize it with something about you. 'Sloane Ferrell, skilled and compassionate LA Hope nurse, going above and beyond the call of duty.' Something like that."

"Because it's good press."

"Because you did a good thing, Sloane. I told you that before—I meant it." Micah met her gaze directly and saw the suspicion there. "Sure, it would be good press. But it's also good news at a time when there's bad news everywhere you turn." He thought of the crisis team tagline: *"When tragedy strikes, we're there."* "What's wrong with taking some personal credit for a good deed? Sharing it with the public?"

"So if it's not public—if I don't share—it doesn't count."

"I'm not saying that." Micah couldn't curb the frustration in his tone. He was getting nowhere. "But maybe you could look at it a different way. On a more practical level. You're a new hire. It doesn't hurt to impress the powers that be. You did a great thing for that girl. Some people are even saying it was heroic. Maybe it's only fair that it also helps you and—"

"Stop," Sloane warned, her face coloring again. She took a step toward Micah. "That girl didn't stay long enough to get a Band-Aid. There was nothing 'great' about what I did. It didn't change her life, and a dumb-luck incident in a hospital parking lot won't *ever* change mine. It's not like one random event can just pop things back into perfect alignment."

A faraway look came into Sloane's eyes, one that Micah had seen before. With trauma victims. What was going on with this woman? He was trying to remind himself that it was none of his concern when Sloane shook her head and the fire was back.

"Zoey Jones is gone. It's over. Done." She glanced up at the clock on the wall. "I need to be gone too. Back to work. I can't hang around here."

"Okay, but . . ." Micah hesitated, unsure how to proceed. "There are still those queries from the press. Fiona will need to respond."

"I can't stop that. But I won't offer anything to make her statement personal. I have a right to privacy."

"Of course," Micah agreed, thinking of the photo he'd seen on Coop's camera when they were having lunch, one he'd snapped during the parking lot incident. Coop had been double-checking to see if there was anything helpful to police regarding the identity of the car. There wasn't because he'd been focused on the people: Sloane kneeling beside Zoey Jones. A dramatic image but useless since he hadn't been able to cover the story. Micah was fairly certain Coop deleted it. He had, hadn't he? Probably should give him a call and—

". . . if the hospital goes ahead anyway, I'll do it," Sloane was saying, her expression suddenly a mix of defiance and something that looked a lot like fear. "You can tell that to Fiona, and she can pass it to the 'powers that be.'"

"I'm sorry—what?"

The blue eyes held his. "I said I won't have any of my personal information made public. No photos, no contact information. Nothing. If the hospital does that, I'll be forced to take action."

Legal action?

Sloane snatched a muffin from the tray and strode out.

"I think that's going to do it," Sloane told Harper while adjusting the CPAP mask over their patient's mouth and nostrils. The sixty-two-year-old wholesale manager, highlighted auburn hair still stuck to her forehead from sweat, dozed now. Her color was much improved, and her respirations—though still moist—were far less labored, and slower. Twenty-two breaths per minute according to the overhead monitor, with an oxygen saturation of 95 percent. Her blood pressure had stabilized as well. The paramedic crew had done a good job getting the ball rolling, and the ER team had taken it from there with nitrates, vasopressors, and ventilation support—no need to tube her. Overall, this was a vastly different picture from what she'd looked like on scene at the Fashion District warehouse: gray and wringing-wet skin, panicky, gasping for air, and choking on copious, frothy pulmonary secretions. A fashionable woman . . . *drowning*. Sloane winced at an unwelcome image of her mother. "She's ready for transfer as soon as ICU can take her. Looks like we did the p.m. shift a big favor on this one."

"You bet, and it's a good way to end our day. Crazy there for a while." Harper smiled at Sloane. "So glad you got back here when you did, pal."

"Me too."

Sloane had been almost grateful for a fulminating case of acute heart failure. She'd heard the sirens even before she made it back to the ER from the administrative offices and had been running every minute since. A perfect distraction. No time to rehash what had happened with Prescott, overthink the possibilities, or answer questions from—

"You never said why the PR department wanted to see you," Harper said, assessing the patient's catheter bag for output. "Something to do with the Face of Hope campaign?"

"You seem to be obsessed with faces."

Sloane cringed. Had she really said that . . . and worse?

Harper met her gaze, a teasing grin on her face. "Spill it: are they going to make you the talk of the town?"

"Hardly," Sloane said, despite her stomach's nosedive. "It was nothing, really. The PIO needs to respond to the press about that incident in the parking lot." She decided against mentioning Micah Prescott. "She wanted to know if I had anything to add. Routine, I guess. And I didn't. So that's that." Sloane dredged up a smile. "Got a muffin out of it."

Harper laughed. "I think I'm going to answer the call of those sea salt and chocolate cookies at Misfit. A perk of foot modeling is that nobody's pointing a camera at my waistline. A couple of the outpatient surgery nurses are going too. You could come along, if you don't have that class tonight?"

"I do, actually. Do we need to empty that urine bag again?" Sloane asked, eager to dodge any further questions. She just wanted to get out of here, go back to the cottage, lock the door, and shut everything out. Like the thought that just came to her—what Micah had said about a dozen people calling 911. Which meant a dozen opportunities to snap cell phone pics, play amateur reporter. And of course, two actual reporters had been there with Prescott yesterday.

"Bag's good," Harper reported, then leaned sideways and squinted toward the doorway. "I think that was Fiona walking by just now with our clinical coordinator. Must be something else going on. We're like the hot news magnet these days."

Twenty minutes later Sloane reported off to the p.m. nursing staff, grabbed her tote bag, and headed out the ambulance bay doors—escaped. It hadn't happened soon enough. That the PIO had passed her in the hallway with only the barest of nods made things even worse. Obviously Micah had told Fiona about their awkward meeting and the way it ended. How Sloane spat out that *"I'll be forced to take action"* line like she was rejecting his marketing pitch with a crack of a Dodgers bat.

Sloane halted at the edge of the building, queasy at the truth: she'd threatened hospital administration. Even if she hadn't said the words, Prescott would assume Sloane was implying legal action. A new employee, still on probation, threatening to sue the hospital. What had she been thinking?

She leaned against the sun-warmed stucco and squeezed her eyes shut. The whole thing was almost laughable. There was no way she would contact an attorney. She'd barely even cooperated with the police yesterday. Calling attention to herself was beyond dangerous, and she had too much baggage in her own dark history to go around whining "unfair." People like Sloane didn't get to play that card. It had been that way for as long as she could remember. A new identity, or even six months of "classes," hadn't changed that. Hadn't really changed her. Lashing out at Micah Prescott was a defensive move, survival instinct. It was a stance that, in various forms, had become a signature for Sloane Wilder—and had netted her nothing but trouble and heartache. Obviously it still was.

She stepped away from the hospital wall, watching the palm trees for a moment, the way they rose out of a harsh urban landscape of cement, lava rock, and carelessly tossed cigarette butts. They swayed in the breeze, tall, strong, even beautiful. A tree from an ashtray. Maybe Sloane's own situation wasn't all that different. She could count only on herself.

If the too-handsome and too-clueless marketing man tossed her like raw meat to the powers that be, she would land on her feet. She always did. But just maybe her bogus threat had caused Prescott to take a step back. After all, he'd agreed she had a right to privacy, hadn't he? Making her a hero to benefit LA Hope would backfire if he had to drag her into that dubious honor kicking and screaming. It would be bad press, and from what Sloane had heard, this hospital didn't need any more of that.

Sloane had probably imagined the dismissive expression on the PIO's face and was simply borrowing trouble. This was a 24-7 news world and Sloane's fifteen minutes had elapsed. There had been no identification of the would-be abductor or his vehicle, and his victim—the only true eyewitness—had disappeared. Sloane didn't have to waste another minute worrying. It was over, done, exactly as she'd told the marketing man. Now she could go home to her safe little hideaway and—

"Sloane . . . hey."

She turned and peered back toward the ambulance doors. Then saw the girl step from behind a stucco pillar.

Zoey.

"What . . . ? Why are you here?" Sloane asked, following her to a more discreet spot at the edge of the parking lot. It was clear Zoey didn't want to be seen. She was dressed in the same clothes, dirtier, with the newsboy cap pulled low over her eyes. The abrasion on her cheek had begun to scab. "Are you having problems with your injuries?"

"Hip's sore. I haven't really been able to clean up."

Or eat, Sloane would bet. "Did you want someone to look at it?"

"No." Zoey glanced at the ER doors. "I skipped out last time without paying. I know how it goes; they won't roll out the welcome mat for someone like me."

"Someone like me." Sloane's throat tightened. "Then what—?"

"I was sort of hoping I could borrow a few bucks," Zoey admitted, resting her hand over her stomach as it rumbled. "Talk about good timing. I haven't eaten since those turkey sandwiches. My backpack is in that creep's car. My wallet, ID . . . everything." She glanced over her shoulder, tugged her cap lower as two employees walked by. "I would pay you back, I swear. Give me your home address and I'll mail it. I don't need much. Something in my stomach so I can get back out on the road."

"I don't know. . . ."

"Right. Hey, forget it." The tough-girl look was back, hardening Zoey's waiflike features. "No big deal. I get it. Some trashy girl tries to hit you up for—"

"No. That's not it. It's just that I don't carry more than a few dollars to work and I spent that for lunch." Zoey didn't need to know she didn't have an ATM card either—another eraser swipe at her paper trail. What this girl needed was food and . . . "Wait," Sloane said, remembering. "I have a gift card to a Mexican place maybe ten minutes from here. That would work."

"Um, yeah." Zoey nibbled at her lower lip. "I can walk it. Which way?"

"I'll drive us." Sloane was still hearing her say, *Some trashy girl . . .* It hit far too close to home. "C'mon, my car's right over there."

Zoey hesitated, caution in her blue eyes.

"The card has enough for both of us, and I'm hungry too. Let's go."

"Okay, I guess. Thanks."

"No problem," Sloane told her, feeling better than she had all day.

The gift card had been presented to her by LA Hope a few weeks back, when she'd been named ER's employee of the month. Twenty-five dollars' worth of tortillas, refried beans, pico de gallo, guacamole, or whatever. Mexican food and a Hallmark card signed by everyone in the department from nurses to janitorial staff. *For our highly valued teammate.* It had taken Sloane by complete surprise; she wasn't sure how to handle it. *Valued.* Nothing like that had ever happened to her before. Except for a lifetime of cereal.

She shook off the thought and pointed to her car. "That's me, there. The green Volvo."

"I'm already tasting a beef burrito."

"Good." Sloane was glad she'd remembered the gift card and could share it with this girl who'd appeared out of nowhere. She thought of her conversation with Prescott. His words: *What's wrong with taking some personal credit for a good deed? Sharing it with the public?"*

Well, she was sharing now, with someone as wary of public recognition as she was. The marketing man would undoubtedly think the gesture worthless. Something about that felt good. Very good. Sloane smiled.

"Here," she said, reaching into her tote bag. "Let's call this an appetizer."

She handed Zoey the muffin.

6

"ADMIT IT. You're stalking me."

"Busted." Coop pointed a tortilla chip at Micah. "But you're no challenge, Prescott. Turn off the location setting on your phone if you don't want everybody and their dog to know where you are."

"Good point." Micah nudged the salsa cup closer to Coop; the tabletop already looked like a crime scene. "I'll fix that."

"But then, everybody and their dog showing up at Manuel's is a good bet anyway," Coop added. "It's practically a hospital annex."

It was. Micah usually avoided it because of that. And because of the crowds; it was packed in here. But there was nothing in Micah's refrigerator except a zucchini the size of a manatee from Fiona's mother's never-ending harvest. He'd opted for a table rather than takeout because he'd needed a cooling-off period before hitting the freeways. It was safer to grind his teeth on a taquito than take out his frustration on the SUV's gas pedal. A last-minute meeting with Fiona—and their decision not to pursue promo surrounding Zoey Jones— had been the disappointing capper to a bad day.

"What's bugging you?" Coop asked, loading a chip with guacamole. "You look like someone asked you to do a feature on pumpkin patches." He grimaced. "Don't ask. Seriously, man, what gives?"

"No big deal. Work. The new campaign."

"Face of Hope," Coop said, avocado dotting his own. He grinned. "If I could, I'd nominate that feisty little brunette from yesterday. The woman in the parking lot. Hard to forget her, even without the drama. I don't see the hardship in sorting through faces like that."

Micah was tempted to say pumpkin patch duty was a lot more appealing than sparring with a litigious ER nurse. As luck would have it, Sloane had been nominated. An e-mailed form arrived in his in-box not ten minutes after she stomped out of their meeting.

"I won't have any of my personal information made public. No photos, no contact information . . ."

"It's Sloane, right?" Coop asked. "Sloane . . . Ferrell?"

"I'll be forced to take action."

"Yeah," Micah confirmed, wishing Coop didn't have such an infallible memory. He had envied it during their college days, but now . . . Micah glanced at the bulky camera case sitting at his friend's elbow. "You deleted those photos you took in the parking lot?"

"One photo. Your nurse and the kid with the bubble-gum hair."

"That one." Micah reached for his best offhand manner. "You got rid of it? Because the story dead-ended and—"

"Now you have me curious. Why are you suddenly so interested in what's on my camera?"

There was no way to get around the truth.

"Sloane doesn't want any media attention," Micah told him. "No mention of her name. Nothing."

"Heroic and shy?"

"Not exactly. She threatened legal action."

Coop's brows shot up. "Curiouser and curiouser."

"Don't," Micah told him, bordering on anger now. Lately it didn't seem to take much to move his general irritation from simmer to boil. "Let it go, Coop. There's no story."

The reporter smiled. "There's always a story."

"Not this time. I can't have that kind of trouble. It's the last thing I need right now. You told me yourself it's not news anymore. There was no license plate on that car and there are thousands of models exactly like it. The girl took off without giving a statement."

"And the nurse with fiery eyes will sue LA Hope."

"Yes." Micah hadn't bothered to tell Fiona; it seemed pointless now that they wouldn't be pursuing a statement from Sloane. "Look, just delete the photo."

"I already did."

Micah released a breath. Good. It was over.

———

"If you want another steak burrito, no problem," Sloane said, thinking once again that she wished she'd had a choice of where to take Zoey. Half a dozen people in scrubs had walked through the door. Fortunately no one she recognized, and she'd slipped her sunglasses on as soon as they left the hospital and hadn't taken them off. "We still have seven dollars left on the gift card."

"I'm good. Stuffed like a turkey, but good."

Zoey had managed to tuck her hair up into the dark cap. No telltale pink, thankfully. Her eyes met Sloane's. "I meant what I said. I'll pay you back. I have a job lined up in Bakersfield. Write down your home address for me. Maybe on a napkin or this food wrapper—that would work. Here, take it. I'll go borrow a pen from the cashier."

"Finish eating. We'll take care of that later."

"But . . ."

"Eat."

Zoey must have mentioned repaying the dinner cost three or four times. Clearly settling a debt was important to her. Integrity with pink hair. Sloane suppressed a smile. She'd write down the hospital's contact information. Good intentions or not, no one got to know where she was living. Too much of a risk.

"At the YMCA," Zoey said after licking some green sauce from a fingertip. "With kids."

Sloane scrunched her brows. "What? I thought you were staying with a friend."

"No. I meant where I'll be working. A special program for underprivileged kids."

"Oh . . . great," Sloane said, trying to reconcile the certainty in this girl's work plans with the sketchy fact that she was now hitchhiking with no ID and no money. Life knew how to deliver a mean curveball. No one knew that better than Sloane. "Sounds good."

"Yes." Something like sadness flickered across Zoey's face, then disappeared as quickly as it had come. "It will be."

"Your friend," Sloane began, voicing one of a dozen thoughts that had refused to quiet. "She knows you're hitchhiking?"

"No." Zoey set the remains of the burrito down. "I'm fine. It's only another couple of hours. I told you I'm careful."

An injured girl fighting for her freedom.

The memory came in an instant: Sloane at fifteen, in the garage with her stepfather. Her face stinging from his unexpected slap. Her whole body shook as she'd issued the strident promise: *"You can't hurt me—you're nothing. Do you hear me? You're going to die a big fat zero. And I'm . . . I'm out of here. I'm gone."*

". . . at the freeway on-ramp. I-5 north," Zoey was saying as she tucked strands of pink back into her cap. "Drop me there. And write down your address—I need that. I have to have that."

"Okay. Sure," Sloane agreed, tempted to offer to drive her to Bakersfield. She couldn't stand the thought of some man forcing himself on Zoey again. Maybe convincing her she really was that "trashy girl" worth nothing and deserving nothing good or even hopeful. It was the kind of cruel legacy that would leave her alone, hitching a ride through life with a hardened heart and too-thick skin.

"Great," Zoey said, standing. "I'm on my way then."

"You are," Sloane agreed, her voice choked by sudden and unwelcome emotion. She'd always conquered that before. Slapped it into submission or, at the very least, shrugged it off with a sneer. When had she become such a weak sister? Hadn't she argued with Micah Prescott only hours ago to protect her right to privacy, her own precious autonomy? She'd even threatened to sue for it. Zoey Jones deserved the same right.

To make a mess of her life? To live lonely and apart? No, please . . .

For a fleeting moment, Sloane almost wished she could pray—that God would hear it. That unexpected thought alone proved she was losing her edge.

"Let's go." Zoey stepped away from the table. "I'm ready if you are."

"Sure," Sloane lied. She had nothing to offer this kid. Only an example of what not to do. Best to end this now. "Let's get out of here."

"You got anything going tonight?" Coop asked, setting his sucked-dry cola cup on the table. "Once I'm done changing out a truckload of kitty litter and making sure Grams has a cheesy Christian romance novel on her Kindle, I'm a free man. Pumpkin patch research can wait a couple of days. Are you down with some hoops, then maybe catch a band at—?"

"Can't. Sorry," Micah said, though he wasn't really. He was a regular at the gym and usually welcomed an opportunity to dunk a few against Coop. But . . . "I'm on call tonight."

"Oh, right. Your volunteer gig. The crisis team." Coop shook his head. "Show up after suicides, drownings, baby deaths? No thanks."

"It's not for everyone," Micah admitted. "Big investment of time in the training." He fought the emotion creeping into his voice. Coop would never understand. The concrete truth in that made Micah wonder why he bothered to foster the friendship at all. "But someone's got to be there for the survivors when those things happen. When their lives get torn apart and nothing makes sense."

"Like what happened with your cousin," Coop said, lowering his voice. He'd been around on the periphery back then. Saw the damage to the Prescott family.

Even after years, the surreal image of that body bag still rose. Anger piggybacked on the memory. Always.

"Like Stephen," Micah agreed. "That kind of senseless loss. Crisis responders can't change it, but somebody should show up."

"I hear you." Coop rested his hand on the camera case. "I guess that's a big part of why I'm doing what I'm doing—or trying to do. Only I 'show up' with a bag full of lenses and a recorder. To tell the story, find the justice, and make some sense of things that way. Put a face on the headlines."

Micah smirked. "Even if it's a pumpkin face?"

"Hey, not fair!" Coop scraped his fingers down his beard. "So much for glory."

"You'll get your byline," Micah told him, feeling a twinge of guilt. Coop was Coop. "I'll be saying I knew you when."

"Remember that. And—hold on," Coop said, lifting his ringing cell phone from the table. He squinted at the screen. "Oh, cool. It's my source at State Prison."

Micah finished the last of his iced tea, trying his best to ignore one-sided snatches of the phone conversation. Coop was head down, scribbling notes on a salsa-splotched napkin.

Despite Coop's hit-or-miss sensitivity, Micah didn't doubt his friend's commitment to journalism or his dogged determination to finally get his byline on a big story.

Micah's thoughts were interrupted by a glimpse of two young women making their way through the café crowd toward the exit. Coming closer to his table now. The second one, a few strides behind the first, wore scrubs and sunglasses.

Sloane.

She slowed and stared at him for an instant, then picked up her pace.

"Hey," Coop said, leaning across the table. "Was that her? Ferrell?"

"Uh . . ." Micah hesitated, realizing what he'd just seen. "I don't think so."

"Scrubs. Like a military uniform. Everybody looks the same." Coop chuckled, then returned to his call.

"Right," Micah said, though he didn't agree. Despite the generic scrubs and sunglasses, he'd recognized Sloane immediately. And wasn't surprised by the pinch of her lips as she connected with his gaze. Nor by the fact that she'd made no polite effort to acknowledge him. Considering their history, none of that was unexpected. On the other hand, Micah had been unprepared for who Sloane was with.

Zoey Jones.

7

A DEATH NOTIFICATION.

Micah had barely arrived at his condo—a seven-mile commute made transglobal by the infamous LA traffic—when the crisis team's text buzzed his phone. A request from LAPD for volunteers to make a death notification visit to the wife of a man struck and killed by a vehicle. Micah had been halfway expecting it because Coop monitored emergency calls and he'd received an alert as they were leaving Manuel's Café.

"It's fire dispatch . . . truck vs. pedestrian . . . older guy . . . No, wait. He wasn't walking; he was sitting at a table? This driver crashed into a sidewalk café!"

Wise's Deli was an old mom-and-pop place, aiming for trendy by adding a few tables and plastic chairs outside. Along with vases of fake flowers and a new hand-lettered addition to the sun-faded *"Se Habla Español"* sign: *We have vegan.* The tofu alfresco option to lure more customers hadn't much worked. Micah passed by the place every Sunday on his way to church and had always planned to stop in. For a goodwill gesture, not soy curd. And now . . .

Six other people had been injured, two of them seriously according to the TV news. Including the Wises' college-age grandson, who helped out at the deli. He'd been taken to surgery. The fatality, a man fifty-eight years old, was pronounced dead on scene by paramedics. It had taken more than an hour to extricate his body from the undercarriage of the speeding truck that jumped the curb, mowed down tables, and came to rest in the deli's front window. Crushed, then dragged. The TV news had shown the property destruction in full-color HD but fortunately hadn't photographed the victims or identified them by name.

"I won't have any of my personal information made public. No photos, no contact information . . ."

Micah frowned and pushed away the intruding thought of Sloane. He grabbed his crisis team jacket, ID, and car keys. Then double-checked he had all pertinent information supplied by dispatch regarding the victim and the surviving spouse. In truth, he was triple-checking; he couldn't imagine anything worse than showing up on the wrong doorstep with a death notification.

No, that wasn't true. Showing up at the *right* address with this kind of news was the worst. Micah would never forget what they'd said about death notifications during his California Crisis Care training: *"In this one instance, the crisis responder is the cause of a survivor's trauma. You are bringing unimaginable news into their ordinary day and will forever change their lives."*

It had been crisis responders who brought the tragic news to Micah's aunt and uncle all those years ago.

Micah checked his gear bag to be sure he had the list of local resources, his small chaplain's prayer book, bottled water, and several packages of Kleenex. No teddy bear today since no children were involved. It was scant equipment compared to Coop's heavy bag of cameras, tripods, and lenses.

He thought of what he'd said to his friend at the Mexican café. *"Someone's got to be there for the survivors. . . . Crisis responders can't change it, but somebody should show up."*

Tonight that somebody would be Micah. Bringing the worst possible news and offering the only thing he could: himself. A compassionate listener, a calm and caring presence.

Micah hefted his bag and made his way to the door. He'd try with all he had to do that, listen and support, with the requisite calm. And without letting his own experiences get in the way. No judgment, no anger. It wasn't going to be easy.

The driver of the truck was intoxicated. Another life claimed by a worthless drunk.

———

"This is good. Anywhere along here," Zoey said. "Just pick a place to let me out."

"Right."

Sloane steered down a street dotted with vintage clothing shops, produce stands, the occasional tattoo parlor or vaping supply store. Neon signs had begun to glow and palms wrapped with tiny white bulbs blinked along the bustling sidewalks. Somewhere beyond, miles of hills would turn pink and lavender under the waning Southern California sun. Sloane had heard somewhere that smog enhanced the intensity of sunsets, pollution spawning splendor. She wasn't sure she believed that. After all, while there was every reason LA air should smell of orange blossoms, suntan lotion, and crisp one-hundred-dollar bills, it actually reeked of—

"I don't want to be caught hitching too close to the free-way," Zoey added.

Stinking reality. It was the scent of Los Angeles air and the current truth. This kid with the pink hair, tough-girl atti-tude, and sad eyes was about to be swallowed up by it again. Suffocating, cruel reality was the real pollution, and there was nothing Sloane could do to stop that. Mostly because Zoey wouldn't let her; she'd accepted the food out of basic necessity.

Sloane steered to the curb after a truck loaded with surf-boards pulled away. "How's this?"

"Perfect."

Zoey unbuckled her seat belt and slid her hand into her jeans pocket. She pulled out a crumpled piece of paper. The burrito wrapper. Then a stubby pencil. "I swiped it off a table when I went to the restroom." She handed them both to Sloane. "Your address. Write it down."

"I . . ." What was Sloane going to say? That she wouldn't give anyone her address because she'd been stupid enough to get involved with a lying, cheating con man? And because she was such a fool, she'd been hounded by creditors and threat-ened by gangsters?

"You think I won't keep my word," Zoey said, snatching at her cap. Her hair, tangled and Disney-bright, fell around her face. "That's what you're saying, right? 'Why bother to give this ghetto girl my address? She's not worth—'"

"Stop." Sloane pinned her with a look. "Don't say that again." She smoothed the burrito wrapper across her thigh and saw an immediate oily stain on her scrubs. She touched the pencil to the paper, then hesitated.

"Forgot your address?" Zoey asked, her tone implying her accusation had been spot-on.

"No." Sloane set the pencil down. "Look, I'm not going to be the second person in a week to hold you hostage in a car. But I don't like the idea of you, of anyone, hitching a ride out there. At least not after dark."

"I'll be okay."

"You probably will. And then maybe you won't." Sloane tried not to imagine how bad it could be. "You need a shower. Those abrasions need cleaning up at the very least."

"You're going use the last seven bucks on your Mexican food card to get me a motel room?"

"No." Sloane managed a small smile. What *was* she saying? Was she really going to—? "My place is minuscule. But I have a shower and soap. And a couch. It comes with a cat, but you're welcome to bunk there tonight. Get cleaned up, have some breakfast in the morning. I'll buy you a bus ticket—loan you the money. You can pay that back too."

"I don't know. . . ."

Sloane took a slow breath. "Suit yourself. I guess there's no reason you should trust me, either."

"I like cats. And I know I stink. I'll take your couch."

"Good."

Sloane reached for the gearshift, her hand trembling. Her whole insides were jittering. She'd probably regret this idiot idea. She needed to be working on her statement for the parole board. And there was the meeting tonight. Right now, as a matter of fact . . .

"You see yourself as some sort of guardian angel?"

"Nope." Sloane's grip tightened on the steering wheel. She pulled out of the parking space. "No angel here."

"Hmm." Zoey wadded her hat and wedged it against the window, using it as a makeshift pillow. She closed her eyes. "Good. I wouldn't know how to handle that."

Me either.

Sloane lowered the window and breathed in the air. It definitely wasn't a Rodeo Drive fragrance, but it wasn't all that bad. Asphalt, motor oil, too-ripe fruit . . . hot dogs, bacon. Reality, but only borderline stinking. She wasn't sure exactly why she'd done what she had—offered this kid her home—except that she'd had to. Couldn't not do it. Any more than she could have stopped herself from running into the parking lot to save her from the would-be kidnapper.

"You did a good thing, Sloane. I told you that before—I meant it."

The marketing man, trying to convince her to go public.

He'd seen her at the restaurant tonight. Maybe he recognized Zoey, too. Surprisingly, Sloane didn't really care. She was breaking her own rules for something that felt important. One thing, one night. Not a huge deal.

"There was nothing 'great' about what I did. It didn't change her life, and a dumb-luck incident in a hospital parking lot won't ever change mine. It's not like one random event can just pop things back into perfect alignment."

Sloane was no Yoda, but what she'd said in that office was the truth. She'd done what she'd had to. It wasn't remarkable and, in the grand scheme of things, didn't really matter. Someone like Micah Prescott wanted fanfare; he needed to put a marketable face on every action. Get some tangible value from it. He'd never understand—

"What's its name?" Zoey raised her head from the window, eyes sleepy.

"Name?"

"Your cat."

Sloane smiled. "Marty."

———

"But I packed a dinner for him," the woman told Micah, denial replacing shock in her expression. Kathryn Fontana was about his mother's age, attractive. Her eyes were red-rimmed and dazed as she twisted the dish towel in her lap. She'd been making a pie, and the house smelled of apples bubbling in cinnamon. Cindy, Micah's crisis partner tonight, had discreetly turned off the burners and oven as Micah got Mrs. Fontana settled on the living room couch and pulled up a chair opposite her. Cindy was in the dining room now, checking with the coroner's office regarding details.

"A Waldorf salad," Mrs. Fontana continued. "I made a big bowl of it because I had leftover apples and because it's our daughter's favorite too." She gestured toward a framed photo on a bookshelf, a graduation shot of a dark-haired girl chin-deep in a flowery ruff of leis, her arms linked with her parents'. "It's Brandi's first year at OSU. Her cousin's a junior. They're driving down for the weekend. Tomorrow. They'll be here tomorrow afternoon." Tears welled.

Micah leaned forward a little, his throat tightening. *Listen. Just listen.*

"You see, Jim eats his dinner in the shop's break room along with his employees," she explained as if convincing Micah of that, telling him these details about her family, would change everything. Erase the unimaginable. "It's a small company, almost like family, and he likes to encourage that relationship. Ask about their kids, hear any concerns, and talk sports and that sort of thing. Jim had his salad tonight. And some broiled chicken—no salt. Doctor's orders. I'm careful about that."

Micah nodded, waiting for the question he knew was coming.

"It doesn't make sense that he'd be at the deli. Because I made his dinner." Her knuckles whitened on the towel, eyes pleading as she finally voiced it. "They're sure it's him? My Jim? It couldn't be a mistake?"

Please, Lord, be here. . . .

Micah held her gaze. "Your husband had his wallet in his pocket, Mrs. Fontana. His work ID badge was clipped to his shirt." He tried not to imagine the kindhearted man grabbing a forbidden pastrami, maybe even joking with the Wises' grandson while some irresponsible drunk climbed behind the wheel. *Deep breath. This isn't personal.*

"I wish it weren't true," Micah finished, "but the police have no doubt your husband was hit by the truck. And died from his injuries."

"*Say* died. Dead. *Not* passed away, gone. *Leave no room for confusion in the survivor's mind.*" The crisis training was clear. The reality painfully complicated. Always.

Mrs. Fontana's voice was a ragged whisper. "Jim's . . . dead."

"We'll help in any way we can," Micah assured her. "Cindy can make calls for you, if that helps. I'll explain what's going to happen and what needs to be taken care of. I'll walk you through each step. One thing at a time, no rush."

She began to tremble. "This is happening. It's real."

"Yes. Here . . . you're shivering." Micah grabbed a lap blanket from the arm of the couch and settled it around the new widow's shoulders. Before he could return to his chair, she grasped his hand. He sank down onto the couch beside her.

"Thank you," she said, tears spilling over. She glanced toward the dining room, then back at Micah. "Both of you. I can't say how much it means to have someone here right now."

We must never forget that when we make that connection with a survivor, we forever become part of the event too. Part of the pain and, God willing, a first step in the healing as well.

"I don't think I could do this alone," she added.

"You don't have to." Micah gave her hand a small squeeze. "That's why we're here. Let's get you some water and we'll work on a list of calls."

"We have a pastor."

"Good. We can start there."

Forever part of the event . . .

Micah thought of Sloane's insistence that the parking lot incident was "over and done." That her actions wouldn't change anything. And yet there she was with that girl tonight. Helping her again, probably. It was a good bet she didn't want any credit—or visibility. Which was the reason he'd brushed off Coop's question about seeing her. He wasn't going to breach her privacy when it came to the media; Micah would respect that. But he had more than a few concerns about how it could reflect on the hospital. And he had a gut sense she'd waded neck-deep into trouble.

8

"I DON'T HAVE NATURALLY PINK HAIR." Zoey sank her finger-tips into her shower-damp roots. She tossed Sloane an impish smile. "But you probably guessed that."

"Probably. But I'm the last person who should go all preachy on the subject of hair," Sloane admitted, unable to block the intruding memory.

"Absolutely not, sir. She's six years old. You won't find any reputable beautician willing to bleach that child's hair. . . ."

"That's not your natural shade?" Zoey asked.

"Natural as it's been in years. But six months ago you'd've been looking at spikes," Sloane added. "Burgundy."

"Yeah?" Zoey returned to studying her hangnail.

The cottage grew quiet again; the only sound was the tumble of the dryer in the hallway beyond. Zoey's clothes.

Sloane peeked at the wall clock, thinking for the umpteenth time that she was crazy to have brought this girl home. Zoey was a complete stranger and Sloane never invited *anyone* here. Still, she'd reconciled herself with that. And it wasn't as though this girl seemed dangerous in any way. Squeezed tight as a bedbug into the other corner of this too-small plaid couch, she looked more like a detainee than a serial killer. It was just that this was so excruciatingly *awkward*. Worse than awkward. More like two people with no social skills stuck in an elevator. In an abandoned building—holding empty plastic cups.

"Hey!" Zoey laughed as the black cat leaped into her lap, collar tags jingling. "You little acrobat."

On the other hand, her cat was the best idea Sloane had ever had.

"Named after some guy?" Zoey asked, scratching under his chin. She lifted an ID tag. "Marty. A boyfriend?"

"No." Sloane's heart cramped without warning. Too much history. Sacramento and the furtive, failed romance, San Diego and the accident . . . "It's short for Save Mart. I found him at an animal shelter. Marty's whole litter was tied up in a grocery bag and tossed off a pier."

"Seriously?" Zoey's brows pinched, making the small metal piercing glint in the lamplight. "Just like that?"

"Yeah. But they didn't figure on the low tide."

The blue eyes met Sloane's over the top of the kitten's head. "Or on you."

"I didn't save him," Sloane said, immediately reminded of that awful meeting with Micah. "I just brought him home."

Zoey smirked. "Seems to be a pattern with you."

"Not really."

This girl didn't need to know how far from the truth it was. Sloane could recite the names of a dozen people who'd swear on Bibles they'd never met anyone as self-centered, cagey, and irresponsible as Sloane Wilder. If someone else hadn't stepped in when she dropped the ball, Marty would have gone from grocery sack to the shelter's gas chamber. Sloane had told the marketing man the truth. She was no hero.

"You think my clothes are dry?" Zoey gave the cat one last pat as he hopped down. She sat up, grimacing as she stretched out her leg.

"What's wrong?"

"That scrape on my hip. A little sore."

Zoey had refused to let the ER physician examine it. Wouldn't even lower her jeans a few inches. When Sloane offered her a shower—and use of the washer and dryer—the girl initially said no. Sloane hadn't pushed, simply pulled out some clean sweatpants and a T-shirt and laid them on the couch. "Did you soap that abrasion in the shower?"

"I tried." Zoey stretched the waistband on the sweatpants and peered at her hip. "It's sort of red. Swollen, maybe. Hard for me to see."

Sloane hesitated, then told herself the worst that could happen would be for Zoey to tell her to butt out and head back to the highway. Sloane would be out some comfort clothes but free from this awkward evening. "I could look at it for you."

"No need."

"Whatever . . ."

Sloane wondered if she'd been as stubborn at Zoey's age, then wondered why she'd even wondered. Of course she was. Stubborn, secretive. A rule breaker. She'd have successfully blackened four bedroom walls if her stepfather hadn't confiscated the spray paint. And then all the black Sharpie pens she'd stolen from school.

"I have some bacitracin," Sloane offered. "And Band-Aids so your jeans won't rub against it. Suit yourself. But two hours on a bus seat . . ."

"Okay." Zoey stood and surprised Sloane by hiking the sweatpants down just enough to expose the spot, high on her hip. "Does it look infected?"

"It's definitely red," Sloane told her, less impressed by the abrasion than by a scarlet-and-black tattoo, boldly inked at an angle across the girl's pale skin. It was only partially visible because of her tight clutch on the fabric, but Sloane could make out twin dollar signs and lettering that spelled *PROPERTY OF—*

"I don't see any pus," Sloane said quickly. "I'll put some ointment on it."

"I'll do it." Zoey let the waistband snap back into place. "Is all that first aid stuff in the bathroom?"

"Yes. In the cabinet below the sink," she confirmed, dozens of questions swirling in her brain as she watched the girl amble toward the hallway. She was an enigma at the very least.

Zoey had revealed next to nothing about herself, but more and more Sloane was getting a feeling about her. And it was troubling. Like the way she explained away leaving the ER because she couldn't pay, yet it had been only moments after the police arrived. Or the fact that she'd never mentioned family. Or the too-convenient—hard to trace—last name of Jones. Now the tattoo.

PROPERTY OF . . .

Sloane walked toward the kitchen, the memory coming

back. That voice, so deep to a small child's ears. Stale breath, lips too close, hands inescapable . . .

"You're my little angel. You belong to me. Don't ever forget that."

Her hand trembled as she opened the kitchen cupboard and reached for a plastic tumbler. Then looked up. The wine-glasses, on that shelf above the rooster canisters, beckoned like a sliver of light beneath the door of a dark closet. Their shiny surfaces whispered escape was possible; secrets would drown. It would *always* be that way for someone like Sloane. So why not—?

"My clothes were dry," Zoey said, walking through the doorway wearing them. Her hair had dried too, shiny, clean, and piglet pink. "I'm beat, though." She yawned. "Seriously whipped. Is there an extra blanket, maybe a pillow? For the couch?"

"Sure." Sloane closed the cupboard harder than necessary. "Right. I'll get them."

"Thanks."

She had to stop herself from jogging from the kitchen.

There was a bus to Bakersfield at 6:30 in the morning. The fare was nineteen dollars one-way. Sloane would spring for a cab to the station too. It was worth it. There was no way she could drive through the merciless LA traffic and make it to work on time. Sloane was still on probation and, considering the whole lawsuit-threat situation, this was not the time to ruffle the feathers of the powers that be. She frowned, remembering Micah's term. For all she knew, he'd already told them he saw her with the runaway patient. She sighed and pulled a blanket and pillow from the hall closet shelf. What would be would be.

She'd done what she could for this girl. Very soon Zoey really *would* be gone.

What's that?

The clock read 2:30 when Sloane jerked awake in darkness. It took her a full minute to remember about Zoey. And the entire walk to the kitchen to get her galloping heart settled back down.

"Oh, sorry." Her guest looked up from the small sponge-painted table. "Hungry."

"That's . . ." Sloane's gaze skimmed the open cupboards. "No problem."

"Are you, like, a food hoarder?" Zoey pointed at the sliding pantry doors that occupied the small space between living room and kitchen. "There's three shipping boxes of cereal in there."

"No." Sloane's face warmed. "I mean yes, there are."

She had a sudden image of Paul, when she finally ended that relationship, hauling his things from her house in General Mills boxes.

"Well, you got gypped." Zoey poked a spoon around in the bowl. "Or do you special order Lucky Charms *without* the marshmallows?"

"No." Sloane hesitated, then told herself she was never going to see this kid again. What did it matter? She settled onto a chair. "I pick them out of the boxes. Because I don't like them."

"If you don't like that kind, then why—?"

"I won the cereal in a contest when I was six. A lifetime supply." Despite a wave of queasiness, Sloane smiled at the incredulous look on Zoey's face. "Yes. That would be twenty-six years of cereal. So far. Actually, they owe me one shipment. I should be getting another box any day now."

"What kind of contest?"

"Uh . . ." Sloane suddenly wished she'd admitted to hoarding. "Beauty pageant."

"For real?" Zoey's gaze skimmed Sloane's face, lingering, it seemed, on the scar. "Sure. I can see that. You *are* great-looking." She spooned up some soggy cereal. "You mean those pageants where they put tons of makeup on kids? Fake teeth and hair and then make them act all flirty and age inappropriate?"

"Shake that sweet little booty, Angel. . . ."

"It was a long time ago," Sloane said, hearing the strain in her tone. She was getting a headache.

Zoey chewed for a moment. "The truth is, I came in here looking for a drink. A bottle of wine. Or a beer."

"You don't look nineteen, let alone twenty-one."

Zoey shrugged. "I always get that." She glanced toward the cupboard. "You have wineglasses."

"I don't drink."

"My luck. I've got to bunk with a straight edge."

Sloane nearly laughed aloud at the irony, then started to say Zoey didn't *have* to be here at all. And that if anyone had a right to complain, it was the person not getting any sleep because—

"You've been really decent to me," Zoey said, the sarcasm gone. She blinked up at Sloane, a drop of milk on her chin. "That doesn't happen much."

Sloane's throat tightened.

"I'll be seventeen on Christmas Eve," Zoey added, her voice not much above a whisper. "I won't be watching the mail for a card from my family—it's not too great there. It's not great away from there either. I just do what I have to. To get by."

"Like thumbing a ride to Bakersfield," Sloane said, certain there was so much more to the story. She knew she'd never hear it; this child had already learned to drown secrets. "To stay with a friend. And work at the YMCA."

"Right." Zoey touched a fingertip to a marshmallow charm on the cereal box. "We can't all be beauty queens."

Sloane was up well before dawn, thinking she would use the bathroom first; Zoey might want to shower again this morning. After seeing the girl wolf down that cereal, she was toying with the idea of scrambling some eggs, toasting a bagel. She'd send her unexpected guest off with a decent meal in her stomach. Sloane thought she had enough eggs in the fridge. She'd better check.

Still in her pajamas, she padded barefoot from her bedroom past the open bathroom door and down the darkened hallway. Then paused at the entry to the still-dark living room, seeing lights on in the adjoining kitchen.

Marty meowed, wrapping himself around her leg.

"Shhh," Sloane whispered, reaching down to lift him into her arms. He bumped his head beneath her jaw, purr rumbling. She squinted toward the couch as her eyes adjusted. Nobody sleeping there, just the rumpled mound of pillow and blanket.

"Zoey?" she whispered, peering toward the kitchen. "You up?"

She crossed the short stretch of wood flooring, then stood in the empty kitchen, confused.

"Zoey?" she called again, turning in a circle to look around the tiny living space as if it were remotely possible to have missed her somewhere. She ignored an anxious prickle, set Marty down, and was about to go check the front porch and driveway when she saw it on the kitchen table.

The rooster flour canister, its lid upside down beside it.

"I just do what I have to. To get by."

Her stomach sank at the obvious. Zoey had ripped her off.

Eight hundred dollars for the rent—due in three days. A week's grocery money and some extra cash Sloane intended to use for the cab and bus ticket. About a thousand dollars total. And . . . She walked to the table and peered into the empty canister.

Mom's necklace. The engagement ring.

She groaned aloud.

Could she really have been so stupid? She couldn't have moved it to her bedroom? Or—

There was a note.

Sloane reached for the paper lying beside the canister. It was nearly glued to the tabletop by a soggy glob of cereal.

IOU
Z.
Find a better hiding place.
You don't look like the cookie-baking type.

9

"MISSING SUPPLIES." Sloane lowered the department memo, looked at Harper, and frowned. "Great. I worked that day."

"We both did. Word is, the instrument set was missing from the room where we put that girl from the parking lot."

Sloane's lips tensed.

"You have to admit it looks suspicious that she ran off," Harper added.

Almost as suspicious as an empty flour canister.

There was no way Sloane was going to admit that one. Definitely not to the police. A theft report could start them digging around, and law enforcement agencies were only a computer click apart nowadays. The freeway accident investigation in San Diego was ongoing, and Sloane didn't want to be questioned about it again. She'd worked too hard at dodging

Paul and those mobsters chasing him—*and chasing me?* Were they? The SDPD detectives tried to make that connection and she'd done her best to act clueless. If they got wind that she'd changed her name, it would wave another red flag. No, she wasn't going to report Zoey's theft. Losing the money and the valuables was a gut punch and a hardship. But it was better to take a financial hit than risk becoming the target of a much-scarier one.

"Hey," Harper told her, "don't look so worried. It's a reminder memo, not a pink slip. Besides, I'm the one who yanked you out of the room to get ready for our stabbing victims. You didn't exactly have time to tidy up. I'm sure most of us have accidentally donated an LA Hope hemostat to the local roach clip collectors."

Roach clips. Hemostats could hold burnt-down marijuana joints. Paul had joked more than once that he knew folks who'd be very happy if Sloane could slip a few of the surgical instruments into her purse.

Were drugs Zoey's game? Sloane didn't want to believe that.

"I don't think one light-fingered patient will take you off the Face of Hope nomination list," Harper teased, moving out of the way of a tech pushing a mobile X-ray machine. "Rumor has it your name's on Prescott's radar."

Sloane frowned, refusing to entertain the idea of another bout with the marketing man.

"Well, I don't have the time for rumors. Or the interest," she said, regretting her tone instantly. "Sorry. I had sort of a rough night. Not a lot of sleep."

There was kindness in Harper's eyes. "And now you're picking up extra shifts."

"A few."

Until I make up for the stolen cash.

For the first time in a long while, Sloane wished she had someone she could confide in and trust, even with the secrets that refused to drown. Someone who could handle the truth and not run the other way.

"I get that about extra shifts," Harper told her. She glanced down at her iodine-stained running shoes. "That's why these glamorous feet are posing for the camera. Bills to pay."

"Right." Sloane looked at the memo again. "I'm just lucky they don't garnish pay for missing supplies."

"For sure." Harper shook her head. "You know, I didn't get that sense about her. But then I guess we can't always understand what people are dealing with."

Micah had watched Sloane walk from the ER to the hospital gift shop, make a selection from the display of energy bars, and then head through the lobby toward the main exit. He'd decided to talk to her about Zoey Jones and had almost intercepted her a couple of times but stopped himself. He liked to think it was out of caution and respect for hospital decorum. He certainly wasn't going to admit to outright cowardice. Now Sloane was walking toward her car in the parking lot. A dark-green Volvo.

He'd noticed it before because his parents always had Volvos; Micah had learned to drive in one. Sloane's was an older model with borderline tires, paint that said it had been parked on the coast for a time, and a collage of bumper stickers. They were thickly layered, some peeling and faded, and proclaimed the whole gamut of boasts, credos, and causes, from "My kid is an honor roll student" to Mary Kay, Bruins Mom, and even Greenpeace—fighting for space with the NRA. Obviously not all Sloane's doing. More likely they were part of the car's history and not hers. But the stickers made Micah all the more aware he knew next to nothing about this woman, except—

"Are you following me?" she asked, turning to face him.

"No." The look in her eyes was more gunfire than Greenpeace. "But I did want to talk with you for a minute."

"That's about all the time I can spare. I have a . . . class."

"No problem." He wished she weren't so beautiful; his usual skill with words failed every time he got close. "It's about Zoey Jones. I saw you with her last night."

Sloane waited. Like a sniper lining up a shot.

"What you do on your time off is none of my business," Micah hurried to say before she could. "Or the hospital's, really. Though, since you're an employee, you should consider—"

"What?" Her eyes narrowed a fraction.

"She gave false information. All of it, from what we can tell. Her address, birth date, and even her name."

Sloane's lips flattened.

"And it appears she may have taken some hospital equipment," Micah added, almost wishing Sloane would say something. There was no way to tell what she was thinking.

"Which means she isn't worth the price of a meal?"

"I . . ." *Words, c'mon.* "That's not what I meant."

"Wait, now I get it," Sloane continued before he could. "Helping someone like that doesn't fit with the image of Los Angeles Hope. You know, that pesky mission of mercy and hope."

"No one is saying that."

"Of course not." Sloane pinned him with a look. "Hospital image wasn't even discussed when you told Fiona and 'the powers' that you saw me eating tacos with a liar and a thief."

"I didn't tell anyone," Micah said, remembering the moment when Coop thought he'd recognized her. He realized he'd felt a need to protect Sloane then. And again today when he'd opted not to say anything to the PIO. The idea that this nurse could need his protection seemed ridiculous. And exactly when had he moved from irritation to concern? "Besides," he finished, "you didn't know then what you know now. About her."

"And if I had known? I should have—what? Notified the police?"

"Maybe. Or found another kind of help. If she needs that."

The warning flush rose on her cheeks. "You're going to tell me there are social services for things like that, right? Or churches? Maybe *your* church, even? Good folks who go once a month to hand out sandwiches and clean socks to the homeless—then out to IHOP afterward to eat waffles with whipped cream and pat themselves on the back."

"Sloane . . . hey . . . ," Micah tried, but there was no stopping her.

"You're right. I didn't know anything about that girl. But I've known about *you* all along. Slick, charming, with all the right words to get exactly what you want. Your agenda, your priorities. That's all that counts. People like Zoey are a waste of your time—worse, an embarrassment. A stain on your spotless, high-achieving record."

What the . . . ?

"Wait," Micah said, scrambling to unkick this hornets' nest. "You're not letting me—"

"No. I won't buy into this stupid pretense. You go around saying you want to honor the compassion of your employees, celebrate the 'face of hope,' but that's a big lie. All you really want is to use everyone you can to cover up an ugly incident that put a crimp in the hospital's revenue." Sloane's lips twitched with a smirk. "With the hope you'll get some big celebratory bonus. Where's the compassion in that? Some scared kid gets assaulted in the parking lot and you fix it by turning her over to the police?"

"Whoa," Micah warned. "Hold it right there."

"No way. Campaign all you want, Prescott, but I'm not buying it. I can't." Sloane's eyes shone with sudden tears; it only seemed to make her angrier. "You don't get it about people. You can't just pick who's the best, who's worth your time, and then drown the rest of them like some scroungy batch of kittens."

She choked a little on the last words, and Micah found himself at a complete loss for how to do this. Clearly, nothing he'd tried was working. And now . . . He took a slow breath and reminded himself that he was a skilled listener.

"Okay," he managed. "Was there anything else?"

"Yes." She lifted her chin. Somehow, the tears defied gravity and didn't fall. "If I'm still working here, I'd like you to keep your distance. Please."

"I can do that."

"Good."

Sloane had her keys out in an instant, climbed into the old Volvo, and pulled away.

Micah got one last look at her bumper and decided the NRA sticker overlapped Greenpeace. By a mile.

———

What had she done?

Sloane lowered the hairbrush and stared into the bathroom mirror, sickened. The face staring back at her looked very little like Sloane Wilder. The old spiky, burgundy-tipped hair was a deep, healthy brown, baby soft and halfway to her shoulders. Her eyes were still that startling blue, but she no longer lined them or layered mascara onto her black lashes. Face makeup and powder had given way to a simple sunscreen tinted in a "natural" shade that Sloane Wilder would have called "buck naked." The scar, its triple lines fanning out from the corner of her left eye, hadn't turned the pearly white a consulting plastic surgeon promised. It was still as pink as the memory of the accident was painfully fresh in her mind. Sloane wasn't convinced either would fade.

She touched a fingertip to the scar, remembering the feel of the stitches and dried blood—and all the pain and confusion of those long days in the San Diego Hope SICU. There was a scar on her abdomen, too, from the emergency splenectomy and then a second surgery after a bleeder cut loose and Sloane nearly bled to death. None of that had been worse than hearing that two people had been killed in the pileup. And an ER teammate was fighting for her life. Sloane's reckless behavior had set the entire tragedy in motion. It hadn't been the first time death punished her offenses. A new name and address couldn't change that.

Still, Sloane had dumped the short skirts and thigh-high boots at Goodwill before she hit the interstate and hadn't hoisted her backside onto so much as a pizza place stool in six months' worth of evenings. Yet today, in the parking lot with that marketing man, Sloane Wilder had risen like a phoenix. Sassy tongue, sharp nails, and bad attitude.

"But I've known about you all along. Slick, charming, with all the right words to get exactly what you want. Your agenda, your priorities. That's all that counts."

She groaned and squeezed her eyes shut. Even if what she'd said was true—and everything screamed it was—Sloane should have kept her mouth shut. She wasn't named employee of the month because her nursing skills came with a side order of cheekiness. She'd done her best to leave Wilder behind and let Ferrell lead the way. Now she'd sacrificed that progress to go to bat for a girl who had stolen from her. A teenage girl who, right here in this house, ate her cereal and . . .

Reminded me of me.

The was no denying it. The girl's prickly attitude and tough talk, her wariness, that hint of her troubled home life . . . even the tinted hair and blue eyes. All of it was so much like Sloane at that age.

"Find a better hiding place. You don't look like the cookie-baking type."

Zoey had pegged her, too. It took one to know one.

"People like Zoey are a waste of your time. . . ."

It might have been wrong to unload on Micah Prescott, but Sloane had been right about that one thing. That was how people like Zoey and Sloane were seen. Defined by so many mistakes, labeled. And used.

"Out there on that stage, you're the little angel, but we know better, don't we, darlin'? You're really the devil's plaything. That's who you are."

No.

Sloane dropped the hairbrush and walked away from the mirror. She grabbed her car keys and purse, hauled open the heavy wooden door, and hurried toward the driveway.

Celeste called out, looking up from her garden bed. "Class tonight?"

"Yes."

Traffic was horrible, making Sloane more than twenty minutes late. In truth, she was late most of the time. Maybe every time. But nobody said anything about it, wouldn't have cared if she'd walked in for the last five minutes. Maybe that was one of the reasons she did show up. No judgment, no pressure. Just a room with rows of folding chairs, a big pot of coffee, and a handful of other people who'd shown up too. For their first time or after thousands of times. People who knew exactly why they were there. And other folks, like Sloane, who still weren't close to sure.

She slid into a chair, not too near anyone else, the same way she always did.

"Hi, everyone," a fortyish woman said, rising from her seat in the front row. Wearing a tailored twill jacket over a white blouse and nice jeans, she looked like a professor addressing her class. "I'm Jocelyn. And I'm an alcoholic."

10

"YOU SAVE MY LIFE," Oksana moaned, her accent made thicker by a mouthful of bacon double cheeseburger. She hunched forward on the unmade motel bed, her hazel eyes meeting Zoey's. "I was like starving dog here. Can't make soup with cold water."

"Doesn't sound hopeful."

Zoey frowned at the scant few instant ramen containers sitting on the dusty window AC unit. One of them was wedged against the matted belly of Oksana's beloved teddy bear. Next to it, boxes of prophylactics were stacked a dozen high. This smaller motel room, adjacent to the "work" rooms, was used primarily for storage by the girls' employers. The blackout curtains had been pulled against the LA sunlight, and the air stank even more than the last time Zoey had dared to visit.

Oksana had limited access to phones and no reliable way to communicate when the coast was clear. Or to get help if she needed it. She'd been sixteen when she was lured to the States by the promise of a job as a nanny for a wealthy American family. But . . .

"You're healing up?" Zoey asked, glancing at the bit of iodine-tinged tape visible above the drawstring of her friend's pajama bottoms, a blue polka-dot flannel so different from her working attire. The bear and the pj's were Oksana's favorite things, beyond "American cheeseburger."

"From the surgery," Zoey continued. "And infection—it's all better?"

"Not all." The burger bliss left Oksana's eyes. "I get a checkup eight thirty tonight. So I can start working again. I guess no guy going to notice a bandage in the dark."

Or care.

"Viktor says I am laying around too long—more trouble than I am worth."

Zoey tensed. The implication wasn't good. "But . . . the pain."

"What's little more pain?" The girl shook her head, long layers of kinky blonde hair brushing her pajama top. Oksana was not quite eighteen now, but she looked tired and defeated. "Life is pain. I wish I had more appendix to pop. Then I can believe in that mercy God."

The church people must have been around again. More promises, tempting as that nanny job. With a bigger lie: *"God loves a sinner."* Zoey hadn't bought it either.

"You still good?" Oksana asked, nibbling at a pickle. "With your Mr. Stack?"

"Sure."

It wasn't completely true, but how could Zoey complain

when she knew what her friend faced? Every day and night. She shifted in the chair, swore she could feel the tattoo on her hip. Stack had rescued her from a life like Oksana's after she'd only had a few weeks of "training." It had been more than enough time for Zoey to know anything else, anywhere else, was better.

"It's good, easy," Zoey told her. "Pawn stuff. Fake some IDs, follow the UPS guy around and grab packages. Scout some scams."

"Get face all scratched."

"Yeah." Zoey touched the scabbing abrasion on her face. When she finally reconnected with Stack, he'd been concerned. As much as he was capable of that. His concentration, his ability to care about something, never lasted long. His top priority was himself. What Stack wanted. Period. He was no Sloane Ferrell. Zoey battled an uncharacteristic wave of guilt. "Sometimes I mess up."

"Sometimes you do good." Oksana lifted the remains of her burger. "My life is happy now."

Happy? Zoey's throat constricted. It shouldn't be this way. Where was that "mercy God"?

"You go now." Oksana's brows scrunched. "If Viktor—"

"I'm gone. Don't worry. Just rest, get better." Zoey grabbed the teddy bear and settled it in Oksana's arms. "Here." She pulled a few bills from her pocket. "Take this. Pay somebody to go out for more food." She studied her friend's face, still bothered by what she'd revealed about Viktor's displeasure. "And be careful. Promise me?"

"Okay. Sure." Rare tears shimmered in Oksana's eyes. She patted her heart, causing Sloane Ferrell's money to brush the bear's shabby ear. "Thank you, sister friend."

"No problem."

Zoey peeked out the door, checked both ways, and then glanced back at Oksana before leaving the room. Her friend was tucking the cash into her hiding spot, a small seam opening under a ribbon on the neck of her teddy bear. Hamburger cash. A little something to make life happier. Stealing was worth it for that.

Strange as it might sound, Zoey imagined Sloane Ferrell might understand. She'd bet the ER nurse had seen some trouble too.

———

Sloane stared at the envelope on her kitchen table, still stunned—unnerved. She'd worked so hard at covering her trail. She hadn't left a forwarding address anywhere except with the state board of nursing and the Feds for taxes. And the cereal company, something she still couldn't quite explain. But this small manila mailer had arrived through the Hope hospital system, not the USPS. It had been forwarded from the emergency department in Sacramento to San Diego to LA Hope. And might even have been tossed in the trash here, except that Sloane's supervisor remembered she'd initially applied for the nursing position under the name Ronda Sloane Wilder.

The name was penciled on the envelope inside. The original date stamp was nearly three weeks ago. With a return address of California State Prison, Los Angeles County.

Sloane's stomach churned. She'd never given Bob Bullard her address, never given him the time of day since she spat the final words of her testimony at his manslaughter trial. But he'd found her. The short note began with no salutation, no attempt at *Dear* or *Hi there* or *Hey, girl*—at least she was spared that.

It's been a long time.

I don't know if you heard, but I'm up for early release. The board meets on 10/17.

I guess you don't want to hear that. Or hear from me at all. I understand.

But I need you to know that a lot of things have changed.

I've changed.

I hope we can talk about that. A phone call, if that's okay.

Okay?

Sloane held the paper, hands trembling, and breathed slowly through her nose. It did nothing to diffuse the anger eating her alive. Like she'd swallowed some merciless demon with claws and fangs.

Drown it. You know how.

She glanced toward the kitchen cupboard, wondering how awkward it would be to ask Celeste if she could borrow a glass of—

No.

Sloane closed her eyes and drew in another slow breath. She wished for a moment that all the "Higher Power" lip service at the AA meetings were real. There was a time years back when she'd thought it was possible, when she'd held her breath and gone under the baptismal water to a chorus of hallelujahs. But then her nose got rubbed in the truth all over again: there was no forgiving God of love for someone like her. Or her mother.

Sloane thought of the necklace Zoey stole. A tarnished silver cross given to her mother by the handsome, blue-eyed soldier who'd promised to marry her. His mother's necklace, perhaps. Sloane's mother didn't know anything about his family. But the one thing she'd known for sure was that her soldier was a brave, kindhearted man who could have been a real father to Sloane—changed everything for both of them—if he hadn't been killed by friendly fire in a training exercise in the Nevada desert. Or at least that had always been her mother's sad, romantic story. Several dramatic versions with the same basic Romeo and Juliet theme. Except that Sloane's mother had lived beyond the tragedy. And the story had become the excuse, the bedrock, for her delicate and dreamy nature, her disconnect from extended family, her sick headaches, and her endless string of awful, self-destructive choices. For herself and for the child she'd given that soldier's name. Wilder.

"You have his eyes . . . movie-star eyes . . ."

Her mother had said it a thousand times—slurred it, sobbed it—holding that cross and alternately praying to and cursing at the cruel God who'd ruined her life. Who'd stolen her chance at a happy ending. Forcing her to settle for so much less.

Like booze and sleeping pills. And a series of loser boyfriends, including the one who couldn't keep his dirty hands off her small daughter. And finally . . . Sloane stared down at the note, bile rising in her throat. Her mother settled for marrying the insensitive and controlling man who took her into the hot tub that awful night.

"And killed her," Sloane said aloud, her voice almost a growl. "You let her slip under the water and—"

She shook her head, fury blurring her vision. Bob Bullard wanted to call and tell her how much he'd changed. How he should now pay less of a price for the evil he'd done, and how he deserved his freedom. Was that what her stepfather wanted? For Sloane to show up at his hearing and ask the board to be merciful?

She laughed so hard tears rose. The irony was too funny, too sweet. Her stepfather had no idea that she'd already arranged to be at his hearing. Where she would stand up and deliver a well-planned speech. Mercy played no part whatsoever in what she was going to say. Bob Bullard deserved as much compassion as he'd shown to his wife.

Sloane folded the letter and slipped it back into the envelope. She was glad she'd accomplished the name change and had managed to keep such a low profile. Bob Bullard didn't know her address. She paid her bills with money orders. What little mail she got came to Celeste's place. She'd never told her coworkers exactly where she lived and rarely gave out her phone number. After what Zoey had pulled, it was an easy bet she wouldn't be retracing her steps back here. Sloane was picking up some extra hours in the ER tonight to help make up for the loss of that money, but she knew she had it good here. She'd be okay. With each passing month, she worried less and less that Paul Stryker would show up on her porch to—

She jumped at the sound of the doorbell.

11

"IT'S A *BEAUUU-TIFUL* PRINCESS," Piper explained, carrying the crayon drawing as she followed Sloane to the kitchen. She was wearing her karate outfit, white belt sagging low over one tiny hip. "Grams says all it needs is some tape. And a friendly fridge."

"I happen to have both." Sloane shook her head, smiling. There couldn't be more of a contrast between this visitor and her last.

"It's a princess with wings," the girl added once they stopped walking. She touched a fingertip to the drawing, indicating twin frills rising from the crayon figure's back, more like crinkle fries from a purple potato than anything with feathers. "Angel wings."

"Oh. I see," Sloane told her, hating that a simple word had the power to drag her back to a beauty pageant stage.

"*Angel Aames. It's a perfect name. Says purity . . . and puts you at the top of the alphabet. You're on your way, baby. . . .*"

Sloane turned her attention to the drawing. "Angel wings and . . . She's carrying a sword?"

"She's a princess angel ninja warrior."

Sloane chuckled. "I'd say that covers the bases."

"Yeah." Piper's quick nod made a curl bounce across her forehead. "I'll trade you."

"Trade?"

The child wrinkled her nose, something in her eyes saying she was testing the water. Deciding. "Not really. You can have it. It's a present. But . . ." She held out the drawing, glancing toward the pantry doors. "We only have Cheerios at my house." Her shoulders rose and fell with a melodramatic sigh. "No marshmallows."

"Ah." Sloane was about to see that fateful cereal on her table for the second time in forty-eight hours. There was apparently a downside to hoarding. She took the drawing and walked toward the kitchen drawers. "Let me find some tape for your picture. Then maybe we can see if I have a snack you might like."

"You do—I *know* you do. Lucky Charms!" Piper's grin blossomed. "And maybe there's chocolate milk."

"Chocolate?" Sloane laughed, warmth spreading across her chest. If ever there was an example of hope on a sugar high. "You're probably pushing it there, kiddo."

"It's okay. I can have reg-lar milk."

"Good to know." Sloane dug around in a sectioned drawer looking for the tape dispenser. She saw a vacant space in the clutter and discovered that her small stash of quarters was gone. Zoey had taken them, too. But she'd left . . . *my AA chips*. Sloane lifted the one designating six months sober and questioned, once again, if day after day of "showing up" would really make any difference at all. *Recovery* was as tough a word as *mercy*.

"Ah," she said, dropping the chip to snag the elusive tape, "here we go." Sloane turned around to find Piper staring at the door of her refrigerator with her hands on her hips.

"You don't have any pictures," the child reported.

"I didn't have anybody to draw me one, until you."

"No," Piper explained. "I mean no pictures of your people."

My people?

"You know," the girl said, tugging at her sagging belt. "Everybody has pictures. Taped up. And also on those things that stick up there without tape."

"Magnets," Sloane offered, a foolish little ache crowding her throat. "Photos on magnets."

"Yes. Those things. Family. And dogs. Friends, stuff like that." Piper's gaze swept over the bare front of Sloane's refrigerator, a sad look dampening her sweet face. "But yours is all empty."

"Until now," Sloane said, lifting the princess-angel-ninja. "Now I have this. My first fridge picture."

"Let's put it up," Piper said, her expression moving to happy-eager again.

They worked for a few minutes, getting it just right, and then Sloane opened the refrigerator and took out the carton of milk. She crossed to the pantry doors, knowing she'd have to open a new box of cereal. One she hadn't yet cleansed of marshmallows.

"You could take a picture of Marty," Piper suggested, her tone pensive as she settled onto a kitchen chair. "And tape it up there. I think Grams has an extra one of me. They took it at the end of kindergarten. Last year. It's old, because . . ." She held up her fingers. "I'm six now. But she might let you have it."

Sloane smiled, touched by the gesture. She opened her mouth to say she'd love that and—

"I think God has the new one. With me being six and with my lost baby teeth," Piper told her with confidence.

"God?"

"My picture. For his fridge. In heaven."

Sloane wasn't sure what to say.

Piper didn't seem to notice. "My mom read it in a book," she explained. "She said if God has a fridge, my picture would be on it. Her picture too. And Grams's." She nodded with profound six-year-old certainty. Then pointed at Sloane. "And yours, too."

Sloane decided there wasn't anything she could say.

"God's got my picture," Piper reiterated, "taped right up there on his big, big, *giiinormous* fridge." She smiled. "Because he's *crazy* about me. And about you, too."

"Me?" Sloane blinked against a ridiculous rush of tears. "I don't know. . . ."

Piper tilted her head, long curls tickling the tabletop. Her innocent eyes went wide. "Don't you believe in God?"

"Things like this," the older PD officer told Micah, "can shake a man's faith, for sure—leastways, his faith in mankind." He swept stubby fingers through his silver hair, then raised his voice over the sounds of receding sirens. "What little faith he had in the first place. I don't mind telling you, mine's about dried up right now." He glanced toward the clutch of evidence techs working the alley crime scene. "Scumbag left her drowning in her own blood. Never seen one still alive like that."

Micah hadn't either and hoped he never would again. This kind of violence was incomprehensible. A young woman, no more than a girl, found in this garbage-strewn alley with her throat sliced. He'd only caught a glimpse as the paramedics worked. Blonde, far too pale, blood . . . everywhere. The sight, coupled with the overripe stench of Dumpsters, had nearly made Micah lose it. He rarely got to a crisis call this fast, but he'd been having coffee within walking distance.

"They're taking her to LA Hope?" Micah asked, tearing his gaze away from the bloody asphalt. "To the ER?"

"That's what I heard." The officer cocked his head as his radio squawked and then silenced again. "Can't imagine surviving something like that." A muscle bunched along his jaw. "Wife and I have a granddaughter about that same age, I'd wager."

Micah nodded, reminding himself that even seasoned first responders weren't immune to critical incident stress. The crisis team had been called to assist a kitchen worker from an adjacent Vietnamese restaurant, the young man who'd made the grisly discovery on a smoke break. But it wasn't only regular citizens who were shaken by this kind of violence. Micah had seen the emotional impact before on responding firefighters, paramedics, and police.

"Ariel," the man said, a hint of a smile on his lips. "Started college a few weeks back. In Montana. Wouldn't take no for an answer. Perfectly good schools here. Where she could live at home and have family keep an eye on her." His gaze moved to the evidence techs, the smile gone. "Kids. They think that it can't happen to them."

"Yeah." Micah pushed down an image of his cousin. "It's hard not to see ourselves, our own, in something like that."

"Yep."

Micah waited. His job was to listen, though he suspected there was little more this veteran cop would say. Toughness tended to come with the badge. The police department had chaplains. This officer mentioned faith . . .

"You're day shift or swings?" Micah asked.

"End of watch right about now." The man's laugh was half groan. "After all the paperwork."

"I hear you on that."

The cop's gaze swept over the crisis team logo on Micah's jacket. "How long you been doing this, Prescott?"

"Almost six years."

"Can't be easy mopping up after stuff like this. All that mess of emotion. Survivors wailing and cursing." His forehead wrinkled. "Why do you do it?"

"Because . . ." Micah thought of that night with his cousin, of his family's unimaginable pain. "Because someone has to. And someone did it for my family once."

The officer nodded, cuffed Micah's shoulder. "You going to the hospital?"

"Probably." He knew what the officer was saying. There could be a death notification to be made. "See if any family shows up."

"Could take a while—she's a Jane Doe."

And somebody's daughter.

"I'll see what else I can do for the witness here; then I'll go," Micah told him.

"Well . . . I'm out of here." The officer hiked his thumb over his shoulder in the direction of his squad car.

"Paperwork?"

"Yeah. Then home. Wife's making stuffed pork chops." The man smiled. "Maybe we'll Skype with Montana."

"Sounds like a good plan."

The officer took a few steps away, then looked back. "Hey, thanks."

"No problem."

Micah watched him walk away, then took a slow breath. Despite the shock factor of this grisly scene, he was glad he'd been close by when the call came in. For the restaurant worker, surrounded by his workmates now, and especially for that stoic officer. Grandfather with a badge. A man who, whether he'd admit it or not, would be dealing with his own "mess of emotions" tonight. Being here was more than worth it for that alone.

"Things like this can shake a man's faith. . . ."

Micah closed his eyes, said a prayer. For the LAPD veteran, the first responders, witnesses . . . and for Jane Doe, the critically injured young woman who was by now lying on a trauma bed at Los Angeles Hope, where Micah would soon be headed. Not in a coat and tie this time.

He shook his head. It didn't happen often—Micah's volunteer persona butting up against his day job. Coop would put a Clark Kent and Superman spin on that. Thankfully, it was the reporter's night to be on scene with his grandmother's kitty litter drama.

"Oxygen's still falling at 78 percent," Sloane reported, straining to be heard over the chaotic trauma room din. "We're suctioning like crazy, but the field crike is plugging with clots. And this hematoma's—"

"I can see that!" the doctor shouted, leaning over the gurney again. His frustration ended in a short curse as he stared at the morbidly pale assault victim. Her neck was grossly swollen and distorted by an increasing accumulation of blood in the tissues. Two surgical hemostats protruded from the wound, the doctor's desperate attempts to clamp bleeders and slow the girl's exsanguination. He turned, yelling over his shoulder, "Is the OR ready? It'll take too much time to trach her here."

"Two minutes and we can roll," the clinical coordinator told him. "Anesthesia just arrived."

"Okay then." The doctor whipped back around and pointed at the respiratory therapist. "Keep bagging and let's get things ready to move." His gaze met Sloane's. "What are those last vitals?"

"BP 78 over 40, heart rate 138." She grimaced, noting the monitor display. "And 74 percent on the O_2 now." Sloane looked down at her unconscious patient and saw the ominous glazed look in her half-closed eyes. The neck gash bubbled with each mechanical breath the therapist delivered and was accompanied by an awful gurgling burp. The girl's lips grew increasingly gray-tinged. Jane Doe had suffered horrifying violence and was now dying before their eyes.

"Anybody find any ID?" a clerk asked, poking her head into the room. "Wallet or a cell phone we could use to track it down?"

"Nothing," one of the techs reported, getting the portable monitor ready for the move to the OR. "She arrived in those pajamas; that's all. No nothing. Except for that tat on her hip."

The tattoo.

It was one of the first things Sloane had seen when the paramedics slid the girl onto their trauma room gurney. Those ominous rag doll–limp arms and legs, then the hip tattoo.

Sloane's heart had stalled. Bold red and black, inked diagonally across her pale flesh: *PROPERTY OF V.*

No double dollar sign. A black crown instead.

Sloane's breath had escaped in a whoosh as she glimpsed the rest of the girl. Blonde, curvy . . . *not Zoey.*

"A tattoo doesn't help me," the clerk said, skillfully averting her eyes from the gurney. "Unless it's got her Social Security number or—"

"Everybody set?" Sloane interrupted, releasing the brake on the gurney. She nodded at the respiratory therapist, double-checked that the IV's pumps looked secure. "Okay. Let's move!"

"The crisis team folks are here. Maybe one of them can find me something," the clerk said, continuing to talk as she stepped aside to accommodate the ER team's exit. "So weird to see Mr. Prescott like that."

"Our marketing guy?" Sloane asked, hugging close to the gurney as they moved through the doorway. The oxygen monitor continued its insistent alarm. "Why is he here?"

"With the crisis team," the clerk explained, grimacing as she caught an unwelcome glimpse of their mutilated patient. "He's, like . . . a volunteer, I guess."

Huh?

Before Sloane could suggest the improbability of that, they'd propelled Jane Doe into the outer corridor for the last short leg to the OR. The gurney squeaked and clattered past a detective, a uniformed female officer, and two crisis team volunteers in their familiar jackets talking with the hospital chaplain. One of the volunteers was short, Hispanic, and the other . . . Sloane's eyes widened as he met her gaze.

The other one really was Micah.

12

"STILL NO CONCRETE MEANS of identifying that poor child," the hospital chaplain told Micah as she sank into the chapel chair with a sigh. Probably in her early fifties, Lydia Chalmers wore her hair pulled back in dozens of tiny braids, had an infectious laugh, and scooted around LA Hope like she was on roller skates. "I imagine law enforcement will eventually release at least a sketch."

"Or a photo of the tattoo," Micah added, unable to block a memory of Stephen's bloodstained personal effects. To spare his aunt and uncle, Micah had been the one to first view the body at the medical examiner's office. The truth was, they might not have been able to identify Stephen with certainty if he hadn't been carrying his wallet. "One of the officers said she may not be a local, or not for long enough to establish an identity here."

The chaplain adjusted her red-framed glasses. "Which could be by intentional design. If she's a victim of human trafficking."

Micah knew it was more than possible. The FBI put Los Angeles in the top thirteen areas of child trafficking in the nation. The crisis team had specially trained volunteers who worked with that situation, helping victims who managed to get out of the sex trade. It struck Micah once again that his role as a crisis responder was nothing like what he did in the hospital marketing department.

Lydia met Micah's gaze, the chapel's subdued light reflecting in her glasses. "I can't tell you how heartening it is to see hospital administration involved in this kind of community outreach—your efforts with the crisis team, Micah."

"It's far and apart from my official position," he admitted, thinking she'd read his mind.

"Maybe so." The chaplain offered him a small smile. "But I still like it. It says a lot about you."

"But I've known about you *all along. Slick, charming, with all the right words to get exactly what you want. Your agenda, your priorities. That's all that counts. . . ."*

Sloane Ferrell wouldn't raise a finger to second Lydia's sentiment. But she'd certainly done an impressive double take when she'd spotted him in the hallway outside the ER an hour or so ago. Something told him her spin wouldn't involve Mr. Kent or the Man of Steel. And it didn't matter.

"It's important to me. Working with the crisis team," Micah heard himself say. "I wasn't sure I could do it at first." He winced. "That scene in the alley today had me second-guessing myself again."

"But you keep coming back."

Micah nodded.

"Because it feels like the most important thing you've ever done."

"Yeah," Micah agreed, unexpected emotion thickening his voice. He thought of the woman he'd had to bring news of her husband's death. Of that police officer tonight who'd needed to talk about his college freshman in Montana. Short, important moments in time that were made different because he'd been there. "Yeah," he repeated, "that about says it."

Lydia's phone buzzed. "I should go upstairs," she said, scanning the text and reaching for her briefcase. "We have a young cancer patient. I want to be there for his parents." She met Micah's gaze again. "Are you going to stick around for a while?"

"I told crisis dispatch I wanted to wait for word from surgery. And in case any family or friends show up for . . . Jane."

"I'll probably see you again, then."

Micah told the chaplain good-bye, then grabbed a cup of coffee from the pot at the back of the chapel. Along with packaged graham crackers, it was something the hospital offered for visitors who found themselves waiting. Micah's stomach growled as he opened the crackers; this would be dinner for now. He thought of what he'd said to Lydia about being here in case someone showed up for the young woman in surgery. The chaplain had referred to her as a child. She was probably right. Even with all the blood, what he had glimpsed of the victim's face looked very young.

Micah grimaced, remembering the one personal item they'd found next to Jane Doe in the alley. A crime scene tech had been sliding it into an evidence bag as Micah was leaving the scene.

A blood-soaked teddy bear.

———

"She needs to get *out* of there," Zoey insisted, catching Stack's attention as he dealt cards onto the musty bedspread for another of his endless games of solitaire. Slap them down, grumble, curse, crow with pride—the same, hours on end. The only thing that changed was these crummy motel addresses. "She's still all cut up from surgery, but those pigs are already planning 'dates' and—"

"Forget it." Stack stubbed his cigar on yesterday's pizza box, shooting her the look that said she'd gone too far. "Not gonna happen. Count yourself lucky it's not you, kid. It could be. Or have you forgotten your little tattoo?"

A smirk teased Stack's lips, making his gray-green eyes narrow in the way some girls would probably find sexy. He had those *Bachelor* TV show kind of good looks, with decently cut hair, a faint stubble of beard, and a lean, hard-belly build. Good teeth. Appealing, probably, if you didn't really know him. Stack's looks were just generic enough that he could change them in a minute if he needed to: cowboy shirt and boots, hoodie and ball cap, Army fatigues—requiring a buzz haircut—coat and tie, and even a priest's collar once.

"You don't remember I saved your skinny behind from that life?" Stack said again, close enough to the darkened window that the motel's neon sign lit his hair as pink on top as hers. His grin spread slowly. "Saved you from unholy sin and degradation?"

"So you keep telling me," Zoey fired back, knowing just how far she could go with a smart remark before she'd pay for it. Not that Stack would hit her—or touch her. She was sixteen and he was pushing forty, and he'd told her a thousand times she was a punk kid not worth a real man's time. He wouldn't hurt her physically for disrespecting him. But he'd absolutely let Zoey go hungry, leave her to thumb rides, and then remind her again and again she could easily be on the menu at every truck stop they passed. Or end up back home. *Was it really worse than this?*

Stack "saved" her because she was useful. Small enough to slip through windows, quick enough to jam out of there if she got caught. Neutral enough to pass for a boy and—with a dress, heels, and a good layer of shoplifted makeup—pretty enough to distract a man. She could cry on demand and lie with the best of them. Zoey was a good actor and an easy keeper, sharp-witted, and most of all, she had nowhere else to go.

"That pink hair," Stack said, lighting another cigar. His smile crinkled the corners of his eyes. "It's not half-bad."

"On top of a cotton-candy cone." Zoey gave him a look just shy of a glare. "When can I ditch it?"

"Well . . ." Stack blew a perfect smoke ring and began laying down cards again. "Tonight, if you want. It's served its purpose. Go boost yourself some Clairol."

"Okay. I will." She stood, glad for an excuse to get out. "I won't be long. There's a CVS two blocks down."

Stack lifted her half-empty bottle of beer. "You over the legal walking limit?"

"I'm good." She offered a thumbs-up. "See ya in a few."

Stack regarded her for a moment, then reached for his wallet. "Hang on. I'll give you some cash. You did good on that last job."

"Thanks."

Zoey took the money and headed toward the drugstore. It was a short walk down a street dotted with stunted and sickly palms. The night sky was shot through with half-dead neon, and the air reeked of gasoline, cheap Mexican food, and back-alley hookups. Too many cars had the bass on their sound systems dialed way too low, like an earthquake starting. She auditioned hair colors in her mind and tried to ignore the small jab of guilt over Stack's compliment.

"You did good . . ."

Zoey shoved her hand into the pocket of her baggy jeans and touched the slithery-cool chain of the necklace. It was something she'd found herself doing more and more since she took it from that flour jar. She'd given Stack the diamond ring and most of the money from her unexpected score at the nurse's house. But not the silver cross. Zoey wasn't sure why, but she'd decided to keep it. Beyond that, she'd better play it straight with Stack. Had to.

She was a liar, a thief, and a con artist. She had nobody, nothing—and was worth less than that.

But Zoey still had it better than Oksana.

"Anyway, I saw you sitting here and thought you were probably waiting for word from OR," Sloane explained after she'd given Micah the update on the knifing victim. "I thought you'd want to know."

"I did—I do. Thanks," Micah said, relief mixed with genuine surprise to see Sloane standing beside him in the chapel. Her voice sounded tentative and there was no hint of impending fireworks in her eyes. She simply looked concerned. And beautiful. "If Jane Doe has 'stabilized,' that means she's going to be all right?"

"It's too early to tell. The bleeding's under control and

they're keeping her oxygenated. So far, she's holding her own." Sloane's fingers moved over her stethoscope. "Most of us thought we'd lose her before we could get her to the OR. There was so much damage."

"Scumbag left her drowning in her own blood."

"I've never seen anything like that. Outside of a war zone," Micah heard himself say. Then realized it wasn't entirely true. He'd seen Stephen.

"Earlier," Sloane continued, "when those people came in from the restaurant near the crime scene . . ." She'd lowered herself to half perch on the chair next to him. "I saw you talking with them. Helping that old woman who was so upset."

"A cook, the great-grandmother to the young man who found the girl," Micah explained. "There was a language barrier, but from what I heard, the assault brought back memories from an incident in her village in Vietnam. Not surprising. Crisis situations can do that. More people are affected by traumatic stress than we'd think."

"Yes." Sloane held Micah's gaze long enough to make his breath snag. "I didn't know you were doing that," she said finally. "The chaplain work."

"The crisis team is part of California Crisis Care. We don't really call ourselves chaplains in this group."

"Same thing. Whatever you call yourselves. I saw it in Sacramento. And San Diego." Something in Sloane's eyes said she regretted mentioning it. "Anyway, I was surprised to see you here. I had you pegged . . . well, not anything like that."

"Slick, charming . . ." Sloane Ferrell didn't have him merely pegged; she'd tried her best to nail him to the wall.

"I guess I was wrong," she admitted, "when I said that you don't get it about people. With what you're doing out there, it seems like you'd have to." Her lovely lips pressed together. "So I'm sorry. About that part."

"No problem," he told her. A total lie because he now realized her words had been grating on him since their last run-in. It suddenly felt like he'd passed some essential test. "Thanks."

"Okay then," Sloane said, a small sigh hinting she'd checked an unpleasant chore off her list. "This is supposed to be my free Saturday, but I said I'd come in for a few hours. My relief is here, so I'm going to head to my car."

The old Volvo with all the at-odds bumper stickers. It seemed like peace was finally possible. . . .

"Hey," Micah began, deciding not to overthink it. "Want to go out and get something to eat? Or maybe some coffee?"

13

"YOU MEAN NOW? Go out somewhere?" Sloane asked, not sure she'd heard it right. Apparently she had a language barrier too. "With you?"

"Yeah. That's what I meant." Micah's quick smile was more of a wince. It made his face look boyish. "Sounds crazy, I guess, considering that you hate me."

"Mmm." The man didn't need to know that she only half hated him now.

"I'm still on call," Micah added. "We'd have to drive separately. Go somewhere I could wrap up my food and run if I had to. So it's not like this is . . ." His brown eyes held hers. "It's food. You. Me . . . Sushi?"

He is. He's asking me out.

"Uh . . ." Sloane floundered. It wasn't only a language

barrier; it was the piled-high bunker she'd carefully built over the span of nearly three years. The string of zip codes, the new name, and all the precautions she'd taken to keep herself physically safe. But most of all, the wall she'd built around her heart.

"If you don't like sushi, it doesn't have to be that," Micah offered, the look in his eyes—chaplain's eyes, whether he claimed the title or not—saying he got this too. But he wasn't going to let it go. "It could be anything you want."

It occurred to Sloane she didn't really know what that was.

"Thanks, but I'm going to pass," she said finally, feeling a strange twinge of regret as she rose from the chapel chair. A chapel, a chaplain—more than a language barrier. She was a foreigner in a foreign country. "I just wanted to let you know about the girl."

Micah released a breath. "I appreciate that."

She started to turn away, then glanced back at him. "For the record: I do like sushi."

"Good to know."

It took her less than twenty minutes to get home. The late-afternoon sun had begun to wane, and once again Sloane realized how much she'd lucked out by finding this place. Celeste had chosen it with her own commute in mind, all those years she worked at LA Hope. Sloane smiled to herself, remembering something else Piper had said during her visit: she might become a nurse one day too. After she got her black belt in martial arts.

Sloane switched off the ignition, pulled the parking brake, then grabbed her purse and slid from the car. Her stomach rumbled as she locked the Volvo's door. She hoped there was more than cereal for dinner. She'd never checked the carton of eggs she'd planned to use for breakfast before Zoey raided her flour canister and took a hike.

Sloane cringed, remembering the tattoo on Jane Doe's hip. Too much like Zoey's.

The detectives had photographed the lettering and the small inked crown, talking among themselves about gang tattoos and trafficking. Sloane wanted to believe it wasn't the case with Zoey. But after all that had happened, it was more than hard to swallow the girl's story about a friend in Bakersfield. And that she'd be working at the YMCA, helping "underprivileged kids." Still, Sloane wouldn't have believed Micah Prescott had a heart for volunteer service either. That had completely blindsided her. Almost as much as his invitation for dinner.

She stood beside the car, letting it wash over her again. She couldn't remember the last time a man had asked her out.

No, that wasn't true. She *chose* not to remember the last several times. Men on barstools getting far too friendly for the price of a watered-down drink, telling her she was movie-star gorgeous and that their wives didn't understand them. Saying their lives could be so much better with someone else, and ". . . *maybe it's you.*"

Lines only a complete fool would buy. And she'd shopped like it was a price drop at Walmart. Not anymore.

Sloane glanced toward the guest cottage windows, saw the lamp with the auto-timer switch on. Security measures. Her new reality didn't include impromptu dinners with men. Even men who surprised her in a good way. She couldn't afford the risk. Not with her sobriety, her heart, her safe—

"Miss Ferrell?"

Sloane whirled around, heart thudding.

"It's Jerry. From the hospital . . . Jerry Rhodes." He stepped out from the shadow cast by Celeste's dwarf peach tree. "I'm sorry if I startled you."

"What . . . ?" Sloane glanced toward the main house. Her pulse was pounding in her ears, confusion making her dizzy. The man was carrying a shovel. "What are you doing here?"

"Working. Setting some stakes for Ms. Albright's beds. She wants some new ones."

"Beds?"

"Her garden." Jerry pointed with the handle of the shovel. "Two more next to the other one. One for winter vegetables, she said. The other for her pumpkins. Hundred-pounders, the little girl told me." He chuckled. The pencil was behind his ear like this was just another day at the hospital. "Ms. Albright didn't tell you I was coming?"

"No." Sloane's mouth was dry. "She didn't."

"Well . . ." Jerry's amiable smile scrunched his dark eyes. "We've got ourselves a draw. She didn't tell me you were coming for a visit either."

"Uh . . ." If he was telling the truth, she couldn't hide hers. "I rent the guest cottage."

Jerry glanced toward the lit window. "You have a cat. I saw her in the window playing with the curtains."

Sloane didn't correct him about Marty's gender. She didn't like this conversation; it felt like too many steps backward in her sense of security.

"Small world," he said. "But I guess that's the way it is with hospital folks. Ms. Albright needing help and asking round LA Hope. Me being a handyman on the side. And now you—"

"I keep to myself, Jerry." Sloane met his gaze directly. "I

value my privacy. I don't give out my address or phone. I'm sure that's why Celeste didn't say anything. Out of respect for my wishes."

"Yes, ma'am." Jerry's expression turned somber. "I understand."

"Thank you," she told him, thinking that he couldn't possibly. She wouldn't want him to. She didn't trust anyone that much. "Well . . . good night."

"Good night, Miss Ferrell." Jerry changed his grip on the shovel handle and looked toward the main house. "I'd better give the wife a call and head home myself."

"Drive safely," Sloane said, knowing she'd sounded blunt before.

"You bet."

She watched as Jerry walked toward a pickup truck parked on the gravel beside her landlady's driveway. A heavy-duty wheelbarrow was secured behind the cab, its handles sticking up like the proverbial sore thumb. Sloane hadn't even noticed it before, proof she was letting her guard down. She was getting too comfortable and making mistakes. Like striking up a friendship with Harper, bringing Zoey here . . . and considering having coffee with Micah Prescott. Had she? Had she really been tempted to do that?

She remembered how intent he'd been in his efforts to help the distraught Vietnamese woman. Doing his best to put her at ease. Micah was probably still at the hospital, conferring with the chaplain about Jane Doe. There had been warmth in his eyes when he'd invited her out. It was hard to deny she found him attractive. Even harder now that he'd revealed another side of his character. But . . .

Even if Sloane weren't forced to hide away, the truth

remained that every mistake she'd made and every disappointment she'd been handed involved trusting a man. It wasn't as if she could erase that. But she could be on guard and stop it from ever happening again by swearing off men like she'd sworn off alcohol. Another sort of twelve-step program—twelve steps and then run like crazy. Men and alcohol: she couldn't trust herself with either. And in combination . . . deadly.

Sloane paused on the porch and peered toward the pickup truck. She could hear the sound of an idling engine. And see a small illumination in the darkened cab—a cell phone probably. Jerry calling his wife.

She went inside and locked the door behind her. Marty meowed at her from his perch on the back of the couch. Sloane smiled. Their start had been rocky, but they'd been soul mates from the get-go.

"Hey there, big guy. I'm all yours for the evening. Who cares about sushi?"

She climbed onto the couch and chuckled as the lanky cat responded to her attention in blissful excess, sprawling out and then rolling onto his back to offer his belly for rubbing.

"There you go," she said, obliging. "How's that, you spoiled thing?"

Marty's purr rumbled and Sloane's shoulders relaxed, her heart settling at last. She was home. It was okay now.

"I'm going to scramble us some eggs. Then load up an old movie in the DVD player. Maybe Cary Grant and Kate Hepburn. *Philadelphia Story*. You love that one, don't you? And then we'll—"

What's that?

The lamplight hit the window, highlighting a collection of smudges. Sloane frowned. Celeste was a stickler about seasonal cleaning; she'd had her window guy in only last week for the main house and Sloane's cottage. She'd obviously wasted her money. The man had missed this whole section.

Sloane leaned closer, studying the dozens of oval smudges. And sort of longer dragging smears. Almost like someone—

Her stomach lurched.

"You have a cat. I saw her in the window playing with the curtains."

Jerry Rhodes's fingerprints? Had he climbed through her bushes, up to her window, and—?

Sloane's cell phone buzzed.

She checked the screen. No ID, but a perfectly timed distraction.

"Yes?" she answered, tearing her gaze away from the disturbing fingerprints.

"Sloane," the deep voice began. "Hey, babe—long time."

No . . .

"It's me. Paul."

──────

"I figured I should check it out, for sure," Coop continued after taking a last slurp from the straw of his Big Gulp. His grandmother kept her thermostat cranked way too high, he'd complained. Changing kitty litter was like shoveling sand in Death Valley. "This could all be playing right into my hands, you know?"

Micah glanced across the hood of his car toward the lights of the ER entrance. Several police cars were still parked near it. "You mean for a story?"

"A tie to my prison research." Coop lowered his voice as if there were reporters in the cars nearby eager to steal his idea.

"Fat Russian kingpin pulls strings from behind bars. Little blonde sex slave pays with her sad, hopeless life."

Micah frowned. Coop was doing his best to get ditched as a friend. "Nobody knows for sure she's involved in that."

"Then 'nobody' is fooling himself."

"And she's *alive*," Micah corrected, resisting the urge to give him a solid thump. Plotting human interest stories wasn't even close to being a compassionate human. "She's in the SICU on a ventilator. Holding her own," Micah added, remembering Sloane's words. "They're replacing the blood. Protecting her airway. She's critical but stable."

"Still Jane Doe." Coop's expression was close to a pout. "And not talking."

"Not possible with her injuries." Micah tried not to imagine the implications of what little medicalese he'd understood. Trauma to the windpipe, cartilage, vessels, and a nick dangerously close to the girl's spinal cord.

"*Won't* talk, I mean," Coop clarified. "Even if they patch her up enough and she can plug off that trach thing to speak, Jane won't talk. Because she's supposed to be dead and she knows it. And she knows way *more*. That's the problem. Why do you think they have cops guarding her?"

Micah had heard about the officers. But he wasn't going to encourage Coop. As a crisis volunteer, he was expected to honor confidentiality. Plus, there had been enough reporters around. Still were. He had a horrible feeling a shot of that bloodied teddy bear would end up on the Internet.

". . . crown's big with them."

"What?" Micah asked, realizing he'd tuned Coop out.

"The tat on her behind. A black crown. The Russians have a few select symbols they like to use."

Micah wasn't going to ask him how he'd found out about Jane Doe's tattoo. He'd only say he had "a gift for gleaning."

"The point is," Coop explained, "someone screwed up. What happened to that kid was amateurish. That she's still alive. And that she was found at all."

Micah shot him a look. "Most people call it a blessing."

"All I'm saying is that a big mistake was made. Either her 'bosses' decided she was a liability and somebody did a sloppy job, or some 'customer' turned substandard Jack the Ripper. Either way, our Jane Doe's in a bad spot."

"Her throat's cut. She's tied down to a hospital bed and surrounded by strangers." Micah didn't try to temper his tone. "I don't think *bad* is a strong enough word."

"Okay—I get it." Coop raised his palm. "But as soon as she wakes up, there's going to be another pile-on. Everybody will be asking that girl questions."

"And you wish it could be you."

"Pointless. I'm the Lifestyle guy, remember? Besides, they're not going to let media get anywhere near Jane Doe. The cops will be doing the asking. And she'll lie."

"So why are you here?"

"Gleaning information, taking notes." Coop tapped his shaggy curls. "Putting it together, right up here. I'm going to track it all backward and look for the bigger story. Connect the dots—and tats."

"Back to State Prison?"

"Clear back to Moscow, if I need to." Coop smiled, then rattled the ice in his cup. "Hey, want to grab something to eat?"

Gleaning info and eats. Coop was a pro.

"I'm still on call," Micah hedged, despite the fact that he was hungry. He had no interest in any more conversation with

Cooper Vance. "I want to check in with dispatch and make some notes first. And I need to round up my teammate. He's still here somewhere."

"No problem. I'm going to head out. Score me a burger. Talk later?"

"You got my number."

"Sure."

As Coop walked off, Micah pulled out his phone and checked for text messages. Then realized how stupid that was. There wouldn't be a text from Sloane. She hadn't given him her number or asked for his. And she'd turned down his impulsive invitation.

"For the record: I do like sushi."

Apparently Sloane was okay with dragon rolls, sashimi, seaweed, and wasabi. But not with him. She'd made that clear on a number of occasions. His volunteer jacket didn't really change things even if she'd shown kindness by giving him an update on Jane Doe. And offered an apology for some of the things she'd said before.

Micah thought of that long moment when Sloane's eyes met his. When she'd asked about his work with the crisis team, after they'd both done all they could to stem the hemorrhage and pain left in the wake of that merciless attack. As improbable as it was given their history, at that moment it was like they knew the tragedy connected them. Maybe even saw each other through different eyes. But . . .

Micah frowned, slipped his phone back into his pocket. A beautiful woman shows him a hint of a softer side and he reads it as a sign of interest? Asks her out? Complete idiot move. He wouldn't make that mistake again.

14

"HOW DID YOU GET THIS NUMBER?" Sloane asked, certain she was going to be sick.

"That's your big question? After all this time apart?" There was an amused laugh. "Not 'Where are you, Paul?'"

Where?

Sloane stared at the smudged window. Was it possible?

"My turn," he said. "Where'd you come up with Ferrell?" He knew she'd changed her name.

"You're married?" Paul prodded.

"No. Not that it's any of your busi—"

"Good, great news," he interrupted. "But it's not your father's name or your mother's or your jailbird stepdad's, and it's sure not *mine*."

"Yours?" Familiar anger rose, bitter as bile. Sloane told herself it was crazy, dangerous; she warned herself to stop, hang up, but—"That was never going to happen, Paul. And you know it."

"I know I put a diamond on your finger."

"The ring?" Sloane's voice choked on something that felt like a laugh. Mixed into broken glass. But it was the first sliver of mirth she'd felt since yesterday morning when she discovered that tacky, empty rooster jar. She glanced toward the kitchen now. No diamond. No cross. Plenty of plastic tumblers. It was dark, sick, but so *truly* funny.

"Is that what you want?" she asked, almost relieved. The last time they'd spoken it was about the ring. It had been appraised once at four thousand dollars. Money for gambling—Paul would get that any way he could. "Because if this is about the ring, you're too late."

"Pawned?"

There was probably a lot of truth to that assumption.

"None of your business," she told him. "It's gone. Not that you had much to do with buying it anyway." He'd made a few payments. She paid the balance. In the end, she'd paid a much higher price considering all that happened. Maybe she was paying still.

"I would have married you, Sloane."

She closed her eyes, hating that the words hurt even a little. It was probably true. Paul might have married her eventually. His "nurse with a purse"—his smartest investment. The old joke had worn thin, almost as thin as his insistence on an "open" relationship. She'd known it from the beginning and told herself he'd change. She bought herself a diamond ring. And a humiliating lie.

"I stuck by you," he added, "even after the whole mess with that married—"

"Don't!" she shouted, the outburst making Marty spring from the couch. "Don't you dare."

"Okay, okay. I don't want it to be like this, babe. I only wanted to—"

"Tell me where," Sloane demanded, looking at the smeared fingerprints again. Were they Jerry's or . . . ? "Where are you, right *now*?"

"In a motel. Alone."

She waited. He knew what she was asking.

"I left Mexico a couple months back," Paul explained. Then summoned his easy laugh. "Any longer and I'd be Mayor Pablo."

"They found you. And you ran."

Those faceless people who'd harassed Sloane with phone calls, written nasty slurs on her car, and then sent her hurtling over a cliff. The mobsters who very nearly killed her. Because they wanted Paul.

"No. That's not it," he told her. "I swear. I'm squared with those guys. All simpatico now. It's good." It sounded like he cleared his throat. "*I'm* good, babe. That's what I called to tell you. I'm a new man. Got my priorities straight. So maybe you and I . . . ?"

"Don't say it." She rose from the couch, dizzy. "Where are you, Paul?" Sloane held her breath.

"West Coast," he told her. "Moving around. You know me. But say the word, and I'll be there."

"Stay. Away."

"I need to see you, Sloane. It's important."

"No."

"It's the only way I can prove to you that things are different."

"I don't want to see you." Sloane paced to the kitchen, opened the cupboard door, and stared up at the shiny wine-glasses. "Don't call again."

"You're involved with someone? Is that it?"

Sloane jabbed the Disconnect button and threw the cell phone into the sink. She struggled for a breath, strangled by anger. Then she reached into the cupboard and swept the entire set of plastic tumblers from the shelf, watching them hit the counter with hollow, pelting thwacks, bounce to the floor and roll and roll . . .

"No." She hunched over, shoulders shaking to loose tears she couldn't let come. Paul Stryker wasn't worth tears, wasn't worth this old thirst threatening to consume her. She couldn't let him do that. *Wouldn't.*

She pulled her phone from the sink, checked the time. Her usual AA meeting was over. She'd never bought into the idea of a sponsor, didn't even know what she'd done with the phone list they'd given her. There was no one she could call. Except Harper maybe.

No, too risky. Sloane could end up revealing far more than was safe. But being here alone wasn't good, either. She'd get in the car, drive somewhere for coffee or . . .

"It could be anything you want."

Micah? Far easier to keep her guard up with him.

They hadn't exchanged numbers, but . . .

Sloane tapped her phone, brought up her e-mail, and checked the few unsent drafts. She'd written an e-mail after the meeting in the PIO's office, a rant she knew better than to send. But it had the address. Yes, there.

She tapped the keys:

Craving creamy tomato udon. Your fault. Thinking downtown.

Sloane hesitated, then added her cell phone number.

She fed Marty, showered, and slipped into cropped jeans, a white shirt, and flip-flops. She switched to a pair of TOMS ballet flats after getting a glimpse of her chipped toenail polish. Then she dabbed concealer over her scar and applied some light mascara, all the while telling herself the strange flutter in her stomach was nothing more than hunger. Maybe adrenaline ebb after the unexpected intrusion by Jerry Rhodes. And Paul. She was hungry and needed to get out of the house. Simple as that.

Besides, she thought as she grabbed her purse and keys and walked toward the door, the chances that the marketing man would check his work e-mail after hours were—

Her phone rang. And her stomach did that flutter. It couldn't be, could it?

"Hello?" she managed.

"Little Tokyo is good for sushi," Micah told her. "There's a great sort of hole-in-the-wall place that has your udon. It's called—"

"Marugame Monzo."

His laugh seemed to warm her ear. "That's the place."

Sloane took a slow breath. "I'll meet you there."

———

"The TV said there was no identification," Zoey reported, stepping through the doorway of the adjoining rooms for the third time in the last ten minutes. Stack was barely listening, probably on the verge of telling her to stuff it. "They said blonde, maybe late teens, and—"

"That could be *you*, two weeks ago. Or tomorrow," Stack said, shaking his head. "Get real. There's a blonde on every corner. In every crummy alley. Stop obsessing, for pete's sake."

"But—" Zoey's stomach shuddered with dread—"Oksana said she was going for a checkup tonight. It didn't sound right. What doctor does checkups on a Saturday night? And then Viktor said that thing about her not being worth the trouble."

"Keep this up," Stack warned, "and maybe I'll start thinking the same thing about you."

Zoey knew he didn't mean it. As a real threat, anyway. But these past weeks, she'd started wondering. Was this—her "freedom"—worth it? She didn't feel free. More and more, she just felt guilty . . . worthless.

Stack shoved aside the laptop. He'd been studying maps for an hour or more, grumbling to himself. He always got that way until the next job came together. He suddenly jabbed his finger toward her. "I've told you before: stay away from those girls."

"It's just Oksana. I knew her from before."

"I don't care if you shared a baby crib with her and had the same loser mother." Stack scraped a hand through his hair, the exact auburn shade of hers now—from the last of her Clairol bottle. He'd touched up his sprouting goatee, too. "I can't have you mixed up with that again. You get that?"

"I'm not. You know I'm careful," Zoey said, hearing the faint whine in her voice. Stack had taken her phone away more than once. She needed to make sure Oksana was safe. "You said it yourself," she continued, forcing a smile. "I'm like a cat. In, out. Nobody sees me."

"No!" Stack lurched toward her, grabbed her wrist. Hard.

"Hey," Zoey said, disbelief edging on panic. "You're hurting me."

"And you're forgetting your place and why I bother to keep you around. Keep you fed, safe."

"I haven't forgotten," Zoey told him, feeling anything but safe. She'd started to tremble. "I swear."

He stared at her for a moment, then loosened his grip. "That business, those dudes—it could bring a world of hurt down on me. I can't have that."

"I hear you." Zoey's legs went rubbery with relief as he let go of her. "I promise, Stack."

"That's better."

She nodded, taking a shuddering breath to try to slow her pulse.

"The new hair color is good on you," he said. "We look like brother and sister or . . ." He grimaced. "Father and daughter. We could work that somehow."

"Sure," Zoey agreed, ignoring her throbbing wrist. "Why not?"

"That's my girl." Stack pointed to her room. "Now go shut off that TV."

"Okay."

Zoey walked back through the doorway, telling herself it *would* be okay. It was harder to believe after what she'd just seen in Stack. She had to question if she really was better off than Oksana. Maybe "okay" only meant alive. Not free, not safe, just here. For now.

She switched off the TV, then slid her hand deep into her pocket to feel the cool, solid presence of the silver cross. Stolen comfort. It was all she had.

15

"YOU *WERE* HUNGRY," Micah said, enjoying the rosy speck of tomato sauce on Sloane's chin. The sheer pleasure in her eyes could be a powerful marketing shot for a review he'd read about this place: *"Crazy good seafood—sexy noodles."* Clearly Monzo's tomato cream udon fell into the latter category. "Pretty good, huh?"

"The best," she said, dabbing away the evidence. Sloane set the napkin down and lifted her small, patterned cup of green tea. She inhaled slowly as if savoring its fragrance. The tea and possibly the very air: hot sesame oil combined with pungent aromas of fish, sizzling meats, steamed rice, vinegar, chili pepper, and vegetables. "I don't splurge like this very often," she added.

Micah decided to fight about the dinner check later. He

liked that Sloane was frugal. It showed in the way she dressed, too: simple, fresh—classic, his mother would say. His mother? Where had that thought come from? It wasn't even in the realm of imagination that he'd be introducing this woman to his family. Truth was, he didn't have a clue why she'd changed her mind about meeting him tonight. Still, it was another respectable hop forward from their dubious history. He'd take that.

"Before I really knew LA," Sloane said, watching as a chef in a white apron and skullcap expertly whacked udon noodles with a huge hinged knife, "I imagined it was all palm trees, fancy cars, and movie studios."

"And Valleyspeak," Micah agreed, referencing the tired cliché about bubbly, tedious Southern California chatter. "Endless sun and freeway gridlock."

Sloane looked at him over her teacup. "It's true about the traffic. Um, like . . . *totally*."

He laughed, surprised by this playful side of her. That she'd shared very little made Micah curious to learn more. Beyond their mutual appreciation for Japanese food.

"Sort of small enclaves in a big city, I guess," she continued. "Like here in Little Tokyo, with the gardens and the Japanese American museum and the Asian theater. All that and still so close to city hall. And then there's the Olvera Street Mexican marketplace. And the harbor, Fashion District, Dodger Stadium."

"All that," Micah agreed, imagining her in a ball cap. "And everything that comes with so many diverse people elbow-to-elbow, trying to make their way." He frowned. "And stay alive."

Sloane met his gaze. "Jane Doe."

"It's hard to get that scene out of my head. Sorry; not a great side dish."

"Hey . . ." Sloane tapped her chest. "ER nurse. Hard to destroy our appetites. Besides, I couldn't eat another noodle. Stuffed." Her expression softened. "I used to be a flight nurse, which dropped me into some rugged trauma scenes. I can imagine how awful it must have been in that alley."

Micah wished he'd never brought it up. "Flight nurse?"

"Medevac choppers. In the Sacramento area, out of UC Davis Medical Center. Until . . ." Sloane seemed to hesitate. "I left it to work in the ER at Sacramento Hope. For a while, anyway." She shrugged. "Not going to bore you with the CV."

Micah couldn't imagine anything about her being boring. But he had a sense Sloane didn't want to talk about it. He understood that feeling.

"What do you say?" he asked. "Want to go walk around a little? Let our dinners settle?"

Sloane looked down at her teacup, quiet for a beat, and Micah was sure she'd say something about needing to get home.

"Sounds good." Her smile did something unexpected to his pulse. "After we split the check."

"Uh . . ."

She produced a small roll of cash from her purse, then peeled off enough for her half of the meal. And the tip.

Micah wanted to argue but thought of every time they had. And how that had ended. Some things were worth a fight. This wasn't one of them.

———

Sloane liked that Micah didn't need a constant stream of conversation. He seemed okay with simply walking along the night-lit Little Tokyo sidewalks, taking in the colors, sounds, and scents. This area of downtown was a sort of cultural collision of Japanese historic and SoCal contemporary. Red paper lanterns and exotic hand-calligraphed banners stretched overhead and along storefronts, complementing glass-and-steel high-rises and a rainbow array of neon advertising.

"Street musician," Micah said, gesturing past a gigantic Hello Kitty sign to the street corner opposite. A young woman in a flowered skirt, thigh-high boots, and an Asian-print bandanna played the guitar. "She's good. Classical guitar isn't easy. Nylon strings, finger picking."

Micah stopped to watch and Sloane sneaked a chance to peer up at him. Nearly a foot taller than she was, he had a stronger jaw than she'd given him credit for when she'd spat that awful "slick, charming" slur. She was right that he didn't look lumberjack burly, even with those nice shoulders. No, not rugged. But definitely masculine and attractive. With that clean-shaven and chiseled profile, the trendy glasses and gray-checked shirt, and the way his sandy hair was sort of teased by the evening breeze . . .

"What do you think?" Micah asked, glancing at her.

"About?"

He smiled. "The guitar."

"Right." Sloane felt her face warm. What she'd been thinking was that "classical" would have easily described this man too—classic good looks. And now she'd been caught staring. "It's great."

"You want to grab some coffee? Sit and listen awhile?"

"Sure." Because she didn't want to go home.

She hated to imagine what Micah would think if he knew he was taking the place of an AA meeting. But even if he was her unwitting sponsor for the night, it wasn't as if she would confide anything remotely personal.

They found a small sidewalk table and Micah asked Sloane to sit down so they wouldn't lose it. She agreed, though something classically male in Micah's expression said it was more about a chivalrous opportunity to pay for her order. She wasn't going to argue this one. It was a bistro chair and coffee, not a dark corner booth and tequila shots. Her stomach sank at the realization: she couldn't remember the last time she'd done this sober. It could be a big mistake.

———

"Here we go," Micah said, setting Sloane's coffee down and taking a seat next to her. His eyes met hers. There was something in her expression . . . "Everything okay?"

"Yes," she said quickly. "I was just thinking. Your family is into music, right? Harper mentioned something. She said they were really popular. Concerts and records?"

"Ah." Micah glanced toward the street musician as he took a sip of his coffee. It was almost as if she'd read his mind. He'd just been thinking how nice it was to meet someone who didn't automatically ask.

"My father's side," he told her. "Uncle Clay . . . and his family. By Grace."

Her brows pinched.

"By Grace is the name of the group. Sort of a double meaning. My aunt Grace is the songwriter, and it's a contemporary Christian band."

"Ah," she said, borrowing his word. "I'm not that familiar with the genre. I'm sure I've heard of them, but . . ."

"They're still popular but haven't toured much in the past

few years," Micah said, appreciating her kind vagueness. He couldn't count the times people hadn't been. Kind or vague. *"Oh, right. A Jesus jam. No thanks."*

"And you?" Sloane asked. "You seem to know about guitar strings. 'Picking'—is that what you called it? Did you inherit the Prescott music genes?"

"Probably," he admitted, grateful for it. Music had always been there for him, lifted him up in tough times. "I play some guitar. Not anything to brag about."

"Here. Give me your hand," Sloane said. "The left one."

Smart girl. She knew—

"C'mon," she said, reaching out. "Gimmee."

Micah's pulse hiked as Sloane took his hand in hers. Skin to skin. Warm, soft.

"Let's see now." She spread his palm and gently examined his fingertips.

Examined, right . . . Micah tried to put his mind in medical mode.

"I thought so," Sloane said, lightly brushing her fingertips against Micah's. It did something to his senses that didn't feel clinical at all. "Calluses. Well-developed. You don't just play guitar 'some.' You have a serious relationship with that . . . What kind of guitar?"

"Acoustic," he said, remembering by some miracle. "A Martin."

"Martin?" Sloane laughed, still cradling his hand. "I have a cat named Marty."

He started to say something trite, like "small world," or idiotic, like "cats are cool," but her touch had made him mute.

"So . . ." Sloane released his hand to reach for her coffee. "You sing, too?"

"Like a bullfrog. With the croup."

"Sure." She rolled her eyes. "It's a good thing you aren't doing your own marketing campaign. Better stick to the Face of Hope."

"Really. I don't sing. But I'm trying to convince my aunt and uncle to compose a song in honor of the winner. And perform it at the gala event." His heart thudded. He hadn't confided that to anyone outside of his family. "I'd like to see By Grace in front of a live audience again. A sort of comeback."

Sloane swirled the stir stick in her coffee. "Why did they stop doing concerts?"

He swallowed. *Why . . . ?*

"I'm sorry," she said, meeting Micah's gaze again. "Maybe that's none of my business."

"No. It's okay. Most people know already if they follow Christian music." He took a breath. "Their son, Stephen, my cousin, was killed in a car accident a while back." Almost ten years. A decade and Micah still had trouble talking about it. "It hit my aunt and uncle hard—hit all of us hard."

There was understanding in her eyes. "You were close."

"Yes. My folks went to Oregon to be near them and stayed on. Dad got a job transfer."

"But you didn't go?"

"I was finishing up college. Communications at UCLA." He thought of Coop, still running with that ambition. "I graduated and then took a little detour to the Middle East."

"You were in the military?"

"No." Micah shook his head, wishing he'd never started this conversation. His crisis training taught him to listen, but suddenly he couldn't stop talking. "My uncle had some connections. I was offered an opportunity to go to Afghanistan with a TV news team." He mentioned the name of a prime-time television news personality and Sloane's eyes widened.

"Really? You were an embedded journalist on his team?"

"More gofer than legitimate journalist."

"I remember some of that coverage. It was dangerous."

It was. Micah had gone half a world away to try to forget the carnage that ended his cousin's life, only to find far too much of the same. Gruesome death, shock, grief . . .

"It was the first time I saw chaplains in action," he told her. "There was this corpsman, son of a Vietnam War chaplain. He called it 'the bloody boot ministry.'"

"Like that old saying 'There are no atheists in foxholes' . . ."

"I don't know. Maybe." Micah wasn't sure why he was saying all of this. "But I saw how much it meant to survivors. To have somebody be there for them."

"You wrote about it?"

Micah shook his head. How did he explain that he'd come home and stumbled around for an entire year, not sure of what he wanted in life? Not even sure what he believed anymore? He couldn't explain it to himself.

Not even now.

Sloane saw something in Micah's eyes that hinted at sadness. A depth, almost world-weary, that was completely at odds with his hospital persona. But then, so was his crisis work.

"I didn't do any essays or war features," Micah continued. "I had some calls from editors, some serious interest. Blew a big opportunity, maybe. Or so I've been told—more than once."

Sloane caught Micah's fleeting frown. She could understand

that feeling of not living up to someone else's expectations. Or in her case, confirming their worst over and over. "You started working for the Hope system after you got back to the States?"

"No. Not until a couple of years ago. When I got back, I did some marketing work for a local magazine, then a few years with a big health insurance company, and . . . now I write hospital ad copy," Micah finished with a shrug of his shoulders.

"Yes. And you . . ." Sloane had to stop herself from taking his hand again. The sudden need was as strong as the one earlier when she'd stared at the wineglasses. "You put yourself in that alley tonight," she said, unable to keep emotion from her voice. "I'm no journalist, but I'd say that's worth a lot more than a series of war features."

Micah's eyes held Sloane's long enough to make her heart stall.

"Plus, you play the guitar," she added quickly.

"Yes." A teasing smile tugged Micah's lips. "Some."

His eyes, warm and brown as their coffee, wrinkled at the edges as his smile spread. The light from the red paper lanterns strung overhead cast a soft, rosy glow over his hair, shoulders, and the very faint stubble of beard beginning to show along his jaw. It was almost like a freeze-frame from one of the countless old, romantic movies Sloane's mother had sighed and wept over. The sappy stories of a good man with a big heart able to see beyond the troubled heroine's mistakes. The hero in *Breakfast at Tiffany's*, kissing a tearful Holly Golightly as she clutched her lost cat in that soaking downpour.

"We should probably get going," Sloane said, crumpling her napkin. "The music is over. You're on call. And . . ."

I'm a stupid fool.

"You have to work in the morning?" Micah asked.

"No. But I have some things to take care of."

Like going over the draft of her prison speech, getting to an AA meeting . . . *cleaning mysterious fingerprints off my window.* Sloane bit her lip to keep from groaning aloud. Micah Prescott wasn't the slick charmer she'd expected, but that discovery did nothing to wipe away all she'd done and who she was. It only pointed it all out, her mistakes and shameful secrets strung like tattered lanterns across the night sky.

Micah's phone buzzed on the table and he reached for it.

"Crisis call?" Sloane asked, not sure if she'd feel relief or regret.

"The Jane Doe situation," Micah reported, scrolling down the text message. "Some people have shown up at the hospital. Folks with missing daughters. Runaways."

"You're going there?"

Micah nodded. "The detectives plan to show photos to them. We'll be there for support. Two responders have already arrived. I'll back them up."

Sloane thought of those awful moments in the ER when the girl struggled to breathe despite the vicious, strangling throat slash.

"I think they're trying to hold off releasing a picture to the media as long as possible," Micah said. "There might be a link to local human-trafficking activity. I'm thinking they don't want to go public and give the gangsters a heads-up to get away."

"They found you. And you ran."

Sloane shuddered, remembering her accusing words to Paul. His link to organized crime was gambling loans, and that was up north in Sacramento but—

"Are you all right?" Micah asked, concern in his expression.

"I was just remembering Jane Doe. I hope one of those people at the hospital is her family."

And I hope Zoey Jones is in Bakersfield.

"Me too," Micah said.

Sloane took one last sip of her coffee, thinking she might as well swallow the truth, too. The troubled little thief had as much chance of being safe and doing good works at the YMCA as Sloane had of finding that big-screen happy ending. She was no Holly Golightly. But at least Zoey had a few bucks in her pocket now. And thanks to the marketing man, Sloane had swum through one more night without giving in to the temptation to drown her secrets.

"Hey, Stack . . ." Zoey walked through the adjoining doorway and blew on her drying nails, a shade called Black Swan. "I've been thinking."

"Thinking?" He drained the last of his beer, belched. "That must be a strain."

"Yeah." She reminded herself to be as careful now as she'd been when she slid the polish into her jeans at Whole Foods—dark lacquer sharing pocket space with a Jesus cross.

"What is it?" he asked, back to fiddling with his laptop.

Her pulse quickened. "I guess it's been like four months since we hooked up."

Stack tossed her a look. "Don't go all girlie-stupid about celebrating anniversaries."

Celebrating? Nothing could be further from the truth. Especially with the bruise on her wrist and no word about Oksana. "I was just thinking about my mom."

Stack raised his brows. "The druggie who moved you into her boyfriend's place? Then grabbed the dope and left you behind when his biker buddies broke down the door in the middle of the night? That sainted woman?"

"They're putting her through rehab in jail. She's probably clean now."

"And I'm Billy Graham." Stack shook his head. "Kid, people don't change."

She shoved her hand into her pocket, risking the new polish to feel that cool, hopeful metal. "I don't feel right about what we're doing."

Stack's eyes narrowed. "You want to work for Viktor?"

"No." Her throat tried to close off. "I want to go home. See for myself how she is."

He shifted on the bed, staring at her. "And maybe tell the cops about me?"

"No way." Zoey struggled to keep new, rising fear from her voice. "I don't even know your whole name. Besides, that would be totally stupid. I'm as guilty as you are."

"Bull's-eye." He raised his hand and pointed in a way that looked too much like a gun. "Don't forget it."

"I won't." She leaned into the doorway, willing her legs to hold her up. "I need to go, Stack. I can't do this anymore."

He closed the laptop, gestured to her. "Come here."

"Stack . . ."

He patted the bed. "Here. Now."

Zoey tried not to think of that girl, throat sliced in an alley. She tried to remember if she'd ever seen hope in Oksana's eyes. She wished she believed any of the things those church people said about the piece of metal growing so heavy in her pocket.

"Good," Stack said as she perched on the edge of the unmade bed. "Now stop shaking like a neurotic terrier and listen to me."

"Okay."

"I've got something big going," he said, capturing her gaze as easily as he'd grabbed hold of her wrist a few hours earlier. "Something I've been waiting on for a long time." His expression softened. "It's what I want, kid. Sort of like the way you want to go home. This is that for me. Understand?"

Zoey nodded.

"All right then," Stack said, the old cockiness back in his voice. "One more job—I need you for this. Then I'll buy you a plane ticket home. I'll give you some cash to get you started. I'll even send a box of chocolates to your loser mom. How's that? You with me?"

Zoey found a smile. "What color hair?"

———

"At least we had some time before a call came in," Micah said as they neared Sloane's parked car. He'd insisted on walking her there, though their vehicles weren't far apart. "Saw a few sights."

"Walked off some noodles."

"Yeah, there's that."

Sloane turned to look at the sculptures sprouting up in this part of the district; all of Little Tokyo was maybe five large city blocks. In the distance was the space shuttle monument commemorating a Japanese American who'd been part of the *Challenger* team. Nearer, rising high and white in the darkening sky, was the sculpture called the Friendship Knot. Her eyes followed it from the base to the top.

"It looks like two huge drinking straws," she said, "sort of tied in the middle. Or maybe breadsticks playing Twister."

Micah laughed, touched his glasses. He didn't always wear them, probably had contacts, too . . . "It's been there since the eighties." He stepped close and Sloane got a hint of his scent: the coffee, a lingering sesame fragrance from the restaurant, and sort of a woodsy clean. Micah regarded the knot. "It was originally from the Netherlands."

"Guitars, sushi, and . . . sculpture?" Sloane's eyes met his again. "You know everything?"

"Not even close." He shrugged. "Crisis responders are sometimes on scene for big events. I've been here during Nisei Week and heard the spiel. The sculpture was moved to this site during a renovation, to represent the joining of two different cultures." He smiled. "Or breadsticks playing party games. Whatever does it for you."

Sloane nodded, thinking that this man's smile did it for her, no matter how much she wished it weren't so. She'd accepted the invitation for coffee because she'd been afraid of what she might do if she were left to her own temptations. They'd shared a meal, laughed, and then shared some things about themselves, he much more than she. Admittedly, the things Micah said had changed Sloane's impression of him. Even gotten under her skin a little, the way no man had in a long, long time.

"I've enjoyed this," he said, bringing Sloane's attention back. "Getting to know you outside work. Though I think I was the one who monopolized the conversation. Next time, I'd like to learn more about you."

Sloane's stomach quivered. He wanted to see her again.

"I mean I'd like there to be a next time," Micah amended, his voice soft and deep. "If that's okay with you."

"I . . ." Sloane hesitated.

What was she doing? They were as unalike as the cultures in that sculpture. Two very different people thrown together by some maniac in a parking lot. She'd simply be chalking up one more mistake if she—

"Maybe," Sloane heard herself say. "I think so."

Micah chuckled. "I'm going to take that as a yes. At least do a marketing follow-up." He extended his hand.

Sloane reached hers out, hoping it wasn't as trembly as she felt. The feeling increased, seismically, as Micah's fingers grasped hers. Warm, strong, but gentle, too.

"Thanks," he said, not yet letting go.

"Thank you . . . for the coffee," Sloane responded, suddenly feeling like she was on a journey without a map. She was standing in near darkness with an attractive man who clearly stirred her senses with a simple touch of his hand. She didn't know what to do with it. No, that wasn't all true. She knew what she'd always done with it, but she couldn't let that happen now.

"Let's get you to your car," he said, letting go. "I need to go on to the hospital."

"Okay."

Micah watched her get in, waited while she started the engine, and then walked to his own car a few rows down.

Sloane sat there, engine idling, waiting to see his car pull away. But mostly she was trying to make sense of what she was feeling. It was confusing, scary, but somehow good. Scary-good, maybe. And so unexpected. Only yesterday, she'd had nothing but contempt for Micah Prescott, certain she knew everything about his self-serving motives. She'd asked him to keep his distance. And now she'd agreed to see him again.

Not in a desperate attempt to escape demons, like tonight, but because she was tempted by something that felt like nothing she'd known before. Something she'd stopped hoping for long before her car went over that cliff. She reached up, touched the scar on her face, and her breath snagged at a realization.

She felt new and different for the first time in the six months she'd been struggling to put her past behind her. She hadn't accomplished it with the Volvo that replaced her demolished car, Marty's adoption, the move to LA, her job at the hospital, all the chips from AA cheering her tenuous grip on recovery, or even the employee of the month honor. None of those had done what this short time with Micah Prescott had. A few sober hours with a man who wanted to *know* her, not simply . . . *have me*. Sloane's throat tightened and she closed her eyes against the sting of tears. She wasn't going to cry. She wasn't going to spoil the first time she'd felt this way. As if she'd never been Sloane Wilder, never—

Her phone buzzed with a text. She smiled. Micah had said he'd check in. He couldn't have been two blocks away yet. She picked up her cell, realizing she hadn't put his number into her contacts, and . . . Her stomach lurched.

Paul.

Call me. Have news.

Sloane jabbed the Delete button. How was she ever going to feel new, clean and hopeful, with her ugly past stalking her?

She shoved the Volvo into reverse, backed out, then cranked the wheel and sped away.

16

"NINETEEN CANDIDATES NOW." Micah glanced at Fiona over the small printed sheaf of employee nominations, information carefully filled in under the campaign's bold header:

The Face of Hope. Maybe It's You.

The PIO had stopped by to offer him some of her mother's gluten-free persimmon cookies—begged him to take some. She hated them but couldn't bring herself to toss them out.

"The candidates are mostly nurses," Micah continued, "and two staff physicians, but there are some others, too: the woman who runs the dietary department, the discharge planner, and . . ." He touched the topmost paper. "Here's one for a housekeeping supervisor."

"Nice diversity." Fiona adjusted her glasses. "I ran into Howard Brill this morning and he mentioned something about his niece?"

Brill was a hospital board member and his niece was a newly hired, newly licensed nurse. Micah decided not to say the board member had mentioned something to him, too. Apparently Brill, a prominent local businessman, was running his own side campaign.

"Brittany Brill," he confirmed, setting down the papers. "Newborn nursery."

"I've met her. And I could probably tell you her NCLEX scores, her weekly Fitbit steps, and her favorite foods." The PIO shook her head, smiling. "Howard tried to get me to do a press release when she was hired. Proud uncle."

Nuisance was the word that came to Micah's mind, but he'd keep that to himself too. He needed this job.

"How long will you keep the nominations open?" Fiona asked, casually adding another lumpy orange cookie to the oily napkin on his desk. "You're aiming for a spring announcement, right?"

"Late February or early March. Billboards, video, posters, mailers, and a star-studded gala. Timed to coincide with completion of the first stage of construction for the new wing." Micah tapped the stack of papers. "I'm taking nominations through October."

"And then there's the interviews," Fiona added. "FYI, my arm can be twisted to be on the panel."

"If I take these cookies off your hands."

Fiona smiled. "Everyone has an angle."

Micah laughed. "So I'm discovering."

"Well," Fiona said, brushing crumbs from her fingers, "it's

a fabulous campaign. It should go a long way toward polishing up the community image of LA Hope." Her expression looked sincere. "We probably don't tell you often enough, but your efforts for this department are highly valued, Micah. Personally, I think you're brilliant."

"Don't go overboard—I'm taking the cookies."

Fiona sighed. "Brilliant and merciful."

When Fiona left, Micah turned his attention back to the campaign paperwork. He flipped through the printouts, thinking there would undoubtedly be more nominees; he'd done everything but spray-paint reminders on employee lockers. He was making steady rounds to all the departments, talking the campaign up. The winner would receive star treatment, media exposure, a significant cash award, a designated parking place, and hopefully a song from By Grace written in his or her honor. With those incentives there would be plenty of candidates to choose from. Micah would absolutely take Fiona up on her offer to be part of the interview panel; she was sharp, savvy, and fair. He liked what she'd said about diversity.

And now he needed to decide on some essay questions for the finalists . . .

Aside from your hospital work, what do you consider your true passion?

If it were possible, what advice would you give your younger self?

Micah laughed under his breath, thinking he'd have to amend that last one if Brill's niece actually made the cut; her younger self would still be playing with LEGOs. Regardless, everyone had an equal chance to be chosen as the employee who "most personified the spirit and values of LA Hope." As long as they passed their background checks and—

Micah paused as he read the name of a nominee from the emergency department: Sloane Ferrell.

She'd given no indication that she knew she was being considered for the Face of Hope. Micah's best guess was she wouldn't want to be. Sloane had made it more than clear in the incident with Zoey Jones that she wanted no publicity. He was grateful their relationship had moved past threats of lawsuits. Warmth spread through his chest as he remembered their time together on Saturday. He'd thought about it more than a few times over the last four days. And thought of calling her again but had held back. He didn't want to come on too strong. After all, that she'd contacted him the other night had been more than a surprise. It had been great discovering new things about her. The quick wit—he smiled, remembering her silly imitation of a Valley girl—that she had a cat and had once been a flight nurse. And . . .

And the way something about her made Micah want to talk, share. He hadn't done that with a woman—with anyone—in such depth for a long time. He'd lain awake that night, thinking of what she'd said when he admitted to never putting words to his war experience.

"You put yourself in that alley tonight. . . . I'm no journalist, but I'd say that's worth a lot more than a series of war features."

Sloane's words, the emotion in her voice, had touched Micah deeply.

And when she'd taken his hand to check his fingertips for guitar calluses . . .

He'd wanted to kiss her when they were standing in the parking lot in Little Tokyo. Not simply take her hand for a moment but draw Sloane fully into his arms, hold her close, breathe her in, and then kiss her thoroughly. He hadn't wanted anything as much in a long time. But it was too soon.

Micah had known women, knew them still, who'd be okay with moving fast. Women who'd make the first move themselves and be proud of it. That aimless year after he returned from the Middle East, he'd drifted from one non-relationship to another, his euphemism for what were more often than not one-night stands. And an excuse for promises he didn't keep. It was like he'd traded military-issue Kevlar for a flak jacket against real intimacy. It was lonelier than being alone. And at complete odds with every value Micah had always held close. He didn't want that anymore.

Sloane Ferrell was complex, intriguing, and cautious. A strong woman with firm opinions and, from what he'd glimpsed, a caring heart. But she was protecting her heart like he'd protected his. Micah respected that and was willing to take the time to win Sloane's trust. Get to know her better. He knew very little about her right now.

He glanced down at the notes he'd been making about the timeline for background checks and the essay portion of the entry. He doubted Sloane would allow her Face of Hope nomination to go that far, but he had to wonder. How would she answer those questions?

Sloane frowned, scanning the questions she'd inserted into her parole board statement. She'd been working on them since she got home from the hospital. This still wasn't right. . . .

Was my mother's life worth nothing?

Did you care what her death would do to me?

Too emotional. Of course he didn't care. Her stepfather cared about order, control, maintaining a tactical advantage, and running his home like it was simply one more garrison for Sergeant "Bulldog" Bullard. It hadn't taken him long to discover that his beautiful, capricious, volatile, and too often melancholy wife was going to have a problem "shaping up, making muster." That she came with a mouthy adolescent daughter who'd learned to trust no one was yet another obstacle.

"You think you're smarter than me? You think you're going to win this battle? Little girl, I've been to hell and back. You are just a rookie."

Their final skirmish left Sloane with a handprint on her jaw and the excuse she needed to shove a few things in a backpack and go AWOL.

Her mother was dead barely three years later.

Sloane closed her eyes, remembering her mother's face, her touch, and the way she'd tenderly brush Sloane's hair. Her breath would smell of mints, her voice a throaty soft slur. *"Fifty strokes. They say it was a beauty secret of the classic film actresses. I don't know. I only know that I love to brush my beautiful baby's hair. . . ."*

Marty leaped onto the table, nudged Sloane's chin, and began a purr that rivaled the Volvo's engine. She stroked his silky fur. Adopting him was one of the few good choices she'd ever made. Both she and her mother had made far too many bad ones. And lately Sloane's seemed determined to come back to haunt her. There had been no further message from

Paul, but knowing it might come at any time had her constantly on edge.

She glanced at her phone lying beside the draft of the parole board speech. How had he found her number? She'd shared so little information about herself, was practically living like a monk, and—

A knock on the door interrupted her thoughts.

"Sloane. It's Celeste." There was a giggle. "And Piper."

Sloane crossed the room, Marty trotting behind.

"I hope we're not disturbing you," the landlady said when Sloane opened the door. Celeste was wearing her gardening clothes, a set of faded surgical scrubs she'd begged from a retired nurse friend. Complete with a scrub cap. "I wanted to see if you had some antibiotic ointment I could borrow." She wrinkled her nose. "Grandma fail. If I'd run out of Fruit Roll-Ups, they'd have revoked my membership completely."

Sloane glanced down at Piper, busy petting Marty, who'd ventured onto the porch. "Did she get a scrape?"

"No." Celeste gestured toward the garden area. "It's for Jerry Rhodes. He donated for the blood drive this morning, and the needle site was oozing a little. He said it was no problem. But I insisted he have a new bandage if he's going to be working with dirt."

"He brought his dogs," Piper announced, her eyes lighting. "Wiener dogs. I mean, doc-sunns."

Celeste smiled. "Long-haired dachshunds. So sweet and comical. They're named—"

"Gibbs and McGee," Piper blurted, squeezing her hands together with obvious delight. "After the TV show. You know."

Sloane nodded. "I do."

She looked toward the garden and saw Jerry there. Cargo

shorts, John Deere T-shirt, shovel in hand—and glancing their way. The nagging concern Sloane had felt before returned. "You knew Jerry from the hospital?"

"No. He's new there. He transferred from the Hope outpatient surgery center." Celeste watched as Piper ran off in his direction. "Jerry's taking on extra jobs to help with the cost of moving his wife's mother out from Florida. They're hoping to get her into the Hope senior living complex." Celeste shook her head. "I was concerned I couldn't afford to have the work done. But Jerry was like 'No problem. Just pay me what you think it's worth.'"

"That's . . . nice."

Celeste looked toward the work area, where a radio was playing country music. "More than nice. I needed help; he needed work. I'd say it's more of a God thing than coincidence."

Sloane's nod was polite. She had no clue about "God things," but she was definitely rooting for coincidence. She didn't want to think that Jerry's being here had anything to do with her.

"Oh, dear," Celeste said. "Is it okay if Marty leaves the porch?"

17

"AAAGH, NO WAY!" Micah groaned, staring in disbelief as Coop's wild rim shot was swallowed by the basket. He drew in a heaving breath. "You *didn't* just make that."

"Did—hold the presses!" Coop laughed and staggered, shoes slapping the cracked asphalt, to recover the ball. His curly hair was plastered to his forehead with sweat. "You now owe me street tacos *and* a beer."

"You mean you're quitting?" Micah swiped his forearm over his face to keep the stinging salt from his eyes. They'd been at it for nearly an hour and his lungs were burning, but he wouldn't let this reporter, at least four inches shorter, think he'd gotten the best of him. "Wimping out? Can't last long enough to—"

"Can't watch a gone-soft corporate lackey die in front of my eyes. I'm far too humane."

"Right. Take the easy out," Micah said with a smirk, telling himself that the "corporate lackey" jab wasn't a three-pointer. And that fielding yet another e-mail from Howard Brill wouldn't become a permanent part of his job. "I'll let you have this one."

Coop walked toward him, basketball balanced on his fingertips. He glanced toward the sunset beyond the palms that lined the recreation pad of Micah's condominium complex. "Seriously, I can take a rain check if you're on call for the crisis team. Or, much better, have a hot date. Someone should have that."

"No. Nothing definite," Micah said, Sloane immediately coming to mind. He hadn't called her yet. Overthinking it, probably. Time to fix that. "But I can't believe you'd pass up a free meal."

Coop's eyes did that reporter-smelling-a-story thing. "I have something going with my research. I was thinking of taking my resource out for a drink."

"The organized crime thing?"

"Yeah."

"There." Sloane secured the gate on the small fenced side yard. Marty was already rolling in sun-warmed cedar mulch, his dark fur dusted cinnamon red. "He's fine there. I've been letting him outside a little each day to sort of stretch his boundaries. But I think he's better off behind the gate today."

"Because of the dogs," Celeste said, finishing her thought. She glanced to where Gibbs and McGee, one a light tan and the other black with red, seemed to be happily competing for Piper's attention.

"What's that she's doing?" Sloane asked, watching as the child struck some dramatic poses alternating with dance steps. "It doesn't look like her usual martial arts."

"Oh . . ." Celeste shook head. "Poor Jerry. She's practicing her show routine."

Sloane's stomach dived. "Show?"

"Talent show. Though she's not sure if she wants to juggle oranges or hula dance or—"

"I'll get that ointment," Sloane interrupted, ducking back inside. "It'll just take a minute."

"Thank you."

She walked the short distance to the bathroom, telling herself it was okay. A talent show wasn't a beauty pageant. And even those were run far more responsibly these days. Plus, Piper's mother wouldn't take any risks with her daughter's safety. She was a single mother but seemed to be handling things well. Celeste filled in the gaps.

Sloane grabbed the ointment from the bathroom cabinet, fighting a wave of queasiness. It didn't help that the last time she'd shared this ointment had been with Zoey. That infected scrape on her hip. Near the tattoo.

PROPERTY OF . . .

"You're my little angel. You belong to me. Don't ever forget that."

Sloane gritted her teeth and made her way back to the door.

"Here you go." She handed the things to Celeste. "There's some Band-Aids too. Don't worry about returning anything. I get samples from the drug reps."

"Perfect. Thanks again."

Sloane closed the door and returned to the table. She

stared at her parole board speech without seeing a single word. Sergeant Bob Bullard was the horrible, angry man who caused her mother to drown. But at least he'd never . . .

The shameful secret surfaced, gasping for air.

Sloane had always worn white for the pageants. Head-to-toe white, sometimes with a halo her mother painstakingly fashioned from dozens of pearlescent pipe cleaners. It was secured with white bobby pins—the kind, her mother said, that nurses used to pin on the caps they wore way back when. The pins pinched but they kept the halo on, and Sloane secretly liked the idea that she shared something with nurses. Graceful white feather wings—when Sloane was nearing six and her mother's boyfriend Phillip came into the picture—completed the pageant ensemble. He tracked down the materials and hired a seamstress to make them, saying, in his soft, spellbinding Southern lilt, that "an angel needs wings, and anything that makes an angel's mama smile is my purest pleasure."

Sloane's mother did smile that year. Laughed, sang, danced in the kitchen, and bloomed like a flower in sunshine. It was as if Phillip's attention erased the "friendly fire" sadness that had always been a part of their lives, their home. Sloane finally began to understand what family felt like. "Uncle Phillip's" thumbs-up enthusiasm, not simply tolerance, for their pageant bond was like frosting on a cake they'd hungered after for far too long.

Her stage name was Angel Aames, the double-*A* spelling chosen in hopes of getting Sloane to the top of the entrant lists. It worked. Time after time, Sloane, beginning at age three, had tiptoed onto stages first. Her trademark blend of "purity and playful pout"—soulful eyes, cherub lips, and a single wayward curl—included a lisping rendition of "Pennies from Heaven," during which she tossed a few into the audience. She followed it with a wave that ended with her hands clasped in prayer position. In a crowded field of baton twirlers, cowgirls, acrobats, and tap dancers, Sloane was a sweet standout. But not often a tiara winner.

Uncle Phillip vowed to change that. First with the wings, then with a few suggestions here and there to "sass it up," and finally with hands-on coaching to help Sloane straighten her posture, cock her hips, roll a shoulder . . .

It was the spring she turned six that he first slipped vodka into her fruit juice. It would help, he promised, to loosen Sloane up before she went on stage. Just a few sips, and don't tell Mommy.

"Shake that sweet little booty, Angel. . . ."

It worked. Sloane won a trophy taller than she was, the long-awaited crowns, and then a lifetime supply of cereal.

"This is what you won, baby. For your whole life—that's quite a net worth. Wait now . . . no marshmallows until you give Uncle Phillip a little sugar. . . . Ooh, yes, there's my good luck charm."

It was shortly after Sloane's big win that Phillip coaxed her mother into taking the swing-shift summer job. He'd babysit, no problem. It was a perfect opportunity to do some additional coaching. He turned their garage into a studio, painted it a sunny yellow, then papered two walls with hundreds of photos of pageant stars and child models. He mirrored the other walls, put in a small fridge for Popsicles and juices, set up a sound system and a video player. Then added a cozy futon so they could all sit and watch his recordings of Sloane's practice sessions. But since her mother worked, it was mostly the two of them.

The week of July 4 he bought her a new, star-spangled two-piece swimsuit, tasseled boots, and sparklers. Phillip had Sloane dance while holding them. He showed her how to be careful, how the metal part could burn, but if she followed his instructions, the bright, glittery sparks would bounce against her skin like happy Tinker Bell kisses. It was the day she learned a whole new meaning of "friendly fire."

"Angel Aames . . . you truly are the devil's little plaything."

The fruit juice made her sleepy. And dizzy. She didn't like the new swimsuit; it was pinchy and too tight. But Uncle Phillip said it was cooler in the summer heat, and she should sit with him on the couch. Give him a little sugar . . .

When Sloane struggled, he said she was an ungrateful and shameless tease. He held her harder. When she cried and said she'd tell her mother, he threatened to kill their cat and—

"Marty," Sloane uttered aloud, new concern smothering the awful memory. Her pulse hiked as she remembered where she'd left him. She was out the door, down the porch, and at the gate in moments. She yanked it open, scanned the yard.

Empty.

No, please . . .

"Marty?" Sloane called, stepping through the gate. She checked the fence top, the roof overhang, and—

"There you are," she said, relief choking her as he emerged, blasé and yellow eyes blinking, from beneath a bush. He wrapped himself around her legs, offering an "I'm right here, big deal" meow.

Sloane knelt on the cedar bark, tamping down the panicky scenarios that had run through her head. Her cat chased by dogs into the street. And under the wheels of a car.

"Hey, troublemaker," she said, lifting him into her arms.

"Next time, Mom's staying right here. These eyes—on you. Get used to it."

She carried him back to the door and paused, glancing toward the garden. The radio continued its nonstop loop of country music, volume a little louder now. The dogs, Gibbs and McGee, lay side by side, one resting his fuzzy chin on the hip of the other. Jerry was kneeling down, measuring something. Sloane had seen him in that same pose dozens of times at the hospital. Celeste and Piper had returned to the house. Nothing at all out of the ordinary.

Marty nudged his nose into the crook of Sloane's elbow and began to purr. *He's fine. . . . I am too. We all are.*

She reached for the door, then stopped as the breeze carried Jerry's music her way. At first she wasn't sure, so she listened a moment longer. Her throat tightened; she knew this one. Willie Nelson. One of her mother's favorites.

"So leave me if you need to, I will still remember
Angel flying too close to the ground . . ."

Sloane carried Marty inside, set him down, and locked the door. She'd open the window a couple inches, let him peek through the screen. That was good enough for now.

Sloane retrieved a plastic tumbler from the cupboard, filled it with water, and returned to the table spread with her parole board notes. She glanced toward the pantry, its sliding door open just enough to reveal the stacked boxes of cereal.

In the end, it had been her mother's outrage against a much-smaller violation that spared her. The week after their family outing to the fireworks display, Phillip decided angels should be blonde. When no hair salon would do it—and her mother was at work—he held Sloane over the bathtub to attempt it himself. The bleach caused an extensive and painful chemical burn to her left eye. When the emergency physician mentioned a Child Protective Services report, Uncle Phillip disappeared.

It was weeks after the eye patch came off and about the time her damaged and shorn hair began to grow back that Sloane finally told her mother the truth. She figured she had nothing to lose since their cat had never been found. Phillip hadn't returned either. Maybe Sloane felt some safety in that. She'd wondered many times since if she'd waited mostly because she feared what it would do to her mother. Because the smiles, the laughter, the fleeting sense of family had almost been worth it.

Like the reward of marshmallows had almost been worth "a little sugar."

She told her mother, and the angel wings disappeared into the garbage. The smiles and laughter were replaced by fury, then tears, then vodka—lots of it. Her mother never told the authorities; she let the ugly secret simply drown.

Sloane took a long swallow of her water, then picked up the pencil. She looked toward the couch; Marty was already pressing his nose to the screen. She shook her head and turned her attention back to the notes she'd made. Just under two weeks until the parole meeting. She might need that time—this was harder than she'd thought. She'd been right to scratch out the emotional pleas. They weren't going to help. She'd present the facts as she knew them.

Sergeant Robert Bullard's treatment of her mother had been callous, insensitive, and at least emotionally abusive. The prosecuting attorney might have failed to prove he actually held her head under the water that night—waited as she struggled, strangled, suffered—but his irresponsible actions were absolutely the cause of her death. His claim that she screamed at him and demanded he get out of the hot tub and out of their lives was no excuse—and unwitnessed. He killed Sloane's mother. She'd present only the facts, without emotion.

But in her heart, Sloane knew the truth. Her stepfather put a final end to their hope for a family. His was the friendly fire that ended it all. There wasn't a punishment on earth harsh enough for that.

Sloane tried to swallow down the old ache. Even if her mother had made some really bad choices, it should never have happened. None of it. There was nothing Sloane could do about the fact that somewhere out there, Phillip was still at large. Whether he'd ever pay for what he'd done or might still be doing was an unknown. But her mother's husband had been convicted and sentenced to twelve years behind bars. He couldn't be allowed to get by with less.

Sloane slid the envelope—with its many forwarding stamps—from beneath her papers. She stared at the State Prison return address and familiar, neat handwriting. She closed her eyes and felt the sting of Bulldog Bullard's slap, heard her mother's tears. And then remembered that awful moment she'd heard the news.

"Drowned? No, you're wrong. She couldn't have . . . She can't be dead."

Sloane's fingers trembled with a rush of anger. Bob Bullard had written the letter and asked for her phone number because he wanted her to support his early release. He believed he deserved that. He'd probably been an exemplary inmate. What was it the prison office assistant had said?

"Let's just say that Mr. Bullard's early release would come as no surprise."

Well, maybe Sloane had a surprise for him. She'd almost done it once but changed her mind at the last minute because she couldn't put herself through it. But now . . . She picked up her phone, searched the call list, and tapped Redial.

"Marcie Dumler."

"Yes," Sloane said, her pulse accelerating. "This is Sloane Ferrell. I need to make arrangements for a visit."

18

"THE ANNOUNCEMENT AND CEREMONY will be last of February or early March," Micah said, brushing his thumb over the metal guitar string. He'd showered, pulled on some old jeans and a T-shirt, and had just picked up the Martin when his mother called. "I don't want to press the issue, but has Uncle Clay said anything?"

"Nothing definite, but . . ." There was a smile in his mother's voice, the same one that accompanied every "It will be okay" encouragement she'd gifted Micah since he was a kid. Even during that reckless year he'd betrayed his family values as well as his soul. "Grace has been doing that thing she does when she's expectant with song."

"Song nesting," Micah said, remembering. His heart tugged. He missed them all—Oregon was too far. "What wall did she repaint?"

His mother laughed. "The stair risers. To look like a stack of classic books. I'm serious. She saw it on Pinterest. *Little Women*, *Pride and Prejudice*, *Gone with the Wind* . . . Your uncle nixed *Grapes of Wrath* as 'not conducive to peace and harmony.'"

Peace. It had been so elusive after Stephen. For him, far longer than the others, it seemed. They'd all searched, each in different ways. Maybe Grace being "expectant" with song and taking a paintbrush to the stairs were signs she'd finally found it. Micah had hoped settling into the hospital marketing position would do that for him, but . . .

"Grace is also volunteering with the Every 15 Minutes program here," his mother said, her voice growing somber. "It's like the one they have in LA."

"Right." Micah was familiar with the program. In fact, the crisis team helped put it on.

The emotionally charged event centered on the topic of drinking—more recently texting, too—and driving. It targeted teenagers and offered real-life experience without actual risk, featuring powerful, graphic reminders about personal safety and the responsibility of making mature decisions when lives were involved.

Like Stephen's life that night . . .

"It's rugged for her every time," his mother continued. "But Grace thinks her honest reactions only make it more real, and if she's able to keep one student from dying, convince him to call for a ride instead of getting in that car . . ."

"Call for a ride." Micah's gut twisted.

His mother sighed. "She says it's more than worth it."

"Yeah."

There was a long pause and Micah heard music in the background. His father's Beatles collection. As far back as he could remember, it had been as much a part of home as Sunday pot roast, sharing couch space with aging beagles . . . and his cousin.

"You're good?" his mother asked.

"Fine."

"Seeing anyone special? You know I have to ask—for Grace."

Micah laughed, surprised by a thought of Sloane on the Prescott couch with a graying dog chin on her thigh and humming along to "Hey Jude."

"Well?" his mother asked.

"Assure *Aunt Grace*," Micah teased, "that when and if that happens, I won't keep it a secret."

"You're incorrigible."

He smiled. "And you're the best."

They said their good-byes and Micah disconnected. He resettled the Martin in his lap and picked out the notes to "Hey Jude." Strumming a C chord, he felt the response of the sound-board and enjoyed the feel of the instrument in his hands. It had been Stephen's, and at first it had been impossible to pick up, the sadness too hard to bear. But slowly the connection became comforting. And nowadays it was the one thing guaranteed to relax Micah—take him away from all else. Except . . .

Why hadn't he asked Sloane out again? The truth was, he might have never met anyone as "special." Beautiful, sure, but much more than that. The narrative nominating her for the Face of Hope had pretty much nailed it. He glanced to where he'd pulled it up on his laptop:

She treats every patient with dignity, whether they are rich or poor, highly educated or seriously challenged. They all have worth, and she gives them her best.

Admirable, absolutely. So why the hesitation?

Micah picked the strings, reminding himself that Sloane's *"Maybe . . . I think so"* response to his question about a second date had been delivered with a smile. The ball was in his court. There was no reason to make it a bigger deal than it was; they were only in that polite, cautious, do-you-like-sushi?, where'd-you-grow-up? phase.

Except Sloane, beyond the sushi, hadn't actually revealed much. Was there some reason for that?

He frowned, strummed the strings, willing the music to do what it was supposed to do. Relax him, take his mind off things.

It wasn't as if Sloane had been overtly evasive. He hadn't pressed for details; a first date shouldn't be an interview. Micah thought of Coop. He would have wasted no time in asking Sloane all about herself, ferreting out the details. And oversharing his own. Coop was sharp, tenacious as a police dog with a mouthful of prowler pant leg, but also painfully honest. To his detriment at times: very few women on a first date were ready to hear that dinner couldn't exceed thirty-two dollars because his credit card was over the limit and he used the rest of his paycheck to bail a former girlfriend out of jail.

Micah shook his head, humming along as he picked the notes of the Beatles song: *"Take a sad song and make it better . . ."*

Being with Sloane Saturday night *had* made things better. The inexplicable and persistent irritation he'd been feeling these past months seemed to suspend itself during those hours. He'd laughed, enjoyed the meal, the humor. Sights he'd seen before felt new in her company. All of that was good. And hopeful. There had been red lanterns, spontaneous music, and Micah thought, a real mutual attraction. Maybe the prospect of a kiss . . . on hold for next time.

The truth was, Micah wanted that next time. Even if, in the light of day, he'd been left with more questions than certainties.

Sloane was a real person with life experience, history. The same was true of Micah. These were the things, far beyond "Do you like sushi?" that built the framework for a strong, genuine relationship. He didn't want a social media meme. He wanted . . .

He set the guitar down and grabbed his cell phone, tapped the contact number. His pulse hiked when Sloane answered and said his name.

"I hoped," he told her, "I could tempt you with coffee and dessert. I know a place in Brentwood that has those Rice Krispy treats we ate as kids, but takes them to another level."

"Rice Krispy treats?"

"Yeah," Micah said, already imagining the bliss on her amazing face as she tasted one. "Cereal, marshmallows . . ."

There was silence, so long that he thought their wireless connection had been dropped. "Sloane?"

"I'm here." It sounded like she cleared her throat. "I can't. I mean, I appreciate your offer, but I have to be someplace tonight."

"Sure," he told her. "No problem. Maybe another time."

"I'd like that."

He disconnected and lifted the Martin back into his lap. He hoped it would do its job and distract him. Keep his mind from leaping to the next logical question: Where did the enigmatic Sloane Ferrell have to be tonight?

Sloane slid into the room just as people were taking their seats. She sat close to an exit door, leaving a cushion of several empty chairs between herself and the others, the way she always did. Three months now at this site; she'd shopped around for a meeting place the first few months in Los Angeles. AA advised that. Or maybe it was her excuse to avoid getting to know people—or be followed. But she'd settled finally. Not always the same day of the week, but usually this same place. It felt familiar now. That in itself was progress.

When Sloane attended her first AA meeting, it hadn't been anything like she expected. She probably assumed she'd find a group of down-and-out people with desperate expressions, hangovers, shakes, all the things she'd seen so many times with patients in the ER. There were a few people who fit her initial assumption, but the majority looked like somebody you'd see at Target or Safeway. There were also men and women in expensive business clothes, a young woman in yoga wear, several senior citizens, and even a man Sloane was sure she recognized from a local TV morning show. The first time, that first meeting, she'd actually walked back outside to double-check she had the right room.

Sloane hadn't expected, either, to find jokes, laughter—lots of it—lively conversation, and a sort of all-pervasive positive energy. It was like she'd crashed a congenial cocktail party without the booze and boozers. AA felt like a club, open to anyone, with slogans and catchphrases instead of clever handshakes: *First things first. One day at a time. Meeting makers make it. Easy does it. You're only as sick as your secrets.*

But there was order, too, a sameness to each meeting that

reinforced, without question, the reason these people were there and kept coming back: to stay sober and help other alcoholics in their recovery journey. Sloane also found—hung on to it like a life preserver—that she could utter the words "I think I'm just going to sit and listen this time," and they would be respected. There was never pressure to share anything personal.

"God, grant me the serenity to accept the things I cannot change, courage to change the things I can, and wisdom to know the difference."

Sloane mouthed the words along with the group, the way she did at every meeting. God, a "higher power," was part of this too. She'd accepted that but applied the "sit and listen" disclaimer there as well; the thought of tossing out a resounding *amen* felt as phony as those old feather angel wings. She simply wasn't the type.

"You don't look like the cookie-baking type."

Not a baker, not a steadfast believer—or at least, not anymore. If there was one thing Sloane had learned from her messy life, it was that God didn't want to hear from someone like her.

The meetings wrapped up on time, and as always, Sloane slipped from her seat five minutes before the end and headed to the parking lot. She saw nothing helpful about joining hands for the closing prayer. If she stayed, she'd soon find herself with a cup of coffee and involved in some awkward conversation about—

"Hey there."

Sloane turned, recognizing the group member who'd shared at the last meeting. Jocelyn. A well-dressed woman with teal-framed glasses and a casual ponytail today, who'd talked openly about her struggle with depression after the suicide of her twin brother. According to her story, she'd turned to "substance therapy," leading to tabloid-worthy behavior that ended her career at a prestigious financial firm. She'd not only slept with the company's married CFO, destroying his marriage and her own, but had attempted check fraud that put her behind bars for six months. The bad decisions didn't even end there, but Jocelyn eventually reclaimed her life and went on to become the head of a large charitable organization. The work brought her peace and enormous satisfaction. She'd finished her compelling story by saying something about net worth being "more than a bank balance."

"Hi," Sloane said, returning the greeting while wishing she'd left ten minutes early. This was exactly what she'd tried to avoid. Especially with this woman. Something about her, a toughness despite the casual polish, said she'd cut right through any load of—

"You're Ronda?" she asked, extending her hand.

"Right," Sloane said, guilt swirling as she briefly took the woman's hand. On the few times she'd offered her name, Sloane gave her formal one, the one she rarely used.

"I'm Jocelyn."

"I remember you. You spoke last week."

"Yes. And you . . ." The woman's eyes met Sloane's. "Come in late. Avoid people. Then leave early."

Oh, great. What now? AA detention hall?

"I . . ." What could Sloane do? Match her 193 days to this pushy woman's ten-year sobriety? She lifted her chin, returned Jocelyn's gaze. "I bought that 'anonymous' part."

"I'm only saying what I see," Jocelyn continued, no judgment in her tone—no syrup, either. "And if you do that—sit apart, leave early, and never share, you're going to drink."

And right now you are driving me to it . . .

"Here." Jocelyn pulled a sheet of paper from the pocket of her jacket. "In case you lost the list we gave you a few months back. Phone numbers—people you can call anytime."

Rescuers. The last thing she needed.

Sloane battled a memory of an ER coworker taking her car keys in that San Diego bar the night of the accident. How furious it had made her, how horribly it had ended. And it was only a small part of her regrettable history. Did being part of this "club," staying sober, mean she had to confess it all? She wasn't going to do that. She'd come here but—

"No thank you," Sloane managed, certain this woman could sense her thirst. It only added to her growing irritation. "I have the list. I don't need another one."

"My number's there too," Jocelyn told her. "Or you can shop around for a sponsor."

"Sure . . . right." Sloane nodded.

"When you're finally ready to get serious. About a disease that's going to kill you."

"Bingo!"

"No thanks, I'm giving it up," Micah said in response to Coop's excited phone salutation. He set his guitar aside and tapped his cell into speaker mode. "Ask your grandmother to go with you."

"Dude," Coop continued, unfazed, "I'm saying that I got it!"

Micah hoped it wouldn't involve something he'd rather not know about some woman he'd never meet. It occurred to him that he'd never introduced Coop to his parents. Had to be something significant there. "What did you get?"

"My source at the prison. She came through for me. Big-time."

Micah waited, wondering about ethics and confidentiality.

"There's a connection—has to be—between my Russian up for parole and what happened with the girl in the alley."

"Jane Doe hasn't said anything." Micah nearly groaned at the idiocy of his statement. The girl still couldn't physically speak because of the damage.

"But her tattoo did. That's what my resource heard. There's a tat on her hip that's distinctive to girls being trafficked. And to a gangster named Viktor." Coop's voice had risen to an octave he probably hadn't achieved since puberty. "Who has ties to my inmate and maybe to other 'businesses' up and down the coast! I can't believe how rich this vein is—prison gold, just like I told you. I'm making myself blind googling news stories. There's an open investigation for a multiple vehicular manslaughter incident in San Diego that was suspicious for Russian involvement. And there could be a link to a gambling operation in Sacramento that was hot a few years back. It's a lot of loose ends, but they don't call me the Ferret for nothing."

"Right," Micah agreed, relieved that Sloane's private life was no longer the focus of this overeager reporter's interest. Even if Micah still had unanswered questions himself. "Sounds like you're headed toward that byline."

"Count on it. I'm not letting this one go."

19

"I BROUGHT SIR GEORGE to see you ladies." The rusty-haired medic grinned as he clattered his stretcher past Harper and Sloane. A bearded and rumpled man lay supine on a hazmat sheet, one arm draped over his forehead. A passing whiff—stale urine, filthy socks, and cheap whiskey—explained why both men on the ambulance crew had surgical masks dangling around their necks. Stink, not contagion. "Where do you want him?"

"Room 22A. Your nurse will be Morgan," Sloane directed, recalling the run report: forty-six-year-old male found unresponsive in a community park by joggers. When roused, he'd complained only of "foot problems." Sloane turned to Harper, who was tapping an entry into the computer. "'Sir George'?"

"Frequent flier," Harper said with a sigh. "Alcoholic, mostly

homeless. Sometimes charming—" she wrinkled her nose—
"always smelly. Claims he was a professor of poetry at Oxford.
And knighted by the queen."

"Anybody google that?"

Harper smiled. "It's LA; he probably *played* a university
professor in some B movie. And hustled toothpaste ads to pay
off his student loans."

Sloane glanced down the hallway, watching the stretcher's
progress. She recalled Jocelyn's story—and then that awkward, one-sided conversation after the meeting. *When you're
finally ready to get serious. About a disease that's going to
kill you.*" Sloane had been completely unprepared for the
exchange, shaken. By the time she arrived home, it had all
morphed to anger. The incident had been a clear ambush, so
unfair. And way off base. Jocelyn didn't know Sloane any more
than the paramedics or hospital staff really knew this poor
homeless guy. Even if he was a "frequent flier."

"It could be true. That he was a professor," she heard herself say. Then caught Harper's expression. "What?"

"You," she told Sloane. "I love that you're giving him the
benefit of the doubt. But FYI, Morgan's not going to thank
you for the room assignment. He's in a custody battle with his
ex and he's been cranky. Once he gets downwind of your good
knight, he'll be whining to go back to the SICU." She lifted a
brow. "Having fun yet, fearless leader?"

Sloane had been asked to take charge today when the clinical coordinator called in sick, something she neither expected
nor wanted but that could help her performance review. Even
if she had to wrangle this "cranky" nurse they'd borrowed for
a few hours from the intensive care unit. "Jane Doe's there,
in the SICU."

"Still no name, no visitors. And in a drug-induced coma for now."

Sloane nodded. "While they assess her for brain damage. Too long without decent circulation. She almost bled out." She thought of Micah and how he'd said the scene was hard to get out of his head.

"They still have police outside the doors," Harper said. "Everyone thinks they're working it as a trafficking case. Especially after that other killing last night."

Sloane's stomach quivered. A car had been found in a thickly wooded area in the Hollywood Hills. Abandoned, no plates. Doused with accelerant, set afire—with an unidentified man's body in the trunk. It felt too familiar. The stolen car that ran Sloane's off the cliff in San Diego, killed and injured others, had also been found abandoned and burned. The MO had immediately raised the suspicions of San Diego law enforcement for organized crime involvement.

Paul had been more than suspicious. *Those Russians. They like fire.*

"Such a nightmare," Harper added. "After all that poor girl went through, they think this guy got whacked for not doing the job well enough." She rubbed her arms like she'd felt a chill. "It's scary to think we're going about our regular lives when, at the same time, there's all this bad stuff happening. Who's to say anyone is really immune? One little something might tip the scales and—"

"Morning, ladies." Jerry Rhodes rolled a cart laden with pipes and tools toward them. He met Sloane's gaze only briefly. "I'll be doing that work on the waiting room water fountain."

Sloane nodded, then watched him rattle away. She turned to Harper. "What's wrong with the drinking fountain?"

"Not kid friendly." Harper smiled. "That man is a prime example of the good stuff. He clocked out, but he's staying to adjust the smaller fountain. He saw a little boy crying because the water kept going up his nose. Jerry promised him he'd fix it. Now he's doing it on his own dime."

"Just pay me what you think it's worth."

Sloane felt a prickle of guilt over how she'd felt when she first spotted him in Celeste's yard.

"Well . . ." Harper stepped away from the computer. "Time to go check on my patient lineup."

"Same here," Sloane agreed. "I'll see how Morgan—"

"See how I'm doing with Sir George?" Randall Morgan appeared beside her. Despite what she'd asked, he was still wearing his SICU jacket. And a decided scowl. Like the medics, he had a surgical mask hanging around his neck. His eyes narrowed a fraction. "I should know by now that the joke's always on the new guy."

"Joke?" Sloane told herself to stay cool. This guy wasn't worth losing her temper.

"Foot problems?" Morgan's laugh was caustic. "The only foot problem that guy should worry about is my shoe against his butt when I kick him out of here. Except I'd have to throw my shoe out afterward. So much for our tax dollars."

Sloane's jaw tensed.

"Soon as the doc gives the green light, I'll get a tech to roll him to the bus stop," Morgan continued, oblivious to the stares of the two women. "His pants can dry in the sun. I'm not digging through your holy donation closet for clothes. He actually asked for that and told me his waist size. And then he tried to order a lunch tray like he was sitting in his favorite booth at the Polo Lounge." Morgan's lips twisted in a sneer. "I told him sure, why not start with appetizers? And then I ripped open a few alcohol wipes and dumped them in his lap."

Sloane stared. "You . . . did that?"

"Yeah." Morgan laughed. "It was great. You should have seen the look on his—"

"Shut. Up." The words seethed through Sloane's teeth. "And get out."

"What the—?" Morgan blinked, his expression morphing from smug to Taser-stunned. He turned to Harper. "She can't take a joke? What's going on?"

"It's *you* that's going," Sloane repeated, not caring that people were watching. Or that one of them was Micah. She'd just caught a glimpse of him out of the corner of her eye. "Get your things and leave this department."

Harper nodded. "She means it, Randall."

He uttered a low curse and mumbled something about his union rep, then stalked away.

"And now what?" Harper asked.

Sloane sighed. "Now I find my new patient some clean clothes—and a meal tray."

"They burned him alive."

"Nah. Probably shot him in the head first." Stack glanced away from the TV. "You gonna eat that fajita?"

"No. Take it." Zoey pressed her hand to her stomach; it did nothing to ease the queasy churning. She watched as Stack chewed a seared chunk of beef. "You think it has something to do with that girl in the hospital?"

"Don't know. Don't care." He reached for his vintage-style

reading glasses, then dragged his laptop closer. "Why are you asking?"

"No reason. Thinking out loud."

She'd made dozens of furtive calls to Oksana's cell over the past week—a phone shared by several of Viktor's girls, under a watchful eye—and finally got an answer early this morning. Fortunately this girl remembered Zoey, and her "supervisor" was currently training one of the new girls. The thought of that made her sick. She filled Zoey in as best she could in a low whisper.

It *was* Oksana in the hospital. None of the girls knew her condition other than what little had been reported in the news, and they mostly got that secondhand. Viktor had heard Oksana was making noises about running away, encouraging the other girls to get on board. The alleged doctor's appointment had been Viktor's plan to dump a bad asset. His man screwed up and now he'd gone missing. Something was going down. The number of "dates" had dwindled significantly, and there was talk the girls would be moved out of the city. They were scared and taking turns watching all night for signs of fire—one of Viktor's men had been seen "checking" the smoke detectors.

"You still driving yourself crazy about that Jane Doe?" Stack asked, making some notes on a sheet of paper.

"No." Even if her stomach didn't always cooperate, Zoey could credit Stack with her talent to look someone directly in the eyes and lie. "I'm too busy looking after my own skin."

"Seriously?" Stack peered over his glasses at her. "I'd say I'm the one who's been doing that. You could be busy with dates. Remember?"

Zoey refused to let him get to her. Not anymore. She was

a short-timer now. "I remember you said you're going to help me get back home. After one more job. Then I'm done."

"That's right." Stack's smile spread slowly. "One more job. It's taking a few days to get the details in place, but we're close now. Go check my closet, kid. I got you a new outfit."

"It's as simple as that," Micah explained to the handful of ER staff gathered in the employee lounge. The room smelled of burnt coffee, mustard packets, and perfume that defied the employee handbook's prohibited list. "You come up with a name of someone you believe is worthy of consideration and submit it to the marketing office. Use the printed form or do it online through the LA Hope website. Either way is fine. That's it—they're officially nominated."

A young woman wearing a flowered top and a clerk's badge spoke up. "Can we nominate ourselves?" She frowned when a teammate poked her. "I'm serious. Can we?"

"Yes. Absolutely." Micah pointed to a flyer pinned to the bulletin board. "That's why it says 'Maybe It's You.' We tagged the campaign that way because it could be anyone. Every employee has an equal chance at this honor." He thought of what he'd seen in the ER waiting room. The maintenance man fixing a water fountain, involving a little boy in the process. "It doesn't matter what your position is or what duties you perform. That's the whole point of this campaign." He met the clerk's gaze. "For instance, when a patient arrives in the ER, you're probably the first person he meets, the first step in his treatment. Your competence and compassion—your face, if you will, becomes his first measure of hope."

The clerk sat a little taller. "I never thought of it that way."

"Well, that's exactly what *we're* thinking," Micah said, proud of the campaign despite his misgivings about his job as a whole. He was giving this project his best shot. "And it's what we want to get across to the community."

"That sounds good but . . ." A balding man in scrubs raised his half-eaten banana. "Isn't the real goal to make folks finally forget what happened with our old chief of staff?"

"Right," a middle-aged nurse said, speaking before Micah could. "I came on right after that mess. He committed vehicular homicide, then used his power and position to effect a cover-up. I heard like a dozen staff were involved. Huge scandal."

"It was," Micah interjected, knowing he needed to refocus the discussion. "A mess, a scandal, and an awful tragedy. I wouldn't even try to sanitize that. There were inexcusable mistakes made and very real consequences for staff involved. They are no longer here. But you all are. We're proud of you. And we're proud to be an organization committed to a mission of compassion, competence, and caring—for *everyone*. We've made that promise to this community and we're keeping it." He made himself smile. "In five months we're going to throw an epic party to celebrate exactly that, and we'll applaud the one of you who will represent us all. Cash prize, media coverage, parking place—your face on a billboard. Maybe more."

The man with the banana cocked his head. "Open to everyone?"

"Yes," Micah assured again, "every employee is eligible for nomination. There will be a selection process, of course, and—"

"Micah?" The door cracked open and Howard Brill peeked in. "Sorry. Am I interrupting?"

"No, I . . ." Micah checked his watch. "I've taken enough of these folks' time. Give me a minute and I'll be right out."

He thanked the staff for their attention, made sure there were enough printed nomination forms, then stepped back into the emergency department corridor, where the board member was waiting.

"Micah, good to see you."

"Mr. Brill. Same here, sir."

"It's Howard, please."

Micah accepted the man's offered handshake, thinking it might have been the first time he'd ever seen this man in this area of the hospital. At least since the groundbreaking ceremony for the new wing and hospital tour a couple of months back. Of course, trauma and everyday maladies didn't have the lure of Hollywood superstars and the Lakers. Howard Brill must have been going to or coming from a business meeting; his well-cut suit and spotless white shirt made him look like a foreigner in this sea of scrubs.

"I'm on my way to a Rotary meeting," the man said, confirming Micah's impression, "but I wanted to stop by and see Brittany." He patted his pocket. "I promised her aunt I'd snap a few pictures of the big day."

Micah scrunched his brows.

"Brittany Brill, my niece." The board member's nod looked like a bullet point. "Niece, godchild, and more of a daughter since my brother's passing."

"Yes, I remember."

"She works in the newborn nursery. They love her there—the staff, the patients. She's highly valued. Ask anyone. Britt's new, but she's already making her mark. Making a difference." There was obvious pride on the uncle's face. "And today she's taking a huge step in responsibility. Showing her leadership skills."

Micah waited.

"She's demonstrating a baby bath in a video for the new mothers. It will be used throughout the Hope hospital system."

"Ah." *Baby bath?*

Micah didn't doubt it was a good thing, a valuable tool. But . . . He had an image of Sloane facing off with that male nurse in defense of a foul-smelling homeless man. Leadership, dedication, compassion . . . with fire-and-ice eyes. No comparison.

"It's scheduled for 2 p.m.," Brill was saying. "You might drop by and talk with some of her coworkers. We'd be delighted to see you there."

"Thank you," Micah said, offering his hand again. "I'm sure you're really proud."

"Newborn nursery. Twenty minutes."

Micah watched the man walk away and then headed back through the emergency department, fighting an uncomfortable feeling not unlike that awkward moment when he'd had to discuss the old chief's drunken act. The staff nurse had been spot-on with her comment: *"He . . . used his power and position . . ."*

Something about the exchange with the board member left a similar bad taste in Micah's mouth. And reminded him that this job was far different from what he accomplished as part of the crisis team. But he wasn't going to let the conversation with Brill get to him. He'd invested a huge amount of time and effort in this campaign and—

"I'll finish up here." A voice floated out from the open doorway of a treatment room. "Then I'll see if we can find you some clean clothes."

Sloane. With that homeless man.

Micah paused and caught a glimpse of her inside. The man was talking, Sloane listening intently. He shouldn't be watching, but he couldn't look away. Sloane was washing the man's feet. A basin of water, towels. Gently, carefully.

"Did you need something?" Sloane asked, noticing Micah there.

"No . . . Sorry; I didn't mean to interrupt."

"No problem." Sloane peeled off her gloves, patted her patient's knee, and walked toward the doorway. "I need to go check on my staff—the ones I haven't already run off." Her lips quirked. "I guess you saw that little skirmish earlier."

"Yeah." Micah glanced toward the man in the treatment room. "I'd say your patient won."

Sloane's smile smacked at his heart.

"Now if I can get through the rest of the shift without raising the hackles of the nurses' union or blowing my probation." She shook her head. "It's been that kind of day."

"I get that," he said, imagining Brill drumming his fingers as he waited for Micah to show up for the baby bath. It wasn't going to happen. He wouldn't waste time on that phony, transparent ploy. Micah wanted something real.

"Look," he heard himself say, "I've had more than enough of this place myself. When you get off shift, want to grab some dinner with me?"

Her eyes met his and she hesitated; Micah told himself to breathe.

"I could do that. But . . ." Sloane glanced down at her scrubs, damp in places from the bathwater. "I'd need to go home first. Shower, change."

"No problem," he assured her, feeling better than he had

all day. "I'll jot down some ideas for places to eat. Run them by you later. Then you can let me know when to pick you up. And where."

Sloane's brow puckered.

"Your address," he explained, hoping that her expression didn't mean she was changing her mind. "So I can swing by and get you?"

"I . . ." Sloane took a breath. "I'll text it to you."

20

"I CAN'T BELIEVE WE'RE DOING THIS," Sloane said, a giddy laugh rising. Giddiness warring with nerves; it had been a worthy duel since the moment Micah walked up her driveway. No, from the instant she gave him her address. She'd met him on the porch dressed in her worn-soft denim skirt, a peasant-style top, and sandals. She'd had to take more than a few slow breaths to diffuse the jittery mix of excitement and anxiety.

"The quintessential Hollywood Hills . . . tailgate picnic," she said, tossing him a teasing smile. She raised her paper cup. "The ad man gets points for originality."

"What can I say?" Micah popped the top on a second bottle of sparkling pomegranate juice as Sloane settled herself on the tailgate of his SUV. "You're really okay with this? All cheesy tourist?"

"Yes and yes. I'm fine, and it *is* cheesy." She let him fill her cup, then surveyed the Mulholland Drive overlook. "Postcard cheesy but still very cool."

Sloane gazed out across the panorama nestled in the hills: the Hollywood freeway winding like a child's snapped-together LEGO creation through trees, red-tile roofs, and on toward the hazy high-rise cityscape of downtown LA. If she closed her eyes, she could hear the *thrum-honk* of the endless freeway commutes, catch a whiff of asphalt and smog, but up here, even next to the highway, there was a breeze and an almost-delicious sense of escape. As if she'd actually satisfied that deep yearning at last. Sloane pointed, picking out the familiar, iconic landmarks. "Hollywood Bowl . . . Griffith Park . . ."

"Don't forget the sign," Micah teased, pointing to the nine famous white letters perched high on Mount Lee. "As if you could miss them, at thirty-some feet wide and—"

"Forty-five feet tall," Sloane finished, remembering. "And there were originally four more letters to spell out *Hollywoodland*, for a new real estate development."

"That's right." Micah shook his head, laughed. "Now *there's* an ad campaign. Nine decades and still going strong." He looked sideways at her. "I didn't take you for a trivia geek."

"Not me. My mom," Sloane explained. "She knew everything about films, Hollywood, and movie stars. It was sort of her passion, I guess." In an instant, memories floated back: her mother brushing her hair with fifty strokes, her red nail polish and the rose-and-lily scent of face cream. Sloane took a sip of her juice, swallowing against the old ache. "We had bookcases full of videotapes, mostly the really vintage films. *Casablanca, Gone with the Wind, Giant, Philadelphia Story.*"

She decided against admitting she and Marty had watched that one recently. *"An Affair to Remember . . ."*

"Classic romance," Micah said, refilling his own cup. "I didn't hear *The Dirty Dozen* or *Red Badge of Courage* anywhere in there."

"No action movies or war films." Sloane pushed aside an image of that old crucifix in her mother's hands. "Tragic romance, romantic comedy . . . movie magazines piled knee-high, and dozens and dozens of framed black-and-white celebrity photos. That was us. For the longest time, I thought Elizabeth Taylor was a relative."

"I would buy that," Micah said, holding her gaze for a long moment.

A flush crept up Sloane's neck. She reached for a sprig of grapes, only a minuscule part of the food Micah had assembled when the prospect of a dinner reservation proved daunting. He'd thrown himself on the mercy of the Whole Foods deli: a loaf of artisan sourdough, Brie and Humboldt Fog cheeses, fig jam, fresh fruit, chilled pinwheels stuffed with herbed chicken, and a small assortment of chocolates wrapped in jewel-colored foils. It was a picnic that would have fit a scene in one of her mother's movies. Though, amazingly, there was no wine. No temptation to drown her jitters. All the while she'd been dressing for the date, she'd agonized over how she'd refuse a drink but never had to say a word. If Sloane even half believed God had a soft spot for someone like her, she'd have shouted, *"Hallelujah."*

"We had Oscar parties," she said, filling the short stretch of silence. "She'd wear sequins. I'd help her glue on false eyelashes. We'd set up TV trays, make popcorn, roll little wieners in crescent rolls, and write our picks on Post-it notes. Mom even had some red JCPenney throw rugs that we'd line up end to end, and . . . Me on a red carpet." Her heart tugged. "It was a rented house in Fresno, but that night she made it Hollywood."

"Did you ever drive down here to visit? Do the studio tours?"

"Once. She took me to Disneyland when I was seven." *After Phillip* . . . Sloane swirled the juice in her cup. "We took the Universal Studios tour. Went to the Walk of Fame. I think she used two whole rolls of film of me on that marble sidewalk with Marilyn Monroe, Michael Jackson, and Lassie. She even made a movie of me pretending to tap-dance down a line of stars." Sloane shook her head. "She'd read the names out loud, tug me along to the next one. It was only us, but it felt like we were at this huge family reunion."

"Just the two of you?" Micah asked, his voice tentative.

"Yes." Sloane would be a fool not to expect that question. After all, she'd started this line of conversation. Opened herself up. "My father died before I was born."

"I'm sorry."

Sloane inspected the grapes. What was she supposed to say? That she was sorry too? Sorry she inherited her father's "amazing" blue eyes and her mother's fatal weakness for booze? Or that she wished her mother never had a boyfriend who bought her angel wings and—?

"So . . ." Micah handed her a chocolate. "You're a tap dancer?"

"No," Sloane said, grateful for a laugh. She'd said far more than she'd intended, than she ever thought she could be comfortable with. But there was something about Micah. "There's no Hollywood star with my name on it. Not a singer, dancer, or actor."

"I'm surprised," he said, unwrapping his own chocolate.

The sun had begun to sink lower, casting a glow over their picnic site. It turned Micah's shirt a little pink and lifted Oscar-gold highlights in his sandy hair. His smile spread slowly. "Considering all that red carpet experience."

Sloane returned his smile and told herself she was doing fine. Better than fine, really. She'd accomplished a hurdle she thought wasn't possible. An impromptu picnic in this un-expected setting could have spurred tears, an ugly flash of anger, or any number of inappropriate responses. Alcohol had jerked the strings of those humiliating performances count-less times. Instead, she was holding up her end of a conversa-tion with a man who treated her with nothing but respect. A decent man who'd sought her company because of a genuine interest in who she was *now* . . . not because he was tempted by a one-night stand. For the first time in forever it almost felt like Sloane's mistakes and all those secrets were as far away as the big white letters on Mount Lee.

"She's still in Fresno?" Micah asked. "Your mother?"

———

The immediate change in Sloane's expression made Micah wish he'd never asked the question.

"She died when I was eighteen," Sloane said, finding renewed interest in a grape stem she'd picked clean. When her eyes rose once again to meet his, there was a sort of deci-siveness in her expression. "She drowned."

Ah, man . . . He searched for something to say, but she wasn't finished.

"They tried to say it was her fault because of pills and al-cohol. Because she was that kind of person." Sloane raised her chin, reminding Micah of that moment in the ER when she'd confronted the nurse. "It took a while, but her husband, my stepfather, was finally convicted of manslaughter. He's at State Prison in LA. They'd moved here a few months before it happened."

"I don't know what to say," Micah told her honestly.

Sloane attempted a small shrug. "It's been almost fourteen years."

"That thing they quote about time and how it heals all wounds?" Micah sought her gaze. "I think it's overrated."

"Probably."

"But then chocolate," he said, grabbing one wrapped in blue foil, "earns every bit of its good press." He held the candy out to her, wishing he were holding her instead. "Medicinal."

She smiled and took it. "You could sell snake oil, you know."

"Thanks—I think."

He watched Sloane unwrap the chocolate, wondering if her quip was closer to the truth than he'd like. It probably was the way people saw it. That his job was simply to hawk the hospital, put a positive spin on anything that didn't otherwise vet. He couldn't deny it was the carefully calculated reason he'd pitched the new campaign to the board. A plan to honor employees he'd never actually spent that much time with until . . .

"I think it was great what you did today," Micah said, "for your patient."

Sloane's tongue swept across her lower lip, catching a bit of chocolate. "You mean doing battle with that nurse from the unit?"

"That too, but I meant taking the time to really care for that homeless man. Personally, when you could have easily handed it off to someone else."

"Not so easily. Sir George has a reputation."

Micah had overheard plenty to confirm that—graphic details that made him especially glad his office was way upwind of the ER. And he'd heard enough about the man's history of DUI arrests to stir his own bias.

"Still," he insisted, "you took him on when you didn't have to. And went more than the extra mile. I saw what you were doing for him."

"Cleaned him up a little, that's all. It wasn't like I was saving his life."

"No, but . . ." Micah hesitated, remembering her washing the man's feet. The image had hit him hard in the gut. A small task but so full of compassion. It was like he was seeing a physical embodiment of what drew him to crisis work. "It's not the first time people have noticed that about you."

"What do you mean?"

"She treats every patient with dignity, whether they are rich or poor, highly educated or seriously challenged. They all have worth, and she gives them her best."

"Things I hear. Things like . . ." Micah cautioned himself against revealing that she'd been nominated for the Face of Hope. Sloane would probably hate it. "What you proved today. That every patient is worthy of the best care regardless of their circumstances. Sure, it's not a new concept. It could be the hospital's mission, printed on a T-shirt—probably has been, by some eager-beaver marketing man way back when." He shook his head. "But more often than not, that's simply *talk*. We all wish it weren't so, but it is. And you . . . you walk the walk, Sloane. You work like you're carrying the banner of the Golden Rule. People notice."

A flush rose on her cheeks. "Maybe I'm a better actor than I give myself credit—"

"No." Micah cut her off. "I'm not going to let you do that. Even if you don't see it, other people do. That man today did. That kid, Zoey Jones, she saw it."

He reached out, gently lifted a dark, silky length of hair framing Sloane's forehead and then trailed his fingers slowly down. From the small, intriguing scar at the corner of her eye to the sweet curve of her jaw. Soft, warm . . . "I see it too. You're special. The more I learn about you, the more I want to know."

Sloane stiffened, her breath catching.

"I'm sorry," Micah said, letting his hand drop. "I didn't mean to make you uncomfortable."

"You didn't. No problem," she said, the breathless relief in her voice making Micah feel even worse. "I just don't know what to do with all that, I guess. I mean, it's nice, but . . ."

"But the last thing you need is a campaign from a snake oil salesman." Micah found a smile.

"I'm sorry I said that. Which makes us even, if we're counting apologies—which I'm not." She looked around; the parked cars had dwindled now. "Does this place close at sunset?"

"Yes," he confirmed, smart enough to get the hint. "You need to get home."

"Not really." The golden light had turned her eyes an incredible shade of violet. "I was thinking it might be nice to put this food away and take a walk down to the Bowl. But I guess we can't now."

"I know a side path," he told her, feeling hope rise like he was a Hollywood actor walking the red carpet.

"Sounds good."

Zoey clutched the cell phone and held her breath, listening as the number rang a second time. Her hands were shaking. Would someone answer? It had gone to voice mail the other two times she'd tried, and she'd hung up without saying anything. Stack could be back at any time, and he was already bugged that Zoey complained about this latest job. It felt wrong, and she didn't want to be a part of it. He'd laughed at her, dropped Viktor's name again, and asked if that "job" was more to her liking. Then Stack gave her a new bit about how things were turning around for him, how it was finally coming together and this would be their last job. And how he wasn't going to let anything or anybody screw it up.

Zoey peered through the open door to his side of the motel rooms, her pulse quickening. He'd check her call list; he always did. But this time she didn't care. This time it would be worth the fight and—

The voice mail greeting: "This is Susie. Do your thing."

Zoey squeezed her eyes shut against a rush of tears, told herself to disconnect, but . . .

"It's me, and . . . happy birthday, Mom."

21

"IT'S AMAZING," Sloane said, meaning it. She turned her head, drinking in the incredible view of the Los Angeles skyline, gone all *Star Wars* galaxy in the purple night sky. Taillights zinged like red strobes on the freeways, streetlights pooled golden on asphalt, and twinkling high-rises were silhouetted in the fuzzy far distance like they'd breached the end of the planet.

Millions and millions of lights. Earthly dazzle vying with the heavens . . .

"People always expect the Hollywood sign to be lit at night," Micah said, glancing in its direction. From where they sat on the outlook beyond the trail, its pale letters were discernible but without fanfare. "That's a residential area, though."

Sloane's skin shivered unexpectedly as Micah moved and his shoulder brushed hers. There was just enough of a breeze to lift a thatch of his hair, let her catch a hint of his scent. Masculine, clean like a freshly ironed shirt, and maybe a little cologne. With juniper . . .

"I remember Mom saying something about the last time they lit it," Sloane said, hauling her senses back in check. "The mayor and Jay Leno flipped the switch." She chuckled. Her mother never missed a celebrity detail. "It was a millennium celebration, part of the fireworks show. She said they lit the sign up in all these colors."

"Right, New Year's Eve 1999," Micah agreed.

The year I ran off . . .

"We were living here then. Burbank," Micah said. "By Grace was asked to appear at a combined worship service for one of the big churches. Everyone was predicting there'd be a huge computer blackout. The whole date-bug Y2K scare. Stephen and I expected we'd be picking our guitars in the dark. I told him to sing and pretend it was me so maybe I'd get a few fans for a change."

"You were performing with them?"

"Once in a while," Micah said, shrugging it off. "Anyway, no power outage, no computer crash. No fan club."

"And Jay Leno lit up the sign," Sloane added, trying to get past the contrast of Micah playing worship music in front of thousands and her shoving her dead father's crucifix into a backpack before crawling out her window.

"Yep," Micah said, his shoulder brushing hers once again as he turned to gaze at Mount Lee. "People came up Beachwood Drive by the thousands to see it, creating a traffic jam that basically trapped everyone in the canyon. And prevented first responders from getting in too. A lot of folks up there still cringe at the memory of '99."

"I'm sure." Sloane wished there were a way to pull the plug on her own bad memories of that year.

They were quiet for a moment, looking out at the lights. Sloane tried to remember the last time she'd done something like this. Something so simple.

"Were you still living in Fresno back then?" Micah asked.

Simple? Was she that much of a fool?

"No . . . not Fresno," Sloane told him, weighing how much she could say without directly lying. Being sober had stolen that dubious talent and left too many raw feelings in its wake. She wasn't always sure the trade-off was worth it. AA addressed it, of course: *"The trouble with feeling better is that you* feel *better."*

"I left home when I was almost sixteen," Sloane admitted. "When things heated up with my stepfather. I went to live with my godparents. I finished high school there."

"Where?"

"Up north. The Fort Bragg area. It was good, I guess," she said, feeling a twinge of guilt. She couldn't remember the last time she'd talked with them. "No movie stars. No red carpet walks—except in church." Sloane shook her head. "I was baptized in Mendocino. Never thought it would happen. Not to someone like me."

———

Micah wasn't sure how to respond. This woman was an intriguing mix of strength and vulnerability. So complex . . .

"He said something about that," Sloane said, her tone wistful in the near darkness.

"Who?" Micah asked, suddenly very aware of Sloane's physical presence beside him. The way the pale overhead reflection—city lights, maybe stars—played off the planes of her face. Cheekbones, sharp chin, straight nose . . . lush lips. "Who said what?"

"Sir George." Sloane hinted at a smile. "Feet-soak wisdom."

Micah was struck again by that humble image of a critical care nurse . . . caring. "What did he say?"

"Something about birds. And God." Sloane's voice was soft. "He thanked me. And at first he said a few things about rescue missions and how no one knows how to make real gravy anymore. Then he started talking about sparrows. I thought it was a poem." She shrugged. "He's been telling people he was a professor of poetry. Occasionally I try to give people the benefit of the doubt."

Except me. You weren't going to do that for the ad man. Micah hoped he was past being her exception now.

"Anyway, I was soaping his feet and expecting a poem, but I think he was quoting Scripture. He said something about the price of sparrows being two for a penny. And 'your Father's care' . . . and then he said we shouldn't be afraid, because each of us is 'worth more than many sparrows.'"

"Book of Matthew, I think."

"Yes. It rang a bell from my non-Hollywood red carpet days." Sloane rubbed her arms, stared out at the cityscape, quiet for a stretch. Then she turned to Micah. "Do you believe that?"

"You're not asking if I think Sir George is a poet."

"No," Sloane said. "I meant, do you believe everyone's worthy in God's eyes?"

"I do."

"I'd like to think it's true. But I don't know."

"I think I get that," Micah said, pretty sure he knew where Sloane was going with the thought. "When we see bad things happen. Like to that girl in the alley, my cousin . . . your mother?" He hoped he hadn't stepped too far. "I think it's part of the reason I work with the crisis team. I can't do much about the victims, but showing up for the survivors is important. Listening, showing them they matter. Even in the middle of chaos, even when everything seems so lost." Micah cleared his throat. "I think it's part of God's plan, bringing people together that way. Like you and the poet today. That man had a full belly, clean clothes, and happier feet because you were there. At that moment in time, *you* were proof of his worth to God."

Sloane's eyes lifted toward Micah's, huge and shiny with tears.

"Hey," he said. "Did I say something wrong?"

"No. Maybe too right. For someone like me."

"I can't believe that." Micah realized he'd taken her hand, or maybe she'd reached for his. Either way, it was making it hard to breathe, let alone talk. "From what I've seen, you deserve far more credit than that."

Sloane made a small sound; Micah wasn't sure if it was a sigh or groan.

"I meant what I said before," he continued. "You're special, Sloane. I've never met anyone quite like you."

"It's . . . complicated. You don't know me."

"But I want to. That's the point." He drew her hand against his chest. "I'm saying I like you. I'd like to see more of you." Micah smiled. "Imagine that as a poem."

Sloane found a laugh, a miracle since her heart had escaped her chest and lodged somewhere in her throat. This sudden dizziness had nothing to do with the Hollywood Bowl trail. Micah was holding her hand against his shirt, and she swore she felt his heart beneath the fabric.

"I want to kiss you," he said very simply. "You might say . . . right now *I* am the face of hope."

She smiled, equally afraid she was about to cry or to grab him and make an even more complete fool of herself.

"Maybe?" Micah asked, leaning in a fraction.

"Very poetic," Sloane said finally. "And yes."

"Well then . . ."

She was still struggling to recall if any man, ever, had asked permission to touch her when Micah cradled her face between his hands. He studied her for a moment before dipping low and touching his lips gently to her cheek. Then her forehead.

"You're so beautiful," he said, leaning back a few inches but still close enough that his breath warmed her skin. "And soft and . . ."

She closed her eyes, felt herself begin to tremble as Micah's lips met hers. Lightly at first, then more thoroughly as his hands moved to the nape of her neck, holding her and guiding her into his kiss. His mouth was warm, gentle but firm, and tasted a little like the chocolates they'd shared.

She slid her arms around his back and tipped her head, responding to his kiss. Eager to give herself to the moment and yet edgy-anxious that this couldn't be as new and wonderful as it felt—that in the end, nothing would be different. Because Sloane really wasn't. Couldn't be.

She drew away, ending the kiss. "We should probably head back to the car?"

"Ah, right," Micah murmured, his voice husky. He traced a finger along her face, tipping her chin up again to give her one last, quick kiss. "LA traffic. Work in the morning. Reality is overrated."

"But there's still some chocolate left in the car," Sloane reminded. "For incentive."

"Yes, well . . ." Micah smiled, his thumb brushing her lip. "Nice try. No comparison."

"He'll be back. You should leave," Char insisted, sliding her hands from the gel nail dryer. She glanced at the door, chewing her lower lip. The jittery redhead looked so much younger without her usual heavy makeup. But then, she was probably no more than sixteen. Dabs of concealer dotted her pale forearms, an attempt to hide needle marks. They might as well have been handcuffs. "Vladi might remember you," she warned Zoey. "I don't want anything to happen. Please."

"I'll go. In a minute."

Zoey blinked against the pervasive scent of acetone. The manicurist at the station next to Char's turned on a nail drill. She and Char were both on tight leashes; Stack had called to say his business was taking longer than expected. He told her to get something to eat on her own tonight. He'd sounded distracted, irritable. She met Char's gaze. "I need to know what you've heard. About Oksana and everything that's going on."

Char checked the door again, then leaned over the dryer toward Zoey. "She's still on all those machines. They're thinking maybe she has brain damage."

Zoey's stomach lurched.

"Viktor's hoping it's true." Char checked the door again. "You should really go."

"But what about the rest of the girls? Do you think they're going to move you out of LA?"

"Looks like it, but . . ." Char's teeth tortured her lower lip again. "Some of the girls are talking about getting away first."

"Away?"

"Out. That plan Oksana was working on. There are people who want to help."

Zoey's skin prickled. "Can you trust these people? Who are they?"

"Church folks maybe? I'm not sure. But after Oksana, we're scared that—" Char gasped, staring at the doorway. "Go. Move—it's Vladi. Oh no, too late. He sees you."

———

"Turn here?" Micah slowed the SUV as he approached the corner. "This is your street, right?"

"Yes . . . here." A small halt in Sloane's response said she'd be more comfortable if he let her out to walk the rest of the way. "At the end of the cul-de-sac."

"I remember," Micah said, stealing a glance at her. Nervous, obviously. It hadn't started out that way; in fact, after the kiss—kisses—she'd been the one to reach for his hand on the walk back to the car. They'd made small talk during the drive, but the closer they got to her community, the more she'd begun to perch on the car seat, mention being tired, hint that her house was a mess. It seemed clearer each minute that she wasn't okay with the idea of inviting him in.

"Here we are," Sloane said as Micah slowed to pull into the drive. "I wish I'd bought some coffee."

"No problem," Micah said, braking to a stop. He shifted into park and reached for her hand. "I don't need coffee.

You don't have to entertain me, Sloane. I should get home too."

"Okay." She relaxed with a small, relieved sigh.

Micah thought once again that this lovely woman was unlike so many others he'd dated. He'd hoped she might ask him in, for no other reason than he didn't want the evening to end, but this was okay too. Sloane was worth all the time it took to get to know her.

"Oh, there's my landlady," she said as the main house's motion sensor lights blinked on. "And . . ."

Micah caught a glimpse of the woman. With a man who almost looked like—"Is that guy one of our hospital maintenance staff? Jerry something?"

"Jerry Rhodes," Sloane confirmed, watching them talk on the porch. "He does some work on the side. He's helping Celeste with garden boxes." They'd glanced toward Micah's idling car, still talking. Her brows pinched. "Well, I should probably go in."

"I'll walk you."

"No need. I'm fine."

"All right," Micah told her, getting it. Rhodes was a fellow employee; he didn't seem like the type to spread stories, but the last thing Micah wanted was to make Sloane uncomfortable.

"Thank you," she said, her dark lashes blinking. "The picnic, the view, everything. It was great."

"I think so too." Micah lifted her hand, pressed a light kiss on her fingers. "We should do this again. See more of each other."

She'd turned once more to peer toward her neighbor and Rhodes, who'd begun to walk toward a truck parked close by.

"Thank you, really," Sloane repeated, sliding her hand from his. "Good night, Micah."

"Good night."

He resisted the urge to get out and open her door, certain Sloane wouldn't want that. So he simply watched her hop down from her seat, give a quick wave in the direction of her landlady, then walk toward her door. The porch light switched on as she climbed the steps. She reached into her purse for her keys, then turned and waved. Her smile made his heart turn over. *Oh, man . . .* He was so hooked.

Micah watched her disappear into the house, remembering what she'd said earlier when he'd tried to tell her how special she was. *"It's . . . complicated."* She was wrong. This was very simple: Micah wanted to know everything about her—and he'd make that happen.

———

Sloane closed the door and leaned back against it, her senses still swirling. Micah hadn't even kissed her good night, but just the brush of his lips against her fingers was enough to make her question if her legs could carry her to the porch. Her pulse was still fluttering. It had all been so simple, but crazy romantic. The picnic, the chocolate, that view . . . his kisses. No, nothing simple about Micah Prescott's kisses. But it had been much more.

"You're special, Sloane. I've never met anyone quite like you."

Did he really mean it? And there were the other things he'd said about her being deserving of "more" . . . that he believed everyone had worth in God's eyes.

She couldn't believe she'd talked with Micah about God.

Or about her mother and her stepfather. How was that possible? She'd never shared those things with anyone. Not even Paul, to any real degree. What was it about this man that made her feel so safe?

"I think it's part of God's plan, bringing people together that way. Like you and the poet today."

And like . . . *Micah and me?*

The thought was far too staggering to wrap her mind around. But everything that had seemed impossible, too far out of reach just six months back, was becoming a reality. That she'd survived horrific injuries, been sober since, and found a safe place to live.

She walked into the living room, cautioning herself not to overthink anything. Hope had never been more than the name of a hospital system that cut her paycheck. Regardless, there was still reason to celebrate. She'd navigated a first date without a drop of liquid courage and with her self-respect intact. She had a job where, apparently, people valued her efforts. She had this great house, a silly cat who was always—

"Marty?"

Sloane glanced around the living room, then took a step in the direction of the kitchen. Something was off. Any other time, she could barely get in the door before Marty wrapped himself around her legs, begging to be petted and fed. A rescue cat with a red carpet ego. She loved that about him. "Where are you, guy?"

So strange.

"Marty?" Sloane propped her hands on her hips and scanned the small living space again. He had been perched on the back of the couch in front of the window when she went out to the porch to meet Micah. She'd left the window open to the screen a few inches, like she'd been doing lately, to sort of expand his house cat horizons. . . .

Wait.

Sloane tensed. *Is it possible?*

She climbed onto the couch to inspect the window. The screen was pushed out on one side.

She raced to the door, flung it open, and stepped onto the porch. "Marty!"

No sign of him in the flower bed below the window. She peered at the shadows beyond the porch light and called out again. She looked toward the main house, dark now. Jerry's truck gone. It would waste time to go search for a flashlight. Sloane tried to tell herself her cat was a homebody; he didn't have a hunting instinct beyond laser play; he'd be afraid of a busy street.

"Marty!"

There was a rustle in the area of the darkened side yard and—

"Lose something?"

Sloane's throat closed. *No.*

"Hi, babe."

Paul stepped from the shadows holding her cat.

22

"LUCKY I STOPPED BY." Paul adjusted his grip on the twitchy, wide-eyed cat. Marty's ears flattened as Paul attempted to scratch his chin. "She could have run into the street."

"Give *him* to me." Sloane kept her voice steady despite the fact that her insides had begun to seize. She wasn't sure if it was fury or fear. "Hand over my cat, Paul."

"Well now." Paul smiled the smile she hoped she'd never see again. "That's kind of abrupt. I'm not hearing any 'Thank you, Paul,' or 'Good to see you, Paul.'"

"It isn't." Sloane reached for Marty.

"Not so fast." Paul turned away; there was a backpack slung over his shoulder. "I think I should carry him inside. For safety. I know you don't want anything bad to happen to your cat."

"Give Uncle Phillip some sugar, Angel. . . . Don't tell your mom. Something bad could happen to your cat."

"Let me come in," Paul said. "For a few minutes. That's all. Then I'll go. Promise."

Promise? Paul? Sloane wished she could laugh.

"Five minutes," she said, reminding herself that he was a liar, a player, and a cheat—and one of her biggest mistakes— but he'd never once been physically abusive or violent. On the other hand, this man was totally capable of taking her cat hostage. "Bring him in," she instructed. "Then say what you came to say and go away."

"Yes, ma'am. Anything to please my lady."

Sloane turned and reached for the door handle before Paul's smug smile could register a win.

"This is a first," Coop said, lifting a foil-wrapped chocolate from the dash of Micah's SUV. His grin was as effective as an elbow jab. "And fancy. You don't need to try so hard, buddy—I like you just fine."

"Very funny." Micah shook his head, feeling his neck grow warm. He forced himself to concentrate on the traffic; if he started remembering the taste of those chocolates on Sloane's lips, he'd wind up on someone's bumper. As it was, he didn't want to be here at all. But Coop had sent him an SOS text after his battery died in front of Fatburger, asking Micah to drive him to Pep Boys to get a new one. He gave his friend a sideways glance. "Almost as funny as a guy who limps along in a fifteen-year-old car and won't spring for an auto club membership."

"Addicted to risk," Coop slurred around a mouthful of chocolate. He flicked the rolled candy wrapper at Micah. "And you're avoiding the real question."

"There was a question?"

"Implied. Who's the woman?"

The incriminating warmth flared again. Along with a nudge of anger at Coop's intrusion. Sloane had clearly been uncomfortable with her landlady and Rhodes seeing them together; she wouldn't like him discussing her with Coop. But Micah didn't like the idea of secrets. It felt too much like sliding backward to that lousy, lonely year.

"Back-alley deal?" Coop joked.

"No." Micah shot him a look, a sudden image of Jane Doe making his tone sharper than he'd intended. "It was Sloane Ferrell."

"Seriously? The nurse with fire in her eyes?"

Micah laughed. "That would be the one."

"So," Paul said after Sloane had tucked Marty away in her bedroom. He'd set his backpack on her kitchen table, pulled up a chair. His green eyes flicked over her. "When did you start dressing like a nun?"

She wasn't going to answer him. Marty was safe. She'd cut the extorted five minutes to three, then toss him out. She wouldn't deal with all that was Paul Stryker; it was too much like facing a row of fun-house mirrors. Everything changing, nothing real. Except physically he looked pretty much the same. Clean-cut, smoothly handsome, and cocky-confident, tanned from his months in Mexico and dressed, surprisingly, in casual business attire.

"But you're still gorgeous," Paul added, his gaze lingering on her face in a way that made Sloane remember his touch. "Even with those plain-Jane clothes and . . . that scar there, by your eye. The accident, right? I heard it was a bad one. I was really worried about—"

"Don't," Sloane warned, heat rushing to her face. Was he really going to pretend his dangerous associations hadn't directly led to that horrible event? Self-serving con man. She should have called his bluff and never let him in here. Sloane crossed her arms. "Stop with the phony concern. You're here because you *want* something."

"Ouch." Paul tapped his fist to his chest, feigned a grimace. "You wound me."

"Don't tempt me."

"Okay. I hear you. But please . . ." Paul held her gaze for a moment, his eyes softening. "Sit with me, Sloane. That's all I'm asking."

"I don't have any money, Paul. I know that's why you're here. But I don't have any." She almost smiled, remembering the rooster canister sitting empty exactly where his backpack lay now. "There's nothing to get from me."

"You're wrong, babe." Paul reached for his backpack and slid it closer. "I'm here because I have something for *you*."

Sloane's pulse quickened as he unzipped the pack. He'd never been dangerous . . .

"Your favorite." Paul grinned as he produced a large bottle from the pack. "Tequila. Not that cheap stuff, either. I had to fork over mucho bucks at customs for this. But you're worth it." He twisted the bottle to show the label. "Gran Patrón Platinum, top ten list. Get us some glasses, babe."

"No."

Paul cocked a brow. "Pigs must be flying. You're saying no to tequila?"

"I . . . I don't want any." The quaver in Sloane's voice

proved that, in less than five minutes, Paul Stryker had taught her how to lie again. She did want that tequila; she suddenly wanted anything, expensive or skid-row cheap, that promised to make all of this go away. "I quit drinking."

Paul's eyes widened. "Well, well. Another step through the convent doors. Okay, your loss. But you don't mind if I have a glass."

"I do."

He scraped his fingers through his hair, sighed. "Oh, boy."

"Get out of here," Sloane told him. "I don't want your tequila. I don't want you here. Do you understand?"

"Sure. I'll leave. After I give you what I really came to give you." Paul reached into the backpack again. "You're going to want to sit down for this."

"I'm not buying the drama, Paul. I just want—"

He set two hefty stacks of hundred-dollar bills on the table. Sloane sank onto the chair.

His lips quirked. "I thought that might get your attention."

"What . . . ? How . . . ?"

"Returns on a business investment. I haven't been sitting on my rear end all these months, babe. I'm no Trump, but I've made enough to be comfortable." Paul held her gaze. Then took a slow breath. "I want to pay you back. I know I can't make up for the bad times between us, but at least I can give back what I took—and then some." He thumbed a stack as if it were a blackjack deck. "Money for the ring I should have picked out and paid for. A bigger diamond because you deserved that. Enough to repay those credit cards I ran up. Cash to make up for the hit you took on the sale of your house and—"

"Stop." Sloane stared at the money, struggling to take it in.

Paul laughed. "That look on your face. Makes it all worth

it." He held out one of the stacks, his eyes lighting. "Count it if you want. Toss it in the air. Roll in it. It's all yours."

"I can't," Sloane rasped. "I can't take that money."

"You *can*, babe. You need it. And I need you to take it." Paul glanced at the tequila and sighed. "Man, I sure wish you'd change your mind about that drink. I make a much prettier speech when I'm buzzed."

Sloane almost smiled; she'd bet there was an AA slogan for that one.

"I need you to forgive me." Paul's voice had gone earnest, soft. "I need to show you that I'm a different man now. A better man. I wouldn't treat you the way I did before. I'd make you happy. Really take care of you this time."

"Paul, hold on . . ."

"No," he said, grasping her hand. She'd never seen him look so intense. "Listen, please. I'm putting money down on some beach property in Mexico. You'll love it there, Sloane. You wouldn't ever have to work again." He smiled. "You could put one of those tropical flowers behind your ear and spend every day swimming in the ocean, lying in the sun, and getting an all-over tan. We'd get that scar taken care of too. It would be like all that stuff never happened." He gave a small laugh. "Hey, I'll bet the plastic surgeon could even add some enhancements if you want."

"Enough," Sloane said, reeling with the absurdity of this conversation. She drew her hand back and stood up. "Take the tequila. Take the money. I don't want it."

"C'mon, you can't fool me. I saw that look in your eyes."

"I don't want it," Sloane repeated. "I don't want *you*. The only thing I want is for you to go. And never come back."

She headed for the front door.

Paul packed up his things in silence and met Sloane in the entryway. She didn't look at him as she opened the door. He hefted the backpack and stepped onto the porch. The light switched on.

"It won't work," Paul said, all gentleness gone from his eyes. "Here's the deal: you can change your name and the way you dress, you can even play at being sober, but you're still the same. Anybody who really looks will see that. You're Sloane Wilder. A very beautiful, *very* naughty woman who never learned to draw the line. And never will. You'll do it all again. Go after someone's husband, get sloppy drunk, get yourself fired, and—"

"Go *away*," Sloane hissed. "If you come back, I swear I'll call the police."

"The police?" Paul's laugh was sharp as the glass that scarred her face. "Have them digging around in your past?" He smiled slowly, watching her reaction. "Strike a nerve?"

"It was all *you*," Sloane breathed, despite her rising anxiety. "Not me."

"Right. I forgot." A sneer twisted his lips. "You're just the innocent cereal tycoon." He hiked the backpack over his shoulder. "Well, I can take a hint. Worth a try, but I've got a small fortune that needs enjoying. If you change your mind . . ."

"I won't."

Sloane slammed the door and locked it. Then crossed quickly to the living room to switch off the lamp and latch the window. She'd fix the screen in the morning. If she couldn't do it herself, Celeste would probably have Jerry repair it.

She thought of when Micah pulled into the driveway tonight, how Celeste and Jerry had been there. It was only minutes afterward that she'd discovered Marty missing. And then Paul came out of the shadows.

She sank onto the couch and hugged a pillow, trying to get past the sense of invasion. Questions whirled. How long had he been out there? How did he find her address? Her phone number before that? And where did that money really come from? Paul had been up to his eyebrows in debt and then on the run in Mexico because he'd defaulted on those gambling loans. The calls she'd received from "business partners" trying to locate Paul had been more than frightening; she could only imagine what it had been like to feel the full brunt of their harassment. Paul had been living under that shadow for more than a year.

But now he was back and flush with money from an "investment." Confident, comfortable, and planning a future—with her? It was crazy, out of nowhere. And suspicious. Even if Paul had looked the part of a legitimate businessman, Sloane didn't trust it. She was right to send him away and sever that connection. Be free of him finally.

"The police . . . digging around in your past? Strike a nerve?"

Sloane glanced toward the window, the broken screen. If Paul thought he'd scare her with that threat, he was dead wrong. She was safe now. And he was gone.

"Ahh . . . hear that?" Coop closed the hood of his Honda with one hand, sparing the other for the order of chili cheese fat fries he'd begged off Micah when they returned to the fast-food parking lot. "She's purring like a kitten."

"Considering your history with cat litter, you might want to avoid that comparison. Though with the oil spots you've left in my parking space, maybe it fits."

"Go ahead, disrespect my ride." Coop patted the hood. "She'll do till I'm rolling in the big bucks. I'll buy myself a Tesla. Or maybe just hire a limo to take me from TV interview to TV interview."

"When you replace Anderson Cooper?"

"Has a certain ring to it." The reporter wiped chili from his chin. "Out with the old Cooper, in with the new?"

"Maybe," Micah conceded; he'd never doubt Coop's willingness to do whatever it took to get what he wanted. "If audacity scores points."

"Great stories are the slam dunk, my friend," Coop said. "And I'm all over that. In fact . . . What time is it?"

Micah checked his phone, eager to get out of here. "Almost 10:00; why?"

"Meeting my source."

"The woman from the prison? That's getting to be a habit. Is this more than a work thing?"

"Nah. She's old. Like forty-five. And not my type at all. But . . ." He glanced toward Micah's car. "Got any more of that fancy chocolate?"

Micah stared at him. "Really?"

"Hey, cut me some slack. I'm on to something big with this story. I haven't been on my surfboard in weeks. But playing the angles is totally worth it. And it's not like this is hurting anybody."

———

"There's my boy." Sloane chuckled as Marty reached up and batted at a shower-damp clump of her hair. The yellow eyes fixed on hers as he settled against her sleep shirt, his purr rumbling. She stroked his glossy fur. "You're pretty proud of yourself, aren't you? My handsome escape artist. Testing those nine lives."

It could have been far different, considering her cat's history—he and his littermates shoved into a Save Mart bag and dumped off a pier. Their lives had been worth nothing to some heartless creep.

Sloane winced, remembering the visits she'd made to see him at the animal shelter. Small, runny-eyed, with that weak little meow. His more colorfully marked littermates were adopted one by one, leaving Marty's life ticking toward a kill date. Sloane had felt that way herself back then. Sad, angry, hopeless, scared of tomorrow. But all that was changing now. For Marty and for Sloane.

Her phone buzzed on the arm of the sofa. She reached for it, battling a twinge of anxiety.

Then she laughed aloud at the text's photo. The Hollywood sign, lit up in full color.

Micah's message was short:

You put the stars to shame. Red carpet AND galaxy. Thx.

Sloane closed her eyes, letting the feeling wash over her. Sweet as those foil-wrapped chocolates.

"You're special, Sloane. I've never met anyone quite like you."

Paul was wrong. She wasn't the same and she wouldn't make those mistakes again. She was moving on with her life and becoming a new person. Tomorrow she'd start putting one more part of her old life to rest. With her visit to State Prison.

23

"IT'S COMING TOGETHER," Sloane observed, stopping by the garden on the way to her car. She glanced at the redwood frames with tidy mitered corners and reinforcements. She gave the eager doxies, Gibbs and McGee, each a pat. Then met Jerry's gaze. There was a fine sprinkle of sawdust on his cheek. Or maybe crumbs from his ever-present bag of chips. He'd kept his radio down low but was already at work when Sloane awakened. "You're here early this morning, Jerry."

"Yes, ma'am." A speck of cheesy orange dotted the handyman's front tooth, settling Sloane's speculation about the sprinkles on his face. "Ms. Albright wants to get a fall garden going. I told her I could put in some extra time. Saturdays, Sundays after church. And evenings, after my shift at the hospital."

Evenings like last night. Sloane itched to ask him if he'd seen a man hanging around the guest cottage. But that wasn't a good idea.

"Wife's back in Florida for a while visiting her mom," Jerry explained. "So I have the time."

"Ah." Sloane recalled something Celeste had said. "You're hoping to move your mother-in-law into the hospital's senior housing facility."

"That's right. And . . ." Jerry hesitated. "I'm sort of working on an idea. About the new hospital wing. Something I think might be good." He half shrugged and seemed to decide against saying more. "That's me, I guess. Always thinking on projects."

"And helping people," Sloane heard herself say. "That's you too, Jerry."

"I try," he said, modesty in his voice. He slid the pencil from behind his ear and reached for one of his several rulers before it became McGee's chew toy. "Following the best I can after that other carpenter. Long time ago."

Sloane guessed he meant someone Celeste hired in the past.

"Mighty big work boots to fill there," Jerry added, then grinned. "I said something like that to little Piper and she set me straight right away. She said Jesus *always* wore sandals."

"That other carpenter." "Ah." Sloane had no problem imagining the little girl saying that. With the same confidence she had that her picture was on God's fridge. It must be nice to be that certain about anything. Or that naive.

"You're going in to work?" Jerry asked.

"No, I'm . . . I guess it's more of a project I've been 'thinking on.'"

He nodded. "Helping folks. That's you, too."

Sloane said good-bye and headed for her car. She wished she had even a small certainty that her morning's "project" would help. She still planned to be at the parole hearing, but suddenly it seemed important to meet with her stepfather beforehand. Without the formality—and audience. At the very least, a face-to-face meeting with Bob Bullard would allow her to say, without necessary censorship, things she should have said long ago. The hearing would be the finale. Today was her star performance.

———

"Fill me in?" Micah addressed the LAPD officer after taking a look around the vacant store being used as a safe area. Across the street, firefighters were still attempting to battle the motel blaze that had begun just before dawn. Even here, the air was acrid with the scents of smoke and burning plastic. "How many victims?"

"No confirmed number yet." The young officer tipped his head, listening to his radio for a moment. "Arson squad thinks it was an explosion involving about a half-dozen rooms. Maybe long-term renters. We haven't confirmed that yet either. The manager's not saying much; the motel owner doesn't live in the city—big surprise."

Sex workers. Maybe trafficked? This neighborhood was known for that. Micah thought of Jane Doe. He glanced around the room. A dozen or more survivors, several wrapped in bedspreads, clustered around a table topped by a large coffee dispenser and bottles of water. One woman, with gray hair and a portable oxygen tank, sat apart from the rest, holding a box of tissues.

The officer stepped aside to speak with another, then returned to Micah.

"Three bodies," he said, keeping his voice low. "Young women. Unidentified."

Micah grimaced. "Were there injured sent to the hospitals?"

"A few, I think. Smoke inhalation. Some burns. Panic issues, I guess. Medics took them to LA Hope."

Sloane wasn't working today.

"Thanks," he told the officer. "I'll go see what I can do for these folks. There should be a second crisis volunteer here soon."

"Appreciate it," the man said, his expression confirming that. "Don't know what we'd do without you guys."

"Glad to help," Micah said, gripping the officer's offered hand.

He said good-bye and made a beeline for the woman with the oxygen tank.

Sloane sat in her car, wishing she'd read the State Prison visiting rules a little more carefully. She'd followed the extensive dos and don'ts on attire: no wearing denim or chambray like the prisoners, no dressing in colors that looked like the guards' uniforms, no wigs or hair extensions, no gang-style clothing, no sheer clothing or bare midriffs. Sloane had definitely gotten all that right. She hadn't brought any weapons or other contraband. But she'd misread the visiting hours and arrived half an hour early. And was parked outside the closed gates. Thank goodness she had her phone. For now. She doubted she could take it in.

Sloane closed the Instagram app—her few social media

accounts were fabricated identities—and tapped the search icon. Giving in to curiosity, she searched *By Grace musical group*. Links filled the screen, tumbled onto the next page and the next and the next. She went to the group's website and tapped the photo tab. There were countless images of performances, recording sessions, church appearances, and family gatherings.

Sloane scrolled through them, feeling like a voyeur as she gazed at photos that were clearly scanned in from family snapshots. Grace and Clay Prescott—the uncle's features somewhat similar to Micah's—and their only child, Stephen. A beautiful boy from chubby blond infancy to preschool to baptism and . . . *Oh.* Sloane's heart squeezed. Micah and Stephen. Dozens of images of the cousins together. Toy cars in their hands, fishing poles, bike handlebars. Holding serving ladles at a soup kitchen, wearing Scout uniforms, and playing guitars, faces similar enough to be brothers. Stephen had been amazingly handsome even as a young teen. Micah was equally blond and wholesome, but . . . Sloane smiled at the photos. Nerdy. With that gangly build, braces, and glasses—always trying too hard to look cool. Micah had obviously taken time to grow into his good looks. It couldn't have been easy to be compared with Stephen all those years.

Sloane tapped on an embedded video, watched for a moment, then laughed aloud. It was an amateur clip of a cousins' jam session—complete with Micah's vocal attempts. So serious. And seriously off-key. He hadn't been kidding with the bullfrog comparison.

More photos showed them clowning, competing at sports, proudly showing off a new car, and in more reflective moments, with their hands raised heavenward at a church service. Image after image of Stephen surrounded by raptly attentive fans, Micah standing behind him literally in his shadow. And . . .

Sloane's breath snagged. Memorial service photos. The Prescott family, brothers and wives and adult son, at Stephen Prescott's funeral. So many flowers, so many people. But all Sloane saw was Micah. The pain on his face, the sag of his broad shoulders, and that distant look in his eyes.

She clicked on a newspaper link, skimmed the article about the young singer's auto accident. A collision with a freeway abutment at high speed. The sedan carrying Stephen Prescott, driven by a college classmate, had been demolished, Prescott pronounced dead at the scene.

Sloane's stomach twisted as the following information registered:

> The cause of the accident that killed Christian
> music star Stephen Prescott was found to be alcohol
> related. A sample of blood taken from the driver
> showed a blood alcohol level far exceeding the
> legal limit . . . driver has pleaded guilty to vehicular
> manslaughter . . .

A car horn beeped beside her.

"Have a great visit, girl!" The driver smiled from her lowered window and pointed to indicate the prison gates sliding open.

Sloane put the Volvo into gear, trying to swallow a queasy wave of truth. Micah's cousin had been killed by a drunk. An irresponsible, thoughtless, selfish drunk.

Someone like me.

"Those girls," the elderly woman said, a paper cup of coffee trembling in her hands. "Did they get out?"

"I don't have details," Micah told her despite what he'd heard from the officer; a crisis volunteer's job was to support survivors, offer resources, and listen. Above all, listen. Essie Malone needed all of that. "You're a guest at the motel?"

"Guest?" A phlegmy chuckle escaped Essie's lips. "That almost makes it sound like I'd see chocolates on my pillow. Or at least a clean pillowcase once in a while." She touched the plastic oxygen tubing in her nose, then drew in a wheezy breath. "Yes. I stay at the Value Inn. Been there for coming on a year. It's all I can afford if I want to eat too. And it's close to my medical."

Micah made a mental note to be sure she was hooked up to senior resources. And he'd better check that she'd been looked over by the medics.

"It's not Leisure World by a long shot, but I get by," Essie continued. "Folks come and go, but I get to know a few. At least their faces. Like the girls. And those brutes who pick up the tab for their rooms." Her lips pinched, making them go grayish. "Those girls are just children. Scrub their faces and you'd see schoolkids—except they're at the Value Inn, not school. And what are they learning? That they're only worth what somebody will pay." She drew in another raspy breath as tears filled her eyes. "I . . . heard them screaming in the fire. Those poor girls."

Help me help her, Lord.

"Here . . ." Micah scooted his chair closer and offered a tissue. He'd have to let the police officers know that this woman might have valuable information. But for right now . . .

"Thank you," she said, resting a tremulous hand on his sleeve. "I don't have anybody. It's good to talk a little. It helps. But I won't keep you any longer." She glanced across the room. "So many people. I'm sure you need to be somewhere else."

"Right now I'm exactly where I need to be. With you." Micah put his hand over hers. "Let's see what we can do to help you get through this, Essie."

———

Waiting seemed to be the key word here. Sloane frowned at her thought, considering that guards held the keys and most of the men in this prison had been waiting for years. For some reason, she thought of Jocelyn. Even six months behind bars would be awful.

"Mr. Bullard is on his way down," a prison staffer said, passing by where Sloane sat at a corner visitors' table. Maybe four or five other inmates sat at scattered tables with wives, girlfriends, a few children, their visits strictly supervised. "Should be any minute," the woman assured.

"Any minute."

Sloane's stomach tensed. It was easy to imagine him walking past rows of cells, tall, muscular, with that ramrod-straight posture, square jaw, thick hair cropped into the old military cut. Eyes narrowed, always looking for an error, a punishable infraction. He excelled at that. But now *he* was being punished, Bulldog Bullard being read the rules, expected to unquestioningly comply—"no back talk, no excuses, no sassy smirk." How would he have reacted to that reversal of roles, all these years? By becoming dominant in the prison yard? Using his confidence and well-honed strategies to influence the staff?

Or had there been times when Sergeant Bullard lost his commanding self-composure, gave in to his tightly controlled anger, and lashed out? Like that moment in the garage when he slapped Sloane's face. Or that night . . . *when he killed my mother*. How angry had he been that night? What kind of monster—?

"Sloane. . . . Long time."

24

SLOANE STARED, oblivious to the guard's last-minute directives. They'd made a mistake. This wasn't—

"Have a seat, Bullard," the guard instructed, then glanced at Sloane. "Unless you want to stand up, ma'am, for a quick hug?"

"No," Sloane blurted, hearing her stepfather echo the same. She clasped her hands together on the tabletop, struggling to get her mind around it. Trying to control sudden shivers, catch her breath.

"Thank you for coming," her stepfather began, taking a chair opposite her. "I wasn't expecting that."

His voice was different. He sounded and looked *small*. As if over the years he'd shrunk or aged until he was an artist's conception of who he'd be at eighty or ninety. Bob Bullard would be only around fifty-five. Still, he looked frail, his shoulders stooping beneath the blue prison shirt, neck thin, hair sparse and gray. His complexion was sallow, and his eyes . . .

"You look fine," he said, connecting with her gaze. "Grown-up. A lot like . . ."

Sloane stiffened. If he dared utter her mother's name, she swore she'd—

"Like I thought you might look," he finished. He swallowed, the action making his thin neck resemble a snake gulping a mouse. "I know I look different. Hardly recognize myself anymore after the chemo. For prostate," he added, likely reading the question in Sloane's eyes. "Being a nurse, you probably know all about that."

"Why did you want to see me?"

"Direct. Always." His fleeting smile wrinkled the skin around his eyes. "I liked that about you."

Prison had taught him to lie. Obviously.

"You stood up to me," her stepfather said, running his fingers through his remnants of hair. "Tough little girl dressed in black head to toe, like you were on some Special Forces mission." A rueful expression flickered across his gaunt face. "You were, I guess. From the first day I moved in."

"Look," Sloane said after glancing toward the supervising staff. "Your letter said it was important to talk to me."

"Sorry," he said, tapping his forehead. "I get scattered sometimes from the meds. Yes, I wanted to talk with you, Sloane. I have a reason."

She struggled against a sudden wave of dizziness, the scent of motor oil, of car parts soaking in naphtha solvent, cold concrete under her bare feet. That night in the garage when she'd finally found the nerve to confront this awful man with everything that had been festering in her heart for so many years. Finally tell her mother's husband exactly what she thought. And now she'd do it again. . . .

"Let me spare you the spiel," she said, refusing to tremble. "I'm *not* going to help you get an early release. In fact, I plan to stand up at the hearing and give a list of reasons you should be spending *another* ten years behind bars." Her voice broke, betraying her. How could her eyes burn from a memory? Every breath smelled like solvent. Her feet were cold. "If you thought that seeing you looking sick would make me take pity—"

"I didn't." He spread his hands, a motion that almost made him look like he was receiving Communion. "I don't expect that of you. I don't expect anything, Sloane."

"Then why?" A thought occurred to her, more sickening than the intrusive scent. "You're seriously asking me to *forgive* you? For killing my mother?"

He closed his eyes. Swallowed again.

"Is that it?" Sloane asked, lowering her voice after she saw the supervisor watching them. "Is that what you want?"

"I'm not expecting forgiveness." There was the unmistakable sheen of tears in his eyes. "And I'm not going to try to argue my innocence. I wasn't innocent, Sloane. I didn't hold your mother under the water. I didn't do that. But . . ."

Sloane's throat closed.

"I left her alone when it wasn't safe. I let my frustration and my angry, stubborn need to control . . . I let it destroy everything." Bob Bullard's voice cracked. "You don't love that way. You don't raise a child like that. Your mother deserved so much more. She was fragile, troubled by things in her past I knew nothing about."

Sloane stared. Her mother never told him? About her father? About Sloane's abuse?

"*. . . only as sick as your secrets.*"

"I should have made her feel safe enough to share those troubles with me," Bullard continued. "I should have listened more, gotten her help instead of trying to make her 'shape up.' I should have taken her to church. I should have done all that for her daughter, too." He folded his hands, glanced down at them for a moment. "That night, in the garage—I've gone over it a thousand times. I shouldn't have hit you, Sloane. I should never have reacted that way to the things you said. I should have asked myself why. Why you felt that way. You were still a child, and I should have been a much better man."

What?

Sloane didn't know how to handle this. Her plan had been to make *him* listen. Cut this awful man off at the knees, rail at his self-righteous and all-controlling attitude, tell Bulldog Bullard exactly what she thought about the evil thing he'd—

"You don't know how many times I wished I'd died instead of her," her stepfather said. "I'd give anything if she'd lived long enough to get healthy and happy. So she could be there for you. Back then and now that you're a grown woman yourself. A woman needs her mother all her life."

Sloane's heart lugged.

"It's funny," he said, "this time behind bars has made me slow down long enough to do some thinking, some reading . . . and praying." Something in his voice had changed. "Lots of praying. I know now that we were all forgiven a long time ago. By grace. It's like I've been carrying a hundred-pound rucksack all my life, getting more and more crippled by the weight of it. And then I finally find I can put it down." There was a look in his eyes Sloane had never seen. Like a light blinked on. "I can't really say it the way I want to. But I keep trying, every chance I get. So many people need that help, Sloane. They need to know they have value, that there's hope no matter their pasts and current situation. There's no better proof than the kind of company Jesus kept. Liars, thieves, outcasts . . ." He turned his head to gaze around the visitors' room. "Sometimes I even think my being here is part of a bigger plan. That it was meant to be."

"Meant to be"?

Sloane had no idea where he was going. She was talking with a stranger. Maybe this was an effect of the chemo?

"I guess that sounds nuts," her stepfather said, that light still in his eyes, "but I think I was supposed to be here, learning what I have. Helping folks as best I can. Like you having that time with your godparents. And your mother's insurance making it possible for you to go to college and become a nurse."

"Wait . . ." Sloane bristled, finally finding some traction. "Are you saying that it was a *good* thing my mother died?"

"No, *no.*" He hunched forward. "Never. I'd give anything if she hadn't, Sloane." Her stepfather groaned. "I'm sorry. *That's* why I wanted you to come. To tell you I'm so very sorry."

"Don't." She closed her eyes, sickened. She'd heard him say the same words at the trial and didn't let it faze her. Despite all he'd said today, nothing had changed. Even if he'd tried to snatch at her heart, she recognized a con man when she saw one. Paul Stryker knew how to say all the right words too.

"I won't forgive you," Sloane said, rising to her feet. "I can't."

"I understand. But I needed to—"

"Don't bother," Sloane said, loudly enough to catch a

staff person's attention. "I don't care what you need. I only care about what *I* need—for you to stay in prison where you belong."

"Problem here, ma'am?" the staffer asked, glancing between them.

"No," Sloane said. "Not anymore. I'm leaving. Get me out of here."

She left the visitors' room with an escort, endured the checkout process, and finally passed through the last of the doors, all of it in a blur. Coming here had been a huge mistake; she'd accomplished nothing. She'd never recited the long list of reasons her stepfather didn't deserve to breathe the same air as decent people, let alone be released two years early. All she'd accomplished was following Bulldog Bullard's orders once again, to sit there and listen to him. It had always been all about him. It didn't matter that he was sick and looked different, that he claimed to have found God, or even that he admitted he'd handled everything wrong during the years he'd lived with them. It was a new tactic but the same man.

Sloane stopped beside her Volvo, losing a battle to tamp down the anger and confusion. It was there again, the unnerving scent of motor oil and naphtha. Her words that night, his surreal acceptance of them now. Why had she believed seeing Bob Bullard one-on-one would help in any way? Maybe it had been a stupid idea, but she wasn't going to let today derail her. She'd regather her thoughts, make solid notes, and then stand up at that parole board meeting and in a firm voice—

"Sloane?"

She glanced up, saw a man standing beside an old car parked a few spaces away. Young, curly blond hair, scruff of beard growth. He looked faintly familiar.

"Sloane Ferrell, right?" he asked, taking a step in her direction. "From LA Hope?"

She hesitated.

"Cooper Vance," he said with an engaging grin. "We met a while back. When you broke up that kidnapping attempt in the ER parking lot."

Great. The obnoxious reporter. Just what she needed.

"Small world." He glanced toward the prison gates. "Both of us spending a Saturday—"

"I need to be going," Sloane said, cutting him off. "Have a good one."

"Sure. You too."

Sloane had been home barely ten minutes when Jerry rang the doorbell. He was holding a huge shipping carton.

"Oh, hi." He shifted the box in his arms. "I didn't want to disturb you, but I wasn't sure if it was safe to leave this on the porch." He glanced down at the box. "It says General Mills, but . . ." His expression looked sheepish. "None of my business. Sorry."

"It's okay," Sloane told him, grateful this one thing was less complicated than the rest of her last twelve hours. "It's cereal. I was expecting a shipment. But they don't usually come on weekends."

"One of those local delivery vans," Jerry said, nodding toward where it still idled at the curb end of Celeste's driveway. "The delivery person asked if I'd take it. It looked like she was in a hurry. I said I was glad to help."

"The main house is the mailing address," Sloane explained. "Hardly anyone knows I live back here," she added, then realized it wasn't really true anymore. *Jerry, Micah . . . Paul.* "Anyway, thanks. It saves Celeste from having to lug it down here."

"And now you have your Lucky Charms," he said, pointing at the brightly colored leprechaun on the side of the box. "My wife and I are scrambled-eggs-and-bacon folks. Grits too, sometimes." He tapped the leprechaun. "I'd forgotten about these."

Wish I could . . .

"You want me to bring the box in for you?" Jerry offered. "It's kind of heavy."

"No problem. I can manage," Sloane said, taking it from him. It was heftier than usual. Extra samples probably. "Thanks again, Jerry."

"Watch out for Marty. He's right behind you."

"I will. Thank you."

Sloane nudged her cat aside and carried the shipment box to the pantry closet. She'd make time later to move it to the bottom of the stack, for freshness' sake. Which was ridiculous, considering how few times she ever really ate any.

"Are you, like, a food hoarder?"

Sloane gave the box a kick to scoot it the rest of the way in, then attempted to slide the pantry door over it. It hung up halfway, so she kicked the box again. Harder. When the door still wouldn't close, Sloane got down on her hands and knees and shoved the box, both hands flattened against the grinning leprechaun's face. It wouldn't budge, and then she saw the problem: it didn't quite match up with the other boxes lengthwise. It might even be an older box. It looked a little worn. Sloane rolled her eyes. The cereal company was recycling boxes. Next it would be the cereal itself—sending her the broken bits, misshapen pieces, and color goofs. So much for the glamour of a grand prize.

This is what you won, baby. For your whole life—that's quite a net worth.

Sloane sat back on her heels, holding in unwelcome tears. It had been such a pile-on of lousy moments since last night. Marty missing, Paul showing up, and then that awful, nonsensical conversation with Bob Bullard. If it weren't for the fact that she was six months into her AA recovery, it would feel like she'd never left Sloane Wilder behind. As if, even with all those efforts to claw her way out of the dark hole of her old life, nothing had really changed at all.

Her phone rang in her pocket and Sloane stood, pulled it out. Her heart leaped.

"Hey," she said, accepting Micah's call. "What's up?"

"Just needed to hear your voice."

The husky sound of his made her stomach dip. She leaned against the kitchen wall. Micah needed her.

"You're on call today?" she asked, finding her breath. "With the crisis team?"

"Yeah. I'm still at a callout for the motel fire. Did you see it on the news?"

"No. I didn't get to the news yet today." *Too busy battling the old stuff.*

"Sounds like a better plan," Micah said. "Skip the news. On your day off, you deserve only good things."

Sloane blinked against tears again, a whole different kind.

"Anyway . . ." Micah's sigh warmed her ear. "I'm taking some extra call for one of the other responders, so I won't be finished until late. And you work tomorrow morning? Your split weekend?"

"Yes," Sloane confirmed, letting herself hope this was headed where it sounded like it was. "Day shift."

"I'm at church till noon."

Sloane thought of that image on the Prescott website, Micah at his cousin's funeral. She pushed it down, not wanting anything to spoil this moment.

"I'd like to take you to dinner," he said over the distant sounds of sirens. "Tomorrow night. Somewhere nice. With a table, not a tailgate."

She laughed, tempted to say she couldn't imagine anything nicer.

"It's late notice, I know. Again," Micah added, his soft groan apologetic. "Next time I'll get it right, I promise."

"That's fine," Sloane breathed. *Next time . . . promise . . .* Beautiful words.

"So," Micah finished, "pick you up tomorrow evening around six thirty?"

"I'll be ready," she told him, not sure if it was entirely true. She wasn't sure she was ready for any of this. Especially the way she'd begun to feel lately. She *needed* there to be a next time; she *needed* to finally know a promise kept. Sloane suddenly needed those things more than anything she'd ever thirsted for. "Six thirty is fine."

"Great. I'll see you then."

They disconnected and Sloane stood there for a few moments, corralling her senses. Then she got back down on the floor and took hold of the oversize shipping carton, twisting it to a sideways position that fit the closet's depth—and hid the faded but grinning face of the leprechaun. She closed the pantry doors, stood again, and brushed dust from her hands.

"You deserve only good things."

She'd been wrong to think that nothing had changed. Everything was changing for the better. Micah Prescott was proof of that.

25

"THE INVESTIGATORS finally released her photo," Sloane noted as Harper looked up from the newspaper spread between them on the table outside the ER. The SICU staff had done what they could to make Jane Doe appear less ghastly, with minimal success. "I guess they were trying to identify her by that recent surgical incision, but no luck. I knew they'd have to go public at some point."

"Right." Harper frowned. "Especially when she finally scribbled some words in, like, Russian?"

"That's not certain," Sloane said, recalling what she'd heard via the hospital grapevine: the girl had scrawled something that looked foreign. The news hadn't reported it. "I guess one of the night housekeepers speaks a Russian dialect. But she wasn't sure what Jane wrote. They'll have to bring an official interpreter in."

"My money's on an FBI translator." Harper set her juice bottle down. "The Feds are already involved because of the tattoos. It totally smacks of human trafficking."

"It does," Sloane agreed, a prickle of anxiety rising.

"Especially after that motel fire yesterday." Harper grimaced. "They're going to have to wait for dental records on those poor girls."

When Sloane finally saw the TV coverage last night, she'd understood why Micah said to skip the news. It was awful, tragic, and her first thought was of Zoey Jones. She'd tried to ignore it, reminding herself she hadn't seen Zoey's complete tattoo. She told herself the girl was streetwise and had learned to land on her feet. When the nagging worry refused to die, Sloane picked up the phone and called the YMCA in Bakersfield. It had been closed for lack of funding. The nearest Y was in Visalia, seventy-eight miles away. The next was in Miramonte, then Lancaster, Valencia, and on down to Santa Barbara. Sloane called every one within a hundred miles of Bakersfield. None had an employee or even a volunteer named Zoey.

She glanced at Jane Doe's grim photo on the newspaper page, wishing she'd thought to give Zoey her phone number. Then she caught herself, nearly groaning aloud at the truth: the girl stole surgical instruments from the ER, then scored a thousand dollars from Sloane. Why was she beating herself up for not helping Zoey more? She could well imagine what people would think if they knew she'd willingly fed and sheltered someone capable of all that.

"*. . . no better proof than the kind of company Jesus kept. Liars, thieves, outcasts.*"

Sloane dismissed the unwelcome memory of Bob Bullard's words. This wasn't about God's grace or some kind of woo-woo prison revelation. She was simply concerned for a troubled kid.

"Sloane?"

She blinked, turned to Harper. "Sorry. What?"

"You're being waved at." Harper looked toward the doors to the ER. "Cooper Vance."

Sloane acknowledged the reporter with a reluctant nod, then watched him disappear inside the building. It made her uncomfortable. "What's he doing here?"

"Probably nosing around about Jane Doe. The PIO's been fielding inquiries from media since early morning. One of the SICU nurses said some female reporter caught her in the cafeteria and tried to give her a business card. Asked her to call if any family showed up for Jane Doe." Harper raised her brows. "How do you know that guy?"

"Don't really," Sloane said, wishing he'd never spotted her in the prison parking lot. If she'd tolerated her stepfather for a few minutes longer, they'd have missed each other. "He probably remembers me giving him a hard time in the parking lot that day."

"Oh, right. That business with our AWOL kidnap victim. I wonder how things worked out for her."

Me too.

"Anyway," Harper said, gathering up the newspaper and remains of her lunch, "he's probably looking to pester some staff too. Or meet up with Micah."

"Micah?" Sloane's pulse quickened the way it had when she'd received a text from him an hour ago. He rarely came in on Sundays but had offered to help the PIO run any necessary interference with media after the Jane Doe announcement. "You mean Vance would want to question him?"

"Maybe. Or just hang out. They're friends." Harper raised her bottle, drained the last of her juice. "From way back, I guess. Someone said they went to college together."

———

"I thought you'd be lurking around the SICU waiting room," Micah said as Coop finished off one of Fiona's persimmon cookies. "Bribing nurses."

"Not my style."

"Right. Tell me another one."

"Besides, I'm much more interested in what happened at that motel." Coop raised a brow. "Stuff the cops aren't reporting. The sort of details that volunteers on scene might overhear?"

Micah frowned. He was fast approaching the end of his rope with this guy. "You know me better than that."

"There's always a chance I'll catch you at a weak moment." Coop shook his head. "Okay. Snowball's chance in—"

"I thought your new source was keeping you busy," Micah dodged, knowing Coop would be frothing at the mouth to know what Essie Malone might be telling the investigators right about now. The elderly motel resident had seen young girls and their handlers come and go for months. "You said your idea was to work the story backward from Jane Doe to organized crime in LA and points farther north. Connect the dots?"

"I'm doing that. I was at State Prison just yesterday morning to take my source out for breakfast after her night shift. And maybe find out who might be visiting our Russian boss. I'm making good progress. Hey—" his brows lifted—"I saw your nurse there."

"Who?"

"Sloane."

"She was at the breakfast place?"

"No. The prison."

Micah's breath stuck. *What?*

"Visiting an inmate," Coop said, toying with a paperweight on Micah's desk. "Some dude up for parole."

"Her stepfather," Micah confirmed for no other reason than to derail any impending Cooper Vance "gotcha" jab. "He's serving a sentence there. I knew that." *So back off.*

"Twelve years for manslaughter. Hoping for an early release at ten. According to what I heard, he looks good for it."

"Your source told you all that?" Micah asked, torn between an urge to call the prison and have the woman fired and another to seriously lay into Coop for invading Sloane's privacy. "You asked and she just looked it up?"

"No HIPAA laws there." Coop's casual tone said he had no clue as to Micah's irritation. "Visitor logs fall under the California Public Records Act. Though . . ." The paperweight slid off the desk, and he stooped to retrieve it. His gaze met Micah's as he returned the object to its place. "It wasn't that easy to find. They had Sloane listed under two names: Wilder first, then Ferrell. She changed it." Coop shrugged. "You probably knew that, too."

"I've got it," Harper said, reaching for a second bag of IV fluid. She smiled down at the expectant mother, four months pregnant and just beginning to show. Things were crazy in the OB department, so they were getting started in the ER. "We're watering you like a ficus tree in the California drought. I'm betting your veins will make slurping noises."

"Found it," Sloane reported, holding the Doppler in place over the forty-two-year-old's gently rounded abdomen. She adjusted the volume so the woman could hear. And breathe finally—classic first-time-mother worry. "Your baby's heartbeat. Hear it?"

"Oh . . . yes. It sounds good, right?"

"Loud and clear." Sloane's heart tugged as tears filled the woman's eyes.

"Thank you," she breathed, a tear escaping. Her gaze swept toward the ceiling of the ER exam room. "I'm so grateful, Lord."

"Your doctor's ordered an ultrasound," Sloane continued, handing her a tissue. "As an added measure of safety. They'll do that in OB when we roll you down there. We're getting started on replacing the fluids you've lost with the vomiting. We can handle that right here, no problem."

"Yes, ma'am." Harper winked, then pulled up the cotton blanket as Sloane lifted the Doppler away. "The medicine your doctor ordered will lessen the nausea. Perfectly safe. I just gave you a first dose through the IV. That's why you're feeling sleepy."

"I . . . am . . . a little," the woman admitted, her palms spreading protectively over the blanketed mound that was her growing child. "It's better. But I think the best medicine was hearing my baby's heartbeat. Our daughter . . ." Her drooping lids fluttered open again and she smiled. "We found out last week that we're having a girl."

Harper offered a thumbs-up.

"I didn't think I'd ever have a child," the woman continued. "Because of my age. And because I haven't always been responsible with my health. Or my lifestyle. I made a lot of mistakes." Her lids closed again and she sighed. "This . . ." Her thumbs stroked the blanket. "This is my second chance. A blessing and a miracle. A beautiful miracle. She's worth every miserable moment I've spent hunched over that porcelain—" A small laugh escaped her lips. "I was sort of going for Hallmark card until that bit about bathroom fixtures. Tell me it's the meds."

"Definitely," Sloane assured, then reached into her scrub pocket as her phone buzzed. She read the text, glanced at their patient. "And now it looks like you have a visitor."

"My husband?" the woman asked, raising her head from the pillow. "He's finally here?"

"Yes, ma'am. They're sending him back. He should be here any min—"

A rap on the exam room door said he'd set a new record.

"We'll let Dad in and scoot ourselves out." Harper smiled. "This is family time."

They gave the worried husband a quick, reassuring update, then headed back toward the nurses' station.

"I don't mind helping OB out at all," Harper said as they settled in front of the computers. "They get a bigger slice of happy than we do most of the time."

"They do," Sloane agreed, thinking of the woman's reaction when she heard her baby's heartbeat.

This is my second chance. . . . I made a lot of mistakes. . . ."

"Hallmark," Harper added, chuckling. "That was cute. Actually, it could be a pretty funny card, considering how many women have problems with—"

"Hey there." Micah arrived at the desk. Still dressed for church probably: checked button-down shirt, slacks, hair neatly combed, and that same woodsy scent . . .

"Oh, hi," Sloane said, hoping Harper's similar greeting hid the foolish breathlessness in hers.

Micah smiled at Harper, then held Sloane's gaze for a fraction of a moment longer. "Well," he said, giving the desktop a quick tap, "I'm heading home."

"Okay," Sloane said, feeling as idiotic as she sounded.

He patted the desk once more, nodded at Harper, and then strode away.

Sloane tapped the computer keys, almost wishing the air would wail with code 3 sirens. *Oh, please, Harper, don't ask me . . .*

"What was that all about?"

"What do you mean?" Sloane made herself look at Harper.

"Since when does the assistant director of PR and marketing report off duty to *you*? He didn't even have a handful of Face of Hope nomination forms."

"Um . . ." *Sirens. Please.*

"Oh, wait a minute," Harper said, her toothpaste grin spreading. "Because Micah's hoping—"

"He's taking me to dinner," Sloane admitted, ending it. Or beginning it. She wasn't sure. She only knew that for some crazy reason she wanted to share. It was a completely foreign feeling. She probably shouldn't risk it but . . . "Tonight. Some place called Geoffrey's."

Harper's eyes widened. "In Malibu?"

"I guess," Sloane said, glancing around the nurses' station. She lowered her voice. "He said it's on the beach."

"Malibu," Harper said with a decisive nod. "Oh, my goodness. He's taking you to Geoffrey's for a first date?"

Sloane started to say it wasn't the first, but admitting to a tailgate picnic at the Hollywood sign would send her over the edge. And reality was setting in regarding something else entirely. "I have nothing to wear."

"What time tonight?"

"Six thirty."

"Hmm." Harper's brows puckered. "We're out of here in an hour, but traffic would kill us if we tried to go shopping."

Shopping? Sloane stared at her, the tack of this conversation impossible to take in. Only a short while back she'd balked at sharing a happy hour cookie with Harper. She couldn't remember a single time in her life she'd gone clothes shopping with a girlfriend.

"We can handle this," Harper said, her tone as certain as if she were reaching for defibrillator paddles. "You'll follow me home. I'll loan you some things."

"Wha-at?" Sloane choked on a laugh. "Are you serious? Look at us. Do I look like I could wear your clothes?"

"No worries." Harper gave her hand a warm squeeze. "I've got this covered. Trust me."

And *then* the sirens came.

According to the radio, two victims from a family reunion gone wrong. One assault victim with a fractured jaw, another with a knife wound to the thigh, and a great-grandmother who'd witnessed the brawl now complaining of crushing chest pain. Three patients with differing treatment modalities requiring a variety of equipment and unique skills. No problem. Sloane could handle it; the last hour of her shift would fly by. She was relieved to be on familiar ground again.

It was how she'd handle the rest of the evening that had her guessing.

26

"YOU LOOK AMAZING," Micah told her as tiny white lights from the deck's trees danced over the shoulders of the sports jacket he'd paired with nice jeans. "Or did I already mention that?"

"Once or twice." Sloane's skin warmed under his gaze.

Micah couldn't know that the "amazing" part had come much earlier when Harper, like a fairy godmother, pulled a half-dozen dress options from her guest room closet. Most with designer labels, some with dangling price tags, and all so much nicer than anything Sloane had ever worn. Apparently Harper's former roommate, a physical therapist about Sloane's size, had been a maniac when it came to Fashion Center clearance sales. A passion gone wild to the point of stowing shoes in the apartment's under-oven drawer. Last spring the roommate backpacked around Ireland, fractured her ankle on the steps of Blarney Castle . . . and fell in love with her widowed orthopedic surgeon. She was currently auditioning harpists for a traditional Celtic wedding. Her new lifestyle, she'd told Harper in a Skype call, would require far more corduroy, sweaters, caps, wellies, and rain gear—and virtually nothing that was crammed into her Southern California closet. She blissfully flashed her engagement ring and asked her former roommate to mail a few key items, then "do whatever you want with the rest." Which tonight allowed Sloane Ferrell to look amazing at Geoffrey's in Malibu.

"I can't get over this place," she said, giving the floral jersey sheath a discreet tug as she shifted in her basket chair. Her gaze swept across stone-tiled decking dotted with wicker tables and tubs of ficus trees. Towering palms, leafy trees, and lush hedges glittered with tiny white lights and offered privacy for diners. There were gas fire pits, deck heaters, and each glass-topped table sported a candle and small pot of flowers. It was a perfect blend of cozy and elegant, and a mix of contemporary Southern California architecture: rough-hewn stone pillars interspersed with tall rectangles of sparkling glass and long stretches of creamy white metal railings overlooking more dining niches below. It created a sense that they were shipboard, made even more believable by the fact that Malibu beach and the Pacific Ocean stretched beyond them as far as the eye could see. The sun had dropped low, frosting the sand with pink, and . . . Sloane turned back to Micah, swallowing against a swell of emotion. "I don't think I've ever been anywhere so nice."

"It's always been a family favorite," he said with a fleeting bittersweet look. "I'm glad I could share it with you. Special place . . . special lady."

Sloane told herself to believe that, to put away the memories of dates with Paul where *special* meant free drinks, comped rooms at off-strip Vegas casinos, and constant coaching to "flirt with the high rollers and see where that takes us, babe." It had never taken Sloane anyplace she wanted to go. Not one single time.

She hated gambling. Not so much out of a sense that it was sinful; it was more that she didn't believe you could get something for nothing. Everything had a price and life was risky enough without betting on it. Still, she'd go with Paul, bring a stash of hand wipes and a bottle of Visine to combat the damage from cigarette smoke, then start drinking early . . .

Sloane drew in a breath of ocean air, cleansing her mind of the memories. Tonight, here—in this dress and with this man—she really could feel special. There was no reason to worry that the past would be served up like tainted leftovers.

"Ah, here we go," Micah said as the waiter settled their plates in front of them. "I hope you're hungry."

"I am." She wasn't sure she'd ever been so hungry. For exactly this, even if there wasn't a scrap of food. Her nervous doubts and jitters about her old life were giving way to the most delicious sense of safety.

"You're a seafood fan." Micah let his fork hover over his Kobe steak as he glanced at her choices: golden beet salad with tangerine vinaigrette and grilled Pacific swordfish. "There are some great fish places in San Diego. You must have enjoyed your time there."

Enjoyed?

Sloane tensed, the irony hitting as hard as a just-hooked marlin. Enjoyed running, hiding? Being the hospital pariah, a despised "other woman," and finally the trauma victim no one wanted to care for? Great seafood had never factored into those sorry months. If she were to be honest, she'd have to say that the city pound, Marty's sweet face peering from a dirty cage, had been her only joy in San Diego. But she couldn't say any of that.

"Sure." Sloane dredged up a smile, reached for her iced mango tea. "Great city. Incredible food."

"Well . . ." Something in Micah's eyes said he'd seen right through her. Mercifully, he didn't question it. He pointed his fork toward her plate. "Let's see how Malibu compares."

———

Clearly he'd said something wrong, Micah told himself as they exited the restaurant later. Their dinner conversation had been casual, sprinkled with light laughter, and ran toward hospital stories, current events, and football—Niners vs. Chargers. Safe subjects, he supposed; she'd seemed to direct it that way. His comment about San Diego should have been safe too. But the way Sloane stiffened, that look in her beautiful eyes, hinted there was something she wasn't saying.

"They had Sloane listed under two names: Wilder first, then Ferrell."

At first he'd told himself it was none of his business and it didn't matter. But after Coop left his office, curiosity got the best of Micah. He'd pulled up the staff files and—

"Which one?" Sloane asked.

"Which?"

"There." She pointed toward the sleek, highly polished cars lined up by the valets. "Lamborghini, Maserati, Aston Martin?" The playful light was back in her eyes, the same violet-blue color, Micah noticed, as the dress she was wearing. Great dress. Sleeveless, V-neck, the length revealing a modest but very attractive stretch of leg. It fit like it had been made for her.

"It's not every day you see something like that," Sloane added.

"No . . . it isn't." He let his gaze linger a little longer before glancing at the cars. "I can't decide. I'll have to trust your judgment."

"Mine?" Sloane laughed. "You saw my ride. Classic Volvo. Six pounds of stickers on the bumper."

"Which one is yours?"

"The stickers?"

"Yeah," Micah said, suddenly needing one more insight. One clue to who this woman really was. "NRA? Greenpeace? 'Beam me up, Scotty'?"

Wilder, Ferrell?

Her lips quirked. "I'm not sure what to think about a man who stares at a woman's bumper."

He laughed and fought an impulse to draw her close, his concerns for the moment put on hold. He liked this feisty side of her. "Not a member of the NRA?"

"Nope."

He spoke with the valet, and when he turned back, there was a faraway look in Sloane's eyes. "The Volvo's a pre-owned car," she said. "I was just glad to find one I could afford, social commentary or not. There wasn't much choice. My other car was a VW. It was totaled in an accident. In San Diego."

"Whoa," Micah murmured, noting her small flinch; she hadn't meant to let that last geographical detail slip. It could explain her earlier reaction when he mentioned the coastal city. "Were you hurt or—?"

"There's your car," Sloane said, cutting him off. "The valet's driving up."

"Great." Micah stepped to the curb, thinking he'd discovered yet another touchy subject. The nagging sense of concern returned. He'd bet money her Volkswagen never saw a bumper sticker. For some reason, Sloane Ferrell kept a pretty tight lid on her personal life . . . and her secrets?

"I'm sorry," Micah told Sloane as he slid into the driver's seat a few minutes later. He'd stood outside the car to respond to a text message. "A friend's heading out of town for a few days and wants me to take care of some things."

"Plant sitting?"

"I wish." Micah grimaced. "Let's just say cat litter is involved."

Sloane laughed, grateful for the tension release. Why had she mentioned the accident? Stupid, stupid.

"I get that," she said, covertly enjoying the contrast of crisp white shirt cuff against suntanned wrist as he put the car into gear. "Must be a good friend."

"That might be up for debate. But it's for his grandmother. And his last-minute trip is for work. I've learned the hard way that trying to talk sense into a journalist hot on a story trail is like stepping in front of a train. Plus, I can work this to my ultimate advantage." Micah's lips twitched toward a smile. "Now Coop owes *me*."

Coop. Cooper Vance. Sloane rode the wave of discomfort the reporter always managed to stir. It disappeared in a rush of warmth as Micah reached over the console and took hold of her hand.

"Hey," he said, his thumb brushing her skin. "Are you still interested in taking that walk on the beach?"

"Definitely." Sloane had asked Micah if getting down to the beach was a possibility and came prepared. "I brought sandals. But are any of the beaches open after sundown?"

"Zuma. It's a great spot—clean, safe. Probably the best family beach in the area. But it's sort of a hike down to the sand."

"Not a problem. I'm good with that."

"I'd say it's a go, then."

They found a place to park along Pacific Coast Highway and, with the help of street lighting, a large slice of moon, and handrails, made it down the relatively steep steps to the sand. White sand. Crazy beautiful in the moonlight. Sloane's breath caught as they reached the bottom of the cliff and the full vista spread before them. Pristine sand, moon reflected on the dark water, distant dots of light on the cliffs . . .

"It's wonderful," she said after drawing in a breath of briny air. She looked at Micah, saw how the silvery moonlight played across the angles of his face and breeze-ruffled hair. Only Barbie claimed this stuff.

"C'mon," he said, taking her hand. "I promised you a walk."

They did that for a while, holding hands and feet sinking in sand as they covered a stretch of beach dotted with lifeguard towers. They walked without talking. The sounds of the waves, distant traffic up on the highway, and the occasional cry of gulls filled the space of their silence. It felt almost magical. A simple bliss Sloane had never quite imagined. Her hand warm inside Micah's, the contrasting cool speckles of sea air on her bare shoulders, night breeze flirting with her hair . . .

Micah gave a soft chuckle.

"What?"

"The lifeguard stations." He stopped and looked out toward the sea, still holding her hand. "They filmed that old TV show *Baywatch* here. Stephen had a hundred jokes about it. Couldn't let it go. He'd do this dumb imitation of the lifeguards' slow-motion run down to the beach. Remember that? They'd get a rescue call and the camera would go all dramatic slo-mo. Really lame. They filmed right where we're standing."

"Wow." Sloane had never been a fan, but if Hasselhoff had a star on the Walk of Fame way back when, she'd probably tap-danced on it.

"You and your cousin came here together?" she asked, easily imagining the two blond boys she'd seen in her Google search.

"Nearly every weekend—and summers. To surf," Micah confirmed. "Mostly when we were in middle and high school. Up until things got so busy with the music business and I started college. Stephen kept at it longer than I did . . . until his first seizure."

Sloane winced. "Seizures?"

"Epilepsy. Idiopathic, I think they called it. He got good control with meds. But no more surfing." Micah gave her hand a squeeze. "He'd be the first one to give me a hard time for having this conversation on the beach with a beautiful woman."

"Okay then." Sloane's heart turned over as Micah slipped an arm around her shoulders.

They walked a few minutes longer and then headed back to the steps, good timing since the damp breeze had picked up. She hugged her arms around herself.

"Cold?" Micah asked as they reached the foot of the stairs shadowed by the cliff.

"A little." She rubbed her bare arms. "No problem. The car will be warm."

"Here," he said, shrugging out of his jacket.

"That's okay. I'm—"

"Taking my jacket. No arguments," he insisted, holding it out. "Slip your arms in."

She did, feeling a shiver that had nothing to do with the sea breeze. The jacket was huge on her, a rough twill with silky lining, a warm nest that smelled of him.

"There." Micah turned up the jacket collar, then reached out to gently free a length of her hair. His fingers brushed her cheek. "Better?"

"Much," Sloane said in a breathless whisper. He was so close. . . .

"Good." Micah's hands cradled her face. He leaned closer.

Sloane drew in a breath and met him halfway, heartbeat scurrying.

His lips touched hers softly at first and then more eagerly as she responded. His hands slid back, fingers burying in her hair. She slipped her arms around him, rising on tiptoe as best she could with sandals in sand.

His mouth moved over hers, warm and seeking, and—

"Pardon me, folks."

Sloane dropped back with a small gasp, confused as a man in uniform appeared out of nowhere.

"Officer," Micah said, his deep voice both respectful and sheepish. He took Sloane's hand. "A problem, sir?"

"No." The older man smiled. "Making my rounds. Keeping the beach safe. Rousting kids from the coves. The usual."

Heat crept up Sloane's neck.

"That's your SUV up there?" The officer glanced toward the top of the stairs. "The gray Durango?"

"Yes, sir," Micah confirmed. "We were just heading back up."

"I see that." The officer's amused smile faded as he scrutinized Micah's face. "Wait. You're Prescott, right? With the crisis team?"

"Yes. It's Micah." He smiled. "I thought you looked familiar too."

"Glen Abbot," the officer said, offering his hand. "We've called your responders more times than I can count. Can't say how much we appreciate your help."

"Glad to do it," Micah assured, gripping his hand.

"Well . . . sorry to interrupt," Abbot said, giving a respectful nod to Sloane before meeting Micah's gaze again. He patted his service belt. "You want a flashlight for those steps?"

"Thanks, we're good." Micah slid an arm around Sloane's waist. "Plenty of moonlight."

"Right." Abbot smiled. "Best kind of night for a walk."

They said good night, leaving the officer to his patrol. The climb up was a little more challenging than the walk down. Micah still found breath enough for a laugh as they reached the top.

"I feel fifteen years old," he said, choking on a second laugh.

Sloane shook her head. "He had to recognize you, of course. 'Prescott, with the crisis team.'"

"I missed my chance. Should have said I was there on an official callout."

"Oh, sure. That's believable."

"No, really. I could have pulled it off," Micah insisted. He took a few exaggerated steps, knees and arms moving very slowly up and down. "See?"

"What the . . . ?"

"Slow motion." His grin widened. *"Baywatch."*

"Oh, brother."

Sloane's laughter stopped as Micah pulled her close again. A hug, his lips against her hair. She threaded her arms around him and breathed in the clean starchy scent of his dress shirt. Warmth spread, weakening her knees. Her breath escaped in a long sigh.

"I suppose I need to take you back," he murmured against her ear.

"Probably," Sloane whispered, regret tugging. She'd have given anything if her own memories of fifteen had felt this wonderful. But with Micah, it all felt so beautifully new. Almost like a second chance. Like something, *somebody*, she'd been waiting for, for far too long.

Maybe it's you . . .

"I don't want to take you home," Micah said, leaning her away enough to gaze into her eyes. The look on his face made Sloane's heart ache. In such a good way. He crooked a finger under her chin. Then bent low, pressed a brief kiss on her parted lips. "I don't want to end this evening."

"Well . . ." She watched his eyes, pushing down a memory of the last time when she'd nearly panicked at the thought of her landlady seeing his car. "Taking me home means I can invite you in for coffee. And dessert." She smiled despite a tiny tremble. This all felt so cosmically surreal. She might as well continue the roll. "I baked cookies."

27

"CHOCOLATE CHIP," Sloane said, carrying the rooster-embellished plate into the living room. She hoped Micah couldn't hear the doubt in her voice; her first solo baking attempt had been far more challenging than anything she'd encountered in the ER. Thirty-two years old and never claimed a batch of cookies that didn't begin as a plastic-wrapped tube of grocery store dough. Zoey Jones, pink hair and chutzpah, had nailed it: *You don't look like the cookie-baking type.*

Sloane set the plate on the orange crate coffee table next to mugs of coffee, trying not to think of Zoey and Paul in this space. Or her continued uneasiness regarding both. "Here we go," she said.

"My favorite. And homemade," Micah said, lifting one from the plate. His eyes met Sloane's. "You did this just for me?"

"Well . . ." She'd made them for Piper first. Asked her to

be an official taste tester of the first batch. It hadn't gone well, though it had almost been worth it to hear the precocious six-year-old's struggle with diplomacy.

"You tried really, really hard . . . but these are horri-bull." Celeste came to the rescue, correcting Sloane's clueless use of baking powder instead of soda.

"I had the time," she said with a shrug as Micah raised the cookie to his lips. "So I thought why not whip up a batch." She made herself take a breath. "No big deal."

"Mmm."

She smothered a sigh of relief. His expression validated Piper's second batch thumbs-up. Both thumbs—and crumbs on her chin.

"These are great. Only better if you sit down here with me." He laughed as Marty hopped from the arm of the couch onto his lap. "With me and your cat."

The cat Paul threatened and . . . *No, stop this.*

Sloane reached for Marty. "Come here, pest."

"Much better," Micah said as Sloane sank onto the couch beside him. Marty shot them a miffed look and sprang to the floor, tail flicking. "I appreciate your inviting me in, Sloane. I respect your privacy. And that maybe it's awkward because of the hospital." He glanced toward the darkened window. "Because your landlady's a former employee. And—"

"Jerry Rhodes," Sloane finished.

Micah smiled. "We might as well take out an ad."

"Right up your alley," she teased, still turning his *we* around in her head. Her heart. Scary and wonderful. Maybe a sixty-forty split toward scary but . . . "Or a freeway billboard. You could arrange that." She waved a hand in the air. "'Sloane Ferrell baked cookies for Micah Prescott.'"

"Yeah . . . right." Micah's voice sounded tentative. "I should probably tell you that you've been nominated for the Face of Hope." He watched her expression. "I figured you'd react that way."

"I don't like it."

"I'm not asking you to."

"I'm sorry," she said, hating that reality had poisoned things again, bitter as the baking powder in that first batch of cookies. "Take my name off the list. Please. It's flattering, but I'm not comfortable with that kind of thing. You're right about what you said before. I like my privacy. I need it."

"And I happen to think you're a perfect candidate. But I don't want to spend any of our time together hashing that one out. So no worries." He lifted her hand, kissed it. "You won't be getting a copy of the essay questions."

"Questions?"

"Fiona's suggestion. A couple of key questions designed to reveal a little more of the personal side of our nominees. Like 'Outside your work, what do you consider your true passion?' and 'If it were possible, what one important thing would you say to your younger self?' Something like that—I'm still working on it."

Sloane's stomach shivered. *What would I say to my younger self?*

Micah had no idea how that question struck home. But for the first time ever, Sloane wished she *could* let it all out. And trust she wouldn't be judged, viewed only as the sum of her mistakes.

"Although—" Micah reached out to trace his fingers along her jaw—"at some point folks are going to figure out we've been seeing each other. You know how hospitals are."

He smiled. "It would probably look more than fishy if suddenly your face, your name—" Micah stopped, his forehead creasing.

"What?"

"It's just . . . I meant what I said about respecting your privacy. But HR sent employee records over for the nominees." Sloane's heart stalled.

"On your initial application, it listed your name as Wilder." Micah's brows scrunched. "I couldn't help but wonder about that."

Sloane broke the gaze, reached for her coffee. Her mouth was going dry. *Breathe.*

"What's that all about?" Micah asked, something in his voice saying there wasn't wiggle room here. He expected an answer. "You changed your name?"

"Yes," she said, setting her cup down before it spilled. "I did."

———

Micah waited for Sloane's explanation, battling a twinge of guilt. She'd baked him cookies and now he'd started an inquisition? Still, this was too important. He'd begun to care for Sloane. Maybe more than he was willing to admit. But he couldn't invest in any more sketchy relationships.

"I wasn't married, if that's what you were wondering," Sloane told him.

"No," Micah denied with a rush of relief. "Well, maybe."

"Never married." She picked up her coffee again, lifted her chin. A defensive posture he probably deserved. "Wilder was my father's name," Sloane explained. "Not my mother's."

He reached for his own coffee. "So you changed to your mother's name?"

"I . . ."

The cat made a noise in the kitchen and Sloane glanced away; if she'd answered his question, he hadn't caught it. But it made sense she'd take her mother's name. Especially since her death had been such a traumatic one. Micah had opened his mouth to clarify that when Sloane spoke again.

"I guess I needed to feel like I was starting fresh," she explained. There was something in her voice that sounded both courageous and little-girl lost. It grabbed his heart. "Haven't you ever felt that way?"

"I . . . Yeah," he said, thinking of the year after Afghanistan. Maybe he'd have changed his name from Prescott if it offered a way out of that hopeless black hole. If God hadn't found him first. "I know that feeling."

"Micah . . ." Sloane's eyes glistened with tears. "I wish a lot of things were different. That *I* was someone different, but—"

"Don't," he said, reaching for her. "Sloane, don't." He drew her close, his palm against the back of her head. He pressed a kiss on her hair and tightened his arms around her. Her face, her chin, fit perfectly against his neck. Her lips, silky and warm, grazed his skin. "I don't want anyone different, Sloane. I want you just the way you are. You're gutsy and strong. So caring . . ."

Her sigh was half shiver. "You don't know me. Not everything."

"No. And there's plenty about me you don't know yet." Micah stroked her hair. "We'll learn about each other a little at a time. That's the best part. Taking the time to do that. There's no rush." Despite his earlier concerns, Micah knew he meant that. He cared too much to press her any further right now. "I'm not going anywhere." He kissed her ear. "Unless you toss me out—and I'll fight that. Maybe on a billboard that makes me look like a fool."

Her laugh tickled his neck. "Creating a traffic jam on the 405."

"Like, *totally*."

Sloane laughed again, then leaned back to peer up at him. Her inky lashes were damp, dark pupils wide against the incredible violet-blue. Her small smile, like a slice of sun peeking through rain clouds, stole his breath. It only got worse when she rested her palm against his face, thumb stroking his jaw, soft against rough.

"I know about you," she said, barely above a whisper. Her eyes searched his—a longer connection than she'd ever allowed before. "You're exactly who you seem. Smart, loyal, honest. So much integrity and so little ego." She shook her head. "I was wrong about that. I wasted a good rant. Or two."

"Hey, wait . . ."

"No." She touched a finger to his lips, endangering his breath again. "I'm not finished yet. You're devoted to your family. You're a good friend. You work hard and give LA Hope your best. In your spare time, you go into the streets and risk your hide and your heart to—"

"Enough," Micah insisted, grasping her hand. "Or I'll have to jog in slow motion again."

"No." She laughed. "Please don't."

"Deal." He pressed a kiss into her palm. "No more talking about me." He slid his arms around her. "In fact, talking can be overrated in general. So maybe . . ." He hitched her closer, bent down, and nuzzled her neck; her pulse fluttered against his lips. "Maybe we should—"

"Yes."

Sloane's arms were around Micah's neck within the space of a breath, her lips finding his. It was a kiss very much like the woman herself, a perfect mix of tender and passionate. It stirred something in Micah he'd never felt with any woman. That she'd taken the lead only excited him more. He responded to what she began, encouraged by a breathless murmur as his kiss deepened. He drew her closer as her fingers twined into his hair and her lips parted slightly, soft and sweet—an encore of the sugar and chocolate. He leaned her back, wanting the kiss to never end, to never let her go. . . .

Sloane drew away, opened her eyes. Her cheeks were flushed and her lips just-kissed rosy. She looked crazy beautiful but . . .

"Is something wrong?" he asked.

"No." Her voice was a breathless whisper. She slid her arms from his neck, made a small, modest adjustment of her dress. Micah immediately felt like an idiot. Was Sloane worried that he might try to take advantage of the situation?

"Nothing's wrong," she said, meeting his gaze. A laugh rose. "Just forgot to breathe."

"Right. Breathing—good point." Micah smiled, relieved by her laughter. The last thing he wanted was to come on too strong and scare her. "And I'm the one who said no rush and all those things about taking time."

"You did." Her expression made his heart ache. Sweet but nervous, whether she admitted it or not. "But I kissed *you*, remember?"

"Hard to forget," he admitted, chuckling low in his throat. He reached out and gently brushed her hair away from her face, tucking a silky dark strand behind her ear. Then he traced his thumb along her brow and slowly over—

"It's . . ." She flinched slightly. "It's from the accident."

"You mean this?" Micah touched a fingertip to the fine, pinkish scar beside her eye.

"Yes . . . the scar." Something in Sloane's voice said that this moment, much more so than their passionate kiss, had moved to an intimacy she wasn't prepared for. She drew in a slow, halting breath. "The car accident in San Diego."

"Were you badly injured?" There was concern in Micah's voice.

"I was," Sloane breathed, realizing she'd opened herself up to something far more reckless than kisses that led to a walk down the hallway. She'd put the brakes on that, but how much could she let him know without her new life becoming hopelessly unraveled? "I ended up in my own trauma room. Then the OR. Twice."

Micah's eyes widened.

"Ruptured spleen. Then while I was in the intensive care unit, I hemorrhaged again and went into shock."

"You could have died."

"Yes." What would he think if he knew how close she'd come to wanting the mercy of death? Because . . . *I deserved it.*

Micah's warm fingers were gentle on her face again. "And your eye?"

"The windshield or rearview mirror, maybe." Memories came back, sharp as shattered glass. The unrelenting and unbearable pain in her belly as she lay on the gurney, sightless because of the saline-soaked bandages over her eyes. Those surreal moments she'd been a patient, not a nurse. And heard the awful truth from the lips of a teammate: *"None of this would have happened if you'd been responsible enough to find yourself a twelve-step program."*

"They thought I'd lose vision in that eye," she continued, reaching up to touch the familiar scar. "There was an ophthalmologist in the OR, but the damage wasn't that bad after all. They stitched up the lacerations and told me to see a plastic surgeon later. But I haven't. Because . . ." Sloane hesitated.

"You moved here to LA," Micah said, supplying a plausible excuse for the delay. "And you had to get settled and begin work."

She nodded, letting it ride. He wouldn't understand that the scar was a necessary reminder of what she'd done, who Sloane really was. If she ever forgot, she only had to look in the mirror.

"It doesn't matter," Micah said, cradling her face between his palms. He touched his lips to the corner of her eye. "You're beautiful just the way you are—for *who* you are." He kissed the tip of her nose and then grasped her hands again. "It reminds me of something my aunt would always say. I think she worked it into song lyrics somewhere. Let me think. . . ."

Sloane waited, comforted by the feel of her hands in his.

"It was something like 'We see our scars and our flaws . . . God sees the child he's always loved.'"

"Do you . . . ?" Sloane's throat tried to close off. "Do you believe it? That it doesn't matter what we've done? That it's all forgiven? Just like that—a slam dunk?"

Micah studied her for a moment. "It's what I learned," he said, "what I've been told as long as I can remember." His lips quirked. "I don't know about the slam dunk part. I leave that for basketball. We've always called it grace."

She made herself smile at him despite the tremble starting

deep inside her. She'd begun to feel so much for Micah, but she didn't want to talk about this.

"You don't believe?" he asked.

"In the concept of grace?"

"In God."

It suddenly seemed foolish to have worried about her newly acquired moral scruples. Micah Prescott wanted far more.

"Ah . . ." Sloane reached for her coffee; it was lukewarm and she didn't care.

"I'm making you uncomfortable."

"Not really," she hedged after taking a sip. Sloane reminded herself she'd survived a major accident. Though right now a car over a cliff paled in comparison. "I think I told you that a couple of years before my mother was killed, I went to live with my godparents. I was almost sixteen and sort of a mess." She shook her head. "No *sort of* about it. I was a hopeless mess."

Micah's silence encouraged her.

"It was my first real experience with church," she explained. "It was important to them. And they were important to me. So . . ." Sloane's attempt at a shrug was sabotaged by a heart cramp; she'd never known such a true sense of family. There were times she felt the loss of it like phantom pain from a severed limb. "I was baptized—I think I told you that, too. The whole, complete soppy-hair dunking."

Micah smiled.

"And," Sloane heard herself say, "I felt good about it. About God. But . . ."

She caught herself. What was she going to say? That she'd trusted the Almighty to turn her life around? She'd begun to believe it was possible until she'd reported inappropriate advances by a popular youth group leader. And it all turned on her again. The isolation, judgmental looks, and cruel whispers of "a girl like that." Her godparents stuck by her even to the point of leaving their church home.

"I believe in God," Sloane said finally. Firmly. It was the truth. "But I'm not so sure about forgiveness. Your one-size-fits-all grace. I can't believe everyone gets that."

"Because of your stepfather."

Plus all my mistakes afterward . . . Grace doesn't fit me.

"I can understand that," Micah said, kindness in his eyes. "How forgiveness would be hard, considering."

Sloane's breath released in a soft sigh; she'd leave it there and let Micah think this was all about Bob Bullard. Anything more would risk this fragile new beginning with a man unlike any she'd known. She wanted that. *Needed* the way Micah made her feel. Almost as if the scars, even the secret ones, really didn't matter.

"Hey, you," he said, drawing Sloane into a hug. His arms wrapped around her, strong and sure. She nestled her cheek against Micah's shirtfront and heard the soft thudding of his heart. His lips brushed her hair as he spoke. "I put you on the spot there, I know. But I appreciate your honesty."

Honesty?

"Really," he said, stroking her hair. "I think it's important that we always—"

His phone buzzed, sparing her.

———

"It's okay," Sloane insisted. "Check your phone. Are you on call?"

"No," Micah told her, resentful of the interruption that

moved her out of his arms. "That's probably Coop wanting me to shampoo the cats while I'm there."

Sloane laughed. "I'd let you practice on Marty, but . . . Seriously, check the message. I'll freshen our coffees."

He watched her walk toward the kitchen, then pulled out his phone. Coop's text, as usual, was in all caps like a newspaper headline for the Rapture:

MINING GOLD. NOT STOPPING TO SLEEP. NEED 2 MORE DAYS. DON'T DIE OF ENVY.

Micah shook his head. Coop would always be Coop. He'd never stopped harassing Micah for leaving journalism to "sell out and become a corporate front man." Always chiding that Micah would be "battling middle-age spread, gout, and paper cuts" while Cooper Vance penned his acceptance speech for the Pulitzer. He tapped in a quick response, hit the Send button, and then stared at the phone for a moment.

"Corporate front man." He frowned, thinking of what one of the ER staff had said about his new campaign. That its goal was to make the community forget the reckless and criminal acts of the former chief of staff. Micah hated the truth in that. He didn't want to imagine what he'd have done to anyone who'd tried to gloss over or make excuses for the drunk driver responsible for Stephen's death. But he'd accepted this marketing position with full understanding of the requirements. His job *was* to sell the hospital.

"Here we go," Sloane said, setting the cups down and interrupting his thoughts. "Warmed up. No cat hair." Her nose wrinkled. "That I can see. Black coffee, black cat." She nudged the cookie plate his way. "Where is Coop, anyway?"

"In Sacramento." Micah lifted his coffee cup. "Or was. He's taking a couple of extra days. Moving on to San Diego,

I'd bet. He said he struck gold with a story he's been chasing down."

"Didn't you say he writes for the *Times* Lifestyle section?"

"Yep." Micah smiled. "Just covered a local pumpkin patch. But this story is freelance, on his vacation time. Coop's convinced a Russian inmate at State Prison is pulling the strings on criminal activity up and down the coast, including that attack on our Jane Doe. And those girls in the motel fire."

Sloane's fingers tightened on her cup. "They haven't made any identifications."

"No. It's going to require dental records."

"Horrible."

It was. And Micah wasn't going to tell Sloane what he'd heard earlier today. It wasn't official and he always kept things confidential. But the elderly woman he'd sat with after the fire had indeed remembered a few of the girls who frequented those burned-out rooms. Some names had been distinctive, "foreign maybe," and there was another name she'd heard several times. *Zoey*.

"Anyway," Micah said, eager to move on to a less grim subject, "I'll be on call for cat box crises for another couple of days." He shook his head. "What ever happened to letting cats go outside to scratch up the neighbor's flower beds? I'll bet Marty has his eye on your landlady's new vegetable garden."

"Marty's mostly an inside cat." She glanced to where the animal was busy sniffing at Micah's jacket, draped over the back of a chair. "I used to let him out a little, but I don't feel like that's really . . . safe." Something in Sloane's voice said this could be about more than her cat.

Micah realized in a heartbeat that he'd do whatever it took

to make this woman feel safe and cared for. It suddenly mattered more than anything.

"I have a confession," she said, meeting his gaze again. Her chin lifted a bit as if she were gathering courage. "I thought you should know."

What now?

"This was my first time baking cookies."

Micah released his breath in a laugh.

"Are you shocked?" she asked, a giggle teasing her voice. She'd snuggled so close against him that her lips tickled the flesh beneath his jaw as she spoke. "Scandalized and completely disappointed?"

"No way." Micah closed his eyes for a moment, memorizing the feel of her in his arms, breathing her in. Then he leaned her back, just enough to see her eyes. "I'm honored that I'm your first cookie taster."

"Well . . . not exactly."

"Another confession?"

"I tried the first batch on a six-year-old. Total flop." Sloane's nose wrinkled. "She can't lie. Her photo is on God's fridge."

"Huh?"

"Something she told me once. But the point is . . ." Her beautiful face sobered. It was there again, that sweet new openness. "You're not my first, Micah."

"That's okay." He took a slow breath, trying to control the insistent drumming of his heart. He knew the subtext here, but he'd never had such a strong sense that this was meant to be. "I'm here now. And it all went right."

"Yes." She sighed as he cupped her face in his hands. "You are. It is."

Micah bent to kiss her, then hesitated. This felt too important; he had to be honest.

"I've had my firsts too," he began. "And seconds. More than a few 'flops' of my own doing. I don't want that anymore, Sloane. What we're starting feels too good for that. So . . ."

She watched his eyes, waited.

"No expectations here," Micah told her. "No pressure. Cookies, coffee. Then I'm going back to my place. After . . ."

"After what?"

"A good night kiss—or three?"

Sloane's laugh was part purr. "Yes, please."

Micah touched his lips to her forehead, the corner of her eye, then watched her lids flutter shut as he claimed her mouth again.

28

"I SWEAR," Harper teased, peering at Sloane around an IV pump, "you could bottle that and make a million bucks."

"Bottle what?" Sloane set the flow rate for a neon-yellow multivitamin infusion. "This stuff?"

"No. The new you." Harper smiled. "The way you've been acting this week—that look on your face just now. Billboard worthy." She arched a brow. "Speaking of Micah Prescott."

"Which I'm not." Sloane's face warmed. But it was true. In the five days since their Malibu date, it felt like everything had changed. As if her life had gone from dark and cautious to full color, like one of the countless glitter-sprinkled rainbows Piper taped to her grandmother's walls. Sloane had never felt so giddy.

"See? You're laughing to yourself."

Sloane tapped the suspended IV solution. "Banana bags are funny?"

"Right. Hilarious." Harper gave Sloane's shoulder a squeeze. "Seriously, this look is good on you, Ferrell. When you're ready to talk, I've got two good ears. And Ben & Jerry's Coffee Toffee Bar Crunch."

"I'll keep that in mind."

"For sure."

Sloane watched her friend walk away and felt the new bliss diffuse a little. Ice cream and girl talk? She wasn't there yet. What she had with Micah was too tenuous and new. She felt a need to protect it, keep it close—like she did with Marty, checking the screen, watching the door, and keeping him safe. There were still threats.

She touched her fingers to the plastic IV bag, saline solution made vivid yellow by the addition of an ampule of multivitamins. There was folic acid, too, several grams of magnesium, and 100 milligrams of thiamine. It was a mixture designed to protect at-risk patients from a particular type of encephalopathy, dangerous brain swelling. In some cases, it helped ease muscle cramps and "the shakes." Banana bags were emergency treatment for alcoholics.

The woman in treatment room 117 was only six years older than Sloane and way down in a hopeless ditch. The former screenwriter could barely put together a coherent sentence. Her limbs were thin and wasted and her belly bloated; there were sores around her lips, and her tongue was glossy red from poor nutrition and B_{12} deficiency. The whites of her eyes had a telltale yellow tinge. She'd stumbled over a parking bumper outside a convenience store, cracked a tooth, and suffered some minor scrapes and bruises. Fresh injuries among dozens of scabbing old ones. Someone had called the ambulance. She'd wet herself in transit.

"None of this would have happened if you'd been responsible enough to find yourself a twelve-step program."

Sloane grabbed the pump and rolled it through the supply room door toward the corridor. Micah was okay with the way things were right now; he was the one who'd said they'd go slow and take their time getting to know each other. There was no reason to dump details of her past into his lap all at once—or ever, some of them. She'd left all that behind, and once she finished with her stepfather's parole hearing, she'd finally be free. October 17, only three days away. Maybe grace didn't come in her size, but for the first time in her life Sloane felt like it was okay to hope that happiness was possible for someone like her. All because of Micah.

"Here we go," she said, rolling the IV pump up to her patient's bedside. "This will make you feel better."

The writer's eyes met hers. "Like a new person?"

Sloane's stomach tensed.

"It's okay." The woman gave a weak laugh. "I don't believe in miracles. Unless you've got limoncello martinis in that bag?"

"Sorry," Sloane told her, trying for a casual smile. She knew that kind of dark humor; she'd been quite skilled at it during her nights on a barstool. And on the subsequent workdays when she'd nursed a miserable hangover. Brittle, defensive humor. But strangely Sloane suddenly wished she had something to offer more along the lines of . . . She cleared her throat. "Would you like me to call a chaplain?"

"Am I dying?"

"No. I just thought—"

"I *know* what you think. You see me and want to pull out the

God Band-Aid. You feel less guilty about your great life by telling me that I'm worthy of some amazing, unconditional, *holy* love." The woman swallowed, the look in her eyes reminding Sloane of Marty, the first time she'd seen him in the cage of the city pound. "Be honest. You really believe that?"

Sloane glanced away.

"I figured." The woman extended her bruised arm. "Now just stick me with the needle."

———

"That makes forty names," Micah said, scrolling to the end of the Face of Hope nominees on his computer. "The list is growing."

"Did you finalize the essay requirement?" Fiona asked. "The two questions you'll pose to the nominees?"

"Yes. But it's three now. After I had coffee with the special projects manager."

Fiona looked up from her cell phone.

"We've had a program for a couple of years where employees are encouraged to submit ideas for improvements," Micah explained. "It's been sort of hit-and-miss. Mostly miss. But an interesting one came in the other day. From one of the maintenance staff."

"What kind of idea?"

"Something for the new wing, the Excellence in Aging department." It was Jerry Rhodes's suggestion and a good one. He proposed that the wing also house a preschool for the children of employees. "It's a concept they've used successfully in Florida. Alzheimer's patients and other seniors, interacting with the children. Reading, doing crafts . . . talking, listening. It's a benefit for everyone, including the parents because tuition cost is much lower and the kids are here on campus. I think there's a personal element to his idea too. This employee's wife is a preschool teacher. She may want to be involved as well."

"I like his idea. A lot."

"Me too. And," Micah continued, "I'm going to ask each of the nominees to come up with a special project idea as part of their candidacy. I think it shows their dedication, and it helps the hospital. Win-win."

Fiona raised a thumb. "I've said it before and I'm saying it again. You're good, Prescott."

"Corporate front man . . ."

Coop was back, though he'd barely come up to breathe, let alone to mooch food from Micah. Apparently he'd garnered the interest of the *Times*. There was more fact-checking to do, but it looked like his coveted byline might actually happen. Soon.

"Which reminds me," Fiona added, "I'll need to start my search for a gala dress. And a date." She rolled her eyes. "I suppose you've already got that crossed off *your* list."

"Yeah." Micah smiled. "I'm hoping."

Fiona shot him a knowing look. "I've noticed that."

After she left, he forced himself to return a few phone calls and set up some necessary meetings. Micah wanted to have everything in place when the department director came back from his family leave. He also wanted to walk down to the ER and see Sloane. He'd manufactured a half-dozen excuses to visit that department this week; people were starting to notice. He wasn't sure he cared. It was too hard having her so close and still so far. It had been a busy week for both of them, but they'd managed to meet for coffee twice. And in the hospital gazebo scant minutes after sunrise on Tuesday, for a discreet hug and a quick but memorable kiss.

Micah had mentioned Sloane in a phone call with his aunt, which meant his parents would know by now. He'd even allowed himself to imagine what Stephen would have thought. He'd say she was beautiful, of course—"crazy gorgeous." And he'd have had fun with Sloane's dry wit, her spunk. But . . .

"I believe in God. . . . But I'm not so sure about forgiveness. . . . I can't believe everyone gets that."

Grace. A sustaining belief for people of faith. Stephen would have been concerned about Sloane's doubts. He probably would have challenged her in his good-natured and offhand manner to discuss it further. He'd ask her to help him understand her reservations. And he would have listened in that kind and generous way he had. Always putting others first and himself last. A familiar ache spread through Micah's chest. Stephen would have looked at Sloane the way God did.

The truth was, Micah understood what Sloane said about forgiveness. Her doubts that it applied to everyone—or should. He'd struggled with that himself after Stephen was killed. He'd tried to distract himself with the work in Afghanistan and afterward tried to deny his continuing faith struggle in a reckless haze of beer and empty relationships. But the doubts remained. Still.

Not that he didn't believe in grace. He couldn't forgive the man responsible for his cousin's death. That drunken college kid who got behind the wheel of a car and murdered the finest person Micah had ever known. Four years in prison and he was free. Married, kids, and working alongside his father in the family's carpeting business. Stephen was never coming back. Nothing about it was right, just, or fair. Micah had asked God over and over to take away these feelings, but . . .

He closed down the computer screen and glanced toward the door. The last time he'd checked, radiology's supply of nomination forms had been running low. He should probably add a few more and have a brief face-to-face with their department chief. Micah's phone conference wasn't for another forty minutes. Plenty of time to walk to radiology. It was just off the emergency department.

He smiled. He'd promised Sloane they'd take it slow, and he wasn't going to pressure her in any way; he'd be the respectful man he'd been raised to be. He'd learned the hard way that ignoring those values brought no real satisfaction. But it didn't mean he couldn't let himself imagine what might come down the road a ways. Even if that simply meant seeing Sloane by his side at the Face of Hope gala. An amazing woman in a beautiful gown, sharing his joy at By Grace's comeback performance. And meeting his parents. He had no problem imagining that now.

Micah stood, lifted his jacket from the back of his chair. He'd stop by the ER on his way to radiology. It would be his only real chance to see Sloane today. He had a meeting tonight—and evidently she did too.

"I think I'll sit and listen this time," Sloane had said again from her chair at one end of the fully occupied back row. She'd discreetly widened the space between herself and the person next to her. Only a foot or so, but it still felt like a safety cushion. So did the fact that she'd come on a different day than usual. Sloane doubted Jocelyn would approach her again—AA

made it clear that members chose sponsors, not vice versa—
but she didn't want to take a chance. Things were going too
well; she didn't need that kind of aggravation. She was here;
she showed up. That was enough.

Sloane took a sip of coffee from her paper cup and looked
toward the meeting's chairperson. He'd been talking about
the twelve steps. The importance of completing them, one
by one. Because, they always said, sobriety wasn't only about
not drinking; it was about seeking recovery in several areas,
including physical, mental, emotional . . . and spiritual.

"It's okay. . . . I don't believe in miracles. . . ."

Sloane winced, remembering her encounter with the alcoholic patient today. And the woman's cynical remarks.

*". . . telling me that I'm worthy of some amazing, uncondi-
tional,* holy *love. . . . You really believe that?"*

Sloane wasn't here for miracles. She showed up because it
kept her from drinking. Even if she never shared, told no one
her name, never joined the closing prayer, and didn't need a
sponsor. One step was enough. That first one: *"We admitted
we were powerless over alcohol—that our lives had become
unmanageable."*

Powerless was a stronger word than Sloane would have
chosen, and she was managing just fine now. But she wouldn't
be here if she could beat this thing on her own. She'd admit
that much. The remaining items on the list about a "moral
inventory," turning your "will and life" over to God, admitting
to another person "the exact nature of our wrongs" . . . they
didn't fit her any more than Micah's grace.

Sloane drained the last dregs of her coffee. It was time to
scoot out of here. Any minute they'd be making that awkward
prayer circle.

She slid from her chair, dodging glances as she made her way to the door. For the first time there was the smallest twinge of regret in her escape. An awareness that she was an outsider here, too. She'd always blamed that feeling on the isolation that came with drinking. But she was sober now.

Sloane crossed to the parking lot, stopped for a moment, and drew in a deep breath. It was getting dark, and for Los Angeles, the air felt autumn-cool. The freeways hummed in the distance, but there were also the crackly chirps of crickets in trees around the parking lot and a dog yipping in a yard somewhere nearby. All of it felt like a peaceful nightcap to her evening. She rolled her eyes at her metaphor. Then reminded herself that, outsider or not—and despite Jocelyn's morbid warning—there was no banana bag calling her name.

Her phone buzzed, signaling a text message. Micah making plans for tomorrow. A day off, together. She tapped in a grinning emoticon, then walked on toward her car with a real-deal smile on her face.

Micah was changing everything. The way he treated her, protective and respectful, the way he made her laugh, his patience. He'd somehow managed to give her hope that she was finally safe and—

"Hey."

She whirled, heart pounding, as a man stepped from behind a tree.

29

"Paul?"

He was nearly unrecognizable. Face battered, eye swollen closed, blood bubbling in his nose. Anxiety choked Sloane's voice. "What happened?"

"Doesn't matter." He took another step toward her and pressed a palm against his ribs—cracked probably. "No time. We need to get out of here, Sloane. Get far away."

"We?"

His nod sent a fresh rivulet of blood from one nostril. He swiped at it with the back of his hand. "You. Me. We need to go."

He had to be drunk. A bar fight or a nasty dispute over a game of poker. This was insane.

"The only one who needs to go anywhere is *you*, Paul. You

need to go to a hospital and get yourself checked over. You probably shouldn't drive." Sloane glanced back at the church. The AA meeting rarely went late. This was a mess. "I'll call 911. Get some medics to—"

"No!" Paul grasped her arm, agitation causing even the swollen eye to open. "We can't call anyone. They'll find me. They'll check the hospitals."

"Who?" Sloane asked, grateful when he dropped her arm to brace himself against the tree trunk. He definitely needed a trauma assessment.

"Who's looking for you?" she repeated, but the moment the words left her lips, she knew. Her stomach shuddered. "Those men you borrowed money from? For the gambling? They're still after you for those loans?"

He groaned. "It isn't about loans. It never was."

What?

"I got all those calls," she insisted. "They said you owed money."

"I found a bag of cash. Back in Sacramento, when I was setting up those poker games."

Sloane's legs had gone weak. "Found it? What do you mean?" She grimaced, remembering his surprise visit at the cottage. "That money you showed me, it's from that?"

"I had to give 10 percent to the dude who held it for me when I was in Mexico. But even after that, my cut is close to 900K." His pained smile exposed bloody teeth. "There really *is* a pot of gold at the end of the rainbow—I found it."

"You *stole* it." Sloane snatched at her hair, anger rising. "The same way you stole my cat."

"Hey, chill," Paul told her. "We don't have time for this. I'll explain it while we're on the road. We'll stop by your place first."

"I'm not going *anywhere* with you. You're crazy to think I would. If these criminals find you, it's all on you." She took a step away. "I'm leaving."

"You're in this too."

"What? Don't even *try* that." Sloane's lips tensed. "I have nothing to do with your gambling 'business.' I never did."

Paul peered over his shoulder. "The poker games in Sacramento and Tahoe are just chump change for these guys. Kind of a side hobby for some low-level guy named Viktor. The syndicate makes most of its money in New York. Online gambling, international sports . . . all of it leading back to Kiev. And Moscow. Right on home to Mother Russia, babe. It's not just gambling. It's girls, too. Young ones. That's Viktor's real specialty. Let's just say he's not known for his gentle touch."

Sloane's stomach roiled. Viktor. V. The tattoo on Jane Doe. And Zoey?

"He wants the money back. I thought I'd let things cool off long enough; then this past week I started hearing some stuff. I changed up my plans and laid low but . . ."

"He found you."

"One of his gorillas." Paul touched his ribs. "With a lead fist. Now I've got to disappear. If you're still as smart as you were, you'll join my vanishing act. Otherwise, I can't guarantee your safety. I'm sure I don't have to remind you about San Diego."

"No one's bothered me in months," Sloane told him, refusing to let him frighten her that way. "Only *you*. And if you come near me again, I'll call the police." It was true now. She'd do it. "I made a huge mistake trusting you. I won't ever do it again."

"Sloane . . ." Paul coughed, wiped at the bloody spit it produced. "Maybe you didn't hear me: it's almost a *million bucks*!" His expression was intense. "You deserve it, Sloane, all

I've gone through to get this. You're worth it. We can go away somewhere, kick back, and have everything we've always—"

"People will be out of the church any minute," she interrupted. "If you won't call the medics, then you should just go. Before they see you."

"Please . . ." He tried to reach for her hand; she stepped back. "I love you, Sloane. That's what I'm trying to say. I *need* you. Give me another chance."

There were voices now, a clutch of AA members walking their way.

"Go, Paul. Hurry."

She reached for the Volvo's door as someone called out to her.

"Everything okay there?"

"Fine—good. Thanks!" she called back, relieved that Paul was limping away.

In seconds, she put the car into gear and headed for the exit.

"I don't get what you're saying." Micah slid his guitar onto the couch beside him. Coop hadn't bothered to respond to text messages in a week. And now he'd finally called, sleep deprived and amped up on caffeine, to blurt some crazy story? Micah jabbed the phone into speaker mode. "What do you mean 'Sloane is mixed up in this thing'?"

"Oh, man . . . you're not listening."

Micah glared at the phone, ignoring an anxious twinge. "*You're* not making sense."

"Hang on. Let me grab my notes."

Notes? Coop had this garbage written down?

"Got it," Coop said, coming back. "Look, I'm sorry I have to lay this on you. But if you're even thinking things could get serious with this girl?"

Micah had ordered flowers barely two minutes before Coop called and . . . *I think I'm falling in love with her.* Was he?

"Get to the point, would you?" Micah ordered.

"Okay. It's not like this nurse is a Russian gangster. I'm not saying that. But I'm in San Diego doing my research, right?" His laugh sounded incredulous, like he couldn't wrap his fuzzy mind around his sudden fortune. "Man, the timing was laser-perfect, you know?"

"I know I'm going to throw my phone against the wall if you don't explain what's going on."

"I told you she used to go by the name Wilder?"

Sloane had explained that. Mostly. New name, fresh new start.

"Well," Coop continued, "she was a nurse at San Diego Hope. In Sacramento before that."

"I know all this." And Micah also knew he was done with Coop, really done now. This was—

"You knew Sloane was in a car accident in San Diego? A bad one?"

"Yep." He'd traced his fingers over that scar.

"Incredible she survived," Coop continued. "Her car flipping end over end after going off the coast highway. And over a cliff."

Dear God . . .

"Rush-hour pileup, intense cliff dive, ambulances screamin' to the trauma centers," Coop narrated, imagining it in print no doubt. "Scene from an action flick for sure. But the real kicker is the witness statements. All those folks who saw what was really going on. An unidentified car chasing her Jetta. That phantom vehicle was on its bumper like a missile, slamming into it, scraping past other cars to get at it again, then finally forcing the Jetta over that cliff. Bang. Whoosh!"

"What—why?" Micah asked, wondering if Coop had more than caffeine on board. "Road rage?"

"Bingo. Exactly what they thought. At first. But someone got a partial plate. Or maybe there were more than a few cell pics and they pieced 'em together. I'll have to check that for accuracy. But bottom line, investigators matched it to a stolen car that was found a day later abandoned and torched. Russian style."

Micah pressed his fingers to his forehead. "But . . ."

"Why would the mob target your nurse?"

"Yeah, what's the connection?" Micah asked, struggling to understand.

"That's exactly what the detectives asked Wilder. She said she didn't know. But they've kept at it. The FBI and San Diego's organized crime unit have had an open investigation for six months."

The length of time since Sloane left there. And the reason she changed her name?

"The day before I arrived in Sacramento," Coop explained, "there was a break in a gambling case. Big ring of illegal poker games. One of the mob minions made a deal in prison that exposed the name of a bagman who ran the Russian money around. Apparently this guy took a hike with some of the organization's cash. To the tune of nearly a million bucks."

"How could that have anything to do with Sloane?"

"This bagman was her fiancé."

Micah closed his eyes.

"You don't know me. Not everything."

Sloane said she hadn't been married but never mentioned a fiancé. She'd only explained the name change because he'd asked. She said it was because of the circumstances of her mother's death and her stepfather's incarceration. Or had Micah only assumed that? Was her militant insistence on privacy really because . . . ? "Are the police looking for Sloane?"

"They hadn't been. But now that they're looking for her ex, I expect they'll want to question her again. Apparently Sloane and this guy broke up while she still lived in Sacramento. Close to two years ago. It's assumed he's running. He'd be a fool not to. These are evil dudes. They were probably threatening to hurt Sloane to put pressure on her ex. Flush him out. A cliff dive is pretty persuasive." Coop's tone gentled a fraction. "She may not have known what he was involved in, Micah."

He needed to believe that in the worst way. "So they're trying to find this—"

"Paul Stryker."

Knowing his name made it real. Could Sloane still have feelings for him?

"I was right," Coop added, a chest swell in his voice. "It's all connected and traces back. I've been working 24-7 with the paper's senior crime reporter, and we've got it tied together and fact-checked. From the sex trafficking here to the gambling in Sacramento and even that ugly accident in San Diego. Burned-out cars are a mob signature. If they've got their sights on someone, they don't care about collateral damage. There were two on-scene fatalities in the San Diego pileup. And the girl driving Sloane's car was—"

"She wasn't driving her own car?"

"No. The reports showed a coworker was driving. Because . . ." Coop's voice trailed off.

"Because why?" Micah got up from the couch and began pacing. He needed to move to think. "Why wasn't Sloane driving?"

Coop's breath puffed against his phone. "It wasn't in the official reports. But I stopped by San Diego Hope. Sloane wasn't popular there."

"What's that supposed to mean?" Micah asked, anger sharpening his tone. He wasn't sure who he was mad at: the Hope staff for breaching privacy, Coop for baiting them, or Sloane for—"What did they say?"

"It was just one person. And you've got to understand that the other employee, the one who was driving, was *really* well liked. The kid ended up with serious head injuries, months in rehab, and still has some problems. It was pretty obvious this guy I talked to blamed Sloane."

"Why? For what?"

"For being drunk, Micah. So drunk her teammate took her keys and insisted on driving her home. Which essentially put this other employee on that freeway and over a cliff. From what I heard, it wasn't the first time Sloane got that drunk. Her coworkers saw it as a big problem."

God, no . . .

Micah closed his eyes against an image of Stephen's dead body. And the face of his convicted killer in court.

"I'm sorry, man," Coop told him. "I know how this must make you feel."

"You can't know."

"I mean, you dated her and now—"

"Wait." Micah hauled his fingers through his hair; his mind

was spinning in too many directions. "You told the investigators in Sacramento that you know where Sloane is? You gave them her new name? That's why you're telling me?"

"No." Coop sighed. "I probably should have. You haven't said much, but I had a hunch it wasn't just one date. I thought I should check with you first. Hey . . . you're not actually serious about this nurse?"

"I don't know," Micah said with an honesty that made his heart ache. "I don't know what to think about any of this. Obviously I don't know *her*."

"Well, I figured I should at least warn you," Coop said, finality in his tone. "It's an important story. With a link to Jane Doe and the motel fire here in LA, it will be top news in the *Times*. Print and online. TV will pick it up too. The tie to the Sacramento gambling and the unsolved San Diego incident will be exposed. There'll be a photo of Paul Stryker. Along with a mention of the victims of the freeway tragedy. Including Sloane's former name."

Micah's gut lurched. "When?"

"Tomorrow morning."

Sloane pulled Marty into her lap, then drew him up against her, comforted by his softness. His tongue made a snagging swipe at her chin before he blinked his yellow eyes and settled down to the serious task of kneading the sleeve of her pajama top. Barely nine thirty on a Friday night and Sloane was already in her sleepwear. She had seen no point in changing back into clothes after showering; she'd raced to do that the moment she locked the door behind her. There'd been a bloody handprint on her shirt.

She closed her eyes, concentrating on the clean scent of her shampoo and the peaceful rhythm of Marty's paws. She'd come too far to let Paul Stryker's unwelcome intrusion make her feel dirty and drag her back to a lifestyle she'd vowed to leave behind. It was a hateful identity she'd shed, a snake escaping skin left shriveled on the rocks below that seaside cliff. It had taken every ounce of her reserve to walk away and find a new life. Paul Stryker couldn't show up at an AA meeting, claim she was still part of his dark activities, and expect her to simply follow him. Because he'd had some kind of epiphany himself?

"You deserve it, Sloane. . . . You're worth it."

Since when was Paul Stryker the measure of who Sloane was and what she deserved?

She nuzzled her cheek against Marty's fur. She'd meant what she said to Paul. She'd call the police if he showed up here again. It would mean opening herself up to questions. But it would be worth it.

Because of Micah.

She glanced at her cell phone lying on the couch beside her. There were no new messages. Only that one he'd sent earlier about his plans for their Saturday. He hadn't answered her text with the happy face icon. Or the one she'd sent when she'd pulled on her pajamas after her shower. But Sloane wasn't concerned. Micah's work meeting probably went late, and it would be like him to check in with the crisis team dispatcher even if he wasn't on call. Maybe his phone ran out of juice. Or he was playing his guitar and didn't notice.

Sloane pressed a kiss on Marty's head and closed her eyes.

The doors were locked, her bloodstained blouse was soaking, Paul was gone, and Micah Prescott only believed the very best of her. The look in his eyes, his whispers, his kisses, proved she was worth so much more than she'd ever, ever imagined. The best man she'd ever known was planning their Saturday together. Sloane was safe.

Tomorrow was a whole new day.

30

WHAT'S THAT NOISE?

Sloane pulled down the quilt and squinted toward sunshine streaming through her window, then at her bedside clock. Her eyes widened. Nine thirty? She hadn't slept this late since the last time she dragged herself home from partying.

Was someone knocking on the front door?

It flooded back, the reason she'd had trouble sleeping last night: The AA meeting, Paul accosting her in the parking lot, battered and bleeding. And his irrational insistence that she go with him, vanish.

She slid from the bed, grabbed her robe, and padded toward the door, telling herself he wouldn't show up here in broad daylight. She'd made it clear she'd call the police. Paul wouldn't take that risk. He was smarter than that. He'd be out of state by now.

She slid the last lock back, opened the door.

"Flowers for—" The senior-age deliveryman peered around an autumn bouquet and seemed to notice Sloane's attire and sleep-tossed hair. He averted his eyes, finding sudden interest in the wicker vase. "I'm sorry if I woke you, miss. You were first on my route. By some miracle, the traffic wasn't bad, so I'm a little earlier than I expected."

"It's okay," Sloane assured him, relief and surprise making her feel wobbly enough to lean on the door handle. "No problem." She smiled as she caught the sweet fragrance of the brilliant orange, burgundy, and golden roses. "I'm not sure I've had a better wake-up call. Are these mine?"

The man returned her smile. "If you're Sloane Ferrell."

"That's me."

"Then it's my pleasure, Miss Ferrell."

He waved as he ambled back down the drive, leaving Sloane with a vase of flowers and a happy rush of goose bumps. This had to be from Micah. Roses, tiny red berries, and sprigs of eucalyptus. So beautiful. She reached for the card, thinking even a handful of dandelions would beat a shipping carton of Lucky Charms. Then she read the message:

To start our day together. Love, Micah

Love.

Sloane stood in the foyer, door still half-open and vase hugged to her robe, and read the card again. She let her gaze linger on the signature. That he'd had the florist write *love* didn't actually mean he loved her. It was used so often, so easily. She stiffened as Paul's words came back.

"I love you, Sloane. . . . Give me another chance."

No. She wasn't going to think of that, of him. The only chance she cared about was *this* one, this new beginning with Micah. She had it now. Maybe the first chance she'd ever had at real . . . *love*?

She closed her eyes and breathed in the fragrance of the bouquet he'd sent . . . *"To start our day together."* A day, a chance, and a hope—she'd let herself go that far—of something even more wonderful.

There was a tap on the door.

"Sloane? It's Celeste, dear." She peeked her head in.

"Oh . . . hi." Sloane felt her face warm as she tucked the card back into the bouquet. "Here, come in. I'll just put these down somewhere."

"They're beautiful," Celeste said, shifting a small stack of envelopes from one hand to the other. She had a newspaper under her arm, probably to offer Sloane coupons. Celeste read the *Times* first page to last, faithfully. "I saw the florist van, so I knew you'd be up. I hated to disturb you on your morning off. I remember how hard-earned these mornings are."

"No worries," Sloane said as her landlady followed her into the living room. Marty was standing on the table, a piqued look on his face. Breakfast was overdue. "I didn't mean to sleep so late. Have a seat, please. I'll put on a pot of coffee."

"Thanks, but no. I'm fully caffeinated." She watched as Sloane scooped her cat off the table and set the roses on the kitchen counter. "I had this mail for you."

Sloane turned to look at Celeste, caught her expression. "Is something wrong?" She felt an anxious prickle. "Piper's okay?"

"She's fine. All of us are fine. But . . ." Celeste opened the newspaper on the table. "It's this. An article in the *Times* this morning. A feature about organized crime. Russians—it says they're responsible for things that have happened in Sacramento, San Diego, and maybe even here in LA."

No . . .

The blood drained from Sloane's head as she stared at a black-and-white photo of Paul. She sank onto a chair.

"It's just that this man in the photo looks like someone I've seen before," Celeste said, pulling out another chair. "A couple of weeks back. A man was sitting in a car at the curb beside our driveway. I'm not sure it was him. But it's possible."

Sloane fought a wave of nausea. She stared at the article, unable to focus her eyes.

"I'd just pulled up with Piper. We'd been to the store," Celeste continued. "I asked if I could help him. He said he realized he had the wrong address. Then he asked for directions to the nearest Starbucks. He was good-looking, young. Polite. He complimented me on my roses."

Of course he would. Paul was a pro.

"Have you seen any strange cars parked nearby?" Celeste asked. "If I remember right, it was an older midsize sedan, dark. Maybe a Toyota?"

"No. I . . ." Sloane made herself meet her landlady's gaze. She glanced down at the photo again, hating her deceit. "It doesn't sound familiar."

Celeste's finger traced down the article. "It says he's a person of interest. That the authorities, including the FBI, are looking for him in connection with illegal gambling and possibly sex trafficking."

"Girls, too. Young ones. That's Viktor's real specialty."

"It must be frightening," Sloane managed, guilt trying to strangle her, "even to imagine you might have seen him."

"It is." Celeste swept a hand over her hair. "I feel like I have to call the police even if I'm not sure. To be safe. Because of Piper."

"Of course." Sloane felt sick. That precious little girl. She reminded herself that Paul was gone. Also of what she'd told him last night. *"No one's bothered me in months."* It was the truth. And even if Paul had said otherwise, Sloane had no real connection to this dangerous business. There was no reason these criminals would bother with her.

"Your name is mentioned in the article," Celeste said.

No, no . . .

"At least I think it's yours. There." Celeste pointed to some lines halfway down the column. "It mentions a car accident in San Diego. It says a car was forced off an embankment. The passenger was a woman named Sloane Wilder. Was that you?"

Sloane's fingers moved to her scar. She tried to find the lines Celeste had indicated. "I had an accident there. But why . . . ?"

"They think these mobsters were involved. They don't give specific details here." Celeste met Sloane's gaze. "I only guessed it might be you because your rent application was under the name Wilder. I'd almost forgotten."

"Ah."

Relief sucked the rest of the blood from Sloane's brain. Only a few people in LA knew that name. Celeste, the head of Hope hospital human resources, the ER manager who'd interviewed her, and Micah, of course. It had been months; maybe no one would even remember. Micah already knew about the accident.

"Well," Celeste said with a sigh, "I suspect there will be more information when the authorities hold that press conference this evening."

Sloane's stomach churned.

"I heard on TV, just before I came over here," Celeste added, "that they've been able to communicate with that poor girl whose throat was cut. Through an interpreter—Russian. It's amazing they put all this together," she said, rising from her chair. "Apparently this young *Times* reporter has been working the angles for months." She tapped the article. "A big stretch beyond his regular reporting. He usually gets a mention in the Lifestyle section. I think he took some pictures of a pumpkin patch last week."

What?

Sloane pulled the page closer and found the shared byline. Cooper Vance.

"Coop's convinced a Russian inmate at State Prison is pulling the strings on criminal activity up and down the coast, including that attack on our Jane Doe. And those girls in the motel fire."

State Prison. Where he'd seen Sloane in the parking lot. Then probably told Micah. Who found her former name in the HR records. Or took it upon himself to look it up? Sloane's heart stalled. Was this why Coop had been leaving those messages for her the past few days? He'd jotted down his number and left it with the ER clerk. She'd ignored it, certain he was trying to hit her up for information on the girl in SICU. But now . . .

"I should go and let you ease into your day off," Celeste said, gathering up the newspaper. Marty's demanding meow rose from the kitchen. She laughed. "And feed your cat."

"Right." Sloane made herself smile despite her troubling thoughts. "Hungry mode."

"Speaking of which," Celeste said, walking toward the

door, "I'm keeping Piper tonight and she's invited Jerry to have dinner with us. To thank him for finishing our garden boxes. I'm making a pot roast. She's planning an interpretive dance with a gardening theme." She shook her head. "I have no clue. But you're invited, of course." She glanced toward the vase of roses on the kitchen counter. "If you don't have other plans?"

"Thank you. Really," Sloane said as she followed her landlady into the small foyer. "But I do have something planned."

"I'm glad. You deserve something nice."

Sloane closed the door behind Celeste, then leaned against it, wrapping her robe tighter. She was being paranoid. Wasn't she? Why would Micah feed confidential information to a newspaper reporter? Why would he help Cooper Vance dig into details of the Sacramento gambling, the accident in San Diego . . . and Paul? Had Coop discovered her connection to Paul? Did Micah know?

It wasn't possible. The flowers in her kitchen were proof. With a card he'd signed using the word *love*. Still, Micah hadn't responded to her texts last night. Sloane had blown it off; she'd been too rattled anyway. But now she had to wonder.

She headed to the bedroom and grabbed her phone off the nightstand. She'd call Micah to thank him for the flowers. She'd hear his voice and be reassured that everything was—

Her phone buzzed in her hands.

A text. From Micah.

Crisis responders needed after tonight's press conference re: motel fire. Going in early. Could run late. Sorry. Know u understand.

Micah switched his phone to silent mode, biting back a curse. This was the third time in an hour he'd let a call from Sloane go to voice mail. How was he supposed to talk with her—what could he possibly say?

Know u understand.

Really? How could she, when Micah didn't?

Please, Lord . . .

He'd lain awake half the night, chewing on what Coop had said. About Paul Stryker, his ties to organized crime, and his engagement to Sloane. She'd agreed to marry this guy? They'd once shared an address, according to Coop's research. Or at least this low-life Stryker had used Sloane's address on paper. Micah didn't know why he found some comfort in the latter idea, when the fact was that she'd lied. Or kept secrets, anyway. Which amounted to the same thing. And now she'd made the front page of the *Times*.

Micah could well imagine how upset she'd be when she saw her name in the news article. It was there because of Coop. His blasted greed for a byline.

He glared at the reporter's name in black and white. They'd even updated his bio pic. He still looked like . . . what? A traitor? Because he suspected Micah's feelings for Sloane and marched ahead anyway?

Yes.

Coop had apologized before laying out his discoveries, but Micah knew him well enough to suspect the reporter would be ecstatic if he could prove Sloane was a Bonnie to Paul Stryker's Clyde. Or even a modern-day Patty Hearst, kidnapped and brainwashed into working alongside a bagman for a Russian mobster who trafficked in underage girls. And left at least one lying in an alley with her throat sliced. Micah wiped his glasses on his shirt, trying to lose the gruesome image.

Sloane wasn't a participant in any of that—he wouldn't believe it. She'd made a mistake in hooking up with a bad guy. It would be easy to similarly judge Micah's behavior after his return from the Middle East. He hadn't been choosy enough about the company he kept. It had taken him a while to divulge any of that to Sloane; he could understand her reticence. But still, shouldn't he be able to ask her about all of that now? Talk it over, sort it out? Uncomfortable, sure, but doable. Considering how much he'd come to care for her. But . . .

"*. . . it wasn't the first time Sloane got that drunk. Her coworkers saw it as a big problem.*"

Sloane was a problem drinker. An alcoholic probably. That, combined with her poor choice of partners, ultimately made her at least partially responsible for the deaths of two innocent people and the reported maiming of a coworker. Micah couldn't get past that. He'd turned it over and over in his mind those sleepless hours last night. He tried to pray—couldn't. This was far too much like what happened to Stephen. It stirred too much pain. Too much anger. He needed time to sort it out.

He'd never once seen Sloane impaired; in fact, she'd been the first to say, "No thank you" when alcohol was offered. What Coop had learned from the San Diego Hope staffer was hard to imagine, but she was so guarded and insistent on her privacy. Almost to the point of isolation; Sloane hadn't been a joiner when it came to hospital socializing. Wasn't that a sign of addiction? Those thoughts and more kept him awake last night. Far beyond his resentment of Coop's greedy ambition. Even beyond the news that Sloane had been engaged to such a high-profile loser. In the end, Micah couldn't come to grips with—

His doorbell rang.

It rang a second time before he could take two steps. And then again.

"Micah, it's Sloane."

31

"I, UH . . . Thank you for the flowers," Sloane said, afraid she was going to pass out. Her heart was beating in her ears like a bass drum. Why on earth had she come here? Micah had clearly changed his mind about seeing her. "They're beautiful."

"I'm glad you liked them."

His quick smile was a mismatch to the discomfort in his eyes. He obviously wasn't on his way to meet the crisis team: unshaven, mussed hair, wearing a faded UCLA sweatshirt and old jeans . . . no shoes.

Micah swept the door wider, clearing his throat. "Come in. I apologize for the mess."

"It's okay," Sloane said, following him inside the seventh-floor condominium. She tried her best not to dwell on the fact that he hadn't offered a hug, even the smallest of touches. "I didn't exactly give you a warning."

Their plans had included meeting here today, but she'd never seen it before. It was nice, modern, and very different from Celeste's cottage. Glossy concrete floors, high ceilings with open beams, and geometric throw rugs. Micah's notion of messy was nowhere near hers. Unless you counted a couple of dishes on his coffee table and his guitar lying across the couch. The Martin. Her throat tightened at the memory of their first date, how she'd discovered the calluses on his fingertips from the strings.

"Want some coffee?" Micah asked as they walked into the open living room. He glanced toward the kitchen area. "I have a pot going."

"No thanks." Sloane's breath snagged as she saw that Micah's "mess" also included a copy of the *Times*. Lying front page up on the stone-top table next to his coffee mug. She turned to look at him and saw his fleeting grimace. "I didn't come for coffee," she said. "I think we need to talk."

"Right." He gestured toward the leather couch. "Make yourself . . ." He seemed to catch himself. Neither of them were anywhere near comfortable. "Have a seat."

Micah lifted the guitar, propped it against the couch, and sat beside her. "I'm sorry I didn't return your texts. Or phone calls," he said, his expression out of sync with his words. No apology there. He looked sullen, wary . . . *angry?* This was bad.

"Did you really get called in for the crisis team?" Sloane asked.

Micah glanced down at his hands. "I called them—volunteered."

"Is this because of the *Times* article? My name in there because of the accident in San Diego?"

He met her gaze. "You know it's more than that, Sloane."

She made herself ask. "What did Coop say?"

"You were engaged to that guy. Paul Stryker."

"I was," she heard herself say. "But it ended—I ended it—almost two years ago. The relationship was a mistake. I can't tell you how much I regret it." The ache in her throat was making it hard to talk. "When you asked if I'd been married, I should have told you that."

"But it was 'complicated.'" Micah glanced toward the paper. "Because of all he was involved in." There was accusation in his tone.

"Yes." Sloane sat forward. "I swear I had nothing to do with any of that. I knew Paul played poker, but I had no idea how far it went. I thought he was in trouble for money he'd borrowed." Her teeth caught her lower lip; she couldn't say anything more about all that had happened recently. "I'd have sent him away even sooner if I'd known what he was up to. I meant what I said about regretting it. I wish I could go back and do it over."

"I'm sure you do," Micah said, meeting her gaze. "But it isn't only that." He dragged his fingers down his stubbled jaw, groaned. "It's like Coop's suddenly laying all this stuff out and—"

"When?" Sloane interrupted, a new emotion crowding in. "*When* exactly did he tell you about Paul . . . and about me?"

"Last night. But he'd been working on story leads for months. Piecing things together, ferreting out details. That's what Coop does."

"Then he went to Sacramento. And San Diego," Sloane

317

said, beginning to feel queasy. "Places I've lived, worked. How could he 'ferret out details' about me without knowing about my name change?"

"He did know."

Sloane's lips tensed. "How?"

"I think . . ." Micah's brows bunched. "He saw you at the prison. Got curious, I guess."

"You told him about my stepfather?"

"I did. But only after he mentioned seeing you. He was there because of another prisoner. One of the Russians. He got your information from a source he's cultivated there at the prison."

Sloane felt invaded, sick.

"Coop saw the name change on the visitor log," Micah explained. "Then told me."

"You said you'd seen it on HR records because of your marketing campaign."

"I looked it up."

—————

Micah wished he could have avoided admitting that, but it was the truth. He saw her stiffen beside him. "I had access to the records because of your nomination. But I looked it up because of what Coop told me."

"I see." Sloane had perched on the edge of the couch and begun to tremble. Her eyes pinned him with the look Coop had once called "shooting fire." That first time they'd all tangled in the ER parking lot after the incident with Zoey Jones. It seemed a lifetime ago. Everything seemed distant now— out of reach.

"So," Sloane continued, "you and your reporter buddy

think you have it all put together? You invaded my privacy to find all the scoop-worthy dirt. You proved I hooked up with a loser and changed my name because I was running from the Russian mob."

"Sloane, hold on." Was any of this fixable at this point? Should he even try? "I didn't know Coop's research in Sacramento would have anything to do with you," he insisted. "Or that he'd end up asking questions at San Diego Hope. About you. And your accident."

"What?" The color drained from her face. "You mean he got my medical records? That's illegal."

"No—not that," Micah said in a rush, almost wishing it were that instead. "Coop spoke with an ER staffer. Off the record."

"What did he say?" Sloane lifted her chin a little, that tough-girl look he thought he'd seen the last of. "Tell me, Micah."

Please, Lord. I'm not ready. . . .

"What exactly did this employee say about me?"

Micah took a deep breath, let it out slowly. "He said you were drunk the night of the accident. So incapacitated that one of your teammates had to drive your car," he explained, hating this. If only he'd had more time to think it through. And then what? No. He had to do it. "He said it wasn't the first time you were in that condition. And . . ."

"What else?" Her chin quivered.

"The girl driving your car was badly injured and people blamed you."

Tears shimmered in Sloane's eyes. He wished he could reach for her and tell her it was okay. But it wasn't. How could he ever be okay with this?

"What do you want me to say?" she asked, wiping at a tear before it could fall. "That it's a lie? Well, I can't. I was drunk that night. And too many nights to count before that." Sloane hugged her arms around herself. "I got involved with a man who ended up putting me in more trouble than even *I* could imagine—and believe me, I've seen some trouble. I messed up. Really bad."

Micah tried to think of something to say, but she wasn't finished.

"Those people in San Diego," she said, her voice thick with unshed tears, "can't blame me any more than I blame *myself*. It doesn't matter that I've been sober since they cut me free from that Jetta. That I've dragged myself to meetings for more than six months, stacking up those AA chips like . . ." Her voice broke. "Like pennies from heaven. It still doesn't change who I am. Does it?" Sloane met Micah's gaze, tears streaming down her face. "*Does* it?"

"Sloane . . ." His heart ached. Why couldn't he do this? Why was it so impossible? "I need time to think. It's a lot to take in. It's—"

"Like Stephen."

Her words kicked him in the gut.

"I'm no different than the drunk who killed your cousin. Say it, Micah."

"I . . . can't."

"Then deny it." Her voice was a raw whisper, her eyes riveted to his. "You can't do that either, can you?"

The answer wouldn't come.

"I'm going," Sloane said, rising to her feet.

Micah let her go, walk out his door. It made him feel worse than anything had in his life. Since Stephen.

How Sloane got back to the cottage, she didn't know; she didn't remember a single traffic light or turn. She only knew she couldn't look into Micah's eyes for a moment longer. It was too much like looking in the mirror.

"We see our scars and our flaws . . . God sees the child he's always loved."

She'd been foolish enough to hope it might be true. Today proved it wasn't.

Micah knew about Paul. Not all of it, but enough. He knew about her connection to that horrible crime syndicate—not all of that either. She groaned aloud as she stood in her kitchen, thinking how ironic it was that Micah had learned so much about the surreal drama of her past, but it was her drinking that hit him the hardest. Ironic, because it was the one thing she was free of. Paul had intruded into her life, grotesque and ranting, only last night. The mobsters were here, hunting for him. But the alcohol, her all-destructive thirst, was no longer a part of her life.

"I need time to think. It's a lot to take in."

Micah wasn't going to take it at all. He'd given it enough thought to cancel their plans for today and avoid her attempts to contact him. He'd already decided she wasn't worth his time, certainly not his "love." Sloane plucked the florist envelope from the rose bouquet and dropped it into the waste can under the sink. She couldn't bring herself to throw out the flowers. At least not yet. Right now all she wanted to do was curl up on the couch with Marty. . . .

She was awakened by the sound of her phone ringing on the coffee table and glanced toward the window before picking it up. It was dark outside. She retrieved her phone and saw it was Harper calling. Not Micah.

"Hey," she said, sitting upright and stretching her neck. "What's up?"

"Apparently you—over a cliff," Harper said. "Chased by Russians?"

Sloane wished she could laugh; it sounded too much like a Road Runner cartoon.

"It's totally crazy," the nurse continued. "You had to change your name and everything? Is it true?"

Who'd spread it around? Hospital admin? Micah?

Sloane's stomach sank. She was still on probation.

"What are people saying?" she asked, hoping her voice sounded casual.

"Just what I said. The people who saw the *Times* article and think maybe it's you. A lot of folks don't. About fifty-fifty, I'd say. Someone said Cooper Vance was hanging around, asking questions."

Sloane squeezed her eyes shut. Coop. She should've known.

"Your hiring records are private, of course," Harper added.

Right. Privacy.

"So . . . ," Harper said. "Is it true?"

"Partly." Sloane took a breath. "I did recently change my name. I had a very bad car accident in San Diego. But I'm not being chased by mobsters." *They're chasing Paul.*

"Oh, good." Harper's breath escaped in a whoosh. "I didn't want to believe the mafia part. These local guys are so scary. Ruthless. We've got like eight police officers guarding the SICU and the hospital entrances tonight. Because of Oksana."

"Oksana?"

"Jane Doe. Her real first name is Oksana." Harper sighed. "It's Ukrainian. Which is close enough to Russian for me, thank you."

"She can't be talking—speaking," Sloane said, cringing at an image of the girl's horrific wound. The damage to her larynx could be permanent.

"She's writing. Or that's what they're saying. The FBI was up there most of the day. There's supposed to be a dual press conference tonight. The information from Oksana and a statement regarding the identities of the girls killed in the fire."

Sloane squeezed her eyes shut. Zoey?

"Anyway," Harper said, her voice warm, "if word gets out and you get pestered by the media, or you want to get away or talk, anything, I'm home. You're always welcome to come here. But then you're probably seeing Micah."

"No." Sloane glanced at the once-hopeful roses. "He's with the crisis team tonight."

"Well then, call me if you want to get together."

"Sure."

They said good-bye and disconnected. Then Sloane heard her stomach rumble and went to check the fridge. Nothing much there except a carton of milk. She'd planned on being out tonight. No fresh food, but there was always . . .

She opened the pantry doors and glanced down at the shipping cartons from General Mills. She'd forgotten to put the newest box—the faded one—on the bottom of the stack to keep the expiration dates in line. But then again, nothing else in her life was in line either. She stooped down to open the new carton, then caught sight of the cereal box she'd opened for Piper. Lucky Charms, of course.

Sloane poured the cereal into a rooster bowl and carefully

picked out all the marshmallows. Then added milk and reached for her spoon.

"*This is what you won, baby. For your whole life—that's quite a net worth.*"

32

"I SAW YOUR LIGHTS," Celeste explained, "and thought maybe your plans had changed. If you're free after all, you're still welcome to join us. We probably won't sit down to the table for another twenty minutes or so. Jerry's wife, Ann, is here too—she's really a delight. Piper asked them to bring Gibbs and McGee." She caught her breath, laughed. "So the more the merrier. We'd love to have you."

"That's nice." Sloane made herself smile. "But I really have to pass this time. There are some things I need to take care of."

"I understand. No problem."

"Thank you, though," Sloane told her, guilt jabbing as she remembered her landlady's worried expression this morning. The concern that she'd seen Paul. Sloane was glad Celeste hadn't asked directly if she knew him. It was true she hadn't seen his car near the house, so . . . *I told a half-lie.* Somehow that didn't help the way she felt.

Sloane told Celeste to give them all her best, then walked back to the living room, battling her own nagging worries. Micah had never said whether Coop revealed her name and her whereabouts to the authorities; she'd been half-expecting a squad car to pull into the driveway since her arrival home. *"We've got like eight police officers guarding the SICU and the hospital entrances tonight."*

Mercifully, it seemed law enforcement was busy with bigger problems than Sloane Wilder Ferrell. They were expecting serious blowback from the press conference and were preparing for it. To the point of having the crisis responders on call. An official notification of death would be made to the families of the motel fire victims prior to the conference, but the news would undoubtedly have a ripple effect on many other people. A tragedy, especially such a gruesome one, always had unexpected effects.

Sloane glanced toward her muted TV. They were already showing clips of the media gathering for the press conference, interspersed with several shots of Los Angeles Hope. Fiona was there. Alone. Interesting, and telling, that Micah chose to be with the crisis team instead. To support the survivors.

She hugged her arms around herself; she should turn the TV off. She'd hear the news tomorrow—from Harper, if not Celeste first—revealing the victims' names. The press conference would be a sickening finish to this regrettable day. If what Sloane feared about one of those dental records was true, she'd feel like a survivor too.

She turned at the sound of insistent knocking on her front door.

"Sloane! Let me in. *Please.*"

Who . . . ?

She walked to the foyer, opened the door, and stared, mouth gaping. The pink hair was gone—dyed raven dark now—as was the brow ring, but it was the same battered newsboy cap, the same blue eyes.

"Can I come in?" Zoey asked, pulling up the collar of her denim jacket. She glanced nervously over her shoulder. "I know I'm the last person you'd want here, but I had to see you."

"Yes . . . here." Sloane stepped back to let Zoey inside. Relief flooded through her, a thousand dollars' worth.

"Thanks. And," Zoey said, glancing back at the door, "maybe lock it?"

"Of course," Sloane assured. There was fear in the girl's eyes.

Zoey jammed her hands in the front pockets of her jeans, looking around like she was refreshing her memory of the place. "I guess you notice I'm not in Bakersfield."

I thought you were on a medical examiner's table.

"Want some coffee? Something to eat?" Sloane asked, then frowned. "Except all I have is cereal."

Zoey went so pale, so fast, that Sloane grabbed hold of her arm. "Hey, come sit down. You look like you've seen a ghost."

"I . . ."

The girl was shivering as Sloane eased her onto the couch. Marty jumped up beside them and Zoey tried to smile. "Hey, little buddy."

Sloane draped a throw blanket around the girl's shoulders.

"I have to tell you something," Zoey said, the pallor still there. She licked her lips and uttered a small moan. "Everything's so messed up."

"I messed up. Really bad." Sloane's words to Micah only hours ago. There was no way she'd judge this girl.

"If it's about the money you took . . . ," Sloane began gently.

"It's not." Zoey's teeth sank into her lower lip. "I'm sorry about that. And for grabbing those things from the hospital. But it's worse now. Way worse."

"I'm listening."

"That day in the hospital parking lot wasn't real." She nodded at the look on Sloane's face. "I faked that whole bit. To get you out there and . . . to get myself here, I guess. At least it worked out that way."

"I don't understand. So you could steal from me?"

"I did what I was told." Zoey pulled her cap off, began picking at the stitching. "That's how we work things."

"We?"

"Me and the guy I hooked up with. A sort of business deal after he saved my skin." Zoey flinched. "More than my skin. I'd run away from home for this modeling job, but . . ." Her eyes filled with tears. "That girl with her throat cut? She's a friend of mine. And the others who burned up in the fire."

Sloane winced.

"Anyway, this dude and I ran cons, I guess you'd say," Zoey continued. "Stack was always—"

"Stack?"

"The guy I was working with. That's his name. He was always saying it was temporary, 'chump change,' he called it, to tide him over until his big payoff came in. Something he'd been waiting for. For a while, I guess. Before me, anyway." She picked at the cap, her expression anxious again. "He said just one more job and that would be it, and he'd give me some money if I wanted to go home. But I guess some stuff happened that messed with the timing. And then it all went really bad, really fast."

"You got caught?"

"Stack did—beat to a pulp." Her pupils went wide. "I thought he might die."

Sloane fought a wave of uneasiness. "When was this?"

"Yesterday afternoon sometime. Stack looked freaked out. He gave me a wad of money. Said catch a bus, hitch a ride— disappear."

"If you're still as smart as you were, you'll join my vanishing act . . ."

Sloane tried to tell herself there must be thousands of con men in LA, that violence happened every hour of every day.

"I guess he knew you . . . from before, somewhere," Zoey said, her tear-smudged eyes on Sloane's. "He set up the con at the hospital so he could be sure it was you. You looked different, he said. I was supposed to find out your name and anything else I could. We'd been watching for a couple of days, waiting. Stack said if we played it right, you'd run to help me. Because you were that kind of person." Her voice choked. "You were, you *are*. Helping me like you did. He was right."

Sloane's mind staggered; she couldn't find words.

"Things got messed up and I couldn't get ahold of Stack that night, so I hung around the hospital construction site till the next day. Then you took me home. I got your phone number off Marty's tag," Zoey added. "I had your address. I ended up giving Stack more than he asked for." She frowned. "All those months, and I never even knew his whole name."

"It's Stryker," Sloane said, her voice sounding like it was echoing up from the bottom of a well. "Paul Stryker."

"Well, there you go. Anyway, I'm sorry," Zoey repeated. "About everything. I feel *so bad*. I wish I could do it all over."

"He's gone." Sloane grasped the girl's trembling hands. "Paul's gone. It's going to be okay. I'll help you get home. There's nothing more to worry about."

"But there *is*," Zoey insisted, the awful fear back in her eyes. "That's why I'm here. Because in that last job, we—"

There was a noise somewhere outside, thunderously loud.

Sloane yanked back the curtain. Gasped. "My landlady's house is on fire!"

33

"CALL 911," SLOANE ORDERED. When she saw Zoey's hesitation, she pulled out her own phone and heaved it toward her. "Use mine. I need to get over there." She fumbled with the door lock. "Make that call!"

Sloane took off running, inhaling smoke the moment she left the porch. She sprinted across the strip of lawn between the two houses, nearly falling over the garden boxes. Her gaze was riveted on the blaze. Back of the house, it looked like, and flames were already licking toward the roof, orange sparks shooting into the dark sky. The front door was still closed. *Oh, please . . .*

Neighbors were coming from everywhere.

"Is Celeste in there?" someone shouted as Sloane came to a breathless halt on the front lawn.

"Did anyone call 911?"

"Grab a hose!"

"Let's get that door open, guys!"

Sloane started for the front door with the others, heard sirens, and then spotted Celeste and another woman emerging from the side door of the garage. Jerry was behind them, with—*oh, thank goodness*—Piper in his arms. The child seemed to be crying but basically unharmed.

"We're okay," Celeste huffed as Sloane reached them. She was flushed, perspiring, breathless. "We were all in the dining room . . . except Piper. She was changing into her costume in my bedroom when we heard this sound like breaking glass. Then this awful explosion and—"

"Gotta go back in," Jerry interrupted, easing Piper to the lawn next to his wife. His face was soot-smudged, his jaw rigid with determination. "Got to find Gibbs and McGee. Stay put, hear?" He gave his wife's arm a quick squeeze. "I'll be right back."

"Wait . . . Jerry . . ."

"Gotta go."

He took off running toward the house, not leaving a chance for anyone to talk him out of it.

"They were with me," Piper shouted after him, hands cupped around her mouth. "Grandma's bedroom!"

Celeste gathered her close and grasped Ann's hand as well. Then whispered a prayer.

Sloane performed a quick check on Piper, on all of them as best she could, considering that dozens of neighbors were crowding in. The first fire truck had just arrived, siren wailing. The two women were coughing some and anxious about Jerry but seemed okay. Piper chattered nonstop without sign of respiratory distress. The medics would be here soon.

"Oh, thank you, Lord!" Celeste uttered as they caught sight of Jerry again. Charging like a running back headed for the goal line—one wriggling, long-haired dachshund under each arm.

"Safe and sound," he puffed, his familiar grin breaking through.

The firefighters moved everybody farther back and Sloane lost sight of her landlady and guests. But Zoey was there now. Standing in the shadows near the garden boxes.

"Here," she said as Sloane joined her. "Your phone."

"Thanks—and thanks for calling."

"No problem. But what happened?" she asked, her voice anxious as a second fire rig arrived. "A grease fire?"

"It started in the guest room, they think." Sloane took a breath, willing her pulse to normalize. "My landlady said she thought she heard broken glass and then some kind of explosion."

"Explosion? Oh no." Zoey's eyes went wide. "It's *them*. They did it."

"What are you talking about? Who?"

"Those g-gangsters," she said, her chin trembling. She looked toward Sloane's place. "They're after the money."

What?

"What money?" Sloane asked, tugging at her sleeve.

"In your house."

"Look at me." She grasped Zoey's shoulders. "I don't have any money."

"You do. A lot of it." The girl's voice had risen two octaves in her panic. "I brought it here. In a white Uber van. Stack even got me a stupid uniform so I'd look like a delivery person. It was our last job. That's what I was trying to tell you. I had to take the Russian money to your place. Hidden inside a box."

No.

"The cereal company carton?" Sloane demanded, nearly shaking the girl. The faded box Jerry had brought to her door. "Is that what you're telling me?"

"Stack had one of the Lucky Charms boxes. He said it was stuff he'd never unpacked after moving a couple of years back. He got the idea to use it after I told him I'd seen all those boxes at your place."

"I said I was expecting another one," Sloane remembered, her own panic setting in. Nine hundred thousand dollars of mob money . . . *in my pantry?*

"Stack thought you'd go along with it, I guess. He thought he could talk you into running away with him. He even kept that diamond ring. I think he was going to give it back to you. But they caught up to him." Zoey's gaze darted to the burning house. "And now they've set another fire."

"Hold on," Sloane told her, still reeling. "This doesn't make sense. Why would the Russians set fire to Celeste's house?"

"I don't know." Zoey shivered. "All I know is Stack was planning to come over here to get that money. Maybe they found out?"

An engine roared to life from the direction of Sloane's cottage. A dark sedan shot backward, tripping the security lights, then roared again and ripped across the lawn in a reckless U-turn before peeling down the driveway and toward the street.

Sloane stared.

"See?" Zoey clutched at her arm. "Stack. He got the money."

Sloane gritted her teeth. "I'm sure going to find out."

She jogged to the cottage with Zoey close behind, all the while struggling to make sense of how this fit together. Paul running the scheme to put Zoey and Sloane together, his desperate need to vanish last night, and now the fire at Celeste's? She gulped in a breath as they reached the porch, telling herself she shouldn't care if she ever understood this crazy mess. She should be relieved that it was over. The filthy money was gone. Paul was gone.

Except he wasn't.

Sloane froze in the foyer, her heart in her throat.

Paul lay facedown near the pantry doors in a pool of blood.

34

"QUICK, HELP ME TURN HIM OVER. C'mon, get *down* here."
Sloane tugged at Zoey's arm, pulling her to the hardwood floor
and onto her knees; the girl immediately slid in the blood and
shrank back. Sloane snatched her arm again. "Stop that and
grab hold. *Please.* It's the only way we can help him."

Hang on, Paul. . . .

Their combined efforts succeeded in rolling him onto his
back in a deadweight heap.

Ah . . . no, no . . . This is so bad.

His face was a bloodless white, eyes half-closed, lips gone
slack and gray. A trickle of frothy blood glistened at the corner of Paul's mouth. In the center of his faded-blue Hawaiian
shirt—his lucky shirt—was a frighteningly huge bloodstain,
like a macabre blossom among the festive flowers. Bullet
wound. Had to be.

Hemopneumothorax, great vessel injury, cardiac tampon-ade . . . This was so much worse than bad.

"He's dead," Zoey groaned, fingers pressed to her lips. "He is, isn't he?"

"Call 911," Sloane ordered for the second time that night, then leaned low in an attempt to hear or see any spontaneous effort at breathing. *Nothing.* She slid her fingers against Paul's pale neck, going by rote and by protocol. But she knew there would be no pulse. She'd begun to tremble. "Call it, Zoey—here." She slid her cell phone across the floor toward the girl, grimacing as it encountered blood and stuck to the floor. "Tell them it looks like a GSW, gunshot wound. To the chest. No breathing, no pulse."

Zoey averted her eyes and Sloane finished her assessment. She made the decision to do hands-only CPR; there was too much blood in his mouth and throat for rescue breaths to be effective. And Sloane needed to protect herself, too. *Oh, Paul . . .*

"I saw medics next door," Zoey said, nearly as pale as Paul as she swabbed the phone against her jacket. "I'll run over there."

"No!" Sloane balanced on her knees, placing one hand atop the other on Paul's sternum. "They're basic EMTs. We need paramedics, a *helicopter.*" She rocked her weight onto Paul's chest, feeling still-warm blood ooze between her fingers; there was a soft sucking sound as she finished the first compression. "Call 911. Tell them what I said. Gunshot wound to the chest, under CPR. Send the chopper and a trauma team."

"Okay. I'm doing it now."

"Good . . . Good girl," Sloane said, her throat raw from battling emotion. "It's going to be his only chance."

Zoey made the call, then turned back to Sloane. "Should I go get those firefighters now?"

"Yes. We need all the help we can get. But don't tell Celeste or the others if they're still there. They don't need this now."

"Okay. I'll be back."

"Good."

Sloane listened to the girl's footsteps as she hurried away, then resumed counting her cardiac compressions aloud. She performed on autopilot, counting as she compressed Paul's breastbone, repeating the motion over and over to accomplish 100 per minute. She only looked at his face when she had to—clinically, to assess the effectiveness of her efforts—because it was too terrifying to see him like that. And it only proved what she'd known the instant they rolled him over: Paul Stryker needed far more than medics and a helicopter.

Sloane closed her eyes.

God, if you're there . . . please give him a chance.

Micah checked the intersection and accelerated through the yellow light, wishing he had the option of lights and siren. The length of time he'd been driving felt like hours; his heart hammered like he had hold of the bumper, pushing the SUV along. But he'd taken off from LA Hope only seven minutes ago and was grateful—*thank you, Lord*—he'd been so close when the back-to-back reports came in. He'd suited up for a crisis response, then decided to make himself available to Fiona as well, in the likely event of problems after the law enforcement press conference. What he never expected was to hear Sloane's address over the police scanner. A fire at Celeste's house and a shooting at Sloane's?

"*Unidentified victim is male Caucasian, late thirties, gunshot wound to chest. Under CPR. LAPD and fire on scene. No other known victims; no information regarding assailant. Witnesses report seeing a dark-colored late-model sedan . . .*"

Witnesses. Was one of them Sloane? Was she there when the shots were fired? Had she been threatened . . . hurt?

Guilt hit Micah like a fist in the gut; Sloane wouldn't have been home if he hadn't reacted the way he did to Coop's story. If he hadn't heard her side of that story through the filter of Stephen's death.

"I'm no different than the drunk who killed your cousin."

He hadn't said a word to dispute it. He'd let her walk out of his place—his life?—judging her like she was a criminal too. He'd spent all those hours in training, assuring himself he was responding to a calling, and then turned a deaf ear when someone he really cared for was in trouble?

Micah braked hard for a light, tires grabbing, then slammed his palm against the steering wheel. What good was he if he could rein in his compassion with the lame excuse of needing time to think? Did Sloane say that when she risked her own safety to run to the aid of a would-be kidnap victim? Or when she confronted the SICU nurse over his treatment of that homeless man? Was "time to think" ever valid when it came to doing the right thing?

He should pull over and turn around. He hadn't been officially dispatched, and after the hostility he'd seen in Sloane's eyes, he was probably the last person she would want to see right now. But he had to know she was all right.

His phone signaled the tone he'd assigned to the crisis team. He glanced up at the light, still incessant LA red, and went against his usual practice to take a look at the text message. From crisis dispatch:

Shooting at 2147-B Ernest Court. Guesthouse. Support for witnesses. Life Flight dispatched. *Be advised fire on same property, main house. LAFD on scene.*

Micah took a slow breath, accelerating as the light turned green. It was official. He was the responder on scene. Whether Sloane liked it or not.

He pulled up the familiar driveway five minutes later and went directly to the guesthouse, despite ongoing fire containment work at the main house. The looky-loos—and they'd better not include Coop, if he knew what was good for him—were much thicker at Sloane's place. Probably because the helicopter had landed in the empty lot next to it, rotors still turning, cockpit and interior lit.

Micah reached for his bag, mouthing a prayer. *"Help me offer comfort and hope to these survivors. . . ."*

Same prayer, same request for different people in different circumstances. And this time it could be Sloane.

He hustled through the crowd to the front door. It was open, and law enforcement had already strung yellow crime tape. He reached for his ID badge as he approached an officer.

"Crisis response team," he began. "I'm—"

"Prescott," the older man said, recognizing Micah. "We've got to stop meeting like this."

"Ah . . . right," Micah agreed, remembering him as the PD officer who'd been on scene when Jane Doe was found. Micah corrected himself: Oksana Durov. She'd been identified today. She was still incapable of voicing a single word but had become a prime witness against the traffickers. Probably the same organization responsible for the motel fire.

"We got a surprise find here," the officer said, glancing into the house. "The shooting victim is the Sacramento money runner the Feds are hunting."

What?

"Stryker?" Micah braced his palm on the doorframe.

"Yep. Got corroboration from one witness. The other one's been doing CPR. Wouldn't let the EMTs take over. Said she was waiting for the trauma team. She's an ER nurse from Hope hospital. This is her house."

I know. "I'd like to go in. If it's possible."

"Let me confirm." The officer spoke into his radio. "Flight physician has taken over. We're preserving the scene for the evidence team; deputies will tell you where you can be. Go round to the back."

"Right."

When Micah was let inside the back door, he saw Sloane immediately. She was sitting on a kitchen chair pulled into the short hallway leading from the bedroom and bath to the front of the house, with an officer at her side. Maybe only fifteen yards from where Micah stood now. Micah's heart turned over. She looked pale, shell-shocked, and was staring down at her still-bloody hands.

"They're transporting the victim?" Micah asked the officer stationed at the door. "Now that Life Flight's here?"

"Pronounced him dead right there." The officer shook his head. "Our nurse wouldn't quit until the doc showed her the head wound. Two in the chest, one to the back of the head, execution-style."

Micah grimaced.

A second man, wearing a suit, was talking with Sloane. "Is she being questioned?"

"Initial statements, I'd suspect. Several neighbors confirmed the story that the nurse and the girl were helping the fire victims next door when a car went speeding away from the guesthouse. Then, allegedly, they walk in and find the guy on the floor. The nurse starts CPR. The other witness calls 911."

"Who was the other witness?"

"A young woman. Nineteen, she said, but I doubt it."

Micah had to ask. "So why was this guy here, in the house?"

"Can't really say more," the officer advised. "Sort of a 'tangled web,' as my wife likes to say. The Feds are all over this one."

Micah nodded, thinking that was exactly how his brain felt. Tangled, confused. He glanced down the hallway again, knowing he couldn't even imagine all that Sloane had endured. "The fire. Anyone injured there?"

"Don't think so." The officer's brows rose. "Pretty good diversion tactic, maybe?"

For a professional hit.

Micah had no clue how to deal with this—except as a crisis responder. It wasn't his job to investigate or judge or fix, even if all he wanted right now was to wrap Sloane in his arms and protect her. He took a slow breath. "I can't go in there, talk with her?"

"Not yet. She may end up down at the station. The girl too."

"Not as suspects?"

"Doesn't look like it, but can't rule anything out."

Micah wasn't going to start down that path.

"Okay then," he said, pulling a crisis team card from his bag. He jotted a few words on the back. "I'm going to see how things are going next door and maybe talk with those neighbors." He handed the card to the officer. "Give this to the nurse, Sloane Ferrell?"

"Will do."

"Thanks."

Micah glanced down the hallway, and Sloane's eyes met his. She stared at him for a few seconds, then looked away.

35

"I WISH I COULD TALK you into coming home with me."

Harper leaned forward on the bed and snugged the motel room blanket around Sloane's shoulders. It was thin, a graying pink, and smelled of lavender potpourri stirred with a cigarette. It did nothing to stop the chill that had reached Sloane's bones. Harper brought soup—oxtail from a Chinese kitchen on the corner—complete with a plastic ladle spoon; she'd apologized, saying it was the closest she could find to chicken soup on short notice. Sloane had forced herself to eat a few bites, mostly to reassure her worried friend.

"I think you scrubbed half your skin off in that shower." Harper looked at Sloane the way Sloane must have looked at Marty in his shelter cage. Her nose wrinkled. "I hope you wore flip-flops in there. This room is more than iffy."

Sloane's shrug freed more potpourri scent. "Three stars."

"They bribed somebody at Yelp."

Sloane tried to smile but couldn't.

She wondered what Harper would say if she knew this room was paid for by organized crime. Zoey must have tucked the envelope of money into Sloane's pocket at some point during all the chaos. She hadn't found it until she returned to her Volvo after the police interviews. Ten crisp hundred-dollar bills to repay the money Zoey had taken from the rooster canister. A thousand dollars given to Zoey by "Stack," undoubtedly part of the stolen money he'd had squirreled away while he was in Mexico. Gambling money, drug money, trafficking money . . . blood money? Sloane would never know for sure. She only knew the mobsters forced Paul to take them to get it back, then brutally executed him. Her stomach twisted at the thought of him bleeding to death on her floor.

She didn't want anything to do with that envelope of money, but her cottage was a crime scene and she'd needed a place to sleep; without credit and ATM cards, she had no access to enough cash until Monday. So she took on one more shame and let dubious money rent this room. She shivered.

"You okay?" Harper halted her effort to smooth the jacket she was sitting on to avoid bedspread cooties. "Are you injured?"

My head, my heart . . . my soul? And what little pride she'd had left. Micah had been there. At the cottage.

"I'm fine." Sloane shook her head. "The police didn't hit me with rubber hoses, Harper. They just asked questions. There was coffee and toaster strudel."

Harper's magazine-ad eyes studied hers. Truth seeking.

"Okay, it was awful being there," Sloane admitted. "And

considering what I expect is on the TV news right now . . ." She blinked to halt tears. She had no right to cry. If she did, she might not be able to stop. "I'm surprised you'd be here."

"Try and stop me." Harper reached for Sloane's hand. "You did try. And you failed. If I'd been able to get a message to you earlier about my guest room, I wouldn't have taken no for an answer. I've never let anyone I cared about deal with something like this alone."

"You know people who *had* something like this?"

"No. You're the first." Harper's expression sobered. "Have they found your cat?"

"Not yet."

Marty had disappeared. There had been smoke, sirens, gunshots, and strangers tramping through the house. The door was open much of that time. It would have been a miracle if he hadn't run off. But still, Sloane had searched under the beds, in the closets, and everywhere she could think of until the police insisted she go to the station for the interviews. One of the evidence technicians was a cat lover and promised she'd watch for him. Sloane left the travel carrier in the kitchen next to Marty's food bowl. "I walked the neighborhood after I got back from the station but . . ."

It had been a nightmare. There wasn't any sign of Marty, and the neighbors had been too wary to even talk with Sloane, as if their homes would be the next to catch a firebomb. Then a TV reporter spotted her. "Jerry's planning to go over and search around the house a few times tonight. As close as the CSI folks will let him get. Marty has his collar and tags and a microchip. That's good, I guess."

Harper nodded. "And how is Zoey?"

"She's in a safe house tonight. After that, I'm not sure. She wants to go home. But at some point she'll probably have to at least give a deposition."

"Along with Oksana."

"When and if they catch that Viktor guy." Sloane thought of Zoey's tears when she hinted at her experiences with him. "Zoey's dealt with more than I ever did."

"I don't know . . ." Harper hadn't let go of Sloane's hand. "I get the feeling you've had more than your share of tough stuff, pal."

"Ugly stuff, you mean." Sloane closed her eyes. "What are they saying? In the news?"

"I don't think now is the time to worry about that."

"Tell me." Sloane opened her eyes, slid her hand away. "I have to know."

"Well . . . you saw the paper. The TV news took that and ran with it after the press conference. Sex trafficking, gambling money, arson, murder. I think they have most of Southern California piling furniture against their doors to stave off the Russians." Harper sighed. "They're saying you had a past connection to the man who was killed. And Zoey was traveling with him—they didn't use her name because she's a minor."

"But they used mine."

"Yes." Harper grimaced. "Both last names. They said you were a nurse at LA Hope. And you'd been cooperating with the investigation."

"Aaagh . . ." The motel blanket slid from Sloane's shoulders. "My job."

"You have friends there," Harper said quickly. "People who'll stick by you."

"Like Morgan from the SICU?" Sloane groaned, thinking of their heated exchange in the ER. "I'm sure I can count on him."

"You can count on *me*." Harper reached for the blanket. "And there's Micah. Where is he, anyway? I thought he'd be riding in like a white knight."

Sloane's heart cramped. Even real chicken soup couldn't fix that.

"I don't know, man. . . ." Coop fingered his beard scruff, looked at Micah in the driver's seat. Even in the meager illumination of the dash lights his expression appeared agitated. "How was I supposed to know—?"

"That you'd get somebody *killed*?" Micah barely resisted the urge to bash him. He'd come back to the scene hoping to catch a glimpse of Sloane. Finding Coop sniffing around only made things worse. "Get a firebomb thrown into somebody's house? Turn Sloane's life into some blasted three-ring circus?"

Coop raised his palms. "I didn't use her new name. The TV guys did that. And it's not like she's so innocent—hey, man, that's how it reads. To me and everyone else. What's that dumb thing they say? 'Not my monkeys, not my circus'? Well, it *is*, dude. All hers, plus a juggling act. Your nurse made her bed; now she's got to—"

"*Shut up.*" Micah lunged across the seat, snatched a fistful of Coop's shirt, and shoved him against the passenger window. "One more stupid cliché and I swear I'll . . ."

"Hold on; hold on." Coop's eyes showed too much white. He twisted against Micah's grip.

"Go ahead. Give me one more excuse," Micah threatened, his fist trembling in an aftershock of what had been happening in his gut for hours. All he knew was that someone was to blame and—

"Hey, Micah. Easy." Coop had gone pale. His voice rasped from the pressure against his throat. "Let go. Please . . . I can't breathe."

Micah stared, saw that his knuckles had gone white with the ferocity of his grip. *What am I doing? God, help me. . . .*

"Uh . . . better. Thanks, man," Coop managed as Micah moved away.

"Don't thank me. Don't talk."

Micah hunched over the steering wheel and stared out the windshield, barely seeing the tableau beyond. Firefighters mopping up at Celeste's house. Patrol cars, unmarked cars, and forensic vans still in front of Sloane's. The lights were on inside. Evidence was being gathered, photographed, and tagged. Micah had heard something about multiple shipping cartons of cereal. He didn't get that. But then he didn't understand any of this. He only knew that it suddenly felt like he'd taken a bullet too.

Coop cleared his throat. "I can see where you're coming from."

"Right." Micah shook his head. "Don't bother; I'm past punching you now."

"No, really." The reporter did his own survey through the window. "When I heard there was a kid in there . . . I don't know. I was so stoked about this story. I've been dogging it for months. And there it was. Right in my hands." He turned toward Micah, his forehead creasing. "That byline—my name in print. A real feature article. Not a stupid pumpkin patch or lawn watering tips. But . . ."

Micah waited.

"You're right." Coop tugged at the neckline of his shirt. "Even if I never meant for it to happen like it did, some of this is for sure on me. My investigation pressured those Russians. They got to Stryker and forced him to take them to the money. They threw that bomb for a diversion. . . ." Coop exhaled in a half groan. "Somebody's dead—bad guy or not. Doesn't really matter. What if that runaway girl and your nurse had gone back to the house a few minutes earlier?"

Micah's heart stalled out. He'd gone over and over that in his head. The truth was, he could blame Coop—act like a jerk and slam him around—and it wouldn't change the fact that Sloane would never have been there if Micah had handled things better. If he hadn't sent her away this morning.

"I need time to think. It's a lot to take in."

Micah tapped his phone in the darkness, watched the screen light, and looked at the message icon. Nothing. He'd written that note on the crisis card asking Sloane to call him, then sent a half-dozen texts. And left a voice mail. She hadn't responded. One of his LAPD friends said she'd been released after the interviews, but they didn't know where she'd gone.

36

"HOW DID YOU GET HERE?" Sloane asked, shocked Zoey had come.

"Uber. No van. No uniform." Zoey dredged up her impish smile. She'd lost all of her makeup and looked twelve years old. Even her hair seemed less coal-black; Sloane suspected she'd scoured herself in a shower too. Blood washed off pretty well, but the painful ugliness stuck. A smile wasn't much better than a Band-Aid.

"But you said you were in a safe house," Sloane said, thinking this girl must be spending Russian money too. From the small remaining portion that hadn't been so violently retrieved from Sloane's pantry. She fought a shudder, remembering the bits of sugar-frosted cereal scattered around Paul's body. "Don't they take a head count in those places?"

"My head was counted. Before I went out the window. I have great skills in that area—in *and* out. Stack . . . Paul, he made sure of that." There was a flicker of something sad in her blue eyes before she turned to inspect the food carton Harper left behind. "*Eww.* What is that?"

"Oxtail soup. A friend brought it over."

"Some friend."

Sloane smiled, really smiled, for the first time in hours. At odds with everything, it felt better having this outlaw kid here.

"Anyway," Zoey continued, picking at her chipped black nail polish, "you told me where you were staying, and I thought maybe I'd stop by. Kind of decompress. Isn't that what they call it? The shrink version of 'chill'?"

"I guess."

Zoey leaned her backpack against the bed. "Better if you had beer."

"We had this conversation once before. Right before you raided my rooster jar." Sloane raised a brow. "You want the cash back?"

"Nope. It's yours. And I know you don't drink." Zoey boosted herself up onto the mattress. "You had those AA chips in a drawer. I left them for you. They're not easy to come by."

Easy does it.

"Nope." Sloane sat cross-legged beside Zoey. She glanced sideways at the girl. "How'd it go with the police?"

"It went. They'll probably go easy on me because I'm underage and was sort of forced into stealing. At least that's what they said. Because there was always a threat of being sent back to Viktor." Zoey shook her head. "It makes no sense, but it was hard to snitch on Stack." She frowned. "Do you care if I call him that?"

"It's fine."

"Anyhow, I know he was a crook. And sometimes he was a jerk to me. Treated me like I was his snot-nose kid sister."

Relief washed over Sloane. Paul hadn't taken advantage of her in all ways.

"But still, I know he thought I was smart. He said so, plenty of times. And he looked after me in his own way, I guess." Zoey's voice cracked a little. "Like I was worth the trouble. That's something, right?"

Sloane's stomach wrenched. Was that all she'd expected from her own relationship with Paul?

"I told the police and the agents a lot. Stuff Stack and I did. Things he said about what he did with the Russians—he hardly told me anything, really. They asked me what I knew about Viktor." Her lips twisted. "Which is hard to deny with his brand inked on your butt."

Sloane hated that she'd guessed it right.

"So I told them what I knew. How it worked. The 'modeling.'" The fleeting look in Zoey's eyes made Sloane ache to hug her. But the girl kept talking. "I was only working for him a few weeks before Stack got me out of there. Barely out on the street. Most of what I knew I heard from Oksana and the other girls."

"Do you know how much she told the authorities?"

"Not yet."

It would be in the news, no doubt. Sloane hated everything about that. Unless it actually put Viktor away. He was "low-level," according to Paul. So were cockroaches if you compared them to a rabid dog, but they still needed to be taken out.

"You know . . ." Zoey's voice had softened. "When Stack was

coaching me for the hospital job, he told me stuff about you. Like how you used to wear your hair all spiky and purplish." She glanced sideways at Sloane. "And how you were all tough-like, with thick skin and attitude. Because you didn't have a father. And your mom died. A lot of hard knocks, Stack said."

Sloane's throat tightened.

"He wanted me to kind of seem like you. So you'd relate. Feel for me." Zoey gave a small shrug, but there was nothing offhand in her expression. "It was Stack's idea to do my hair pink. And pretend like I'd been kidnapped by a pervert."

She'd never told Paul about Phillip. She'd never admitted it to anyone. Except her mother.

"So I did all that," Zoey said, "and you took me home. Fed me, gave me clean clothes, and offered me bus money. More than Stack even expected. It was one of the times he said I was smart. A great little actress. But I really didn't have to try that hard." Zoey picked at her nail polish for a few seconds. When she finally met Sloane's gaze, her eyes were filled with tears. "The thing is, so far my life has been a lot like yours was. I'm like you. Or I could be, if I ever find my way through this mess. I guess I'm saying I wish I *were* more like you are now. Brave. And really decent."

Sloane's heart lugged. "Aagh . . . you're killing me, Zoey Jones."

"Not actually my name. The Jones part." She brushed at a tear. "It's Atkinson. Zoey Jayne Atkinson from Boulder, Colorado."

"Well, okay then." Sloane smiled and extended her hand. "Good to meet you, Zoey from Boulder."

"Same here." The girl grasped Sloane's hand. "I'm glad I met you. Regardless."

"Yes. Regardless." Sloane nodded. "Is that why you sneaked over here? To tell me all that?"

"And to give you this." She reached into her jacket pocket and pulled out the silver chain and cross. "I shouldn't have taken it," she said, laying it in Sloane's palm.

"Paul let you keep it?"

"I never showed it to him."

"It was my father's," Sloane told her. "I think he gave it to my mother as sort of a promise they'd be married. But he was killed before I was born. Now . . . they're both gone."

"And you wore it."

"I never did. I just kept it."

"Oh." The girl was quiet for a few moments. "I don't know why, but I felt sort of safe having it with me. Protected, maybe. With everything that was going on with Oksana and the girls. And when I felt alone. It's hard to explain, but it made me feel like things could be okay."

"You . . . believe in God?" Sloane heard herself ask, not sure if she was repeating what she'd been asked by Piper . . . or by Micah? She wasn't sure she should have asked it at all but—

"I want to," the girl said as if she'd been thinking about it for a while. "It wasn't part of my life . . . before. I never bought into any of that hard sell, the things some of those church ladies would say when they'd see us on the streets. Calling us sinners and saying we'd be judged. How we'd better get 'clean and purified' before it was too late."

Sloane saw an image of the two of them at Paul's side, blood on their hands, fighting to save him. Her fingers closed over the cool metal of her father's necklace.

"They scared me, I guess," Zoey continued. "It felt more like an extra helping of shame."

Sloane nodded. She'd had it by the plateful.

"But there was this woman once, one of those volunteers who help get girls off the street. I think that's what she was. Maybe part of that crisis team. Anyway, I was in a foul mood. Some creep had kicked me in the ribs the night before. Like I was a stray dog or something."

Sloane winced.

"I told this woman that I didn't need her to tell me I was going to hell. But she said she wasn't there to preach. She wasn't supposed to do that, but since I'd mentioned it, she said she knew for a fact that I was special in God's eyes. Just the way I was. That he loves me like a father because that's what I am—his child." Zoey shook her head, but there was no hiding the wonder on her face. "I didn't trust it. Not with everything I was seeing back then." She glanced down at Sloane's hand, holding the necklace. "But lately I've been hoping it's true."

"You remember that little girl . . . my landlady's grand-daughter?"

Zoey nodded.

"Her name's Piper. Funny, confident, happy little kid. She said something to me once—that God has a picture of her on his fridge. He has a 'ginormous' refrigerator in heaven and he taped her picture on it. Because he's crazy about her." Sloane smiled at the look on Zoey's face. "Yeah, I know. But I think that's a lot like what the volunteer was trying to tell you. In God's eyes, you're more than worth the trouble." Sloane blinked against tears, then held the necklace out. "I want you to have this."

"What?"

"It's yours," Sloane said despite an ache that threatened to choke her. "Because I'm completely sure that if God does have a fridge, your picture—whatever color hair—is right there on it. And . . ." A tear slid down her face. "I don't want you to *ever* forget it. You hear me, Zoey from Boulder? Promise you'll remember that."

"I'll try." Zoey took the necklace and flung her arms around Sloane's neck, hugging her. "Thank you. For this. And for everything."

"No problem."

Zoey gave Sloane one last squeeze, then pocketed the necklace and glanced toward the door. "I should go."

Sloane nodded. "Right. Get back to the shelter before they count heads again."

"Not yet. First, I'm going to look around for Marty."

"With an Uber ride?" Sloane asked, touched.

"I'll have 'em park and wait." The girl shrugged. "I can afford it. And then after that I'm going to the hospital."

"The hospital?"

"To see Oksana. I heard she was moved out of intensive care."

"Even if that's true, they wouldn't let you visit. You're not family, it's late, and there are police posted there."

"Not a problem." The girl's smile was definitely impish. "I've got skills, remember? In, out. You can't imagine how many places I've done that."

"It won't work. Only staff—"

"I have scrubs. Swiped them from the hospital that day we met." She shrugged. "The cops took me to the bus station to get my backpack, so now I have everything I need. They said they'd take me to see her tomorrow, but I'm not going to count on it. Besides . . . I kind of like the challenge."

There was nothing Sloane could do but shake her head.

They said their good-byes and Zoey was gone, leaving Sloane alone with the slim choices of cold oxtail soup, risking TV, or turning out the lights to toss and turn.

Her phone buzzed—a calendar reminder she'd set weeks back for October 17.

The State Prison parole board meeting was only two days away. In the current shambles of Sloane's life, it was the one thing that still felt right.

She glanced at the messages she'd already seen. Then tapped Play to listen to one last voice mail. Her heart turned over at the sound of Micah's voice.

"It's me again. I just need to know you're okay. I have to know if there's anything I can do."

She listened to it again, remembering how he'd looked standing at her back door in his crisis team jacket. As the police swarmed in and out, laying bare the ugliness of her past and exposing her miserable mistakes as graphically as the lifeless body on her floor.

"I wish I were more like you . . . Brave. And really decent."

Zoey was so naive.

Micah wasn't.

Sloane closed her eyes, wishing she could forget the things he'd said before it all came crashing down—how he'd called her special and how he'd said they would take their time and get to know each other. She wished she could forget his kisses, the safety she'd felt in his arms, and most of all, the hope he'd made her feel.

But Micah's texts, his calls, especially this last one, were because he'd been assigned to cover a tragedy on Ernest Court. Her screwed-up life had become tonight's crisis call. He'd left that business card at the scene with a jotted message—*Call me, please*—because Micah Prescott was dedicated and thorough and wanted to know if there was anything left to do. There was. He'd probably already figured it out.

Sloane closed her eyes, held the phone, and whispered the sad truth aloud. "Someone like you should run as fast as you can from someone like me."

37

Monday and still no word from Sloane.

Micah had driven by the house several times yesterday, but the police still had crime tape up. The forensics team wasn't expected to finish before this morning at the earliest. There had been no sign of Celeste either. But she'd told Micah, in his capacity as a crisis responder, that she'd be staying with her daughter and granddaughter for a day or two. Fortunately—if that word could be used in conjunction with a mob hit—the worst of the fire damage was limited to the guest room at the back of the house. The arson team believed an explosive device had been hurled through a window, igniting the carpet, bedding, curtains, and then extending up to the attic space and roof. There had been smoke damage to other rooms. But, thank God, no injuries or loss of life.

Not in that house . . .

Micah stared down at the front page of the newspaper on his desk. It displayed the same image of Paul Stryker and now an old passport photo of Viktor Aristov. Along with brief mention of a teenage girl who'd been at the murder scene and had provided information to authorities. She'd not been named, but Micah knew it was Zoey Jones.

His gaze followed the article to its mention of Sloane, prefaced with "local RN and former fiancée of Stryker." It reported there was no evidence she'd been complicit in these crimes; she'd been cooperative with authorities but was still refusing all media interviews.

"I won't have any of my personal information made public. No photos, no contact information. Nothing. If the hospital does that, I'll be forced to take action."

Sloane's words—her threat—right here in this office. She'd meant business; Micah hadn't doubted that. And all this had made her fair game for countless social media trolls and every tabloid "news" hound in LA. Micah grimaced, thinking of the gossip magazine he'd seen in the hands of a hospital visitor this morning. It had been only a quick glimpse in passing, and he couldn't be 100 percent certain, but a photo had caught his eye. Black-and-white, a little grainy from enlargement, but very recognizable: Sloane. Kneeling next to Zoey Jones— in the ER parking lot. Coop's photo. He'd told Micah he'd deleted it. And now . . . *he sold it?*

Micah clenched his teeth. No way he'd let Coop get away with this. But at the moment Micah was more worried about what he'd just seen here, in the *Times.*

He reread the short addendum to the newspaper article:

According to Los Angeles Hope hospital PIO Fiona Everett, Ms. Ferrell is currently on administrative leave from her position as an RN in the hospital's emergency department.

Administrative leave?

From what Micah heard, Sloane had left a message for the emergency department director late Saturday night saying she wouldn't be coming in this week. Micah was certain she'd felt the need to make a first move before hospital administration insisted on a temporary leave. A preemptive strike was so like Sloane. He had a sudden, daunting image of her eyes that day she ran to rescue Zoey. A woman on a mission, defying anyone to interfere. Who could have known what that day would set in motion?

Only God . . .

Micah's jaw tensed as the too-familiar feeling washed over him. How did the plans of a loving God allow for what happened here? A young runaway at the mercy of organized crime; a family forced to flee their burning home; a man shot dead, while the woman whose only intent had been to help was . . .

Where? Where are you?

Micah had joined Fiona for the press conference this morning. Reporters were eager for word regarding Oksana Durov, especially since there had been hints from law enforcement of a connection to a Russian prisoner being held at State Prison. And then, even as they were assembling for the current feeding frenzy, there was breaking news: Viktor Aristov had been taken into FBI custody outside Modesto, California. While taking him off the streets would do little to thwart the agenda of the mobsters, it was a start. *And he won't be inking his brand on any more young girls.*

After meeting with the media, Micah had stopped by the ER to find Harper. She was assigned to triage and, though the waiting room looked surprisingly empty, told Micah she was busy and could only spare a minute. He had a strong sense she wanted to avoid him altogether; she wouldn't even look him in the eye. She said she didn't know where Sloane was "right now" but did say they'd been in contact and that her friend was mostly worried about her cat. Marty had disappeared during the fracas.

When Micah tried to give Harper his cell number in case she heard anything else, she'd finally met his gaze directly. She was sorry, but she couldn't do that.

He glanced at his phone, not even certain of what he'd say if he did finally reach Sloane. As much as he wanted to know she was safe after such a staggering series of blows, had his concerns, his doubts, changed?

"It's not like she's so innocent. . . . Your nurse made her bed; now she's got to—"

Lie in it? Was that what Micah thought too? He'd gone for Coop's throat to stop him from saying it, but was the anger really because Micah couldn't bring himself to accept that he'd been falling in love with a woman whose choices ultimately put her in this situation? Even if she'd worked so hard to put that past behind, to the point of changing her name, changing jobs, and . . . ?

"It doesn't matter that I've been sober . . . dragged myself to meetings for more than six months, stacking up those AA chips . . ."

Yesterday at church he'd seen mention of an Alcoholics Anonymous meeting in the weekly bulletin. It had probably been a regular Monday night meeting for years, but this was the first time Micah noticed.

The kid who'd killed Stephen had sought out a twelve-step program too. Wrote letters, then met with Stephen's parents and Micah's in person for "amends." He'd asked to meet with Micah too, but there was no way he'd let that happen. Amends? How was that even possible?

"Knock, knock." Fiona tapped on his doorframe, holding out a small stack of papers.

"Oh, hey," Micah said, grateful for the interruption. "What's that?"

"More campaign nominations. They somehow got routed to my desk instead of yours." She released a sigh as she set them on his desk. "I didn't mind. After what's been going on, it's a welcome reminder that hope still exists."

"Good point."

"And I'm off to a meeting," Fiona said. "I feel like Tinker Bell. Sharing some hope, flitting off."

Micah forced a smile. "Somebody's got to do it."

After Fiona left, he thumbed through the nomination forms. She was right; it was a welcome reminder that there was still something positive to look forward to. And a measure of proof that maybe something was going the way it was supposed to.

What the . . . ?

Micah spread the sheets out, ten of them, and scanned the information again. All of it carefully typed, and all—every one—nominating the same employee: Brittany Brill. The board member's niece.

Micah thumped his fist against the papers, biting back a

curse. He was a fool to hope even this one thing would work the way it was supposed to.

———

"'And,'" the prison official continued, reading aloud from an inmate's statement, "'he told me I'm worth something even after all I done wrong. I'm never getting out of here, but my soul is free. That's the promise. Bob Bullard made me see it. I'm not the only one he's helped either.'" The official lowered the paper and glanced at the assembled board members. "That's it."

"Thank you," the leader said. "Are there additional letters of support before we move on to Mr. Bullard's statement?"

"No further letters."

"All right then," the leader continued. "We'll hear from Mr. Bullard. And then go on to the victim statement."

Sloane's stomach tensed and a humming in her ears blotted out all but her own heartbeat. Her clammy hands left little raised fingerprints, like allergic welts, on the papers in her lap. The room was empty except for the board, her stepfather, and three other participants seated in chairs near hers. Any minute the board would order Sloane to stand and—no, they'd *welcome* her. Bob Bullard was the monster who'd growled orders. This parole board was giving Sloane an opportunity to speak out and see to it that he stayed behind bars. It had been her primary goal for months, her one true north. And now it was the only thing she could still make right . . .

". . . I'd give anything if I could go back and change what happened. Undo the wrongs and all the pain I caused."

Her stepfather was speaking now, addressing the parole board and . . . *me.*

Sloane's gaze met his, and she was certain she'd be sick. She tried to summon the shielding anger, but all that came was the scent of solvent and oil and the memory of her shrill rant that night in the garage.

"You can't hurt me—you're nothing. Do you hear me? You're going to die a big fat zero."

Why was she shaking like this? Why couldn't she focus on her statement?

"Miss Ferrell?" The board member repeated her name. "Your victim statement?"

"Uh . . . yes."

Sloane forced herself to stand, one hand on the cold metal back of the chair in front of her in case her knees gave way. Everything was a blur. The paper trembled in her fingers. She fought a wave of nausea as the replay of the garage incident gave way to a more horrifying collage of images: herself hanging upside down in the crushed Jetta, Zoey's hands covered in Paul's blood, and the look on Micah's face when she'd tried to make him understand about her past mistakes.

"You were drunk the night of the accident. So incapacitated that one of your teammates had to drive your car."

She dropped her other hand to the chair back, crumpling the victim statement. The room began to spin. *Please, please . . .*

"Miss Ferrell?"

"I . . . I'm sorry." Sloane's voice emerged in a strangled whisper. "I have to leave."

She wasn't sure how she got out of the room or back to her car. She only knew that she'd failed at one of the last things in her life worth anything at all.

Forty minutes later, Sloane swallowed a mouthful of French roast, black—chosen only for its much-needed caffeine—then took one more covert glance around the Starbucks before sliding her sunglasses to the top of her head. The customers looked benign enough: young women in yoga gear sipping tea, two men in business attire completely absorbed in conversation, and an older gentleman with a graying beard, elbow-patch sweater, dark glasses . . . and a service dog. A few others ordered their coffees to go in the usual morning rush. Mercifully, there was nobody who looked remotely like a reporter. Sloane took one more sip of her coffee, then turned her attention back to her priority task: searching for Marty. She still couldn't explain what happened at the parole hearing, but she couldn't let anything—exhaustion, stress, bone-deep uncertainty—interfere with finding her cat.

She refreshed her laptop screen and scrolled down the page of images posted by the local branch of Los Angeles Animal Services. Sloane had begun the laborious task of calling individual shelters before she'd discovered the Finding a Lost Pet search option online. It let her enter type of animal, gender, age, size, and color. Her heart stalled as yet another black cat stared out from the page.

I am a black domestic shorthair. My name is unknown.
I've been at the shelter since September 1.

Wrong date. Not Marty.
She reminded herself that he had a collar and tags, a microchip, and that he could still be hiding somewhere around the cottage.
She thought of that dark sedan squealing away from her

house. Had those killers left the door open after they dragged Paul in, forced him to identify the shipping box?

Sloane closed her eyes. Did they run down Marty as they sped away? She tried not to imagine how little of a cat might be left in the street after the fire trucks, police vehicles, forensic vans . . . and crisis response. Micah.

Was he at the hospital today? Sloane hadn't watched the news. Couldn't. And she hadn't heard from Harper yet. She'd asked her friend not to tell Micah where she was, grateful that her vague "things have changed between us" explanation wasn't questioned. Sloane couldn't have said more even if she'd wanted to. There really wasn't anyone she could tell it all to. The stark truth of that had kept her awake all night. And left her feeling more alone than she had in her whole life. Especially now that Marty was—

Her phone buzzed on the table. She picked it up and her pulse quickened. Wasn't that the number of one of the animal rescue shelters? *Please, please . . .*

"Hello?" she said, dropping her sunglasses back into place.

"Sloane Ferrell?"

"Yes, that's me."

"Wonderful. This is Sarah at Four Paws Rescue. Have you lost a cat? A young, neutered black shorthair?"

"Yes. Marty." A rush of relief made Sloane queasy. "His name should be on his collar."

"It sure is." There was a smile in Sarah's voice. "And he's been asking for you. Let me give you directions to our location."

38

HOWARD BRILL LEANED FORWARD in the chair, his eyes meeting Micah's across a desk spread with nomination forms. "Exactly what are you saying, Prescott?"

"That these . . ." Micah fought to keep his voice even. It was his job to be diplomatic. Maybe even deferential when it came to hospital board members. Which only made him angrier. "These nomination forms aren't authentic." *Fraud* was a better word.

"You don't believe my niece has such tremendous support?" *Liar* fit too.

"I didn't rule it out, but I did some fact-checking." Micah was suddenly glad a desk separated them. He remembered the sound of Coop's head smacking the window of his Durango. *Cool it—keep it cool . . .* "I spoke with every employee who signed these forms, Mr. Brill. Each one said you spoke with them. And that you were directly involved in completing the forms."

"I don't see a problem there." The shoulders of Brill's well-cut jacket lifted in an unconcerned shrug. "I was glad to offer technical assistance. Frankly, your nomination procedure was less than user-friendly. We should expect better from you. I'm sure your superior does."

Micah's temples began to throb. "Unfortunately, I discovered it was more than technical assistance. You *wrote* these nominations and asked them to sign."

Brill's brows lifted only slightly. "These good people made some complaint?"

"No. They said they didn't mind doing the favor." The board member's smug smile pushed one too many buttons. Micah told himself he should stop but . . . "I got the feeling that if I pressed it, I might discover you'd promised a return *favor*. Parking spaces, maybe? Coffee cards? A good word to their supervisors?"

"Hold on, Prescott. You're *accusing* me?"

"I don't have to." Micah lifted the papers, barely stopping himself from hurling them at the man. "These do."

"I see." Brill glanced toward the closed door, then turned back to Micah. His eyes narrowed. "What do you intend to do with this 'evidence' you believe you've found?"

"I haven't figured that out yet," Micah admitted. He hadn't gotten that far. Too many other things on his mind. "But it's not right for anyone to try and game this selection. To influence the outcome no matter *who* they are." He shook his head, tempering his frustration. "Look, Mr. Brill, I've heard good things about your niece. Beyond all *this* effort." He set the nomination forms on his desk. "I get that you're proud of her. I understand you'd want me to know that. But I'm not personally choosing the Face of Hope winner. It won't be up to me. We're putting together a panel to go over the nominations."

"But it's your campaign. And you have influence. You could put in a word. Or two. If push came to shove."

Push? Shove?

"What does that mean?" Micah asked.

The shrug was back. "Only that it's also a panel that reviews your contract." Brill steepled his fingers; a USC ring glinted in the overhead lights. "The hospital board has a say in keeping you in your position here. Or letting you go."

Micah stared at him.

Brill raised his brows fully this time. "Something to consider?"

———

Sloane needed Marty's cat carrier. She had the key to the cottage in her hands. The forensic team had finished their work. No cars in the driveway, no sign of the media or even the neighbors, but . . .

She sat in her Volvo, frozen to the seat.

I can't . . . Oh, please. How can I do this?

She lowered the window but found no comfort in the breeze. It still smelled of smoke.

There were tarps on Celeste's roof. Ladders on the side of the house, a building contractor's sign pounded into the lawn. A wheelbarrow on the porch—Jerry's wheelbarrow. He'd offered to help, of course. First with building the garden boxes and now with cleaning up Sloane's personal path of destruction.

Celeste had sent a text on Sunday to ask if Sloane was okay.

She said they were all fine and that she would help watch for Marty. She'd also said that she'd ordered a cleaning crew for the cottage. Sloane had simply replied, I'm so sorry.

It didn't begin to cover . . . *anything*. There were no words.

Somehow she managed to make it to the porch and, keys shaking in her hands, open the door, then step inside. The scent made her stomach lurch: chlorine bleach, commercial disinfectant, and something that smelled a lot like Celeste's apple air freshener. Sloane glanced toward the kitchen and saw the spray can sitting on the tile counter. Febreze to cover up—

Get the cat carrier. And go.

But something drew her, pulled her, toward the pantry doors.

In an instant she was sitting on the floor, staring down at the hardwood planks, her breath coming in ragged, shallow pulls.

They'd cleaned up. The dark, congealed pool of Paul's blood was gone. The floorboards were returned to their usual semi-scuffed sheen. Except . . . Sloane spread her palms on the wood and leaned closer. Trying to see. Then swallowed against a gag. There was still blood in the grooves between some of the floorboards. So black that it almost looked like it could be old varnish or garden soil tracked in by a rambunctious grandchild . . . *or even chocolate chip cookie crumbs?* No. Sloane knew better. She'd spent a career dealing with blood; she'd knelt in it right here only two days ago, trying with every ounce of her being to save Paul's life. Praying . . . as if God would listen to someone like her. Just another in a lifetime of mistakes.

She'd found Q-tips and laundry bleach and was on her hands and knees, sponging furiously at the flooring grooves, when Celeste walked in.

"Sloane . . ."

"I came to get the cat carrier. Someone found Marty," Sloane explained, staring up at her landlady. "But then I saw that they missed some of the . . . spill. Just a little, in the grooves. So I thought I could get it with Q-tips." Celeste's face blurred through a film of tears. "I'm so . . . sorry. I'm so very . . ." A racking sob strangled her.

Before she could take another breath, Celeste sank to the floor and gathered Sloane into her arms.

"It's okay," she said, rocking her. "There's no need to apologize."

"I *lied* to you," Sloane said, drawing back. "I should have told you I knew Paul. That he'd been here. It was only one time and I thought I'd gotten rid of him." She glanced toward the pantry shelves and shivered. The cleanup crew had put the cereal boxes back, neat and tidy. "I never thought anything like this could happen. I put you and Piper in danger. Your house is burned." Sloane pressed her fingers to her mouth in a failed attempt to smother what had become a keening wail. "My life is an unforgivable mess."

"No." Celeste gently pried Sloane's hand away. She rubbed it between both of hers as if she were reviving a frostbite victim. "You can be sorry. We're all sorry for something. But I don't allow the word *unforgivable* around here." She offered a small smile. "Ask Piper. She's got an impressive tally of *sorry*s going."

Sloane couldn't swallow past the rising ache. "I've made so many mistakes. Too many bad ones. I thought I could hide here, and that was wrong too."

"Come," Celeste said, tugging Sloane's hand as she stood. "I'm too old to squat on the floor. Come sit on the couch. I'm getting us some water."

"I should go. I need to—"

"Sit."

Sloane settled onto the couch, picked at a few of Marty's dark hairs, and tried not to think of sitting in this very same spot with Micah. Before it all changed.

"There," Celeste said, handing her the water.

"Thank you." Sloane spread her fingers around the cool plastic, wondering why she'd ever hated these tumblers so much. Something about them felt impossibly right. She was so thirsty. . . .

"You don't have a monopoly on mistakes," Celeste said, brushing at a silvery curl. "Or running and hiding."

Sloane peered over the tumbler's rim as her landlady continued.

"When Piper's mom was almost exactly her age, I packed everything I could into a Hefty bag, dressed my daughter in three layers of clothes, and hitched a ride on a produce truck headed for Utah. I should have done it five years before that." Celeste shook her head. "No. I should have had the guts to do it when I was pregnant. The first time he beat me." Tears moistened her eyes. "If I'd done that, there never would have been a first time he hurt my child."

Sloane winced.

"Those were only the first big mistakes I made." Celeste brushed at a tear. "You could say I was somewhat of a pro at screw-up-your-life drama. If they gave out championship belts for life mistakes like they do for those awful TV wrestlers, mine would be *giiinormous*." She smiled. "To quote my granddaughter."

Sloane found a smile despite another rush of tears. "Even still, your picture is on God's fridge. Up in heaven."

"Sure is." Celeste gave Sloane's hand a squeeze. "That's

the promise. That's grace. It's for all of us. Ours for the asking. We run; we hide . . . We're afraid people will discover our mistakes. But the thing is, God already *knows* our secrets. And loves us anyway."

Celeste sipped her own water, than added, "I read something the other day, by Tony Evans, I think. Something like . . . 'God never defines you by the past, but the enemy will try to confine you by it.'"

Sloane stayed quiet, not sure if she was uncomfortable or comforted. She only knew that she didn't feel the need to wield Q-tips anymore. She'd take that for now.

"I'm not here to preach," Celeste told her. "I just wanted to make sure you're okay. And tell you I'm planning to have some work done in the guesthouse, too." She glanced around the room and toward the kitchen. "Rip down that old rooster wallpaper border—it's looking like a henhouse around here. Some nice paint, maybe a new sink. Definitely a new water heater. And flooring. We're going to start with the floor. I told Jerry he could pull it up tonight after he leaves the hospital. Get this dingy old stuff out of here. I said you'd be okay with that?"

Sloane nodded.

"I still want wood planks," Celeste said, "but wider and much lighter. Fresher-looking. Maybe bamboo. Jerry had some great ideas. And I'll want your input too."

"Mine?"

"Of course. You'll be living with it."

Sloane's heart climbed to her throat.

"You might have to shuffle around while the work's being done, deal with plywood underfoot. But we can plan that out later. There's plenty of time." Celeste smiled. "Right now Marty's waiting."

"Oh yes . . . you know your mom." Sarah's dark eyes were warm as melted chocolate as Sloane pressed her fingers to the cage door. Marty's trilling meow morphed into a purr as he rubbed his head against them. The volunteer reached for the latch. "Let's get this sweet little dude out. Here we go."

"Thank you—oh, hey there," Sloane said, arms suddenly full of amorous cat. Marty snuggled his head under her chin, purring even louder. "He . . ." Her voice cracked. "I adopted him from a county animal shelter. His litter had been tied up in a grocery sack and dropped off a pier."

"Ouch." Something in Sarah's eyes said it wasn't a new story.

"He was so tiny," Sloane recounted, remembering the wobbly kitten with runny eyes and a worrisome cough. "And they'd penciled a date on his cage."

"We're a no-kill shelter," Sarah assured her. She scratched Marty's chin. "We're of a mind here that every animal deserves a second chance—as many times as necessary. Now, I should get your paperwork."

"Is there a fee?"

"No fee . . . but donations are always welcome. I'll just be a few minutes. Want to put him in your carrier?"

"No," Sloane said, spotting an overstuffed vinyl chair. "Not yet."

Sarah patted her heart. "I would have bet money on that."

Sloane held Marty on her lap and glanced around the small room designated for cats and kittens. Nicer than the city shelter in San Diego, homey. Her stomach shivered as a dark sense of déjà vu pressed in. A whisper that said, despite her struggle, Sloane was back where she started. No better off than the lonely woman who'd lingered in front of that cage in

San Diego. Then returned again and again, nursing a series of ugly hangovers and peering over her shoulder at her past. All that time she'd fought to find some viable reason not to save a sick kitten from his kill date. Her life had been a wreck; all she'd needed was one more mistake.

No.

Sloane blinked as a barrage of truths hit like a meteor shower. It *wasn't* the same now. Not at all. Marty wasn't facing a kill date; he'd had a good home for a long time. And though Sloane hated how it had come about, she no longer had to hide from Paul and his dangerous associates. And . . . *I'm sober.* Sloane shook her head, remembering the feel of that plastic tumbler in her hands today. The simple glass of water Celeste offered. An ordinary thing, but it had felt so meaningful.

"All set," Sarah said. "One little signature and you and Marty can hit the road."

"Sounds good."

Sloane settled Marty's carrier in the Volvo only a few minutes later. She reached for the ignition, then stopped to glance back at the Four Paws building. She smiled, imagining the kindhearted Sarah's surprise when she opened the donation box and found the envelope with a crisp stack of hundred-dollar bills. Despite the source of that cash, it felt incredibly good to have it support a place founded on second chances . . . *"as many times as necessary. . . ."*

It felt a lot like what Celeste had said earlier. About mistakes. And grace. It made Sloane wonder if the all-consuming thirst she'd struggled with for so long was really for something much, much different.

39

"EMERGENCY MEETING?" Micah asked, not liking the sound of this. He pushed the remnants of his late lunch aside. "What does that mean?"

"I only know that the ER director and some 'key staff' are meeting to discuss Sloane Ferrell's contract." Fiona frowned. "They asked that I be present. I can only assume they want to explore the impact of her current situation on the hospital's image."

"I don't see how that's relevant to her employment contract. She hasn't been arrested."

"I think they're going to claim she's failed to show up for work. A no-show for three consecutive days is grounds for termination. Tomorrow will be the third day." Fiona sighed. "Sloane didn't fill out the paperwork. It's a technicality. She has the vacation accrual. And frankly I think the director planned to offer her the time after all she's gone through. But there's been pressure. The real issue is PR."

"Which is *my* job. Why wasn't I told about this meeting?"

Fiona's brows pinched. "One of the board members complained about your seeing Sloane socially."

"Brill?"

"He thinks it's a conflict."

"Oh, I *agree*," Micah said, wishing he hadn't held back with the man earlier. "Between him and me. If anyone's guilty of doing damage to the hospital's image, it's Howard Brill." He looked at his watch. "When's this meeting?"

"Tomorrow morning at 7:15. Media room."

"I'll be there."

———————

"I really appreciate it, Harper," Sloane said, giving Marty's stomach a rub as he sprawled over the clothes she'd piled on her bed. She shifted the cell phone in her hand. "I'll only be using you as a backup in case Celeste runs into a problem. She's home tonight and she wants to keep Marty, but it might mean shuttling him back and forth between the houses with the work going on. Noise and all that."

"How long will you be gone?" Harper asked, telltale sounds of sirens and ER monitors pinpointing her location better than any GPS.

"Five days, maybe a week. I only have ten days' vacation."

"Uh . . . right." Harper's voice sounded distracted. Work, no doubt.

"So that's the plan." Sloane drew in a deep breath, grateful Celeste had opened all the windows. The cottage already smelled more apple, less disinfectant. "My godfather's in Denver on business this week, but my godmother will be there. I told her to expect me early in the morning."

"It's like ten hours to Mendocino."

"Eight. I'll drive halfway. Stay somewhere." Sloane's throat tightened as she thought of her godmother's response to Sloane's unexpected phone call.

"Of course you'll come. We've been waiting for you, sweetheart."

"I think it's good you're getting away," Harper said, her voice still a little odd.

"It's something I have to do." The idea, like so many other unexpected thoughts, had come to Sloane as she drove back from the rescue shelter. She still didn't know where all of it was heading. "I'm almost packed. I'll leave right after my meeting."

"That class you've been taking?"

Sloane told herself it was time . . . *past time*.

"They're AA meetings, Harper."

Sloane's stomach quivered as she glanced at Jocelyn, sitting next to her in the front row. She smiled and gave Sloane's hand a quick, reassuring pat. Sloane felt sick. And healthier than she'd been in years. If only her heart would stop crowding her throat. If only . . .

"Are there any folks from out of the area?" the chairperson was saying. "Newcomers? Maybe give us your name—tell us something about you. We'd like to get to know you."

Shares.

Sloane's heart thudded. After nearly seven months of meetings, she knew the routine. Serenity prayer, readings from the Big Book, a topic and discussion. And now—

"Would anyone like to share?"

"Yes. Here. . . ." Sloane raised her hand. It was trembling. She took a slow breath and looked around at the faces of the people she'd sat with for months, knowing she was really seeing them for the first time. *Oh, please . . .*

The faces smiled. At least a dozen thumbs raised. There was a wink or two.

Despite the trembling, an achy-good feeling filled her chest.

"My name is Sloane," she said, her voice quavering a bit. "And I'm an alcoholic."

She hardly heard the enthusiastic chorus of hellos, barely saw their faces through a prism of tears. She only knew this was where she was meant to be—and that it might be best to grab hold of Jocelyn's hand. She was kind of dizzy and she'd take all the support she could get.

"I'm not new," Sloane began. "I've been coming here for months. . . . But today feels like my very first day."

Two hours later her bag was packed and her pulse tap-dancing faster than Piper's talent show act—caffeine overload from multiple cups of coffee with Jocelyn. *My sponsor.* Sloane's breath snagged; so much had happened and her thoughts were still tumbling. After the meeting, Jocelyn suggested they go to a nearby café so she could answer any questions Sloane might have. It turned out that she had quite a few. Jocelyn had been her usual keep-it-real self, but also patient and encouraging. They'd talked for nearly an hour, interrupted only by the waitress refilling their cups—and by a quick "night-night" call from Jocelyn's youngest child. She'd been supportive of Sloane's trip to Mendocino, her need to talk with her godmother. Jocelyn insisted, however, that finding a local meeting there must be a priority. As Sloane's sponsor, she'd be only a phone call away.

Sloane inhaled the fresh scent of sawdust, then glanced toward the floor in front of the pantry doors. Jerry had already made good on his promise to tear out those stained boards. A sheet of plywood lay in their place, heralding the repair work to follow. It was exactly how Sloane felt about her life. Under construction. Jocelyn said the twelve steps were her tools to build a new life. And that what she'd done tonight by standing up, speaking the truth, and asking for support was a good beginning. Talking to her godmother, finally confiding some difficult and shameful secrets, would only add to that strong start.

Sloane thought of what Zoey said about her own relationship with Paul. How his attention made her feel "worth the trouble." It had struck Sloane to the core. She'd wondered if that same sad need had been at the root of her own long string of mistakes. Even before Paul Stryker. Had she let the abuse by that long-ago "uncle" convince her she was worthless? Or worth only what some man told her she was worth? Had she lowered the bar on her own expectations? And then set herself up, over and over, to prove she was "someone like that"?

Sloane glanced toward the pantry shelves, saw the shipping boxes restacked by the cleaning team. A lifetime supply of cereal she rarely ate. Why hadn't she put an end to it? Was it more proof that she'd actually bought into that loathsome lie?

"For your whole life—that's quite a net worth."

Her heart cramped as yet another question prodded, fresh as the sawdust that replaced the stains on her floor. She didn't want it to be true, but was Micah Prescott simply one more

attempt in her misguided scramble to feel worthy, special?
Was that all there was to it?

Sloane thought of what she'd told Zoey that night in the
motel room. She'd told the girl to keep the chain and cross,
that *"in God's eyes, you're more than worth the trouble."* At
that moment, holding the lost girl in her arms, Sloane had
believed it with all her heart. Because Zoey was young, her
mistakes not nearly as many or as unforgivable as Sloane's.

"We're all sorry for something. But I don't allow the word
unforgivable *around here."*

Celeste's words, as they sat on this floor now covered with
fresh wood. Under construction . . .

For some reason, Sloane thought of the question Micah
was asking the Face of Hope nominees: *"What one important
thing would you say to your younger self?"*

Had Sloane actually done that when she told Zoey that,
regardless of her past, she would always have worth in
God's eyes? What difference would those words have made
in Sloane's life? What might have changed? Was it too late
now?

An ache rose in her throat as she lifted the twelve-step list
from the table. Her gaze moved to step three:

Made a decision to turn our will and our lives over to
the care of God . . .

Sloane closed her eyes over welling tears, then bowed her
head.

"Please, God, I need you in my life. I can't run anymore.
Take this pain and fear, please. Show me what you want for
me. . . ."

It was after ten when Micah decided to try Sloane's number one more time. She hadn't answered any of his texts or calls for two days now. He told himself to stop, but he had a strong sense that something was going on and—

"Micah?"

"Hi. I . . ." He realized he hadn't figured out what he would say. "I wanted to see if you're okay."

"I . . . am." Her voice sounded different somehow. Micah couldn't put a finger on it.

"Good. That's good. Where are you exactly?"

"Home."

That wasn't good, was it? Alone in that place where so much had happened? He reminded himself he wasn't a crisis responder here. That what he wanted to be was—"I need to see you, Sloane."

"I'm leaving in a few minutes. Going away for a while."

What? His breath caught. "Where?"

"Up north."

"I need to see you," Micah told her again. "I can be there in like ten minutes. Fifteen at the latest."

Please . . .

There was a long pause. He held his breath.

"I have to go, Micah. It's important."

"When will you be back?"

"I'm not sure yet."

Not sure? His mind whirled. Had Brill already convinced Hope hospital to fire her? If that was true, Micah swore he'd make the man regret it.

"I should go," Sloane said. "I want to make good time on the road tonight."

He told himself he could get there in less than ten minutes if he pushed a few yellow lights, risked a red. If he got there in time, he could convince Sloane that . . . *What?* What did he want? Was this only about rescuing her?

"Micah? Did you hear me?"

"Is it okay if I call you up there?"

"I'm not sure that's a good idea. It's complicated."

He closed his eyes, the weight of good-bye pressing down. *Complicated* wasn't even close to a big enough word.

40

MICAH RETURNED TO HIS SEAT at the media room table after refilling his coffee cup, a useless attempt to focus his scattered thoughts; he'd slept less than three hours last night. Every conversation he'd ever had with Sloane had replayed in his head, and then when he'd grown tired of staring at the bedroom ceiling, he'd opted for the boring balm of the late-night movie channel. It turned out to be a marathon of classics, the offering at the time being none other than *An Affair to Remember*. One of the films Sloane mentioned as a favorite of her mother's. It was a cruel jab that led him to imagine Sloane as that child tap-dancing on the Walk of Fame. And left him remembering how, twenty-five years later, she'd raised her beautiful face for his kiss on that amazing night in the Hollywood Hills. Then he recalled every kiss after that, each touch, every laugh.

"I'm leaving. . . . Going away for a while."

Micah glanced up as he heard the ER director say his name.

". . . would like to say a few words before we begin," she finished, nodding at him.

He took another futile sip of his prescription coffee, then rose from his chair.

"I appreciate this opportunity to speak," Micah said, surprised, frankly, that it took so few people to give Sloane the ax. The ER director and her assistant, the day shift clinical coordinators, Harper Tatum—apparently a member of the peer review board and not at all happy to be here, from the look on her face—plus two other senior staffers. Fiona was there too. Howard Brill wasn't, but the more Micah thought about it, the more certain he was that this was the arrogant board member's brainchild. Sloane fired first, then Micah.

"We're glad you could come," the director added, something in her expression saying she understood the idiocy in that statement. He hadn't been invited; he'd bullied his way in. But Micah had always known her as a kind woman. And fair, from what he'd heard. She was clearly responding to what Fiona referred to as "pressure." She folded her hands on the table. "Please understand, however, that the latter part of this meeting must involve only nursing administration." She glanced at the PIO, garnered her nod as well. "Go ahead, Micah."

"Thank you." He glanced around the table. He'd meet Brill's subversion with complete honesty.

"Before I begin," he started, "you should know that Miss Ferrell and I had been seeing each other outside of work." *Had been.* He hoped his disappointment didn't register in his voice. "But that has no bearing whatsoever on what I came here to say on behalf of your teammate. A dedicated Hope employee. I think you know that."

One of the clinical coordinators failed to hide a guilty flinch.

"During the Face of Hope campaign," Micah continued, "I've made a point of stopping by the ER to meet with your team. It's given me a rare chance to see you in action, doing what you all do best." He knew he'd begin with praise—everyone needed that—but he was going to wing the rest of his statement. He was fairly skilled at it. Businesslike and persuasive. In truth, that skill was a big part of why he'd been hired. "Offering not only your technical expertise but your selfless compassion. Day in and day out, in situations that would stop most people cold in their tracks. Including me. It's made me even more certain that this hospital is the face of hope for our community. Because of people like you."

The director glanced down at her paper.

"In all honesty," Micah was surprised to hear himself admit, "it hasn't been easy to take over the task of rebuilding this hospital's image after the scandal involving the former chief of staff. Many of you may know that a member of my family was the victim of vehicular manslaughter related to alcohol abuse." His gut tensed; he hadn't planned to say that. Lack of sleep was taking the reins. Maybe, this time, winging it was a mistake. But he couldn't seem to stop. "Knowing you now and seeing your dedication makes me proud to do this work—makes me want to do it well."

Fiona nodded at him.

"Sloane Ferrell is an example of what I'm talking about. I could cite several instances, but I'll just share one." He looked at the director. "Is that all right?"

"Of course."

"A homeless man came in by ambulance, drunk and apparently a 'frequent flier.'" Micah saw Harper grimace a little; she knew who this patient was. "The patient was a mess. Literally. I won't deny the stench alone made me want to hustle back to my department. He roused long enough to complain of painful feet. Bad shoes, rotted socks, too much walking. Not anywhere near the acuity that requires nurses of your caliber. He was the kind of patient, I think I heard someone say, that staff draws straws over." Micah shook his head. "Well, the short-straw nurse wasn't having any of it. So the nurse in charge, Sloane Ferrell, attended this man herself. She did that without complaint and with the attention and respect you might expect if this man were a local celebrity, a star athlete. Or a hospital board member."

Fiona smiled.

"She washed his feet," Micah said, the image still branded in his mind. "This nurse with so much responsibility, such a high level of training, and not a minute to spare in a busy shift took on the most humble of tasks. She rolled up her sleeves and showed a homeless, hopeless man more kindness and compassion than I'd bet he'd seen in a long, long time." Micah glanced from person to person around the table, not caring anymore that emotion had crept into his voice. "We're a hospital system that sees patient care as a ministry, as God's work. I've included that mission statement in more PR blurbs than I can count. But I didn't really get it until that moment. When I saw Sloane Ferrell washing her patient's feet."

Harper met his gaze and mouthed a teary-eyed thank-you.

There was a stretch of silence. Long enough for Micah to realize that he'd meant everything he'd said. Not only about Sloane but about his job too. It wasn't just marketing-speak.

These people, this hospital, did represent hope for their community.

"Well . . ." Micah looked around the table again, aware only that he needed this personal "campaign" to succeed no matter what happened to his own relationship with Sloane. "I know you have more to discuss. But I'd like to leave you with this thought: I think the primary question isn't whether or not to continue Miss Ferrell's contract. Or even how much skin it would take off our noses to do whatever we can to support a fellow employee who's going through something none of us would want to deal with. No. I think the real question should be, how do we find more people like her?"

Micah left the media room and went straight to the hospital chapel.

He wasn't sure how long he sat there; he only knew that what he'd said in defense of Sloane had pointed out, even more, how confused he'd been feeling about his own actions— or more honestly, his *inaction*. His disturbing inadequacy. He'd sat with Sloane and talked about grace, told her that God didn't see scars or flaws, only a child he loved. He told Sloane he'd believed in forgiveness all his life. Time after time he pulled on a volunteer jacket and waded into scenes of tragedy and chaos to offer a lifeline of support to countless strangers, and yet . . . *I let her go.*

Micah drew in a slow breath that did nothing to ease the ache in his heart. Then bowed his head and prayed.

41

SLOANE ARRIVED AT HER LA EXIT around 2:30, after leaving early Sunday morning and making the eight-hour drive home in one long stretch. She smiled, thinking of her godmother's offer to share the driving and fly back home on Monday. She'd been tempted to take her up on it, not for the driving respite but because she'd hated for their time together to end. It had been all Sloane dared to hope for and then so much more. She'd been grateful and teary at her godfather's return yesterday, but it was the time alone with her godmother that had meant the most. They'd laughed, cried, and left no subject untouched, including her godmother's regret at the estrangement from Sloane's mother and her deep concerns—well-founded, as it turned out—about the relationship with her boyfriend Phillip. They talked of her mother's growing abuse of alcohol and dependence on prescription drugs. Her god-mother spoke of her own heartbreak when she learned of her best friend's drowning, and how very desperately she'd wanted to provide comfort and hope for her troubled teen-age daughter. She confided that her heart had broken all over again when Sloane moved on and then gradually became so distant. She'd been praying all these years that Sloane would find her way "home."

And her godmother listened late into the night—more than one night—as Sloane shared, for the first time, the whole story of her childhood abuse and the confusing and bitter hostility she'd felt toward her stepfather, Bob Bullard. She revealed the tragic details of her relationship with a married man in Sacramento, her own descent into alcohol abuse after-ward, and the fateful journey with Paul . . . that eventually led her back to Mendocino now, fifteen years later. A full-circle return, they'd both tearfully agreed, that was set in motion by God's infinite mercy.

Sloane had finally had time, too, to untangle her un-expected reactions at the parole board meeting. When, just as she was poised to strike at her stepfather, memories of her own mistakes had come flooding back instead. Had she been any less irresponsible than he?

Maybe Bob Bullard's fellow inmate had the best insight: *"He told me I'm worth something even after all I done wrong."*

Wasn't that just what Sloane told Zoey—and exactly what, for most of her life, Sloane had so desperately longed for?

And then, just this morning, as Sloane and her godparents were having an eggs-and-sausage breakfast, they'd even tossed around ideas about what to do with a lifetime supply of cereal. A donation to a food bank seemed in order.

"You don't need cereal to prove how beautiful you are, my darling girl."

Loss, shame, forgiveness, faith, love . . . and cereal. They'd talked about almost everything, Sloane thought as she turned onto Ernest Court. The only thing she hadn't shared with her godmother was her still-unsettled feelings about—

Micah?

Sloane blinked, certain road fatigue was playing tricks on her eyes. But it was true, and her heart staggered. Micah's Durango was parked next to Jerry's truck. What on earth?

The cottage door was open, sawhorses in the foyer. She stepped around them.

"Sloane." Micah set a handsaw down, stood up from where he'd been kneeling. "Harper said you'd be back tomorrow."

"I decided to drive straight through," she told him, having a little trouble breathing. Not only because it had been a surprise to find him here, but because he looked so . . . Her skin warmed as her gaze took in the old plaid shirt with sleeves rolled up, frayed jeans, and work boots. Sawdust in his hair, on his glasses. He looked every inch like the hunky star of one of those HGTV house renovation shows Harper watched.

"What are you doing here?" Sloane asked, finally reclaiming her voice.

"Working." Micah's smile wreaked further havoc on Sloane's vital signs. "Home Depot gofer. Cat-sitter. Talent show practice audience. Whatever's needed."

What Sloane *needed* was to sit down before her knees gave way. What was happening? In her whole time in Mendocino, she'd never mentioned Micah because she couldn't be sure of her feelings. And now he was here, fixing her house . . . and rattling her senses?

"I took some time off," he continued, wiping his glasses on his shirt before setting them on the coffee table. He joined her on the couch. "I told them I had some things to do."

According to Harper, Micah had already done plenty.

"He stood up for you, Sloane. Told them that what Hope hospital needs is more people like you."

And from what Harper heard via the hospital grapevine, Micah hadn't stopped there. He'd gone to the chief of staff and informed him that if Sloane was fired, they could count on seeing Micah's resignation as well.

"It looks amazing." Sloane turned to gaze around the room; if she looked at Micah one minute longer, she'd lose her mind. "Jerry's . . ."

"Checking in at Celeste's, then done for the day. I said I'd finish up."

"Oh." Sloane glanced toward the kitchen. It had been partially painted in a soft bisque color. Even from this distance, she could see a fancy new pull-down faucet. And a new sink, probably. Celeste had said something about that, hadn't she? She couldn't remember anything. Only that Micah was here. And her heart was making a fool of itself. "The kitchen cabinets are being painted, too. Everything's lighter . . . brighter."

"All the barnyard stuff is gone." Micah shook his head. "Piper entertained Zoey with clucking sounds while Zoey scraped off the wallpaper."

"Zoey was here?"

"Supervising mostly. Except for the wallpaper. She said it had to go. Because you aren't 'the rooster type.'"

Sloane's heart tugged. "Where is she?"

"In Colorado with her mother."

Sloane glanced toward the hallway. "And Marty?"

"At Celeste's." He captured her gaze as she turned back. There was kindness in his eyes. "How was it? Your visit?"

"Good. More than good." Sloane's throat tightened as she thought of the times she and her godmother prayed together. They'd asked God, as Sloane had right here in this house, to show her what he wanted for her. Was it possible *this* was part of his plan? "It helped a lot."

"I'm glad. I think having someone really listen makes a big difference."

"It did. It does." There was no option but the truth anymore. "I've made a commitment to really work the program with AA. I have a sponsor now. And I'm going down the twelve-step list, one thing at a time. I think I'm getting a grip on the first three." She took a breath that felt fresh and new as the paint in her kitchen and smiled. "It seems God has been waiting for me, all this time."

"I'm certain of it." The look on Micah's face made her heart ache.

"So," he said, moving a little closer. "You'll be looking at number four, then. Big one. 'A searching and fearless moral inventory.'"

"That's right. How did you know?"

"My church hosts AA meetings," Micah said. "It's an open meeting, so visitors can come. It turns out there are several more open meetings in the city. All times of the day and evening, seven days a week."

"You went to one?"

"I went to three. So far."

"But . . ." Sloane stared at him, confused. "You don't have a drinking problem."

"No." Micah's expression was somber. "But I have a serious problem judging people who do."

"Wait . . ." Sloane hesitated. "If this is about me, don't beat yourself up. I can understand how you'd feel. Stephen was killed because of a drunk driver. And then you find out about my accident and my drinking and—"

"No," Micah interrupted. "It's not about you. It's not even about the guy who was convicted in Stephen's accident. It's about me."

———

Micah hadn't said this aloud to anyone yet. He'd only whispered it to God. Or maybe it was the other way round.

"After Stephen was killed," he explained, "I volunteered with that embedded news team, mostly because I wanted to get out of here. Away from everything and everybody." He shook his head. "Maybe I even had a death wish—it's possible. At the very least, I was looking for distraction, escape. It didn't work. And when I came home, I spent the next year behaving like an irresponsible jerk. That didn't help either."

The look in Sloane's eyes said she got it.

"I moved on with my life. Took that job at the paper, then insurance." Micah frowned. "I didn't think any of that work 'fit,' but I didn't really care, either. Maybe I just settled, the same way I settled for friendship with Coop. He and I have nothing that matters in common." Micah had used similar words when he'd finally had it out with Coop about the photo he'd sold—the lie. It had been hard, but he'd kept his temper in check. "Maybe I didn't think I deserved more than that after Stephen." Micah sighed. "Then I finally found something that made sense. Filled a hole in my life."

"Your crisis work."

"Yes. But I still carried that anger around. A sort of festering judgment when it came to drunks. I saw it all through the lens of what happened to my cousin. It felt justified, a banner I had a right to carry. Maybe even some kind of . . . sacred obligation. And then *you* came along, Sloane. With a history that smacked up against all of that."

Sloane waited.

"I let what Coop said about you derail me," he told her, never intending to make this a speech, but it needed to be said. "Even when I wanted to stop you from going away, something held me back. I couldn't understand. So I went to the first AA meeting, mostly to see what it was all about. The whole big deal about a twelve-step club. I needed to see who these people really were." Micah gave a short laugh. "They were nothing like what my bias was telling me. They were regular people, there to get help. And to help each other."

Sloane's smile was small, knowing.

"So I went back. And pretty soon it felt like I was learning about myself."

Her brows rose.

"For the first time," Micah said, finally ready to put it out there, "I realized what I was so blasted angry about." He tapped his chest. "Me. *My* weakness, *my* failure."

"What do you mean?"

"I told you Stephen didn't drive because of his seizures. He rode to the party with a friend that night. But his friend had to leave early. Stephen said no problem; he'd call me for a ride home. And . . ."

Sloane winced. "You didn't go get him."

"I'd ended up with an unexpected date, someone I'd been

interested in getting to know. I said I'd come if he really needed me, but maybe he could try to find someone else first. Stephen said sure, he could do that." Micah's chest tightened. "I think the last thing he said was something like 'Never accuse me of getting in the way of true love.'"

Sloane placed her hand over his.

"Nowhere close to love. And the truth was, I'd been jealous of Stephen for a long time. His popularity, the way friendships came so naturally for him. Even if I didn't realize it at the time, I was probably envious he was at the beach party that night—maybe it factored in with what happened. I don't know." Micah drew a slow breath. "Afterward, there was all this anger. I know now that it was mostly guilt. Of course, I didn't see it that way at the time. It was easier to blame the drunk. Even after he served his sentence. And joined AA. And wrote letters to all of us."

"Amends. I'll be making a list." Sloane gave a small sigh. Her fingers brushed Micah's much the way they had on that first date, when she'd asked him about his guitar. His heart ached. She was so far ahead of him now, doing the hard work he'd been so stubbornly avoiding for far too long. He couldn't express how much he admired her. He could only pray he hadn't ruined everything.

"I think I understand that," she said finally, her voice soft. She peered at him, blue eyes filled with compassion. "I think it's a lot like the situation with my stepfather. I had some awful things happen to me when I was very young. Abuse by my mother's boyfriend."

Micah's gut twisted. *Ah, no . . .*

"I think I judged my stepfather because of that," Sloane continued. "I was looking for a target for that old anger. And he was there. He wasn't perfect by a long shot, but I think he really cared for my mother—and me, in his own way. Until I did everything I could to poison it." She closed her eyes for a moment. "I was visiting him when Coop saw me at the prison. I went there to tell my stepfather how much I hated him, how I'd do anything I could to keep him in prison forever. Instead he tells me how sorry he is, how bad he feels about neglecting my mother and me. About his irresponsibility the night she died and how long he wished he'd died instead. And how grateful he is now for God's grace." Sloane's lips curved into an incredulous smile. "Behind bars. Way freer than I was. I get what you're saying, Micah."

"Sloane . . ." His heart filled his chest, and before he knew it, Micah was reaching out to cradle her cheek in his palm. "Thank you. You couldn't have said anything better. Except maybe . . ."

"Maybe what?"

"That we can start over," Micah said, taking the risk. "Or keep going but—"

"In a better way," she finished, reading his mind. She'd tilted her head to nestle her face against his palm. "Both of us sort of working on that 'personal inventory.' And being there for each other."

"Right," he managed, hope warming him like the Malibu sun. His thumb brushed her cheek. "And we'll take it slow, like I promised before."

"Um . . ." Her nose wrinkled. "Not quite that slow."

"What?" He laughed at her expression. "What do you mean?"

"It took you *forever* to kiss me."

"Oh yeah?" He'd cradled her face in both hands now. Bent down a couple of inches. "You're complaining?"

"Not exactly." Her dark lashes fluttered. "It was worth the wait."

"Good to know," Micah murmured, brushing his lips against her brow. He leaned back to gaze into her eyes again. Eyes so capable of fire and ice. There was something new and far more beautiful there now. "So what exactly are you saying?"

She smiled. "Only that while 'take it slow' is a good idea, and taking the time to get to know each other is great, wonderful . . ." Her lips twitched. "There's no need to backtrack on the kissing part. Agree?"

"Oh yeah." He bent low again. Smiled. "Like, totally."

"And . . . *for sure*," Sloane added with a throaty laugh. Or tried to add, tried to laugh. Neither was really possible with his lips on hers. He wasn't going to be accused of making her wait forever again. It was pretty clear she was good with it by the way she wrapped her arms around his neck, fingers playing in his hair as her mouth clung to his.

"Did you really do that for me?" Sloane leaned back in his arms.

"Do what?" Micah asked, opening his eyes grudgingly.

"Go to bat for me with hospital management. Compare me to Mother Teresa."

He laughed. "Harper exaggerated that last part."

"But . . ." Sloane's voice was soft, a look almost like wonder in her eyes. "You went there. And you said what Hope hospital really needed was—"

"More people like you."

"I . . ." Her voice cracked a little. "I love that."

And I love you.

Micah almost said it out loud. But it didn't fit with his take-it-slow promise. He'd wait awhile for that. Not forever but . . .

"I'm glad you feel that way," he said. "Because I meant every word. I wasn't speaking just as the marketing man or only for the hospital."

"Meaning?"

"I meant—" Micah hiked Sloane closer in his arms, then pressed a kiss to the corner of her mouth—"I've been waiting all my life for someone. Now I'm thinking . . ."

"Maybe it's me? Like the hospital campaign?" Sloane teased.

"No 'maybe' about it." Micah smiled. "I'm *sure* it's you."

"Oh. That works." Sloane's smile spread slowly. "Great job, ad man."

Her sweet, lingering kiss was even more proof he'd said exactly the right thing.

EPILOGUE

"I'm glad we're doing this," Sloane said, glancing at Micah as he drove. Her heart did the crazy-corny thing it always did, even after five months together. She was okay with that. "A sort of closure and celebration all at the same time. Seeing the first Face of Hope billboard . . . on the heels of your last week as their *assistant* marketing man."

"And speaking of heels, you look great tonight." Micah sneaked a quick but obviously appreciative glance at Sloane's legs, though not much showed below the long, shimmery skirt Harper had insisted she borrow in honor of the occasion. Actually, it had been Harper who'd come up with the whole idea of dressing up for the billboard viewing, part of her never-ending quest to introduce Sloane to the art of fashion.

She'd tried a dozen times to convince Sloane to take the entire contents of the guest closet home; the happy Irish bride wasn't coming back. But Sloane had grown to enjoy the girl-time feel of shopping at Harper's place.

Her friend had been excited to help outfit Sloane for this particular adventure, saying Micah hadn't had nearly enough accolades for pulling off such a great campaign. She'd added that tonight's viewing should feel like an awards ceremony in itself. They'd paired the fancy skirt with a casual tank top, crystal beaded headband, and sparkly flip-flops—very "casual wow," Harper concluded, coining a phrase just for the occasion. Micah had been a good sport and gone along with the hype, especially when Harper gave him a bottle of sparkling cider to use for a celebratory toast. Sloane invited her to join them, but she'd quickly begged off, saying something like "seen one billboard, seen 'em all."

Her loss, Sloane thought, *and definitely my gain.* She didn't mind having Micah all to herself.

"I still can't believe how the timing worked out," he said, signaling for their freeway exit. "My boss taking the transfer to San Diego Hope, then my promotion to director announced the same week as the gala—and the first billboard going live."

"Perfect timing," Sloane agreed, giving Micah her own appreciative glance. He'd acquiesced to Harper's nudge and pulled on his tuxedo shirt and jacket over a pair of jeans. With leather sneakers, a loosely knotted tie, and his hair mussed from Sloane's fingers. A smudge of her lipstick at the corner of his mouth completed his awards-night ensemble. She had no doubt her high-fashion and highly romantic friend would approve.

"Still, even after all those months of planning, it seemed

to happen so fast," Sloane continued. "The final choice for the Face of Hope and then the gala on Saturday." She smiled, remembering the amazing moment when By Grace took the stage. They invited Micah to join them when performing a number in honor of Stephen. There had been tears in Micah's parents' eyes, and Sloane thought her heart would burst.

"And Jocelyn's decision to include California Crisis Care in her fund-raising efforts." Micah nodded. "That's worth a celebration of its own. We're going to be able to do some incredible things with our team."

Our team.

Sloane was still pinching herself over that. But after all she'd gone through and how far she'd come, it seemed only natural she'd be drawn to crisis work. Especially to the area where she planned to volunteer almost exclusively: working with exploited women and girls. Her training was nearly complete—evenings after her ER shifts—and Sloane could hardly wait to start volunteering. A merciful bonus, the training had also gone a long way toward healing her own lingering pain from childhood abuse. She couldn't imagine anything more rewarding than helping these survivors find a true sense of self-worth and, whenever possible, leading them toward new faith.

Several local churches had offered help, and after the motel fire and related tragedies, there was increased community interest as well, initially prompted by a human interest article cowritten by one Cooper Vance. His "amends," Micah had joked. Though they still hoped Coop would eventually grow up, finally get it, they almost never saw him anymore. He'd quit the *Times* and moved to the beach to work on a novel, a venture funded by the modest inheritance from his grandmother. The remainder had been left in trust for the lifetime care of her cats.

"Zoey's all set for summer classes?" Micah asked, accelerating up the highway into the Hollywood Hills. "To get her ready for senior year?"

"She is."

Her mother had been clean for six months now and they'd both been living with Zoey's grandparents, who'd relocated from the Midwest; they seemed stable and loving. Zoey was continuing with counseling, but she hoped to come to LA for a visit before school started in the fall—a whole year since they met in that fateful ruse in the ER parking lot. So much had happened. Oksana was living under an assumed name at a safe house and working with a team who specialized in assisting victims of trafficking. She'd had several reconstructive surgeries on her throat and continued to benefit from speech therapy. She hoped to eventually join a married cousin living in Des Moines, maybe even find that nanny job she'd wanted in the first place.

Sloane's stepfather had been set free, though he'd be the first to say it had happened long before he left the prison gates. He'd moved to Washington State and was close to completing training that would allow him to continue his prison ministry—as an ordained chaplain. He'd told Sloane that the amends letter she'd sent him was one of the biggest blessings he'd ever received.

"Zoey told me she might want to go to nursing school someday," Sloane added, smiling.

"Not surprising. She has the best role model."

"Thank you." Sloane stayed quiet as they climbed farther

into the hills; the sun had dropped low in the sky, giving every-thing a sort of golden glow. *Perfect timing.* All of it. Sloane had never felt anything so deeply and with such a sense of gratitude. After so many painful years, she now knew without a doubt who she was—whose she was. All the mistakes she'd thought so unforgivable had been paid for long ago on a cross. That amazing gift: grace.

"Here we go," Micah said, pulling off the highway and then turning the SUV so that—

"Oh, oh . . . there!" Sloane slid across the seat to stare out the windshield alongside Micah. Her gaze swept the huge, lit billboard looking down on the bustling freeway. "It looks so awesome. And exactly right. The best campaign in the world, Micah—award-winning. Harper's right." She smiled at the familiar face on the billboard. "And he's the perfect choice for the Face of Hope."

Micah pressed a kiss on Sloane's ear before gazing back at the billboard. "You definitely had a hand in it."

"You said anyone could nominate." She chuckled. "Once."

Micah shook his head, thinking, no doubt, of Brill's resigna-tion. Another accomplishment of this exceptional marketing man.

"I love it," Sloane said, grinning at the billboard—as Jerry Rhodes beamed back. "Everything about it. The idea. The selection. The way it looks up there." She leaned forward a little, squinting her eyes. Then picked up the binoculars they'd brought along. She adjusted the focus. "He has the pencil behind his ear!"

Micah laughed. "Of course. Have you ever seen Jerry with-out it?"

"Maybe at the gala?"

"Nah, it must have been there. He probably had a tape measure in his suit pocket."

"I wouldn't be surprised." Sloane thought of him dancing with his wife, Ann, while her mother watched with such a sweet, proud expression on her face. Sloane sighed. "And I wouldn't have it any other way."

Jerry was the finest example of "casual wow." A humble man who helped everyone whenever he could. The guy who'd come up with the great idea for the new day care center. The hero who carried Piper from her grandmother's burning house, then worked overtime to rebuild it. Jerry Rhodes knew, absolutely, his true source of hope.

"Following the best I can after that other carpenter. Long time ago."

"So, my brilliant and very hot PR and marketing director . . ." Sloane tugged at Micah's tie, kissed his cheek. "Should we pop open the bubbly?"

"Not yet." His eyes met hers. "I think we should drive up to the Mulholland overlook. Do it there."

"Ooh, great idea." She kissed him once more and slid back to fasten her seat belt. "We haven't been back there since—"

"No, we haven't." He grinned and started the engine.

In a few short minutes, they'd made it up there; a few minutes longer and they found a parking spot. Hardly private, but then it was LA, and the view more than worth sharing. It still looked picture-postcard iconic. The hills, the Hollywood sign, the bustling freeways below, tile roofs, palm trees . . .

"What are you doing?" she asked as Micah turned the car around, backing toward the view.

"Tailgate picnic."

"You brought food?"

"Deli." Micah switched off the engine. "And dessert."

"Another great idea," she said, loving the playful look in Micah's eyes. Playful and something more, too. Whatever it was, she was on board. "Let's do it."

They walked to the back of the SUV and Micah opened the tailgate.

"What's this?" Sloane asked, spotting the expanse of red terry cloth laid across the cargo space, sales tags still attached. "New beach towels?"

"Yes, but try to imagine them as carpet," Micah said, spreading the towels over the tailgate. He shrugged, not quite hiding the sheepish look on his face. "Sort of a last-minute, jerry-rigged red carpet. Like . . ."

"Right. The Academy Awards," Sloane said. "Because tonight should feel like an awards celebration. Oh, and because when we were here before, I told you about my mother and our Oscar parties." She smiled, touched that he remembered. "That's really sweet, Micah. Thank you."

"You're welcome. Well, hop up there," he said, his hands circling her waist to give her a boost. "Don't want to miss the sunset."

"Not for a second."

Sloane moved over to make room, watching as Micah pulled the cooler closer. Thoughtful, generous, and caring. How could she not love this man?

"Five months since we were here that time," she said as Micah popped the cork on the sparkling cider and reached for the glasses, the sea-glass goblets Sloane had waited so long to buy; she'd let Marty lap water from one in celebration of the purchase. "I'm glad you thought of this. It's perfect for our Face of Hope unveiling. Your Oscar-worthy achievement."

Micah laughed like she'd said something far funnier. Then he set the bottle down. "I thought coming here tonight felt right." He reached for her hand. "First time. Last time."

"Last? Oh, you mean as assistant director." She glanced at the cliff edge and shot him a teasing look. "At least with the car turned around like this, I'm not going to worry about some Thelma and Louise cliff dive."

"You and your movies." Micah shook his head, then raised her hand to his lips. "I guess I meant 'full circle.' Because our first real date was here."

"And our first kiss," she said, knowing she'd never forget it.

"I remember." He cleared his throat and reached for the cooler. "I think we should have dessert first."

"Not a toast?"

"Dessert, then a toast."

"I won't argue. You're the one who knows how to market a moment."

"I hope so." He seemed to hesitate, then lifted something from the cooler. "Here we go. Your dessert."

"What . . . ? You *didn't*." Sloane grinned with delight as Micah handed her a familiar sculpture wrapped in gold foil. "Chocolate? In the shape of an Oscar? Did Harper—?"

"Nope. My idea."

"Too great." Sloane shook her head. "I can't believe you found such a thing. But you're the winner here, Micah." She held it out to him. "This should be yours. First bite anyway."

"I've never felt more like a winner. But that is *yours*." Micah's expression grew suddenly serious. "There's something else there. At the bottom."

"What? Oh . . . I see." There was a niche cut into the base

of the chocolate statue. With something tucked inside. A small velvet . . .

Sloane's heart stalled.

"Open it."

"Micah . . ." She held her breath and slid the jewelry box out. Opened the lid. Then gasped as the setting sun lit the ring's stones on fire.

"It was my grandmother's," Micah said, barely above a whisper. "Sapphires were her favorite—blue like your eyes. And the diamonds were from my great-grandmother's ring. On my father's side. I had the jeweler combine them all in platinum."

Sloane looked up at him, the box trembling in her hands.

"I love you, Sloane. I'm asking you to marry me."

"Oh, Micah." She clutched the box to her chest, seeing him through a blur of tears. She wasn't sure she could breathe, let alone speak. "I love you, too. Much more than I ever thought was possible."

"So . . . that's a yes?"

"Yes . . . *yes!*" A tear slid down her face. It felt like the whole world had just turned Oscar gold. "I can't wait to be your wife."

"That makes two of us."

Micah cupped her face in his hands, brushed his lips to her cheeks, forehead, eyelids . . . and then bent low to claim her mouth in a long kiss.

Sloane curled an arm around his neck, fingers still tight on the jewelry box, and kissed him back like they were sealing their future. Her heart beat so hard it almost sounded like—

"Oh, boy." Micah leaned away, beginning to laugh. He nodded toward the cars parked along the overlook. Horns honked, people clapped. Their news had spread . . . like the promise of hope.

"It's LA," Sloane said, laughing too. "Of course."

"Congratulations!" someone shouted.

Arms waved. "All the best, you two!"

"Kiss her again!"

They waved back, shaking their heads and grinning. Then Micah lifted the ring from its box and slipped it on Sloane's finger. It fit like it was meant to be.

"This," he said, tracing his fingers along her cheek, "*you*, will always be my face of hope."

"Always . . . forever." Sloane raised her face for Micah's kiss, her heart filled to overflowing. With love and with gratefulness beyond measure. *Thank you, God.*

TURN THE PAGE
FOR A PREVIEW FROM

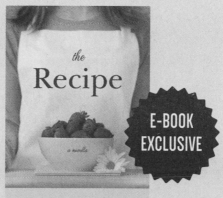

the
Recipe
a novella

E-BOOK EXCLUSIVE

CANDACE CALVERT

ALSO INCLUDED IN

romance collection

CHANCE OF LOVING YOU

terri **BLACKSTOCK** | *candace* **CALVERT** | *susan may* **WARREN**

AVAILABLE NOW IN STORES AND ONLINE

CHAPTER I

LUCAS MARCHAL FULLY EXPECTED his grandmother to show
no interest in her hospital dinner tray; her appetite had
dwindled to almost nothing. But in his wildest dreams he
wouldn't have imagined that her dour, no-nonsense nurse's
aide would lift the dish cover, scream, then stumble backward
and fall to the floor.

He bolted toward her to help, vaguely aware of other San
Diego Hope rehab staff filing through the door.

His grandmother's roommate, chubby and childlike despite
middle age, pitched forward in her bed to utter a lisping litany
of concern. "Oh . . . my . . . goodnethh. Oh, my!"

"Here." Lucas offered a hand to the downed nurse's aide.
"Let me help you up, Mrs.—"

"No need," she sputtered, waving him and one of the other
aides away. "I'm all right. Weak ankle. Lost my balance, that's
all. After I saw that . . . *horrid* thing." Revulsion flickered
across her age-lined face. "On your grandmother's plate."

What?

Lucas's gaze darted to the remaining staff now gathering around his grandmother's tray table. They stared like curious looky-loos at a crime scene. Lucas was all too familiar with that phenomenon, though as an evidence technician, he operated on the other side of the yellow police tape. He turned back to the nurse's aide—Wanda Clay, according to her name badge—who'd managed to stand and retrieve the dish cover she'd dropped in her panic. "What's wrong with my grandmother's dinner plate?"

"It was on the rice," Wanda explained, gingerly testing her ankle. It was hard to tell if her grimace was from an injury or from what she was struggling to explain. "Sitting there on the food, bold as brass." She crossed her arms, tried to still a shudder. "Black, huge, with those awful legs. I haven't seen one of those vile bugs since I left Florida."

A *cockroach*? On his grandmother's food? It could snuff what little was left of her appetite—and his hope that she'd finally regain her strength.

"It's probably scurried away by now." The nurse's aide rubbed an elbow. "That's what they do in the light. But I saw it, plain as can be. And you can bet I'll be reporting it to—"

"You mean *this*?" A young, bearded tech in blue scrubs pointed at the plate. Then made no attempt to hide his smirk. "Is this what freaked you out, Wanda?"

"I wasn't scared," the woman denied, paling as she stared at the tray. "Startled maybe. Because no one expects to see—"

"A black olive?" the tech crowed, pointing again. "Ooooh. Horrifying."

Someone else tittered. "Yep, that's an olive—was an olive. Sort of cut up in pieces and stuck on the rice. A decoration, maybe?"

"Oh, goody." The roommate clapped her hands, her expression morphing from concern to delight. "Can I see? Is it pretty? Can I have a party decoration too?"

"Hey, Wanda," the tech teased, "what form do we use to report an olive to—?"

"I think that's enough," Lucas advised, raising his hands. "No harm, no foul. Okay?" He reminded himself that law enforcement saw its own share of clowning. But . . . "We have two ladies who need to eat."

"Yes, sir." The technician nodded, his expression sheepish. "Just kidding around. I'll get your grandma some fresh water."

"Thank you." Lucas glanced toward Wanda. "You're not hurt?"

"Only a bump." She rubbed her elbow again, lips pinching tight. "Some decoration."

"Yeah."

Lucas watched for a moment as Wanda helped the chattering roommate with her tray; then he glanced toward the window beyond—the hospital's peaceful ocean view—before returning to his grandmother's bedside. He slid his chair close, his heart heavy at the sight of her now. Asleep on her pillow and far too thin, with her stroke-damaged right arm lying useless across her chest. For the first time ever, Rosalynn Marchal actually appeared her age of seventy-six. So different from the strong, vibrant woman who'd essentially been his mother. A woman whose unbridled laughter turned heads in more than a few fancy restaurants, who shouldered a skeet rifle like she intended to stop a charging rhino. A still-lovely senior equally at home in a gown and diamonds for a charity event or wearing faded jeans and a sun hat to dig in her wildly beautiful garden high above the Pacific Ocean. She was an acclaimed painter, a deeply devoted believer. And a new widow. That inconsolable heartbreak had brought her to this point . . . *of no return?*

No.

Lucas watched her doze, torn between the mercy of letting her dream of far better times and the absolute fact that if she didn't eat, drink, move, breathe, she'd succeed in what she'd recently told her pastor and her grandson: *"I'm okay with leaving this earthly world."* Lucas couldn't let that happen even if his grandmother's advance medical directive, her legal living will, required he honor her wishes regarding life support. She'd beaten the pneumonia that brought her to the hospital this time, and the therapists said she still had enough physical strength to regain some mobility, as long as she mustered the will to take nourishment.

"Here's that water," the technician said, setting a pitcher beside the food tray. He cleared his throat. "I'm sorry about that kidding around earlier. It wasn't professional."

"No harm done . . . Edward," Lucas told him after glancing at his ID badge. "I appreciate the help all of you give my grandmother."

"Pretty special lady, huh?"

"The most."

"If you need to get going, I can help feed her tonight," Edward offered. "I know she's on Wanda's list, but I don't mind. I have the time." He shrugged. "And after all that joking around, I'm probably on her list too. Wanda Clay's ever-growing—" The young man's gaze came to rest on the Bible on the bedside table, and he appeared to swallow his intended word. "Her hit list."

Lucas smiled. His grandmother's powerful influence for

good. Even in sleep. "Thanks, but I can stay tonight. Things look pretty decent out on the streets."

"You're a cop, right?"

"Evidence tech—CSI," Lucas added, using the TV term everyone recognized.

"Cool."

"Sometimes. Mostly it's like being a Molly Maid. With gloves, tweezers, and a camera. Not as exciting as on TV."

"Still sounds cool to me." The tech moved the dinner tray closer. He pointed to the tepid mound of boiled rice. "I guess I can see how someone might think that thing was a bug."

Lucas inspected the offensive olive. "You think it's supposed to be a garnish?"

"Yeah." Edward snickered. "Some bored dietary assistant getting her cutesy on."

❊　❊　❊

"It's not like I'm sous-chef at Avant or Puesto," Aimee Curran told her cousin, citing top-ten local restaurants. She tucked a tendril of auburn hair behind an ear and sighed. "Or that I even get much of a chance to be food-creative here. But . . ." She raised her voice over the mix of staff and visitor chatter in the San Diego Hope hospital cafeteria so that Taylor Cabot could hear. "At least working in a dietary department will look good on my application to the culinary institute."

"You're serious about it. I can see it in your eyes," Taylor observed, mercifully offering no reference to Aimee's failed and costly past career paths. Nursing, right up to the moment she panicked, then passed out and hit the floor during a surgery rotation, followed by early childhood education that . . . just didn't fit. "Aunt Miranda would love it, of course." Taylor slid an extra package of saltines into the pocket of her ER scrub top. "She was such an awesome cook."

"She was." Aimee's mother had been a school nurse, but her kitchen was her beating heart. "Apron time" with her only daughter had meant the world to her. And to Aimee.

"If I win the Vegan Valentine Bake-Off, it means admission to the culinary institute with fully paid tuition," Aimee explained. "I can't qualify for more student loans. So this is it."

"I didn't know you'd gone vegan."

"I haven't. Not even close, though Mom taught me to respect organic and local foods. It's just that there won't be so many entries in a vegan contest. It's a calculated risk. And I need to win, Taylor." Aimee's pulse quickened. "It's my last chance to honor my mother with a choice I'm making for my life—my *whole* life. I've got to do that. I can't bear it if I don't."

"I think . . ." Taylor's voice was gentle. "I think that your mother would be proud of you, regardless."

"But it just seems that everyone else has found their calling, you know? You've got your career in the ER. My brother's starting medical school up in Portland, and Dad's found Nancy." Aimee smiled, so very happy for him. "Now they've adopted those two little rascals from Haiti . . ." Her eyes met Taylor's. "The contest is being held on Valentine's Day."

"Your birthday. And also . . ."

"Ten years from the day Mom passed away." Aimee sighed. "I'm going to be twenty-six, Taylor. It's high time I got myself together and moved on."

"I understand that."

"I know you do." Taylor's husband, a Sacramento firefighter, had been killed in an accident almost three years ago. Taking a job in San Diego was part of Taylor's plan to move on.

"So what are you going to wow those bake-off judges with?" Taylor asked after carefully tapping the meal's calorie count into her cell phone. The old familiar spark of fun warmed her eyes. "Some sort of soybean cheesecake?"

"Not a tofu fan," Aimee admitted, her nose wrinkling. "I thought I'd go through Mom's old recipe tin and adapt something—you know, ban the chickens and cows, but keep the sugar."

"And all the love. Aunt Miranda was all about 'stirring in the love.' I think I asked my mom once if you could buy that at Walmart in a five-pound sack like flour."

Aimee smiled. "The first phase is tomorrow. I've got to pass that. The bake-off finals will be televised. Professional kitchen, top-grade tools . . . ticking time clock." She grimaced. "Nothing like pressure. But at least the hospital dietary kitchen gives me a chance to handle more equipment than I have at my apartment and practice my chopping and slicing techniques." She shook her head. "Mostly when nobody's looking, since the biggest part of my job is tray delivery. But I've been known to add a few artistic, signature Aimee touches and—"

"Hey, Curran!"

Aimee turned and saw a familiar young man in scrubs cruising toward them. Beard, husky build. That rehab tech, Edward.

"Hey there," he said, plunking a hand on the edge of their table. He grinned at Aimee, raised a brow. "Was it you?"

"Was *what* me?"

"That cutesy olive on Mrs. Marchal's rice."

"I don't know what you mean," Aimee told him, afraid she did. Why was he making a big deal out of—?

"A black olive, cut up like some kind of decoration? I think someone got pictures of it."

"Really?" She hesitated. Was he flattering her? Or . . .

"Wanda thought it was a cockroach. She screamed like a banshee and fell down on her—"

"What?" Aimee's heart stalled. *No.* This had to be a bad joke.

"Anyway," he said, waving at a passing student nurse, "Wanda's probably gunning for your department. Grumbling about 'malicious mischief' and things like that. Thought you should know." Edward winked, smacked his hand on the table. "But thank 'em for me, would ya? Highlight of my day."

Aimee closed her eyes as he sauntered away. *Please* . . .

"Aimee?" Taylor leaned over the table, touched her hand. "You okay?"

"I . . ." She met her cousin's gaze and groaned.

"Oh, dear." Taylor winced. "A 'signature Aimee touch'?"

"It was a *daisy*. I snipped all those little black petals really carefully. I didn't even know whose tray it was. But I thought it was sort of cheery. And now, when I'm still on probation, I might be accused of doing something malicious . . ." Another thought made her breath catch. "Wanda's pretty old. Do you think she got hurt? Broke a hip or—?"

"I doubt it," Taylor interrupted, her expression reassuring. "Wanda is sturdier than she looks. But I do think you should go over there and explain. Apologize to her. And to the patient, too, if she was upset by it."

"Oh, great. I just thought of something else." Aimee squeezed her eyes shut again. "I think Mrs. Marchal's grandson works for the police department. Can this get any worse?"

ACKNOWLEDGMENTS

HEARTFELT APPRECIATION TO:

Literary agent Natasha Kern—for care and support that goes far beyond career guidance.

The amazing Tyndale House team, especially my editors, Jan Stob, Sarah Rische, and Erin Smith—this author is so blessed by you.

Critique partner and author Nancy Herriman—for "being there" all these years. What a gift.

Kathy Kipp—for your invaluable help in shaping Sloane's journey. And confirming that Girl Scout song about old and new friends: you are truly gold.

Sarah Peer, rescue kitten foster mom—for showing up for Marty yet again, this time on the page.

Reader friend Ann Street—for sharing your wonderful family (including dogs!) as inspiration for my character Jerry Rhodes.

Finally, my family, especially my husband, Andy—you signed on for quite a journey, and I'm ever grateful for your love and support.

And of course, my readers—that you allow me to touch your lives and your hearts with these stories is such an honor and joy.

ABOUT THE AUTHOR

CANDACE CALVERT is a former ER nurse and author of the Mercy Hospital series—*Critical Care, Disaster Status,* and *Code Triage*—the Grace Medical series—*Trauma Plan, Rescue Team,* and *Life Support*—and the Crisis Team series—*By Your Side, Step by Step,* and *Maybe It's You*. Her medical dramas offer readers a chance to "scrub in" on the exciting world of emergency medicine. Wife, mother, and very proud grandmother, Candace makes her home in northern California. Visit her website at www.candacecalvert.com.

More from
Candace Calvert

THE GRACE MEDICAL SERIES

THE MERCY HOSPITAL SERIES

TYNDALE HOUSE PUBLISHERS
IS CRAZY4FICTION!

Fiction that entertains and inspires

Get to know us! Become a member of the Crazy4Fiction community. Whether you read our blog, like us on Facebook, follow us on Twitter, or receive our e-newsletter, you're sure to get the latest news on the best in Christian fiction. You might even win something along the way!

JOIN IN THE FUN TODAY.

 www.crazy4fiction.com

 Crazy4Fiction

 @Crazy4Fiction